ALAA AL ASWANY

The Republic of False Truths

Translated from the Arabic by
S. R. Fellowes

faber

First published in the UK in 2021
by Faber & Faber Ltd
Bloomsbury House
74–77 Great Russell Street
London WC1B 3DA

This export edition first published in 2021

First published in Arabic in 2018
by Dar al Adab, Beirut, Lebanon

Typeset by Faber & Faber Ltd
Printed and bound in the UK by CPI Group (UK) Ltd,
Croydon CR0 4YY

A CIP record for this book
is available from the British Library

ISBN 978–0–751–34760–5

MIX
Paper from
responsible sources
FSC
www.fsc.org
FSC® C020471

2 4 6 8 10 9 7 5 3 1

To my wife, Iman Taymour
and to my children,
Seif, Moatez, May, and Nada

1

General Ahmad Alwany had no need of an alarm clock.

The moment the dawn prayer was called, he'd wake up of his own accord. He'd lie on his back in bed, eyes open, repeating the words of the call in a whisper, then rise and go to the bathroom, where he'd quickly perform his ablutions, comb his black hair (carefully dyed, apart from two thin white streaks of equal length that he left, one on each side), then don his chic track suit and set off for the nearby mosque. The head of his security detail had asked him more than once to put up a mosque inside the villa so that he could be more easily protected, but General Alwany refused. He liked to pray alongside everyone else, just like any ordinary person, so he'd cross the street on foot, surrounded by four members of his guard, who kept their eyes on the road, weapons poised to fire at any moment. At the door to the mosque, the guard split up, two staying outside while the other two stood inside, guarding him while he prayed. During those blessed, radiant moments, General Alwany would leave our world for another. A deep and genuine humility would flood over him, his guards and the other worshippers would disappear from before his eyes, and he would cease to think of his job, or his children, or his wife. Placing his shoes under his arm, like any other worshipper, he would walk, head bowed, to a distant corner, perform the two prostrations of greeting to the mosque followed by two more in accordance with the Prophet's morning custom, and then continue uttering thanks to God and entreaties for forgiveness until the collective prayer commenced. Despite the pressing requests of the other worshippers, General Alwany always refused to lead them, insisting instead on praying in the back row, head bowed in submission, the tears often gushing from his eyes when the imam recited, in a sweet and melodious voice, verses from the Koran. Prayer liberated him, made him feel as though he were a new person. His soul became limpid, his worries drifted away, and a sense of serenity came over him, as though the prayer were a draught of cool water offered him when thirsty, in the heat of the day. The world ceased to have any importance in his eyes and shrank to the size of a gnat's wing. He would wonder at men's struggles over their selfish interests, their panting after passing pleasures. Why all the scrapping and the competition? What was the point of all the lying, the envy, and the plotting? Were we not all merely travellers on the road? Were we not, in the end, all dead men? Would we not, one day, lay ourselves down in the moist earth, while our souls ascended to their Maker that He might hold us to account for our deeds? On that day, neither rank nor wealth will avail us, and nought will save us but good works.

For fifty-eight years, the general had lived as a pious, observant Muslim, never missing a religious obligation or even a voluntary practice. He had never embarked on anything new without first ascertaining whether it was permissible. Not once in his life had he tasted a drop of alcohol or inhaled a draught of hashish. He had never smoked and had never known a woman outside of the marital bed (aside from a few fumbling sexual adventures as an adolescent, for which he asked God's forgiveness). He had, thanks be to God, made the full pilgrimage to God's Holy House twice, and the lesser pilgrimage three times. He was renowned for his charity. Ten whole families lived off monthly subventions that he paid from his own pocket, and when one of these people thanked him, the general would smile and whisper, 'Say, "I seek forgiveness from God!" my lad! Nothing that I give you comes out of my pocket. All wealth is from God, and I am but its guardian. Just promise me, my dear friend, that you'll remember me in your prayers. Hopefully, God will then excuse my shortcomings.' Unlike many of those who hold high rank in our country, General Alwany also preferred that people refer to him by his religious title of Hagg rather than saying 'Your Excellency the General' or 'Basha'.

Now, following the prayer, he returned to his house and sat, as was his habit, on the luxurious sofa in the spacious hall to recite from the Koran. He began with the two 'prayers of refuge' and some of the short chapters, then recited a portion from the 'Chapter of the Cow' including the part of which the Prophet has said, 'If anyone recites it in his house during the day, Satan will not enter that house for three days.' After final praises of God's glory and requests for His forgiveness, General Alwany then took the lift to his suite on the second floor, had a hot shower, put his dressing gown over his naked body, and entered the small kitchen to make his own breakfast – two large spoonfuls of top-quality mountain honey (sent to him, with unfailing regularity, by Yemen's ambassador to Cairo), a few slices of toast spread with a thick layer of the Swiss cheese that he loved, and, finally, pancakes, covered with strawberries and melted chocolate and washed down with a giant cup of milky tea, followed by a cup of medium-sweet Turkish coffee.

And what did His Excellency do then?

There is no call for embarrassment when speaking of matters of which religion approves. General Ahmad Alwany was one of those who feel sexually energised in the morning, a fact attributable to his lengthy labours on the night shift, which had caused him to adopt this matutinal regime. Now, then, he sat on the edge of the bed where Hagga Tahany, his wife, lay fast asleep. Reaching for the remote, he tuned in to a pornography channel, regulated the sound so that it would be audible only inside the room, stared at the torrid intercourse taking place on screen until he could bear the excitement no longer, and, taking off his dressing gown and throwing it on the floor, launched himself onto his wife, kissing her passionately while fondling her body and taken by surprise at her immediate, ardent response (of a nature that suggested she too had been watching the film from under the covers). General Alwany's uprightness, his avoidance of all depravities, his military training, the care he took to keep fit, and his healthy diet had all combined to preserve his sexual capacity without the aid of aphrodisiacs, and, holding images from the obscene film in his head, he was able to gambol and frisk in the bed like a forty-year-old.

Some might ask, 'How could a God-fearing Muslim like General Alwany watch pornographic films?'

A foolish question that only ignoramuses, or the malevolent, could entertain! It is true that watching pornography is an act disapproved of by religion but it is not considered a major sin like murder, fornication, or the consumption of alcohol. The True Religion may allow, on occasion, the commission of an act that is disapproved of if it prevents the believer from committing a greater sin, in accordance with the legal principle that 'necessity permits the prohibited'.

By virtue of his elevated position as head of the Apparatus, General Alwany dealt on a daily basis with the most beautiful women in Egypt, many of whom would have loved to have an affair with him so that they could exploit his influence, not to mention that foreign intelligence services frequently thrust beauties into his path, either so as to be able to influence or blackmail him, or to spy on state secrets. All of these were real dangers that dogged his heels. Hagga Tahany Tuleima, his respected wife, who was over fifty, whose face was under attack from wrinkles, and who refused to have cosmetic surgery because it is forbidden by religion, was all he had as he faced the insistent, imperious charms of women. Hagga Tahany's body had turned flabby and acquired an outer layer of fat, and she now weighed 120 kilos and had an enormous belly that began immediately below her exhausted breasts and reached its greatest girth at her navel before dropping away suddenly to form a hemisphere.

This unique, almost masculine belly would have been enough on its own to put an end to General Alwany's sexual appetite without the porn movies to which he resorted to inflame his imagination. As His Excellency once told his friends, 'If you're forced to eat the same food for thirty years, you have to add a few spices to get through it.'

After the morning routine – prayer and recitation of the Koran followed by breakfast and sexual intercourse with his lawfully wedded wife – it was time for work. The moment General Alwany exited the villa, the soldiers of the guard performed a military salute and one of them hurried to open the door of the black, bulletproof Mercedes. His Excellency settled himself on the back seat and the vehicle moved slowly off, preceded and followed by a car for his guards, the cavalcade led by four motorcycles ridden by armed officers. Covering the distance between the house and the Apparatus's building ought not to take more than half an hour, but in fact took twice that time as the guard commander insisted on changing the route daily to avoid the possibility of ambush or terrorist attack. The general devoted the time to studying the reports that had been issued overnight and issuing urgent instructions by telephone. The moment the car passed through the gateway to the Apparatus's headquarters, a shout of 'Attention!' went up, followed by the sound of rifle butts clattering on the ground as those holding them performed the military salute. General Alwany leapt nimbly from the car and returned the salute of his aides who knew, from long service with His Excellency, that they had to be waiting for him at the door. They could read his face and on that particular morning were aware, from the first instant, that he was in a bad mood. Looking at them with a frown, he asked, 'Did the boy talk?'

'Lt. Col. Tareq is interrogating him, sir,' one of them answered.

Annoyance registered itself on the general's face, he dismissed his aides, and instead of going upstairs to his office on the third floor, he ordered the lift operator to take him down to the interrogation rooms. As the iron gate opened, emitting a gloomy creak, the damp, foetid air of the basement assailed his nostrils. The general walked ahead, returning the salutes of the soldiers one after the other, till he arrived at a spacious chamber with high, narrow windows covered by iron bars and, here and there, metal instruments with arms and wheels, which one might at first glance have taken for sports equipment. A man wearing a blindfold was hanging by his hands from a thick rope attached to a metal ring that dangled from the ceiling. He was naked but for his underpants and his body was covered with cuts and bruises, while his face was swollen and blood had congealed around his lips and eyes. Four police goons stood opposite him and seated at a desk was an officer with the rank of lieutenant colonel, who jumped up and saluted the moment he caught sight of General Alwany. General Alwany drew the officer aside and held a whispered conversation with him, after which they returned to where the man hung suspended, only for the latter to let out a sudden moan, as though begging the newcomer for pity. 'What's your name, sonny?' General Alwany asked him in a gruff voice.

'Arabi El Sayed Shousha.'

'Speak louder. I didn't hear.'

'Arabi El Sayed Shousha.'

'Louder!'

Each time the general told him to raise his voice, the goons rained blows on the man with sticks, causing him to scream louder and louder, then suddenly burst into tears. When this happened, the general gestured to the goons and they stopped the beating. In a calm, knowing voice like that used by a doctor advising a patient, he said, 'Listen, Arabi. If you want to go home to your family, you have to talk. We won't let you go. We'll beat you till you die and we'll bury you here and no one will know where you are.'

In a voice full of tears, the man screamed, 'Basha, I swear by Almighty God, I don't know anything.'

'And I swear by the Almighty,' replied the general almost tenderly, 'that this attitude of yours truly saddens me. Come to your senses, my boy, before you destroy yourself.'

'Have mercy on me, Basha!' the man shrieked.

'Have mercy on yourself and talk.'

'Sir, I don't know anything.'

Furious, Lt. Col. Tareq now yelled, 'You expect us to believe that, you bastard?'

It was a signal. One of the goons bent over a large black piece of equipment resembling an air conditioner and pulled towards him a thick cable that ended in two round metal ends, which he attached to the man's testicles. Then he pressed the button. The man shuddered violently and let out an uninterrupted succession of high-pitched screams that resounded through the chamber. The shock was administered several times, until General Alwany brought it to an end with a wave of his hand and yelled in a voice like thunder, 'We've brought your wife, Marwa. I swear to God, you son of a whore, if you don't talk, I'll let one of the soldiers jump on top of her in front of you.'

'How can you do such things?' the man shouted.

General Alwany glanced at the goons and they hurried out, then returned holding a woman wearing a torn housedress, her hair dishevelled, her face showing signs of having been beaten. As the goons started hitting her, she began to scream, and the man recognised her voice.

'Leave me my honour !' he screamed.

'Strip her!' the general yelled.

The goons fell on her. She resisted valiantly but they were stronger and were able to rip her dress completely open. When her underwear showed, General Alwany laughed and said, 'Now there's a lovely sight! You're a lucky lad, Arabi, your wife has a padded cotton bra. That type was fashionable ages ago. They called it a "straitjacket bra".'

Everyone laughed at His Excellency the general's wit and the sarcastic comments followed thick and fast. Then the general said cheerfully, 'Take off her bra. What are your wife's nipples like, Arabi? Personally, I go for the big, dark ones.'

The goons ripped off the bra, revealing the woman's breasts, and she let out a single, long scream.

The man convulsed and screamed, 'Enough, Basha! I'll talk. I'll talk.'

Lt. Col. Tareq went over to him and yelled, 'You had better talk, you son of a whore, or I'll have the men string her up!'

'I'll talk, I swear by Almighty God!'

'Are you a member of the Organisation?'

'Yes.'

'What district?'

'Shubra El Kheima.'

'Who do you report to?'

'Abd El Rahman Metwalli.'

There was silence for a few moments. General Alwany took a couple of steps towards the door, then gave a wave to Lt. Col. Tareq and called out to him, 'If you'd brought his wife in at the start, you'd have saved yourself a lot of trouble.'

The lieutenant colonel smiled gratefully and said, 'Thank you so much, sir! We learn something new from you every day.'

General Alwany gave him a fatherly look and said, 'Make audio and video recordings of the confession and write your report. I'll be waiting for you in my office.'

*　*　*

The man had been disguised as a woman wearing a full-face veil. He'd been arrested at the Dar El Salam underground station and from there been moved to the police station where he'd almost been brought before the public prosecutor, who certainly would have let him go. However, a fingerprint check showed that he was in the files, though under a different name, so they brought him to the Apparatus, where he made a full confession. He said he was a member of an organisation that was spread over a number of governorates and he'd been wearing the veil so he could visit the families of members who were in detention without arousing suspicion. General Alwany gave instructions to his officers to have the members of the organisation followed and to write daily reports with any new information that might come to light. The case represented a new achievement for the Apparatus and for its boss, General Alwany, despite which His Excellency's officers noticed that throughout the day he remained preoccupied – so much so that after praying the afternoon prayer, he'd wanted to be on his own and had told his office manager to admit no one.

The general lay down on the sofa and began running his prayer beads through his fingers, saying 'I seek refuge with God from lapidated Satan!' Why did he feel oppressed? God's bounty towards him was prodigious: He had blessed him with the sweetness of faith, the strength of submission to His will, and with success in his work. The president of the republic himself had praised the performance of the Apparatus more than once before the cabinet. The year before, when the Apparatus had aborted an assassination attempt against him in Alexandria and arrested all the conspirators, His Excellency the President had ordered that large bonuses be paid to all the Apparatus's officers and then invited General Alwany to the presidential palace, where he had congratulated him with the words, 'Bravo, Alwany! Just so you know, I'd been thinking about appointing you prime minister, but the problem is I can't find anyone else as efficient to take your place in the Apparatus.'

Fervently, General Alwany had responded, 'Your Excellency is the leader, and I am but a foot soldier whose duty it is to follow orders! I have learned from Your Excellency that I must be ready to serve my country in any capacity.'

God had granted General Alwany excellent health and an ample portion of daily bread. He lived with his family in a villa that, in reality, was a huge mansion in the Fifth Settlement, set in the midst of fifteen acres of land and including a swimming pool, a tennis court, and an orchard. He also owned a number of luxury villas on the North Coast, and at Sharm El Sheikh, Ein El Sukhna, Alexandria, Matrouh, Hurghada, and Luxor, as well as a 250-square-metre flat in Paris's Saint Germain quarter, an elegant two-storey house with beautiful garden on Queen's Gate in London, next to Hyde Park, and a spacious and luxurious flat in Manhattan. He had a number of bank accounts too, most of them outside Egypt (in case of emergencies). General Alwany was also blessed in his family: his eldest son, Abd El Rahman, had become a judge, the middle boy, Bilal, was an officer in the Republican Guard, and his youngest child, his daughter Danya, was a student at Cairo University's Faculty of Medicine. His wife, Hagga Tahany – companion in the struggle and good luck charm – possessed, despite her advanced years and excessive corpulence, more energy than younger and lighter women. She was a wife who accommodated her husband's intimate needs at least twice a week and a mother who had raised her children to the point where they were no longer at risk, as well as serving as chair of the board of directors of Start!, an NGO that concerned itself with rescuing street children and turning them into decent citizens. She was, in addition, a committed Muslim, who organised lessons in religion in her home and who had been – through God's grace – behind a number of people finding the right path. Over and above all of this, Hagga Tahany owned a company called Zamzam, which was one of Egypt's largest contractors. True, she'd registered the company in the name of her brother, Hagg Nasser Tuleima, but she'd got a defeasance from him (this was a kind of deed of abdication, which she'd registered with the public notary and then put securely away in her bedroom safe, informing her husband of its location, given that 'all men's lives are in God's hands' and 'no man knows in what country he shall die').

General Alwany never exploited his office – let us give credit where credit is due – in order to gain any advantage for himself or his family. Were Hagga Tahany to let him know, for example, that her company was seeking to acquire a piece of land from one of the governorates, General Alwany would quickly contact the governor in question and say, 'Your Excellency the Governor, I have a service to ask of you,' to which the governor would immediately respond, 'I am yours to command, sir!' The general would now say, in tones that brooked no refusal, 'Zamzam & Co. has asked to have a piece of land allocated to it. This company is owned by my brother-in-law Hagg Nasser Tuleima. The service that I need from Your Excellency is that you treat Hagg Nasser like any other contractor. Kindly apply the law without fear or favour.' The governor would remain silent for a moment and then say, 'Is Your Excellency giving us a lesson in impartiality and integrity?' and the general would interrupt with 'Heaven forbid! I'm just an Egyptian who loves his country's soil, and a Muslim who would never allow his family to become involved in anything dishonest.'

Later, after the land had been allocated to the company, General Alwany would feel not the slightest embarrassment. He had contacted the person in charge and told him to grant him no favours. What more could he do than that?

When his eldest son, Abd El Rahman, applied to be appointed to the prosecutor's office, General Alwany phoned the minister of justice and asked him to treat his son just like the rest of the applicants, without discrimination, and Abd El Rahman had been accepted into the prosecutor's office and was now a judge on the South Cairo Court. And when his son Bilal had applied to join the Republican

Guard, General Alwany had phoned the minister of defence and begged him to apply the rules to his son without partiality, and he'd been accepted into the Republican Guard and now held the rank of major. By such means, General Alwany maintained a clear conscience before Our Lord, Glorious and Mighty and had nothing to hide or be ashamed of. Why, then, had he, since the start of the day, been feeling oppressed?

In his heart of hearts, he knew the reason, but was avoiding thinking about it – it was his only daughter, Danya, or 'Her Highness the Princess', as he called her. After he'd fathered two boys, he'd begged God to provide him with a girl. His wife became pregnant, but in the fifth month had a sudden haemorrhage that made her miscarry and affected her psychologically for a while. When she became pregnant again and gave birth to Danya, his delight was beyond description. He chose as a name for her a word used in the Noble Koran to describe the trees of Paradise. Danya induced in him feelings he had never felt before. Hard as it is to believe, General Alwany had left his work at the Apparatus for an entire day in order to accompany his daughter Danya on her first day at the nursery school run by the Mère de Dieu school. When the day came, he'd handed her over to the nun in charge but hadn't been able to bring himself to leave her there alone. He'd remained huddled in his car in front of the school, following the work at the Apparatus by telephone and calling the nun from time to time to reassure himself about Danya. At the end of the school day, General Alwany had stood in the school garden, watching the door until Danya emerged, in her pink uniform with the little checks and the white collar. She looked angelic. She called out to him, then stretched out her arms and ran as fast as she could and threw herself into his embrace. At that moment, General Alwany almost burst into tears. Believe it or not, this man of steel, who could decide the fate of a family with a word, or even a wave of his hand, was, before Danya, transformed into a sensitive lover who would do anything just to see a smile on her face. Every evening when she was a little girl, as soon as he got back from the Apparatus, he'd hurry to her room to look at her as she slept. He'd contemplate her little fingertips, her nose, her mouth, and her innocent face, even her school bag and her socks and clothes – everything that had to do with her stirred in him deep feelings of tenderness and solicitude.

Naturally, like any father, he loved his sons Bilal and Abd El Rahman too, but his daughter Danya was the true source of joy in his life. Frequently, he'd be discussing with her about some trivial matter and be suddenly overwhelmed by emotion and stop talking and hug and kiss her. Danya had never let him down and was outstanding, both in her studies and in her conduct. She was always a top student, and when she got her secondary certificate, at the Mère de Dieu, she'd wanted to study medicine. General Alwany had made all the arrangements to send her to Cambridge, but Hagga Tahany had started crying and pleading with him not to deprive her of the company of her only daughter. In the end, he'd given in and enrolled her at the medical faculty at Cairo University and bought her a Mercedes, though he feared for her too much to allow her to drive and appointed her a personal driver. General Alwany was careful, as was his wont, not to overuse his influence, so before the exams he'd phone the dean of the Faculty of Medicine to impress on him that he shouldn't give Danya any special treatment, and his daughter had gone on getting top scores till now, when she was a year from graduating. He could imagine how joyful he would be the day she graduated and was forever thinking about the next steps. Should he open her a clinic in Cairo, or send her abroad to get her doctorate? His love for Danya could reach strange heights – so much so that the very idea of her getting married disturbed him. How could a day ever come when Danya would leave the house to live with a strange man and share her bed with him? How could she have a relationship with a man other than himself and become the centre of that man's life?

He knew that that was how life was supposed to be and that his wife would never be completely happy until Danya was married and a mother, but he often wondered whether there was a young man in Egypt worthy of being Danya's husband. Was there even one man, other than himself, capable of appreciating her as she deserved? The One True Religion commanded that a wife obey her husband and made her his ward, but where was the husband who deserved to be Danya's guardian? She was far more refined than any of the young men he saw. She was straightforward and incapable of the cunning and deviousness of other girls and so sincere in her religion that in second year preparatory she'd asked, of her own accord, if she could wear a headscarf. She was good-hearted and pure, assumed the best of everyone and went to great lengths to provide help to all who needed it. What worried him was that Danya's innocence (which amounted sometimes to naivety) would make her easy prey for any bastard of a boy who might take her in with a smile and a word or two and then do with her as he pleased. How often General Alwany had regretted giving in to his wife's tears and not sending Danya to Cambridge! Now here she was, at Cairo University, rubbing shoulders with the offspring of riff-raff who were now her colleagues just because they'd scored high in the secondary school leaving exam. And now he was paying for his error. He could ignore it no longer: Danya had changed. She was still refined and well-mannered, but she was no longer the obedient daughter who, dazzled by him, hung on every word he uttered, who seized on everything he said and acted accordingly. He'd ordered one of his most trusted officers to write regular reports on her movements, and this morning he'd read something that had ruined his day. He'd kept putting off talking to her to give himself time to think, but now he couldn't stand it any longer. He stood up suddenly, ordered his office manager to have the car brought, and a few minutes later was on his way home, having decided to confront her, whatever the consequences.

2

Dear Reader,

You will never know who I am because I shall sign this book with a pseudonym. I am not afraid. I come, thank God, from a family of brave men, generation upon generation. The only thing is that we live in a lying, backward society that adores delusions, and I am not willing to pay the price of others' stupidity. I have lived for fifty-five years, and most of those years I have spent in deep thought, which has led me to comprehend a number of truths, which it is now my duty to both proclaim and document. The theories that I shall put forward in this book would merit academic study, were we living in a decent society. We are, however, in Egypt, where the serious thinker and the brilliant scientist find no recognition, and where glory – and what glory! – goes to liars and impostors. Let me start my theory with the following question: 'What is the essence of the relationship that ties a man to a woman in Egypt?'

What is the point of all those earnest looks, affectionate smiles, yearning touches, and letters full of flirtatiousness and passion? What is the objective of all those whispered nocturnal telephone calls and romantic sessions on the banks of the Nile? Why do women go to such lengths to accessorise and wear make-up that accentuates their charms, and what is achieved by those so-called 'ladies'' shoes with the high heels that set a woman's body a-wobble and bring out its succulence? Why all those dresses and 'ladies'' trousers and skirts and twin-sets? Why do designs and colours proliferate endlessly? Why do even many religious women who cover their hair wear tight-fitting, provocative clothes, as though they would like (if this weren't so very unacceptable) to give men a glimpse of the details of their bodies?

Gentlemen,

This entire dazzling, prodigious firework display has a single purpose: to catch a man and drag him into the marital cage. From puberty on, man suffers from a persistent, painful desire that drives him to chase women and have sex with them and so find relief from the pressure on his nerves from his male hormones. Against this, woman is raised, among us, to think of her reproductive organ as her hidden treasure.

Only in our country does the press describe a girl who has lost her virginity as having lost 'the dearest thing she has'.

Think, my dear reader: the dearest thing that an Egyptian girl possesses isn't her mind, or her humanity, or her life. It is her virginity. That membrane that covers her reproductive organ so as to guarantee that it hasn't been previously used. To acquire the right to make use of that untouched organ, the man chases the woman, so she acts the coquette with him, asking for presents and jewellery, a dowry and luxury furniture and a large flat in a posh neighbourhood. And the man submits to all these conditions, drooling as he dreams of tasting the pearl that rests concealed in the oyster. Then they marry, the ebullience of the early days comes to an end, and the man discovers that having sex with his wife isn't the greatest pleasure in the world, as he had imagined. He will be surprised (in most cases) to find that his wife is sluggish in bed or finds sex disgusting and considers it something dirty, like urinating or defecating, so she'll do it only when compelled, as though carrying out a duty. And the wife may even (and this is the worst) use sex as blackmail, as though saying to her husband, 'If you want to enjoy my body, you will have to cover me in presents and give me any sum of money I may demand, and always back me up in my quarrels with your mother and your brothers and sisters.'

Only then does the husband realise the enormity of the deception: he has spent everything he possesses dreaming of the pearl only to discover that the oyster is empty! But before he can escape, his wife will have borne a child. Egyptian women have children faster than any others on the face of the earth. They use their children as effective weapons to retain their husbands and make them subservient to their will. This is a fact known to every Egyptian husband (even if he denies it). The second fact is that the femininity of the Egyptian woman varies in reverse proportion to her social status. Women of the upper class are (for the most part) nothing but sterile, counterfeit dummies, pseudo-females, sugar dolls with neither desire nor soul.

Only the woman of the popular classes is a natural, complete female, one who doesn't ruin her spontaneity with artifice, knows nothing of the lies and games of the grandes dames, or of the hypocrisy that these imbibe with their mothers' milk. Observe the paintings of Mahmoud Said. This great artist was raised in the mansion of his father, prime minister of Egypt, studied in France, and worked as a judge until he was fifty, after which he dedicated his life to art. Despite all which, when he painted, the sole example of femininity he found before him was the Egyptian woman of the popular classes. The explosive energy that looks down at us from the painting 'Girls of Bahari' is something the young women of the upper classes will never know. In brief, the woman of the popular classes is a woman, and every other woman is fake and artificial, the difference being precisely that between a natural and a plastic rose.

The third fact is that the charm of the woman of the popular classes manifests itself most clearly when that woman is a domestic. When this is the case, she adds to her fresh, overflowing femininity a delicious stamp of submissiveness that puts fire into her allure.

Kindly answer the following question frankly. What would happen if you were to invite your aristocratic fiancée to lunch at an elegant, high-class restaurant and then suddenly say to her, 'Your

body is extremely arousing, my darling. Your well-rounded backside has two halves that quiver in a marvellous way and your full
chest makes me imagine myself sucking on your nipples, causing my
member to go extremely hard and making me want to have conjugal
intercourse with you this very minute.'

What would your fiancée do?

She'd be furious, no doubt about it. She'd revile you. She'd hurry
home to cast herself weeping into the arms of her mother and
curse the luck that threw her into the clutches of a man so vile and
depraved. And she'd probably break off the engagement. Her anger
at your open declaration of your sexual fantasies would be quite sincere. It would never occur to your fiancée that when she chose her
form-fitting dress her goal was precisely to draw your attention to the
curve of her backside and the swelling of her breasts. The rules of the
charade require that your fiancée arouse your lust seemingly without
meaning to, while at the same time you hide your arousal and talk
of other things. The real reason for your fiancée's fury would be that
you have spoiled the charade with your frankness. But the very same
sexual flirtatiousness that angered your fiancée, if directed at your
maid, would probably be considered by her a charming compliment.
She'd coo and laugh, with lovable obscenity and playful gratitude.
Truly, maids are indispensable mistresses for anyone who knows how
to quaff from their sweet, natural springs!

Assembled gentlemen,

He who has never loved the maid has never loved at all!

I, like so many husbands in Egypt, have been the victim of a deception. When I practise sex with my wife, I feel as though I'm eating a
sandwich filled with soap powder: no matter how hungry I may be,
my gorge must inevitably rise at the first bite. When I reached fifty, I
gave up having sex with my wife almost completely. I think she was
relieved, because she had never liked sex and only practised it within
the narrowest of parameters and after every possible excuse had been

exhausted. In this book, I shall present my experience with maids, in hope that this may be of some assistance to the millions of husbands who suffer in silence, having been deceived with the same cruelty and in the same despicable way.

Despairing, amorous husband, The Maid Is the Solution!

What more does a man need than a desirable female residing with him under the same roof with whom he can take his pleasure whenever he wants? Whom he can have sex with straightaway, without any shilly-shallying or wasting time on phone calls and clandestine romantic meetings? A real woman, who knows the value of sex and enjoys it and looks forward to it? Did not our grandfathers, up to the nineteenth century, buy concubines for sexual gratification? Might not a lawfully wedded wife, back then, present her husband with a beautiful concubine, for which gift the husband would thank her and then have sex with the concubine, with the result that he would calm down and his worries would go away? If we could rid ourselves of middle-class complexes, the husband's relationship with the maid would persuade him to bear with equanimity the tensions in his relationship with his wife and lead, as a consequence, to greater familial stability. Naturally, a maid can sometimes present problems, but these are all solvable. There is, for example, that roughness of hand and foot that plagues the maid because of her work. This can be overcome by giving her a monthly sum with which to buy creams guaranteed to smooth the extremities (due care being taken to avoid excessive smoothness, so as not to arouse the wife's suspicions).

Another common problem: your maid-mistress may be afflicted with a case of jealousy that will drive her to provoke your wife and disobey her instructions. On such occasions, you must warn her of the consequences of challenging your wife since, if she decides to throw her out, you will be unable to protect her. There is also the problem of the greedy, gold-digging maid – but in truth, how paltry the sums! What you spend on your maid-mistress in an entire year you may spend on your wife in one night, if you invite her and her family to dinner in a posh restaurant, or you buy her a necklace or a ring for her birthday. In this way, you can enjoy, for peanuts, a superb mistress who will make you forget your despair over your lady wife and her empty oyster.

Beware, though, and beware again! Maid-love is not to be undertaken impromptu, or blindly. It is both an art and a science that call for study and carefully considered steps, which may be summarised as follows:

1. Exploration

It is possible to discover the maid's character from day one. If you feel she is trying to attract your attention; if she keeps passing in front of you for no good reason; if she starts with surprise on finding you at the door to the kitchen and tugs on her headscarf and catches her breath in affected fear; if she bends over in front of you to wipe the floor with the floor cloth and then retreats, proudly showing off her backside; if she leans out of the window opposite you to hang out the wash, then puts the clothes pegs in her mouth and bends over so that her large breasts appear, resting on the windowsill – all of these things are signs that your maid is ready for love. Proceed to Step Two.

2. First Manoeuvre

As soon as you find yourself alone with the maid and well away from your wife, smile and ask her how she is, then give her a lustful look. Look her body over slowly and lewdly. This is a decisive moment, a definitive test. The unresponsive maid will ignore your look entirely, or talk to you about something serious, or call out to your wife to ask her any old thing. The responsive maid, on the other hand, will smile and talk to you coquettishly and may even grant you a generous gift, such as giving you a glimpse of a delightful shake of the breasts, or by passing in front of you while moving her backside like some fascinating pendulum (left, right, and back again). In this case, you are on the right track. Advance!

3. Creating a Secret

At the first opportunity when no one can see you, take out a hundred pounds, thrust them into the maid's hand, and whisper in her ear, 'Don't tell the madam I gave you anything!'

She will nod her head and thank you warmly. This step has two objectives: the first is to let the maid know that her love will not go unrewarded, the second to create a common secret in preparation for your relationship, which has in fact now begun, all that remains being the final step.

4. Attack

Take care before attacking. The maid may be matching you step for step and then, as soon as you touch her, erupt and threaten you with a scandal, or lecture you on morality. A maid of this sort will have a chip on her shoulder and a villainous temperament. She will have an inferiority complex that she wants to compensate for by catching you red-handed in an act of harassment. She seeks to satisfy her vanity as a woman while at the same time enjoying, as a maid, the exercise of moral superiority over her employer. This vicious species of maid is, fortunately, very rare, and can be exposed using a simple test. When zero hour arrives, have her make the first move. Call her over and invite her to sit down next to you, or pretend that your back hurts and ask her to give you a massage. The villainous maid will refuse, but the open-minded maid will come to you. At this point, hug her hard and kiss her and squeeze her breasts with your hands. She may *make feeble protestations or pretend to try to wriggle out of your grasp while clinging to you. Pay no attention to this insincere, fragile denial, it's just for the record. Intensify the attack. Pounce on her. Ravish her. And welcome to the Happiness Club!*

Ashraf Wissa stopped writing and lit a joint, holding the smoke in to increase the effect of the hashish. The book's subject was now clear in his mind. The first chapter would bear the title 'Getting Laid by the Maid: A Guide to the Pleasures of', the second 'Diaries of a Delighted Donkey'. The third would be called 'How to Become a Successful Pimp in Five Steps'. He'd also have a whole chapter describing the farcical scenes that took place in the cinema world. He'd tell everything in this book. He'd print 1000 copies at his own expense and distribute them secretly. No one would ever know he was the author. The original would be written on the computer, not in his own hand, and he'd have it printed at the press belonging to Ahmad Ma'moun, lifelong friend and repository of his secrets from the day they were students together at the Lycée Français.

Unfortunately, though, Ashraf Wissa had discovered that writing was a lot harder than acting. After months of work, the book was still in its early stages and it had taken him a lot of effort to arrive at the right biting, sarcastic tone. He wasn't trying to persuade his readers of anything. He just wanted to show them how many are the lies that we live. It would make him happy to see the effect of the book on all those artificial, arrogant women, devoid of femininity, and all those finicky, fastidious men, oozing triviality and stupidity.

'Yes indeed! Read my book, you frauds, and learn the truth about yourselves! I am Ashraf Nagib Ramzi Wissa, failed bit player and hash fiend, whom you despise and make fun of, or are even so gracious as to pity. My book will deliver a resounding slap on your faces for every pain and frustration you have caused me and for every lie and mean-spirited act.

'I shall leave a copy of the book at the office of Lamei, that pimp of a casting agent who has for so long humiliated me and extorted money from me so that I can get fatuous parts lasting only a few minutes. I shall leave copies on the sets, so that famous actors may read them and realise that I know exactly how they reached stardom. I shall send a copy of the book to all of my 'successful' relatives, so that they know that success in the corrupt society in which we live doesn't merit such self-satisfaction. I shall leave a copy of the book on the dressing table in the bedroom so that my wife Magda can read it. It will give me the greatest of pleasure to shock her out of her pathetic ideas regarding the holiness of the 'facts of life'. My wife Magda is the executioner who has taken on the task of torturing me for a quarter of a century. If I were a Muslim, I would have divorced her a few months after getting married, but we Copts are allowed divorce only in case of adultery. Magda was the least suitable woman in the world for me. I saw her some miserable day at a church party and fell into the trap. My late mother warned me against the marriage so often, but I was a dumb, randy male and sent myself off to my doom. Dear Lord Jesus, glorified be your name, it's as though Magda Adly Barsoum had been created for a single purpose – to make my life miserable, no more, no less.'

Feeling suddenly anxious, Ashraf lit another joint, inhaled deeply, and resumed his memories of life with Magda. How many problems she'd caused! When she had children, she wanted to call the boy Patrick and the girl Kristina, to facilitate their assimilation into Western society when they grew up and emigrated. Ashraf had rejected her suggestions vehemently, because his grandfather Ramzi Basha Wissa had been a comrade of the nationalist leader Saad Zaghloul during the revolution of 1919, selling many parcels of land and spending vast sums of money in support of the nationalist cause. It was inconceivable that the descendants of that great Egyptian should bear foreign names! After violent arguments,

Ashraf had been able to impose two Egyptian names on his wife – Sarah and Butrus.

Life with Magda was nothing but a series of arguments and quarrels, interrupted by long periods of hostile silence, poisonous comments, and haughty refusals to acknowledge the other's presence. She went on at him to sell his grandfather's block of flats on Talaat Harb Street where they lived and buy a villa in 'October' or 'the Settlement' because Downtown had turned, in her opinion, into a plebeian neighbourhood that was beneath their station. What a stupid idea! Yet another upsetting battle to fight! Why should he throw away the income from the building off which, along with additional income from his inheritance, he lived? Where would he find another flat like the one they were in now? Seven spacious rooms with high ceilings after the old fashion, with two bathrooms and two kitchens plus a large balcony that sat ten people easily, not to mention three small balconies attached to the bedrooms. He'd be insane to leave a flat like that! On top of which, he couldn't imagine himself living anywhere else. He had been born here and spent his childhood and youth here, and every corner of the flat had witnessed some part of his life. He couldn't get any of these delicate human feelings through to Magda. She understood nothing about life that couldn't be converted into figures.

At the start of their marriage, she used to go on at him to emigrate to Canada, like so many of their relatives. She'd quarrel with him and shout, 'Give me one reason for us to go on staying in this country!' and he'd always reply with the same words: 'I'd be like a fish out of water. If I leave Egypt, I'll die.'

He had managed, with much effort, to dissuade her from the idea of emigrating, but she had, unfortunately, convinced her son and daughter, and they'd emigrated to Canada as soon as they graduated. That was something for which he would never forgive her. How he needed Butrus and Sarah with him now! He was getting on in

24

years and was entirely alone. Magda would leave in the morning and not get back from work before 7 p.m., leaving all the household chores to the maid. Even when she was home, she avoided talking to him unless she had to. Magda had never loved him and had dealt with him on the basis that he was 'the best option going for marriage and children'.

He didn't mind because he too had never loved her. What truly made him sad was that she didn't respect him. She considered him a failure. She alluded frequently to the fact that she had worked hard and become a chartered accountant with a well-known and successful practice, while he was unemployed, despite all his money, and sat at home for weeks, and sometimes months, before the order to film reached him, when he would spend days in demeaning, exhausting work just to appear in one or two scenes as an extra in a film or a serial. A few days ago, he'd screamed at her that he missed Sarah and Butrus and she'd answered, in a tone laden with significance, turning her face away from him, 'No doubt they're working hard to make successes of their lives,' as though what she really meant was, 'Let them get on with it, so they don't turn out like you!'

How the words had hurt him! Magda considered him spoiled and a failure but that was so far from the truth. Certainly, he lived off the income from his properties, but he wasn't lazy or without ambition. He was an actor who loved his art, and the leading critics and directors had borne witness to his talent. Unfortunately, though, the opportunities had never come his way, because the acting field in Egypt, like everything else in that country, was like a filth-covered swamp swarming with insects and worms. If he'd been a flirtatious actress who gave her body to the director, he would have achieved stardom long ago, and if he'd been a pimp who brought the directors women, they would have given him leading roles. He was, quite simply, however, and like so many other Egyptians, paying an exorbitant price for his talent and self-respect.

Feeling tired, Ashraf turned out the lights in his study and walked down the long corridor to his bedroom, where he stretched out in the darkness next to Magda and soon fell asleep. In the morning, he was awakened by the usual everyday noise and listened, eyes still shut, to his wife as she came out of the bathroom, put on her clothes, did her make-up, and moved about quickly in all directions before checking, one last time, the work-related papers she was carrying in her bag. He pretended he was asleep. He didn't want to talk to her. Now she was turning off the light, closing the door of the room, and leaving. Ashraf went back to sleep and when he woke it was past ten. He went into the pantry next to the bedroom and made himself a large honey and clotted cream sandwich, which he ate with relish, then prepared himself a cup of sugarless coffee which he sipped while smoking his 'top-of-the-morning' – that first joint whose effect was always so wonderful. His mind cleared completely and he became filled with an amazing serenity. He shaved carefully, then surrendered to the hot water pouring from the showerhead, and, having finished in the bathroom, put a cashmere dressing gown over his naked body, squirted himself with a few puffs of his favourite perfume, Pino Silvestre, and made his way to the kitchen, where his other, glorious, life would begin.

3

Good morning, Mazen!

I'm Asmaa Zanaty. I was sitting opposite you at the Enough! movement meeting yesterday. I have long black hair and was wearing a white pullover with a collar and green jeans. Do you remember me? I wanted to talk to you after the meeting, but I was too shy. I got your email address from the secretary and made up my mind to write to you; I always express myself better in writing. I have a BA in English Literature and have made several attempts at writing. Perhaps I'll show them to you one day. Would you like to know what I want from you?

I'm going through a difficult time and I need your friendship. I know that I'm putting my reputation at risk, because if an Egyptian girl asks a young man to be her friend, she brands herself as loose. I'm sure you'll understand me. I'm not loose, Mazen, just different, and being different is the cause of all my problems.

I'm from a traditional Egyptian family. My father, Muhammad Zanaty, has been working as an accountant in Saudi Arabia for a quarter of a century. I only got to know him during the holidays. For one or two months a year I would have a real, 'tangible' father and for the rest of it he was turned into an elided pronoun, a mere idea, a cloudy concept. I can't blame my father for the displacement he was forced to undergo to support us, but he had no impact whatsoever, apart from the sums of money he sent to cover my expenses, on my upbringing. It was my grandfather Karem – my mother's father – who raised me and shaped the way I think. I was so attached to him that I'd often leave our house on Feisal Street and go stay with him in his flat in Sayeda Zeinab, where he lived on his own after my grandmother died and my uncle, his only son, emigrated to Britain. Grandfather Karem was a man of letters and culture, and it was he who made me love reading and the arts and gave me self-confidence. He used to take me to the opera, to the theatre, and the cinema, and he taught me that a woman is a legally competent individual and not just an instrument for sexual pleasure and a machine for producing offspring. He supported me against the reactionary thinking of my family to the day he died, five years ago, leaving me to fight my battles alone. I live on my own with my mother. Our life is one of unending arguments. My mother is my father's representative in the house. She talks to me as though she were he and she believes all his ideas are correct and the essence of wisdom. I love my father and I'm certain that he loves me, but I'm always at odds with him and cause him such worries that sometimes I imagine he regrets having had me. My father is more comfortable with my elder brother Mustafa and my sister Sundus, who is two years younger than me. They, in his view, are normal. Mustafa graduated from the College of Engineering and got a contract in Saudi Arabia, and Sundus covers her hair and obeys her parents. She got an undergraduate degree in commerce, married the usual nice boy, went to Saudi Arabia, had a son, and now she's pregnant again. I, on the other hand, refused to cover my hair, refused to work in the Gulf, and rejected the principle of marriage just for the sake of respectability. I can't imagine sleeping with a man I don't know simply because he's paid the bride money, bought the engagement ring, and signed some legal papers with my father.

Lots of men have made offers for me, and each time my parents pressure me to agree to see the suitor. I refuse and argue, and in the end, I'm forced to see him. The suitor usually comes to our house all dressed up, full of himself, confident in the impact of his well-stuffed pockets. He softens us up with sentences that make passing refer-

28

ence to his possessions – a high-end car (Mercedes or BMW), a chalet on the North Coast and another in Ein El Sukhna, a luxurious flat (generally in Medinet Nasr) with 300 square metres of floor space and two levels. Following this display of wealth, the suitor begins his inspection of the goods (namely me). I feel his eyes exploring my body, bit by bit, slowly. We can't blame him. The man will pay a large sum of money for me, to allow him to use my body for his pleasure (which is the definition of marriage in some religious law books), so doesn't he have the right to a visual inspection of my body so as to be sure he'll be investing wisely? Isn't it possible that I have a club foot, for example, or suffer from some skin disease, or that my breasts are artificial? The suitor has the right to make sure that the goods are in sound order and he isn't being swindled.

How humiliated I feel, Mazen! I feel cheap and without self-worth – just goods displayed in a shop window waiting for the customer who will pay what I cost and take me away. On such occasions, the feeling of humiliation drives me to behave aggressively. I try to prove I'm worth more than just the body that is displayed for sale. I ask the suitor who his favourite authors are and what novels he has read recently (generally, the suitor hasn't read a book in his life, apart from commentaries on the Koran and the set books at school). I feel happy when he reveals his ignorance in front of everyone. Then I lure him into a discussion of politics. I ask him, for example, if he accepts the torture of innocent people at the hands of National Security and the rigging of elections, and whether he accepts the hereditary transfer of rule by Mubarak to his son Gamal, as though Egypt were a battery farm.

At this point, the suitor looks at me in astonishment, as though I were a winged creature just landed from Mars. He is an ordinary Egyptian citizen. He considers himself lucky that he works in the Gulf where, usually, he puts up with the slights of his local sponsor and lives with oppression to secure his livelihood. He really cannot understand, at all, how anyone could concern himself with anything in the world other than making money, plus regular performance of the rites of religion out of fear that his pampered existence will otherwise come to an end.

Despite the interruptions from my father and mother and their desperate attempts to change the subject, I persist with my scheme. I tell the suitor about my participation in the Enough! movement's demonstrations and about the wall magazine I used to write against the regime when I was at university. Then I turn to the topic of religion and announce that I will never ever cover my hair and review the legal opinions that assert that Islam has never imposed covering of the hair on women.

This is the straw that breaks the camel's back. The suitor leaves and never returns. And after each suitor has fled, the arguments with my family – my father and mother, my sister Sundus, and my brother Mustafa – begin. They all think that I'm unbalanced, stupid, and don't know what's in my own best interest. I'm completely convinced of the rightness of what I'm doing but sometimes I get tired. I wish sometimes that I could be in harmony with society, not in conflict with it. All the same, I quite simply cannot be anything other than what I am. I'm sorry to go on at such length, Mazen, but I need to talk. After I obtained my bachelor's degree, I went for two years without work. Then, after numerous interventions by friends of my father's, I was appointed last September as an English teacher at the Renaissance Preparatory School for Girls in Mounira. If you were to see the school, Mazen, you'd leave with an excellent impression: the building is elegant, the walls are freshly painted, and the lavatories are clean. This beautiful outward appearance, so rare in government schools, is attributable to the efforts of the headmaster, Mr Abd El Zaher Salama, who follows up personally on every matter, large and small, at the school and also takes an interest in his girls' morals and how closely they observe the teachings of religion.

Mr Abd El Zaher forbids any of his Muslim students to enter the school with her hair uncovered and halts instruction for the performance of the midday prayer, when he himself leads the male teachers and workers in prayer in the school courtyard, while the girls and the female teachers perform the prayer in their classrooms. The headmaster isn't the only one characterised by such rigorous religiosity: all the male teachers are religiously observant and bear on their foreheads the mark made by frequent prostration, and some of them are bearded, while the female teachers all cover their hair and we have three who cover their faces completely. You may be wondering, how do these hardliners deal with someone like me, who doesn't cover her hair?

On the first day, the principal female teacher, Mrs Manal, said to me, with a smile, 'You look like a good girl, Asmaa, and you deserve to enjoy the comfort of obedience. I have to say, you'll look lovely with your hair covered!'

Mr Abd El Zaher received me warmly, gave me a tour of the school, and introduced me to the other teachers. The following day, he called me into his office, gave me a short pamphlet on covering the hair, then smiled and said, 'Listen, dear girl. Where the students are concerned, I make them cover their hair because they're young, and I'm responsible for them before Our Lord, Glorious and Mighty. As for the female teachers, my duty towards them goes no further than advice. I've provided you with all the legal proofs that the covering of the hair is a religious duty. Read them carefully and Our Lord will, should He so wish, inspire you to do the right thing.'

I thanked him and told him that I would read the pamphlet but that I knew of other arguments to the effect that Islam imposes decency in general terms and does not impose any specific form of clothing.

Mr Abd El Zaher laughed sarcastically and said, 'My, my! So you're a scholar of religion too?'

I tried to list the legal opinions on which I relied but he interrupted me by saying, 'Listen, Asmaa, covering the hair is as much a religious duty as praying and fasting. Any other opinion is wrong.'

I realised there was no point in arguing with him, so I thanked him and left. After that, no one talked to me about covering my hair. I'd put a covering over my head when I was praying at noon with the girls, then take it off, and no one objected. I think they were prepared to coexist with me. I can almost hear you saying, 'What more could you want, Asmaa? A well-maintained model school, and a headmaster and colleagues who are religious but not fanatical?'

That, my dear friend, is how we look from the outside. The truth, though, is that the Renaissance Preparatory School for Girls is nothing less than a gang of criminals, in the full meaning of the word, that includes all the teachers and is led by Mr Abd El Zaher himself. This gang's sole goal is to extort money from the students and force them to take private classes. The school is in the Mounira district, and the girls are poor. If the cost of going to school becomes too much for their families, they have to abandon their education, and my pious colleagues know no mercy. They divide the girls into three categories, starting with the girls who take private classes, who are treated well and get top marks at the end of the year because the teachers help them cheat. This happens with Mr Abd El Zaher's knowledge and encouragement. Cheating is considered normal at the school, where they call it 'helping'. The second category of students consists of those who can't afford the cost of private classes but take 'review' classes. These aren't treated well but the school administration is obliged to make sure they pass their exams because if they fail, the other students won't take the review classes. Then there's the third category, who are so poor that they can't afford to pay for either private classes or review classes. These are the pariahs who always fail. I can't describe to you the lengths to which the teachers go to take *it out on them and humiliate them. At first, I couldn't understand what made them so cruel. Then I realised that they were defending their livelihoods. They have to take it out on the poor girls to keep the machine of private and review classes going. The parents understand that without these lessons and special classes, their daughters will be subjected to humiliation, punishment, and mockery and that they will go on failing till they are expelled from the school. My problems began when I refused to give private classes and review classes. I'm no hero and no saint. However, I am quite simply better off than my colleagues. I'm not married and I don't have children. My needs, too, are simple, and my father helps me by giving me some money every month. From day one, I decided that I'd give the teaching my all, and my students' level began to improve, little by little, until they all passed the mid-year test. Not one student in the three classes that I teach failed English. Such a result ought to be considered an achievement for any teacher, but Mr Abd El Zaher called me into his office and instead of praising me, gave me a lukewarm greeting, and said, 'If you don't change your approach to teaching, I shall punish you. You aren't leaving the girls any opportunity to think for themselves. Pedagogically speaking, that is a very harmful approach.'*

I tried to argue with him but he insisted on his point of view. Then he said, offensively, 'Listen, I don't have time to waste on you. Consider what I've said a warning. If you don't change your approach to teaching, I shall punish you. You may go.'

You cannot imagine, Mazen, how shocked I was. Think of yourself making every effort to succeed at your work and then being punished! Mrs Manal, the principal female teacher, made her position even clearer than the headmaster. She told me, rudely, 'Look here, dear. If you're too rich to need the money from the private classes, that's your business. But every one of your colleagues has a family to support. When you explain everything in the classroom,

33

you're stealing the bread from the teachers' mouths and you can be sure that no one's going to let you get away with that!'

Naturally, I paid no attention to these warnings and continued to do my work in a way that satisfied my conscience. Two weeks later, Mr Abd El Zaher called me in to his office, where I found Mrs Manal and a group of teachers. The moment I walked in, the headmaster accosted me angrily with the words, 'Asmaa! I've decided to give you a final warning in front of your colleagues.'

Before I could respond, Mrs Manal shouted out derisively, 'Which are you, Asmaa? A Muslim or a Copt?'

I said, 'I'm a Muslim.'

The headmaster said, 'There are no Muslim women who do not cover their hair.'

I tried to argue, using my usual justifications, but the headmaster interrupted me. 'Silence! Forget this nonsense! Our function here is to educate and inculcate morals. I cannot permit you to corrupt the girls' minds. Are you or are you not going to cover your hair?'

I yelled in his face, 'Covering one's hair is a personal matter, and no one has the right to impose it on me!'

The headmaster shook his head, seemingly relieved at my answer, and said quietly, 'Fine. Kindly go to your classroom.'

The next day, Mr Abd El Zaher presented an official complaint to the director of the Education Administration accusing me of wearing inappropriate dress at school. He asserted that he had put me on notice more than once in front of my colleagues but that I had treated him with contempt. At the end of the complaint, he demanded that decisive measures be taken against me to preserve the students' morals. Naturally, a complaint of this sort could open the doors of Hell before me. I am to go to the ministry's Legal Affairs department for interrogation tomorrow. I'm not afraid, Mazen, but I feel unjustly treated and demeaned. In what other country in the world do they punish a person for being successful?

Plus, how can the headmaster and the pious teachers be such liars?

Today, in class, I could tell from the girls' looks that they knew about the interrogation. When the girls leave the school, the parents usually say hello and ask me about their daughters. Today, they avoided me completely, though the mother of one of my first-year students shook my hand and drew me aside from the others who were waiting.

'Don't let it bother you, Miss Asmaa,' she said. 'Good luck. We know they're just taking revenge on you because you have a conscience. We're all praying for you, but the parents are afraid that if they stand up for you, the director will persecute our daughters.'

You know, Mazen, the parents' behaviour annoyed me more than being referred for interrogation. I defend their daughters' right to an education and they abandon me because they're afraid they might have problems?

Are all Egyptians now either corrupt or cowards?

What is this swamp that we're living in?

I feel nauseated by all this lying and hypocrisy and corruption. Please, tell me what you think, because I'm really depressed. Thank you for your time.

Asmaa

P.S. I'm writing from an email account that isn't my own. Would you mind opening a new email account just for our correspondence? As you know, we're all watched by Security.

Even More Important Note: If this bothers you, don't reply. I shall understand and shan't write to you again.

4

As the time approached, they gathered, as though they couldn't bear
to wait. They went out to the gate of the villa, men in front, women
behind, waiting for Sheikh Shamel to arrive. All were well-known
figures – businessmen, celebrated doctors and engineers, former
ministers, police and army generals either serving or retired. Most
of them were accompanied by their wives and daughters, and there
were famous actresses, some of them – the ones who had repented
and abandoned acting – with their hair covered, others – the ones
who were still taking their first steps on the path of piety – decently
dressed but without hair covering. The moment the black Mercedes
appeared, a thrill ran through the crowd. Sheikh Shamel always sat
next to the driver, keeping the back seat for the ladies, as he was
usually accompanied by two of his four (fully veiled) wives. As
soon as the sheikh began his descent, men rushed to shake his hand,
some of them even bending to kiss its precious back, though he
would pull it quickly away, saying 'God forgive me!' in an audible
voice. The sheikh's disciples believed that the source of the delightful odour that filled the air as soon as he descended from the car
was not the expensive musk with which he anointed his clothes but
one of the signs of grace that God bestows on those of His servants
whom He loves; the disciples believed in their sheikh that much.
Few knew that he had received no formal religious education and
had a degree in Spanish from Cairo University. He had tried hard,
on graduating, to find a job as a tourist guide, but tourism had been
hit by a recession, due to terrorism. The sheikh had then obtained a
contract from Saudi Arabia to work as an administrator at a sports

club; God had done well by him, and at the mosque he'd got to know Sheikh El Ghamidi, who saw signs of promise in him and imparted to him a generous portion of his learning. Sheikh Shamel had lived for ten years in Saudi Arabia before returning to Egypt, where he made up his mind to devote his life to proselytisation. With a tender smile and in grateful tones, he would say, 'God was generous to me. I sat at the feet of Erudite and Learned Sheikh El Ghamidi, quaffing the religious sciences from that pure spring until my thirst was quenched, and then my learned sheikh – may God reward him well for his selfless service to religion! – granted me permission to teach.'

The Egyptians fell in love with Sheikh Shamel when he appeared for the first time on his weekly show on the Godliness Channel. As his popularity grew, he withdrew from the latter and established the Right Path Channel, which opened before him the way to great good fortune. Sheikh Shamel speaks constantly (as the Koran commands us to do) of the many blessings God has given him: he owns three recent-model black stretch limousines and a fourth sports car that he himself drives on family outings. All of them are Mercedes, the make he prefers because of its solid build and elegance. It is also the case that the director of the Mercedes agency in Egypt is a disciple of his and always gives him special deals. Another of God's blessings on Sheikh Shamel is that he lives in a large villa in 6th of October City, where three wives, each with her children, live in the top three floors, while the sheikh reserves the fourth for his newest, who is always a virgin whom he enjoys in full compliance with holy law and then dismisses with a generous sum, granting her her full legal rights including maintenance, the balance of the bride price, and all the rest. He is said to have taken the virginity of twenty-three young girls, all in compliance with holy law. There is nothing shameful or sinful about this because he has never broken God's canons, and he always gives the following advice to his male disciples: 'My

37

brothers, I advise you, if your means and health permit, take more than one wife, for to do so is to guard yourself against sin and to provide a veil of godly protection to the daughters of the Muslims!'

The sheikh's love of intercourse brings no shame on him as he never exposes his virile member in ways forbidden by religion and is still (he is now over fifty) attractive to women. His body is massive, with broad shoulders. His face is fair-complexioned and handsome, his eyes large, honey-coloured, and lined with kohl, in imitation of the practice of the Prophet, God bless him and give him peace. He embodies the authentic elegance of the Righteous Forefathers – so different from that of the jeans and trousers brought to us from the West – and he wears a floor-length shift of the finest materials (except silk, which is forbidden by religion), covered with a mantle that is made specially for him in Marrakesh. He has dozens of pairs of chic Italian shoes, the cost of any one of which may reach astronomical figures. The white cloth with which he covers his head may be considered the last word in the sentence of his sartorial elegance. Sheikh Shamel never speaks of his attractiveness to women, but he is aware of it and keeps it resolutely in check, lest it should lead (God forbid!) to sin. During the programme he presents, a female viewer will often phone in and shriek in torrid tones, 'I love you in God, Sheikh Shamel! I love you in God!' On such occasions, the sheikh lets his heart be his guide. If he feels that what the caller has in mind is love in the virtuous sense, his features relax into a sweet smile and he says, 'May God fill you with grace and surround you with blessings, my dear sister in Islam.' If, however, he senses a dubious tremulousness in her voice, indicative (God forbid!) of lust, his beautiful face darkens immediately with something akin to anger, and he says, as he resolutely hangs up, 'I pray to God, respected sister, that He may bring us together in blessing on the Day of Resurrection, should He so will.' Continence, uprightness, and godliness are innate traits of Sheikh Shamel's personality.

The disciples now joyfully followed him to where he would give his lesson next to the swimming pool. Sheikh Shamel gives the lesson every first Saturday of the month at General Alwany's mansion. Men sit to the right, women to the left, while the sheikh sits on a broad raised seat made of oak inlaid with mother-of-pearl on which the Most Beautiful Names of God have been carved in delicate letters of great beauty. The seat is a genuine work of art that Hagga Tahany had made specially for the sheikh so that he could sit cross-legged and be comfortable while giving his lesson.

Hagga Tahany, with her corpulent body and ample black robe, appeared enormous. On her chest, she had hung a heavy chain of white gold from which the word 'Allah', formed of flawless diamonds, dangled. She bowed and whispered a few words to the sheikh, then handed him a small piece of paper which he thrust into the pocket of his mantle with a smile, seeming to thank her. Throughout the lesson, Indonesian maids, their hair covered, would circulate with hot and cold drinks. Afterwards, there would be a large banquet for which superb food had been brought in by the Wholesome Bites company, owned by Hagga Tahany. Sheikh Shamel began with whispered prayers before the microphone, then smiled and said 'Peace be upon you!'

Those present returned the greeting in a variety of excited voices. Sheikh Shamel began his talk with the words 'Praise to God, Mighty and Sublime, for His blessings and His favours, and blessings and peace upon the Chosen One, Lord of All Creation!'

Then he said, 'My brothers and sisters in Islam, I shall talk today about the covering of the hair, which is a duty imposed on every Muslim woman who has reached the age of menstruation, according to the consensus of legal scholars and orthodox Muslims. Covering of the hair is known to be a necessary part of religion that needs neither explanation nor debate. What brings me to speak of it is the rabid attack to which God's religion is being subjected by the secularists, those agents of Zionism and the Crusader West. Through God's grace, above all, and then through the grace of our righteous, revered sheikhs, the practice of covering the hair has spread and now predominates among the women of the Muslims, delivering the secularists a severe blow that left them first staggering, then dancing the dance of death. These secularists, with their plots against our Islamic nation, cannot bear to see a Muslim woman adorned with modesty and seemliness. We Muslims are subject to a general conspiracy that aims to distance us from our religion. Be on your guard, then, my brothers and sisters, and beware the cross-worshipping Christians and ape- and pig-descended Jews, and their agents the secularists, who bear Islamic names and live among us and stab us in the back. These secularists, despite the multiplicity of their sects and schools – liberals, communists, socialists – are all, without exception, devoid of honour, corrupt by nature, and worship their desires like beasts. Indeed, I swear there are beasts that show greater modesty than these brazen people with their defence of perversion and group sex (we take refuge with God!). To these acquiescent cuckolds we say, "Why do you hate the covering of the hair?" Healthy instinct imposed the covering of women's hair before it became a divine command. Observe God's creations about us, if you would indeed acquire wisdom! Is not the planet itself wrapped in a protective layer without which all of life would be destroyed? Is not fruit preserved in a protective layer that preserves its freshness? Is not the limb-severing sword kept safe inside a scabbard? Is it not the peel of the apple that preserves it from corruption? Is it not the peel of the banana that preserves it from turning black and rotten? Do we not wrap books and copybooks in jackets to preserve them from dirt? What then when it comes to the women of the Muslims? The secularists want to interfere with the laws of nature and call our women to unveiling and indecency. There is no god but God! As the Koran says, "How then can you be so deluded as to turn from

40

the truth?" I ask you, dear sister in Islam, if you go to buy halvah, and you find a piece that is exposed, for hands to tear at and flies to settle on, and another piece of clean halvah well wrapped in a thick, elegant wrapping, which would you buy? Naturally, you would prefer the clean, wrapped halvah over the exposed, dirty halvah. God is great! God is great! You, my dear Muslim sister, are the piece of halvah and God, great and glorious, wishes to preserve you from uncleanness and keep intact your dignity, modesty, and purity. Would you refuse this generous gift from the Lord of the Universe, Great and Glorious? Would you meet God's grace with rejection and recalcitrance?'

Cries of 'God is great!' rose from the listeners. Sheikh Shamel bowed his head in silence for a moment, then resumed, saying, 'How many of our girls have told me, "I'm not convinced I have to cover my hair. Convince me first, and then I'll cover my hair." Glory be! I put one question to such girls: "Are you a Muslim?" My respected young daughter will reply, "Yes, I am a Muslim. I bear witness that there is no god but God and that Muhammad is the messenger of God." Then I ask her, "Do you love God and His messenger?" and the girl will reply, "Of course I love them." And I say to her, "If you love God and His messenger, obey the command of God and His messenger! You are commanded to cover your hair. You have no choice but to obey. If you are living in a country, do you not obey its laws, which have been set by mortals such as yourself? My beloved young daughter, if you are working in a company, do you not obey your superior's orders? How, then, can you disobey the commands of God, Great and Glorious? Is the Lord, Great and Glorious, of less account in your eyes than a superior in a company? Alas for mortal men! Is it that the hearts of some Muslims are carved from rock that they feel not and seek not the joys of obedience? Alas for those Muslims who quiver in fear at mere mortals like themselves, but, when God commands them to do something, argue and look for proof where none is to be found! This is a command from God, who created us and feeds us and showers us with blessings beyond counting! Which would you rather: obey God, Mighty and Sublime, or place yourselves above His commands and do harm to yourselves?"'

The listeners murmured audibly, asking God for forgiveness. It was clear that they were moved. Even the celebrated presenter Nourhan burst into tears, causing the lady sitting next to her to take her in her arms to calm her down. The sheikh resumed in tones trembling with emotion:

'Brothers and sisters in Islam, say after me the following prayer and memorise it, for, by Him who holds my soul in His hand, I teach it to you only out of desire for the approval of God, Great and Glorious: O *God, make the women of the Muslims, and their daughters, righteous, godly, submissive, and penitent, and make decent clothing and the covering of the hair appealing to them, and implant in them modesty and continence! O God, guard them from the curses of the corrupt and the claims of those who would lead them astray, through Your mercy, O most merciful of the merciful!*'

The listeners repeated 'Amen' after him in voices that rang through the place. Suddenly, Sheikh Shamel cast his gaze on those around him, his features full of exultation. 'O Lord! O Lord! Brothers and sisters, be joyful! I swear I see angels surrounding us on all sides, for in this gathering of ours we mention God's name and worship Him, as God, mighty and sublime, has commanded us!'

'God is great!', 'God grant you His blessings, Master!' were the repeated, excited cries of those present. The sheikh fell silent, then reached into the pocket of his mantle and took out a piece of paper. 'Brothers and sisters in Islam,' he said, 'I announce to you the good news that our daughter Marwa El Giyushi has bidden goodbye to sin forever, God willing. God has conferred upon her the blessing of obedience and she has decided to adopt the hair covering required by religious law. Come here, Marwa!'

A young woman in her twenties wearing elegant, flowing garments emerged from the group. She seemed embarrassed and smiled shyly. Hagga Tahany took her by the hand and stood her next to Sheikh Shamel, whose face lit up as he exclaimed, 'Bravo! Come here, Marwa.'

Marwa moved closer to him and the sheikh gave her the microphone. When she appeared too embarrassed to speak, Hagga Tahany took the microphone and held it in front of her mouth. The sheikh began chanting in a sing-song voice the following prayer:

'O God, You are my lord other than whom there is none other.
You created me and I am your handmaiden.
I seek refuge with You from the evil that I have done.
O God, I seek Your forgiveness from every sin that creates grief and leaves repentance in its wake.
O God, I accept Your favour in overlooking my sins and Your bounty in overlooking my unbelief.
O God, I have wronged my soul, so forgive me and accept me as Your obedient slave.'

The young woman wept during the prayer, and Hagga Tahany hugged her and then placed the hair covering over her head and knotted it below her chin. She gazed at her for a moment and then kissed her on her cheek. Trills of celebration rang out, loud exclamations of 'God is great!' were heard, and cries of joy echoed everywhere:

'Well done!'
'Congratulations, Marwa!'
'Marwa, you look gorgeous!'

* * *

As General Alwany approached the house, he noticed the cars in front of the gate. He knew that today was Sheikh Shamel's seminar

43

but didn't want to see the guests, so he ordered his driver to drive around to the back of the house and went in through the back entrance. There, he rode the lift to the second floor, made his way to Danya's room, and rapped with his fingers on the door. Danya quickly appeared, on her face a radiant smile that roused in him a mixture of tenderness and gloom. She was wearing baggy trousers and a blue satin jacket and had removed her hair scarf, leaving her smooth black hair to hang down around her beautiful face. She reached up and gave him a peck on the cheek, then looked at her watch, pursed her lips playfully, and said, 'Honourable General, you have come home from work early. May I know the reason?'

General Alwany was briefly confused, then cleared his throat and said in a serious tone of voice, 'I want to talk to you about something important.' Her smile broadened and she said as she made way for him to enter, 'We are Your Excellency's to command, sir!'

He decided not to fall in with her joking mood. He would not let her smile affect him. He had to confront her now. Danya's large room was not unlike a luxury hotel suite, being divided into a bedroom, a study, and a bathroom. All the furniture and decorations were imported from Italy and all in either white or green, giving a restful impression of cheerfulness and expansiveness. General Alwany sat on the sofa, looked at Danya, and said, sounding rather like an interrogator, 'Why didn't you attend Sheikh Shamel's lesson?'

'He always says the same thing.'

'Sheikh Shamel is a leading Islamic scholar. We have to show him respect.'

'I do respect him, but I disagree with him.'

'May I know why?'

'Sheikh Shamel has shrunk Islam to covering the hair, praying, and fasting. He never talks about people's real problems.'

'It is the task of a man of religion to teach people the rules of religion.'

44

'When a man of religion sees injustice taking place before his eyes and says nothing, he becomes an accomplice to it.'

General Alwany looked at her angrily and said, 'You're getting some strange ideas.'

'You have always encouraged me to express my ideas frankly.'

'This is more important than ideas. Your behaviour itself has become unacceptable.'

'What have I done?'

'Your Facebook page contains videos damaging to the reputation of the police.'

'Are you spying on me, Father?'

He said nothing, and she looked at him reproachfully and said, 'I would rather you ask me and I tell you than you spy on me. You've always trusted me.'

'Of course I trust you, Danya, but this is my job. It is my duty to defend our country. We keep track of people who publish videos that hurt the reputation of the police and unfortunately you came up. Frankly, it was a shock to me.'

'The videos show officers torturing innocent people, and putting them on Facebook may help to bring them to trial.'

'Tens of thousands of police officers work day and night, giving their lives to protect Egypt. It's not acceptable to sully their reputation because an officer or two, or even a dozen, have made mistakes.'

'Torture isn't a mistake. It's a crime. Plus, telling the truth never hurt anyone. What hurts the police is the presence of criminal officers who torture people and escape punishment.'

'Fine words!' the general said, sarcastically.

She replied, fervently, 'The Prophet, may God bless him and grant him peace, said, "Wish for your brother what you wish for yourself!" I don't think anyone wants his son or his brother to be tortured in a police station.'

'Police officers only beat up criminals.'

'Even if they're criminals, they don't have the right to beat them up.'

'So what are we supposed to do? Give them chocolates?'

'No. They're supposed to face a court of law.'

'Our law is taken straight from French law and isn't suited to our country, and if we were to apply it in full, not a single criminal would confess.'

'Ten criminals escaping punishment is better than a single innocent person being treated unjustly.'

'That's theoretical and won't work in our country.'

'Egypt, like any other country in the world, must be ruled with justice.'

Suddenly the general grew furious and shouted, 'So it's come to this? You're giving me lessons now? It's not your fault, it's my fault for having listened to your mother and, instead of sending you to Cambridge, putting you into Cairo University with the children of the rabble, who have poisoned your mind. I will not permit you to speak to me with such impertinence! Do you understand?'

'I'm sorry,' Danya said, in a low voice, but General Alwany had decided to push on to the end. He took a flash drive from his pocket, put it into his laptop, and pressed some keys. Danya quickly appeared on the screen, sitting with some young people who were talking to an elderly lady dressed in black. 'What's this?' he asked her.

Danya appeared embarrassed for a moment but then said, 'That was a visit I made with my fellow students to the mother of the martyr Khaled Said.'

'So people who die from drugs are martyrs?'

'The late lamented Khaled Said died of torture.'

'Even if he did die of torture, what's it got to do with you?'

'We're demanding a fair trial for Khaled Said's killers.'

'Who's "we"?'

'Me and my fellow students at the faculty.'

'I don't understand. Are you a lawyer or a medical student?'

'I'm a Muslim.'

'We're all Muslims.'

'Islam commands me to defend what is right.'

'Islam says, "Sowing discord is worse than murder".'

'Islam honours the individual and forbids treating him without respect or torturing him.'

'That's the talk of the human rights NGOs, the ones that take money from the European Union. Who told you that Islam forbids torture? Aren't flogging, stoning, and amputation of the hand torture? Islam permits the torture of certain individuals, or even their killing, to keep the country stable. Did you ever hear of a punishment called "castigation"? Under castigation the ruler, on his own, has the right to evaluate a crime, decide its punishment, and carry it out against the accused. That means that if the ruler considers any person a threat to the stability of society, he has the right to punish him by flogging and imprisonment, or even, according to some legal scholars, death. Study your religion before you talk to me about it.'

She hung her head, and he felt a sudden pity for her. 'Think again, Danya!' he said. 'You're being pushed into doing things without considering the consequences.'

As though trying to placate him, she said, 'I visited a woman whose son had died of torture. It was just a humane act.'

'No!' General Alwany responded excitedly. 'It was a political act. The state has been accused of murdering Khaled Said. It follows that for you to show solidarity with his mother was an act directed against the state.'

She didn't answer, so he went on in a quieter voice, 'I'm sure that your intentions are good, but you have to consider the significance of your behaviour. First, by virtue of my position within the state, I can assure you that there is a general conspiracy against Egypt.

And your colleagues who are inciting people against the police are, intentionally or not, helping the conspiracy to succeed. Second, you aren't the same as your colleagues, Danya. In the end, they're just students, nobodies. Your situation is different. All of Egypt knows you're my daughter. Have you any idea how many government departments monitor your Facebook page? Have you any idea how many departments filmed you at Khaled Said's house? Don't you have any idea that I have opponents and enemies whose goal is to spoil my image with the political leadership? This behaviour of yours is a gift to my enemies. Did it never occur to you that you have a brother who's a judge and another who's an officer in the Republican Guard and that their promotions may be delayed and that they could even be dismissed from their posts once and for all because of you?'

She looked stricken, so he hugged her, kissed her head, and whispered, 'Danya, if you love me, promise me it won't happen again.'

5

Ashraf Wissa felt so good as he crossed the hall that he quietly sang to himself, like a bird circling in a clear blue sky. He gazed at the carpet, then at the high ceiling, the lamps, and the pictures hanging on the walls. Everything around him appeared to be full of joy, as though congratulating him on the happiness that was soon to follow. He reached the kitchen, poked his head around the door, and beheld Ikram standing at the sink, washing the cups and plates. At that moment, in her work clothes – a loose garment that covered her head and chest; an old, faded housedress, worn through at the elbows; cloth shoes without socks – she looked like an ordinary maid. She pretended not to have noticed his presence and went on washing the dishes in the hot water. The motion of her hand as she rubbed at the plate seemed to him somehow sexy and, carried away by hashish and arousal, he leapt towards her with a large, celebratory step, as though announcing that the play-acting was over. He clung to her and grasped her breasts, and she let out a gasp and whispered, 'No, please, Ashraf Bey. If Madame Magda comes back all of a sudden, it'll be a disaster!'

Ashraf paid no attention to this feeble objection (of the sort the law would refer to as 'procedural'), held her even tighter, and began slowly and ardently kissing her neck and ears, causing her to produce a low, heated moan. She turned around, gave him a sweet smile (as though the objection of the moment before had never occurred) and whispered, 'Okay. You go ahead to the office.'

She dried her hands and left the kitchen. Immediately, Ashraf set about preparing the theatre of operations. He locked the door to the flat from the inside, turned on the television (to cover the sound of lovemaking so that no nosy parker who happened past the flat would hear anything), and entered his spacious office, where he firmly closed the curtains, took the seat cushions off the chairs, arranged them on the floor, and covered them with two large towels, thereby laying the foundation for the bed of love. Then he lit a joint and smoked it slowly till Ikram appeared at the door. Radiant, she appeared before him in a black, form-fitting nightdress that showed off the curves of her body and opened at her breasts, revealing the shining white beneath. She had applied light make-up to her face and let her smooth black hair hang loosely over her shoulders. How Ikram could be transformed from maid into bewitching mistress so quickly was beyond Ashraf's comprehension. Where did she hide her make-up things, and the nightdress? When did she find the time to take care of her body and make it so smooth? How did she manage, following the lovemaking, to hide her charms once more under her work clothes?

Like a seasoned violinist tweaking the instrument's strings before beginning to play, Ashraf placed light kisses in quick succession on her cheeks, ears, and nose, then devoured her lips in a fiery kiss while his hands roamed slowly over her body. He knew, from long experience, how to pace the waves of desire so that they didn't cast him onto the shores of pleasure too soon. Despite his numerous experiences, he had never seen a maid who was so clean. Even her underwear was the best that Egyptian industry could provide. All the same, her greatest charm, in his opinion, lay in the fact that she was *brut* (a French word meaning raw, or unpolished). With her, he felt as though he had returned to nature – to the jungle or the desert: just a man having sex with a woman to satisfy their lusts, without pretence or lies. She expressed what she wanted with total frankness, asking for certain positions and whispering the names of the genitals without embarrassment. Her shameless behaviour ignited and renewed his lust.

Having come to the end of the first bout of love, they lay on their backs, naked. After he had climaxed and the heavy silence fell, Ashraf would discover his true feelings towards a woman. On such occasions, the naked body that had fascinated him moments before would normally be transformed into a flabby lump, sweaty and abhorrent. With Ikram it was different. The pleasure would come to an end, leaving behind a calm appreciation, a certain astonishment, and feelings of something like gratitude. He would gaze at her face, flushed with the aftermath of love. He enjoyed holding her close, feeling her warm breaths on his chest, and would bury his nose in her hair so he could inhale the smell of soap. This close, sweet-smelling, warm body seemed to him familiar, as though he had kept it company in a former life, then lost it and by an amazing accident found it again. She wasn't just a maid with whom he had sex. Their life was in some way conjugal. His wife Magda, always busy with the budgets of big companies, left in the morning and didn't get back before seven at night. It was Ikram who looked after him, washing his clothes, supervising their ironing, and cooking his favourite dishes. She reminded him about his blood pressure medicine if he forgot to take it, bought razor blades before they ran out, and alerted him that he needed to buy heavy clothes before winter came. They spent the day together, talking, eating, and making love, and then, at the end of the day, carefully removed all traces of the crime. Ikram resumed the appearance of a maid and Ashraf sat and watched television in the living room, so that everything looked normal when his wife returned. He liked Ikram's personality. It was true that she read and wrote only with difficulty and spoke with a plebeian accent, overemphasising the letters and pronouncing some words wrongly, such as saying 'exways' for 'X-rays' and 'Mershedes' for 'Mercedes', yet, despite all this, she was an intellectually and emotionally intelligent and sensitive person who immediately grasped the subtlest ideas. She was also endowed with true self-respect and absolutely never asked him for money. It was he who pressed her to accept his gifts. She never exploited their relationship so as to remove the social distance between them, as other maids did. When he had asked her to call him by his unadorned name, she had done so once, then laughed in embarrassment and said, 'I can't. Your name, sir, is Ashraf Bey.'

'Call me just Ashraf!'

'If you like, but give me a while. It'll take time.'

This simple, uneducated maid comported herself with greater refinement than many upper-class ladies whom he knew. She was dazzled by him. She believed that he knew everything. She'd ask him about any subject and her black eyes would grow large as she listened to him with full attention, like a young schoolchild listening to the teacher explaining. Within a few months his relationship with Ikram was better than his relationship with his wife was after a quarter of a century. Ikram understood him with a single look. She was sensitive to his moods and knew if he was hungry or feeling like sex or downhearted or unwell from smoking too much hashish. Once, after a wonderful bout of lovemaking, she put her head on his chest and whispered, 'Can I ask you a question, sir, but you mustn't get angry?'

'Go ahead.'

'Don't you love Madame Magda, sir?'

'No.'

'Why?'

'We have different personalities.'

She looked at him in silence and he laughed and said, 'Of course, you want to ask me why I go on living with a woman I don't love, right?'

'Right.'

'I'm a Copt, Ikram, and we don't have divorce. If I were a Muslim, I'd divorce Magda and marry you.'

She smiled and asked him coquettishly, 'Go on with you! You're telling me you'd be willing to marry a maid?'

He hugged her, planted a quick kiss on her lips, and whispered, 'Please don't say that. You're better than many women who make themselves out to be great ladies.'

She hugged him hard, as though to express her gratitude.

He'd never forget the first time he played one of the films in which he'd acted in her presence. She was sitting next to him on the couch and suddenly yelled out, 'O my God! You act in films, sir?'

He laughed at her childish astonishment and told her he was an actor. After that, he started showing her the scenes in which he appeared and each time she'd show how much she liked his role, which never exceeded a few minutes. Once she asked him, 'You act so beautifully, sir. Why don't you do leading roles and become famous?'

He thought for a little and then said, 'And you, Ikram, are pretty and young and clever. Why don't you marry a respectable man who knows your worth, instead of all this drudgery you have to put up with?'

Sadly, she answered, 'It's my fate.'

Ashraf smiled and said, 'And that's my fate too.'

Later, he explained to her the corrupt system that operates in the cinema world and he could see in her eyes that she understood him. She grasped that his failure wasn't his fault – if he lived in a decent country, he'd have become famous long ago. Once he waited a whole day where they were filming in order to shoot a scene that lasted two minutes. The next day, they made love as usual and afterwards he stretched out next to her and told her what had happened. Then he said bitterly, 'I'm tired and fed up, Ikram. If I didn't love Egypt, I wouldn't stay here another day.'

She kissed his brow, then placed his head on her bosom and whispered as though rocking him to sleep, 'Please, don't upset yourself,

Ashraf Bey. You live well, you're well off, your health's fine, and you have Sarah and Butrus, God protect them. Praise God, we're better off than most, by a long way.'

At the beginning of their relationship, he'd questioned her about her life, and she'd avoided answering, but he'd pressed her until she did. She'd been born in Hawamdiya, the eldest daughter of a poor family, and she'd lived there with her father, mother, and five brothers and sisters, all crammed into a flat consisting of two bedrooms and a living room; her father had taken her out of school before she obtained her primary certificate and forced her to work as a servant in people's houses; when she reached sixteen, he'd forced her into a common-law marriage with a sheikh from the Gulf, and earned a few thousand pounds; the husband had vanished at the end of the summer, leaving divorce papers, as it emerged, at a lawyer's office; the following year, her father had married her off again, for a smaller sum; the pattern had been repeated, with her husband divorcing her after one month and paying the balance of the bride price; when her father had wanted to marry her off a third time, she'd run away and gone to live with a girlfriend and begun working in houses on a day-by-day basis until she'd married Mansour, who made his living ironing clothes, to whom she bore her daughter Shahd, only to discover that he was a serial bigamist, with children from three earlier marriages that he hadn't told her about; he also worked no more than was needed to earn him the price of the pills and injections of Max to which he was addicted.

Silence hung over them for a few minutes. Then Ikram sighed and said, 'There are women criminals whose luck is good and good women whom God created with bad luck, like me.'

Ashraf said, 'Your father wronged you.'

She looked at him reproachfully and said, 'We have to make allowances.'

He responded vehemently, 'He doesn't deserve allowances. No one sells their daughter.'

She was silent for a moment, then said, 'No one wants to sell their daughter. My father worked putting up reinforced concrete shuttering. Hand to mouth. One day of work and ten at home. And there were six of us kids, plus my mother. Where was he supposed to find the money to spend on us? Poverty is ugly, Ashraf Bey.'

Even her sorrow added to her attractiveness. The day before they had made love wonderfully. They'd soared high and reached climax together, then remained clinging to one another for a while until he'd sat upright and lit a joint. She laughed and said, 'Just so you know, I inhale the hashish you get and at the end of the day I'm so stoned I can't do a thing in the house.'

He took a drag, blew the smoke playfully in her face, and said, 'Our Lord sent us hashish as a blessing, so we can put up with the stupidity of other people.'

He finished the joint and gazed at her naked body. He ran his hand over her plump arm, then fondled her full, smooth breasts and his lust blossomed anew. He took her in his arms and put his tongue in her mouth, to begin a new round of passion. Suddenly, however, they heard a loud knocking on the door of the flat.

6

Dear Asmaa,

Thank you for your confidence in me. Of course I'd be happy to be your friend. I too need a friend who understands me. I often feel alone, even when surrounded by people. Would you believe it if I told you I'd been hoping for a chance to make your acquaintance? Something made me feel comfortable in your presence, and after I read your letter, I came to admire you even more, as a liberated, cultured young woman fighting for change through the Enough! movement – one who isn't on a mission to get a contract to work in the Gulf or find a rich husband, one fighting corruption and demanding justice and freedom. To which must be added, of course, your authentically Egyptian beauty, your long black hair, your black eyes, and that delicate smile that makes your wonderful dimples appear. All these things grant you an irresistible charm. (If you find these words offensive, cross them out and accept my apologies. I've got used to saying whatever I think frankly. Che Guevara has a wonderful sentence: 'Honourable behaviour is always saying what you believe and always doing what you say.' It's something I try to put into practice.) Now I'd like to introduce myself to you.

I'm an only son and have one sister, Maryam, who is a law student. I have left my family's home in El Abbasiya and live in a studio flat on Sherifein Street in the centre of the city, next to the old broadcasting building. Naturally, I visit my family every week and phone every day to check that they're okay, but living apart from them has spared them lots of the difficulties caused by my political activities. My late father, Gamal Saqqa, was a lawyer and a fighter for socialism. I graduated from Cairo University, Department of Chemistry, and I work as an engineer at the Bellini cement factory. It used to be called Eastern Company, and was the largest and oldest cement factory in the Middle East, making more than a billion Egyptian pounds profit every year. Then it was sold to the Italian company, Bellini, the Egyptian government retaining a 35 per cent share, while Bellini owns a further three Egyptian cement companies outright. The Italian company has deliberately neglected the factory and as a result it has begun to operate at a loss and the company has transferred all the new machines to its other companies, because they produce pure profit. I should be considered lucky compared to my fellow graduates of the Faculty of Engineering because when I graduated I was able to find a job in my own area of specialisation. Credit for that goes to the intervention of the factory's manager, Essam Shaalan, who was a friend of my late father and his comrade in the Struggle. Every day, I do battle as a member of the union committee, just as you do at the school, defending the workers' rights against the Italian management, which steals from them brazenly and seeks the aid of National Security to repress them. I agree with you: we are indeed living in a swamp, but we must never give in or despair. We will change this country, Asmaa! I swear to God we will change it! But changing things won't be easy. We will face many difficulties, but shall be victorious in the end.

I'm going to tell you about an incident that changed my life.

One night, I was on the minibus returning from a visit to a friend in Embaba. The officer at the police checkpoint stopped us, made all the passengers get down from the bus, and asked each of us for his ID. In front of me was a young man whom the officer dragged out by his shirt, violently. The young man objected, using a word I didn't hear. The officer got angry and set about hitting him till the blood was running down his face. I couldn't restrain myself and shouted at the officer, 'You have no right to hit him!' The officer turned around and yelled in my direction, 'What do you want, sunshine?' I went up to him, presented him with my Engineers Syndicate membership card, and said, 'Kindly speak to me with respect. I'm telling you that you have no right to hit him. If he has broken the law, hand him over to the prosecutor's office, but don't hit him.'

The officer looked at me for a moment, then took the card, tore it to pieces, and threw it on the ground. I let out a cry of protest but the police goons fell on me and beat me till I fell, then picked me up and threw me into a police vehicle and kept on beating me and insulting me with obscenities till we reached the police station, where I received another round of beating and insults in the detectives' room. I spent the night under lock and key, and when they brought me before the prosecutor in the morning, I asked that the marks on my body be recorded. The prosecutor smiled and said, 'Listen, Mazen. You're an engineer and you look like you're from a good family. I can record your injuries in the report. It's your right. But speaking to you as an older brother, if you get into any kind of a fight with the Ministry of Interior, you'll be the loser. The ministry will never punish one of its own officers even if he commits murder. If you bring charges against the officer, he'll deny that the incident ever took place and they'll cook up a case against you and bring witnesses, at which point I'll be obliged to put you into preventive detention, and you'll stay in prison until the court lets you out, and it may find you guilty. I advise you to accept the officer's apology. Let's put an end to the matter rather than making things more complicated.'

I agreed to a reconciliation and they took me to the officer's desk, and when he saw me, he smiled and said, 'Okay, Mazen. It worked out this time, but let it be a lesson to you to mind your manners. Don't ever challenge an officer again. Got it?'

That was the honourable officer's 'apology'. Can you believe this, Asmaa? Just because I defend a citizen's dignity, I get beaten and insulted and thrown into gaol with the criminals! And in the end,

I go to the officer and instead of apologising, he tells me off! I felt horribly demeaned, as though I had no worth and no rights. I didn't leave the house for a week. I thought for a long time and decided I had two options: either emigrate to some other country where they respect one's humanity, or strive for change. I decided to join the Enough! movement, where I found a group of the most courageous and noble Egyptians. All of them think the way I do. After that came the tragedy of Khaled Said, which confirmed that repression can touch anyone, irrespective of their social class. Naturally, I sympathise with your anger at what happened in the school, but frankly I don't see any reason for you to be depressed. Let us agree on three things: first, our battle isn't with the police officer, the headmaster, or the Italian company. It's with the corrupt, repressive regime that has choked the life out of Egyptians for so long and that must be overthrown if we are to build a respectable, decent country. Second, people in Egypt have lived under dictatorial rule for so long that they have lost any hope of getting justice, so don't blame them if they avoid confrontation with authority and prefer peace and quiet. Third, you, Asmaa, do your work with integrity primarily to have a clear conscience, so you shouldn't be looking for gratitude from anyone.

To be honest, these aren't my thoughts, they're lessons I learned from my father, the fighter for justice who went to prison, was dismissed from his job, and left homeless, but who never regretted for one instant the positions he'd taken. Once I asked him, idiotically and cruelly, 'You've wasted ten years of your life in prison, and still nothing has changed in Egypt. Don't you regret that?'

My father smiled and said, 'I did my duty and what I got out of it was self-respect. Plus, who told you nothing has changed? Every day people's awareness increases and the truth becomes more obvious to them. Someday, their anger will reach a point that drives them to revolution. Even if I don't see the revolution, I shall die with a clear conscience because I did everything in my power to serve the Cause.'

The Cause, in my father's dictionary, meant the struggle for a democratic state and a socialist society. Don't be angry at the parents' reaction. They know very well that you are defending their rights but they are, quite simply, scared of the headmaster. Have patience with them. Little by little, they will learn to trust you and rid themselves of fear. My father used to say, 'People will only love you if they trust what you say, and they will only trust what you say if you get close to them and put yourself in their shoes.'

When I began working at the factory, I found that the workers trusted neither the management nor the engineers, because the latter always sided against them with management. I spent an entire year trying to get close to them before I won their trust, and then they elected me to the union committee, warning the management strongly against rigging the election. If you try to control the workers by using force, they will never love you. It's true that their behaviour can be coarse, and sometimes aggressive, but if you live with them, you will come to realise that they are the true heroes. If the corruption annoys us, it kills them. Every day, the cement worker stands for eight hours in front of an extremely hot oven that you and I couldn't stand in front of for even a few minutes. The cement worker suffers from petrification of the lungs and lung cancer from inhaling cement dust because management rarely buy filters for the chimneys, and if they do buy them, they don't always install them because they affect the rate of production. The same simple worker who faces death every day in a noble battle to raise his children is, in my view, more honourable than the university professors who have sold their souls to the authorities and turned into prostitutes. The factory used to have six thousand workers. Can you believe that the Italian management forced two thousand of them into early retirement? And despite the fact that Essam Shaalan was a friend of my father's and to him goes the credit for having appointed me, he played a disgraceful role in the early retirement issue. He would call in the workers and threaten them, to force them to ask for retirement: 'Do you think you can take on the government? The government wants to retire you. If you say no, you'll be dismissed without compensation and you may even be arrested and thrown in prison.'

Can you believe it, Asmaa? Forty-year-old workers with wives and children finding themselves on the streets with a paltry sum in their hands that will have evaporated in a few months. What is the worker supposed to do then? He can beg or he can steal. It's a real tragedy. Now, we have a strange phenomenon at the factory: many of the workers who were forced into early retirement come each morning and sit in front of the factory gates till the end of the shift, then leave. Management tried every means to get rid of them. Essam Shaalan talked to them politely, then called in the security guards to threaten them, but it was useless. I thought, at the beginning, that their sitting in front of the gates was a way of attracting attention to their tragedy. Then I thought that they expected management would make use of them. I went to them and asked them why they were sitting there like that. One of them said, quite simply, 'We miss the factory. We've spent our whole lives here.'

Another worker said, 'This is our factory. It means more to us than it does to Essam Shaalan or the Italian management. They threw us out, and they still think it's too much to let us sit in front of our own factory?'

Such are the workers. Be patient with people, Asmaa. Don't be too quick to pass judgment on them. Overlook their mistakes and get close to them and you'll discover their amazing human energy. I'm proud of you, my dear friend. Go to the interrogation with your head held high, because you are standing on your own against an entire system of corruption. You are stronger than them because you are defending what is right. Don't be shaken by them or lose your

61

confidence for a single second. Please let me know what happens. Don't get upset, old girl, please! Can you give me a smile, please! I want to see those dimples. That's the way. Bye, champ!

Mazen

P.S. Overlook my mistakes in grammar. I'm not a writer like you. I'm an engineer and I only just got through Arabic Language at school.

More Important P.S. If you want to call, my number is 0127 334 4288.

Naturally, the phone's tapped, so don't talk too much and don't give out any information. Write to me whenever you like at this email address, it's more secure.

7

Egyptians know Nourhan as a TV presenter but they don't know her as a person. Truth to tell, her personal history is ringed about by numerous tales, some true, some lies put about by women consumed by jealousy of her beauty, her intelligence, her chic, her celebrity, and, above all, her magical ability to attract men. The following are some of the things that have been said about her:

1. They say Nourhan attends Sheikh Shamel's classes simply to make a show of her piety and that when she weeps during the class, it isn't because she's moved but just to attract attention.

The truth: from the time Nourhan reached womanhood, as a student at Mansoura Secondary, she was taken in hand by Destiny, shaper of girls' ends, and, softened and rounded, her charms began to stand out, and she became the cynosure of all eyes wherever she went. And she weeps during Sheikh Shamel's lesson specifically when he speaks of the hair covering that she was forced to abandon so that she could appear on screen, a matter that created in her such deep feelings of guilt that she tried more than once to convince those in charge to allow her to appear with her hair covered; however, they refused. Nourhan's tears and her piety are, then, sincere, and she has never in her life undertaken any action, however simple, without first making sure that it is in keeping with the precepts of religion. Here, we may mention a celebrated episode in the programme she was presenting that was titled 'Covering the Hair . . . Custom or Devotion?'

Nourhan took the side of covering. She asserted that it was a religious duty, like praying five times a day and fasting. She beseeched girls and women, however, not to go overboard in covering their hair, for any reason. A viewer called in and asked her how she could defend the covering of the hair with such enthusiasm when she herself had abandoned it. Nourhan bowed her head in silence. Low, sad music was broadcast in the background, the camera slowly moved closer to her face, and Nourhan could be heard communing with her Lord in a tremulous voice, saying, 'O my God . . . my Creator and my Master! Thou knowest that I yearn to wear a covering over my hair, and Thou knowest that I do not possess, at this time, the power to do so. O my Lord, O Thou who hearest my cry, hasten the time when I may cover my hair and do not take me unto You until such time as I have adopted the headscarf!'

That night, Nourhan wept and made the viewers weep, and she had everyone calling on God to bless her with the comfort of having her hair covered.

2. They say she changed her name from Nour El Huda to Nourhan to hide her low-class origins.

Nourhan's origins were humble but not low class. Her father, the late Muhammad Bayoumi, was a police assistant at Mansoura Police Station One. He was poor, with lots of children, but, through hard work and application, he managed to raise them and educate them, and when God took him, his eldest daughter, Nourhan, was in Group Three at the College of Humanities (Geography Dept) while her three siblings were at various stages of the school system. As for the changing of her name, it's a well-known fact that work in the media may require a person to change his or her name, to make it more musical and attractive, and Nour El Huda chose the name Nourhan because it was the closest thing to her real name.

3. They say Nourhan seduced her professor, Dr Hani El Aasar, and snatched him from his wife and children.

Dr Hani is a scion of the ancient El Aasar family, known in Mansoura for its wealth, and a professor of mineral geography at the

Faculty of Humanities. He was a counsellor to the Pearl student activities club to which Nourhan belonged. She caught his attention on the Luxor and Aswan field trip and he befriended her. When her father – God have mercy on his soul – died, Dr Hani stood by her, gave her a shoulder to lean on in her time of trial, and soon was phoning her daily, to check that she was alright. One day he invited her, along with a group of her colleagues, to spend a day at his farm. The next day, he invited her to his office, praised her character and her morals, and suddenly seemed to lose control of his feelings, for he approached her, touched her face, and whispered, 'Nour . . . you're so beautiful.'

No sign of surprise appeared on Nourhan's face, but she removed his hand firmly and said, 'Doctor, I am a Muslim woman. It is forbidden for anyone who is not a member of my family to touch my body.'

The professor had passed the point of no return, and his voice trembled as he moved closer to her and whispered, 'I love you, Nour.'

Nourhan drew back and cried out vehemently, 'Please, Doctor! Enough!'

Then she left in a fury, slamming the door behind her. Dr Hani had been married for twenty years to a teacher in the Faculty of Law and had two boys and a girl.

In the days that followed, Nourhan boycotted Dr Hani completely. She didn't answer his repeated telephone calls and whenever she caught sight of him in the college corridors would avert her face, purse her lips, and knit her eyebrows (making her look even more beautiful). After two weeks of rigorous avoidance on her part, 'Uncle' Abu Talib, the tea man, came to her smiling and said, 'Miss Nour, Dr El Aasar would like to see you in his office.'

She went to see him, with her furious, beguiling face, and said, in a formal tone of voice, 'Uncle Abu Talib tells me that you wish to see me, sir. There's nothing wrong, I hope?'

Dr Hani invited her to sit. She hesitated a little, then sat down on the edge of the chair, as though ready to leave at any moment. Dr Hani smiled nervously and asked, 'Are you angry with me, Nour?'

'Of course!' she replied.

'May I know the reason?'

'I never imagined for a moment that you'd think I was loose.'

'God forbid! I have the greatest respect for you, Nour.'

'If a man respects a woman, does her treat her in an immoral manner?'

Dr Hani inhaled deeply on his cigarette and looked at her. His face looked exhausted, as though he hadn't slept well, and he responded with a speech that he appeared to have prepared in advance. He said that he was an adult, not an adolescent, and that he had given the matter long thought and made sure of his feelings towards her. He respected her uprightness and commitment to her religion but was, at the same time, solicitous of his family and didn't want his children to pay the price in any way for his love for her. Nourhan folded her arms across her chest and looked at the floor, appearing, at that moment, like any woman who has been deeply insulted and awaits the immediate restoration of her honour. Dr Hani lit another cigarette and said that he was prepared to marry her right away, on two conditions – first, that their marriage should remain a secret, and second, that they would have no children. This aside, he was entirely ready to fulfil her every demand. Nourhan said nothing for a while, then stated, tersely, that the offer of marriage had taken her by surprise and she needed time to think. She forced herself to give a wan smile, said goodbye, and left the office with slow, slightly faltering steps (reflecting her confusion), while he followed her with his eyes.

She disappeared again for a whole week, during which she returned none of his calls, which compelled him to summon her to his office again, via Abu Talib. She seemed mournful and worried this time, and when he asked her why she'd been absent, she said she was going through a personal crisis, and had said the prayer for guidance

66

for a number of nights in the hope that God would bless her with the right decision. Dr Hani didn't ask her what her decision was, as though afraid that it might be a refusal. Instead, he repeated his offer of marriage. Nourhan said nothing and averted her beautiful face, as though seeking the appropriate answer. Then she looked him in the face and said that she agreed, in principle, and would leave the bride price and trousseau for him to decide, because she had no interest in money. However, she did have two conditions: first, he must tell her family of the marriage and have them witness it, so that it would be legal from the religious perspective, and second, that Dr Hani should buy a flat in her name in Mansoura. And here, for the first time in weeks, a sweet smile appeared on her beautiful face, and she said, with seeming affection, 'Even if it's just a small flat, it doesn't matter. The important thing is that it's in a decent neighbourhood and registered in my name, so that I feel like a legally wedded wife and not a mistress moving around from one furnished flat to another. I agree, of course, to delaying having children until we agree on the appropriate time. As far as your family is concerned, I swear to Almighty God that I shall be mindful, because I couldn't bear the guilt of distancing you from your children.'

Dr Hani agreed and bought in her name a luxury flat with three bedrooms and a living room in the upscale Tourelle neighbourhood. Then he demonstrated his generosity by paying her a fifty-thousand-pound bride price and buying her, as an engagement gift, a ring with a solitaire diamond. Vows were exchanged at her home at a splendid party that was limited to relatives and close friends. Dr Hani persuaded his first wife that he had taken on additional responsibilities at the college, which required that he work every day until evening, and at the same time reorganised his lectures so that they were all over early. He would go daily directly from the college to Nourhan's flat, then be home at the end of the day. The newly-weds were of one mind on everything, except one.

Dr Hani liked whisky but Nourhan resolutely banned it, because alcohol, being forbidden by religion, drives the angels from the house, as mentioned in a Noble Tradition. Dr Hani yielded to her wishes and made do with drinking with his friends every Thursday. He spent such happy days with her that one day, after he had drunk too much with his friends, he burst out, 'Lads, I'm in seventh heaven! Anyone who hasn't been married to Nour El Huda Muhammad Bayoumi has never been married at all!'

How happy he was then! But when did happiness ever last, and for whom?

Nourhan graduated with honours, her husband having put in a good word for her with his fellow professors. He then worked hard on the president of the university and had her appointed as a teaching assistant. Their life continued as usual, and one day he went to her, they ate lunch, and they made the most marvellous love. Nourhan went into the bathroom, returned with a rosy face, and put her white cashmere dressing gown on over her bewitching body. She sat down in front of him and smiled. Then she said, in a completely normal tone of voice, 'Congratulations, darling! I'm pregnant.'

Dr Hani was taken by surprise and said nothing for a few moments, staring into thin air as though he didn't believe it. Then he reminded her, in a gasping, unsteady voice, that they'd agreed not to have children. Nourhan responded immediately, 'You and I wanted to prevent a pregnancy, but when Our Lord, Glorious and Mighty, wants something, "He says, Let it be, and it is."'

At this, Dr Hani exploded in a rage such as she had never seen before, and started yelling at her and threatening her, accusing her of being a liar and evil and of having tricked him. Nourhan smiled sadly and meekly and didn't answer him back with even one word (since, as a Muslim wife, she was commanded by religion to bear her husband's anger and meet abuse with charity). Dr Hani disappeared for ten days, during which Nourhan made no effort to contact him, then returned. But when she went to embrace him, as was her custom, he pushed her away and sat down on the living room sofa. Lighting a cigarette, he said, avoiding looking at her, 'I've arranged with a colleague at the Faculty of Medicine for you to go in on Monday and have an abortion.'

In that instant, Nourhan was transformed into a raging lioness, and she yelled, 'You want me to disobey Our Lord, Great and Glorious, just to suit you? Impossible! Our Lord has commanded me to obey you in what's right, not what's wrong. No creature may be obeyed if that creature demands disobedience to the Creator!'

He tried to say something, but she cut him off in a voice that echoed off the walls of the love nest: 'Listen, Hani! I'm going to say a few words for you to "wear like an earring". I'm a Muslim woman and will never do anything to anger Our Lord. You're not going to be of any help to me when I'm thrown into the grave and held to account for my sins! And I'll have you know that, even if you divorce me, I have ways to make sure the child in my belly gets its rights. Like they say, "No one leaves the bathhouse the same as he went in," my dear sir!'

Dr Hani submitted to the *fait accompli* after arguments and quarrels and failed attempts to convince her from his side, and yelling and weeping and slapping of her cheeks from hers, and Nourhan gave birth to a beautiful boy child whom she named Hamza (in memory of the uncle of the Prophet, God bless him and grant him peace), and when they celebrated his first birthday, she asked Dr Hani to secure the child's future. This time, he made no objection and opened Hamza a bank account in which he deposited a million pounds, and he also gave him a large orange orchard, which he registered in his name. With Hamza there, it was no longer possible to keep the secret and the news made its way to his first wife (via a brief telephone call from an unknown well-wisher) and Dr Hani was forced into a confrontation with her that ignited a war to the death against both him and Nourhan, who bore the injuries done her by her co-wife patiently and in the hope of heavenly reward, as befits a Muslim woman. Dr Hani's children joined their mother's side and would have nothing to do with him, to the point that the eldest, who was a medical student, was impertinent to him, describing him as 'a skirt-chaser'. Dr Hani couldn't bear all these problems. His blood pressure rose and he suffered a blood clot in the brain that led to hemiplegia. He was taken ill in Nourhan's flat, and she spared no effort in looking after him, staying with him for three whole days in the hospital, during which she consulted a number of sheikhs of proven reliability, all of whom ruled that the best thing for Dr Hani, given his severe medical condition, was for him to be with his first wife and grown-up children.

Nourhan acted in accordance with the opinion of religion and contacted his first wife, asking her to come and look after her husband at the hospital, then quickly departed, to avoid embarrassment. A few months later, God's will was made manifest and Dr Hani's fated end overtook him. Nourhan then demanded her legal share of the inheritance, which she obtained after a number of problems and court cases with his first wife, all of which she won.

Such was her history with Dr Hani El Aasar, God rest his soul, and in what way, pray tell, can Nourhan be said to have committed any sin or violated religion's code? Would it not be better for those who spread rumours about her to fear God and have some shame?

4. *They say Nourhan is a dangerous woman, who messes with men's minds and uses sex to gain mastery over them, then does with them what she will.*

Good gracious! Are merits to be turned into faults? Blessings into punishments? What fault is it of Nourhan's if men like her? Are we to punish her for her beauty? Does she have to be misshapen and repulsive for us to accept her? All her life, Nourhan has dressed respectably, followed the rules of religion, and not allowed any man

70

who was not her husband or a close relative to lay even a fingertip upon her, even when she was fully clothed. As for the sex, would that every Muslim wife would put on half the show that Nourhan would put on for her husband! Is not the Muslim wife commanded by the precepts of religion to please her husband in bed using every method (the two forbidden acts, namely intercourse during menstruation and penetration of the anus, excepted)?

Do not the greatest scholars of religion call on the Muslim wife to be an 'obedient whore' in her husband's bed, so as to satisfy his sexual appetites and preserve him from vice? Nourhan had been a naive, inexperienced girl who knew nothing of sex, so she laboured and toiled to acquaint herself with it. She read a lot and watched dozens of instructional films on the internet until she had learned the arts of the bedroom and practised these (in religiously approved fashion) time after time, until she perfected them. She learned to pluck out the hair on her body (front and back), moisturise her skin using the Moroccan Mixture, clean her intimate areas and fumigate them with incense in the Sudanese manner, and then rub them with a fruit-flavoured perfumed oil (apricot or apple). Had she not learned to arouse her husband (in religiously approved fashion)? How to turn off the bedroom lights and light candles and then burn benzoin resin in order to prepare her husband psychologically for love? How to direct a grave, passionate look at her husband and then bite her lower lip to indicate her desire? How to wear a revealing nightdress and then lean over in front of her husband, apparently without meaning to, to bewitch him with the sight of her breasts? She had bought a belly-dancer's outfit for an exorbitant sum and learned how to dance in front of him with lascivious and loveable abandon. And she had learned, in bed, when to moan, how to whisper thrilling words in her husband's ear, and how to play with 'the seven erogenous zones' of his body, driving him crazy (since we are speaking of religiously sanctioned pleasures, there is no call

71

for prudishness or embarrassment). Nourhan had learned how to give her husband pleasure using her plump, soft behind without performing the forbidden act of penetration. She had learned how to suck her husband's phallus slowly and smoothly – as religion permits her to do – and indeed had even begun offering him fruits, cinnamon syrup, and pineapple juice long enough ahead of intercourse to make the taste of his semen in her mouth more palatable. Are we to blame Nourhan for her efforts and her prowess in the area of sex? Are we to blame her for satisfying her husband and keeping him blameless of sin? Should we not rather blame the Muslim woman who withholds herself from her husband, or neglects him in bed, causing him to fall, God forbid, into vice? Nourhan is a virtuous Muslim woman (we give precedence over God to none!) who abides by the teachings of religion and has never deviated from them by so much as a finger's breadth.

Finally, the only thing remaining where such rumours are concerned is Nourhan's relationship with Eng. Essam Shaalan.

Nourhan was a widow before she was thirty. Alone, she bore responsibility for her son Hamza. True, she had a large monthly income from her share of the inheritance, as well as her salary from the university and her late husband's pension, but she felt that Mansoura had become too small for her and wanted to raise her son in the capital, where everything was better. She therefore laboured persistently until she was transferred to Cairo University. She rented out her flat in Mansoura and lived in a 'new rent' flat in El Giza, then exerted herself until she got a job as a presenter on the People's Radio station, and when the cement crisis hit two years ago, the head of the station charged her with the task of holding interviews about it. She conducted a one-on-one with Essam Shaalan, manager of the Bellini cement factory and so impressed him with her efficiency that he offered her a job as the factory's media advisor at an attractive salary, with easy working hours that would not conflict with her work at the university and the radio. Nourhan accepted the position and did her best to carry out its responsibilities in a way pleasing to God. Unfortunately, however, the same old story repeated itself. Essam Shaalan imagined that she was an easy woman and tried to seduce her, but she taught him a harsh lesson in morals and quit the job immediately. Essam pursued her but she ignored him totally. He then offered to marry her, but she refused and informed him that she had dedicated her life to her son Hamza. All the same, he persisted, striving to persuade her that their marriage would be in Hamza's interest because Essam would be a surrogate father to him. In the end, Nourhan accepted, on two conditions: that he buy her a flat in a suitable area of Cairo where she would live with Hamza, and that it be a common-law marriage, so that she would not lose the late Dr Hani's pension (Sheikh Shamel had given this arrangement his blessing from the religious perspective).

Essam married her at the office of a friend of his who was a lawyer, and bought her the flat she now lives in in the Sheikh Zayed neighbourhood, then used his influence on her behalf so that she could take unpaid leave from the university and be transferred to work as a presenter on TV.

What exactly is wrong, or sinful, about what Nourhan did? She married twice according to the custom and practice of the prophet and messenger of God. So far as the age difference is concerned, the True Religion does not forbid marriage between a Muslim woman and a man twenty or thirty years her senior. And then, isn't it possible that Nourhan really loved Essam? Isn't it possible that she was impressed by his determination to marry her, or perhaps trusted him and felt he was capable of protecting her and taking care of Hamza?

What is certain is that Essam Shaalan is attractive to women. At first glance, he looks strange, off-putting, outside the norm. But – and bear in mind that he is past sixty – he still has a strong, slender body with no flab, thick, entirely white hair, and a dark brown

73

face with hard, rocky features; to these characteristics may be added his loud, gruff voice and the sceptical, searching looks he directs at whomever he's talking to, as though questioning their veracity. This rough, confrontational nature (so often attractive to women) he may have acquired while in prison camp, where a defiant response is the only alternative to being broken, or may be due to the effect of alcohol, as he never goes to bed without first drinking half a litre of whisky. At the same time, as a Marxist since his youth, he despises false, bourgeois refinements and is always completely frank, calling things by their names even at the risk of people considering him insolent or foul-mouthed. He is quite capable of interrupting whomever he is talking to, whatever his position or status, and saying in peremptory tones, 'You have no right to say that!' or 'You're just repeating lies. Shame on you!'

Essam Shaalan had been a leader of the student sit-ins of 1972. The protesters had demanded that President El Sadat come to Cairo University, but instead he sent the minister of youth to negotiate with them. When the students demanded democracy and freedom, the minister was at a loss and said, 'My dear children, it's not my decision to make. I'm just a postman. All I can do is pass on your demands to His Excellency the President.'

Silence reigned for a few minutes, and then suddenly the gruff voice of Essam Shaalan rang through the hall: 'We thought you were a minister and capable of taking responsibility but you say you're a postman. We don't need postmen. Please be so good as to leave.'

Immediately, the students started chanting 'Out! Out!'

The minister left to the accompaniment of mocking comments and the incident came to be remembered as a glorious deed, one that was recounted to prove the courage of Essam Shaalan, who had thrown out a minister sent by El Sadat. Shaalan had never married because he'd spent years on the run from the security apparatuses.

By the time his situation was normalised, he was getting on in years and had grown accustomed to being alone and free. He could no longer tolerate life with a wife to hold him to account or watch over him (he considered his relationship with Nourhan a temporary companionship, not a marriage). At the same time, his conscience would not allow him, at his advanced age, to have a child and then leave it to face the evils of the world while still young. Essam Shaalan withdrew from the political struggle and worked his way up until he became manager of the Bellini cement factory. His material circumstances also improved, though he continued to be influenced by Marxism and was a member of several NGOs for the support of freedom of thought and the combatting of religious fanaticism. He scrupulously signed statements of solidarity with writers whose works were confiscated or who were put on trial because of their writings. He refused to buy a Mercedes because of its bourgeois associations and made do with a spacious recent-model Peugeot. He never wore a tie and wore a safari suit in the summer, with a roll-neck pullover under it in the winter.

*　*　*

One day, Engineer Essam left the factory at 7 p.m. Madany, his driver, took his briefcase, which was stuffed with papers, and, as soon as he had settled into the car's back seat, the engineer said, 'Take me to Sheikh Zayed, Madany.'

As though he'd been given a secret password, Madany drove till he was through the factory gates, then stopped in a side street, lowered the curtains over the windows, opened the boot, and took out a bottle of whisky, an icebox, and a cup full of pickled cucumbers, placing everything on the table attached to the back of the seat in front of Eng. Essam, who swallowed a Viagra, so that its effects would be felt at the right time. Essam spent the time on the road

75

from Turah to Sheikh Zayed drinking and listening to the songs of Umm Kulsoum. Throughout the year and a half of their relationship, he had failed to persuade Nourhan to allow him to drink in the flat. He respected her piety and avoided discussions of religion with her so as not to anger her, and he'd agreed to a common-law marriage for her sake, but he didn't think she had the right to prevent him from drinking in a flat he'd bought with his own money. Essam believed in God, but after extensive reading had been assailed by doubts about all religions and no longer believed that God, the highest, absolute power, could have chosen people like us to speak in His name. Often he wondered whether there really was another life after death. No one had died and returned to tell us what happens. Wasn't it possible that death was just an extinguishing of the consciousness, after which the body would be transformed into some other form of matter? He shared these opinions only with a few of his old socialist friends at their drinking sessions. He'd say to them, sarcastically, 'There are a million rational people in the Rastafarian sect who believe that Haile Selassie, Emperor of Ethiopia, is God Himself and who worship him with utter devotion and sincerity. Note that Haile Selassie has been dead for fewer than forty years. Imagine this creed after four hundred years. There will be millions of people worshipping Haile Selassie and ready to defend their religion to the death.'

Essam viewed religion as follows: all religions begin as folklore, and with time acquire sanctity because people need to have faith in the unknown in order to put up with their hardships and sense of injustice.

Egyptians, as they grow older, turn to religion in the hope of a happy ending. Essam, however, was incapable of self-deceit. He could not practise the rites of a religion he didn't believe in. Despite, therefore, the overwhelming pleasure that Nourhan gave him, he still felt lonely, as though loneliness were his fate. He had lived alone and would die alone. He accepted the idea of death, but feared illness. He didn't want to be in pain or become a burden on people or the object of their pity. He hoped he would die quietly in his own bed and had resolved, in his heart of hearts, to commit suicide if afflicted with a serious disease.

Essam poured himself a fresh glass of whisky, listened to the voice of Umm Kulsoum, and decided to put everything that was worrying him out of his mind. He'd suffered greatly in his life, he thought to himself, and deserved to enjoy what was left of it. By the time he reached Nourhan's building, he was tipsy and had phoned to make sure that little Hamza had gone to sleep. The sound of her voice on the telephone had excited him, and he got out of the car in a hurry, entering the towering building and taking the lift to the tenth floor. Nourhan was waiting for him, the scent of perfume wafting off her, wearing the pink dressing gown that he loved. And the moment she closed the door, she turned to face him, suddenly threw off the dressing gown, which fell to the floor, and revealed that her body was totally naked. Essam stared at her for a moment, then lost control of himself and pounced. She pretended to be taken by surprise and whispered in a weak voice, 'Be careful with me. Please don't hurt me.'

The melting tone in which she said this so kindled his desire that his erection became almost painful. He took her to the bed, where his performance was strong and rough, and she shuddered twice before he reached his own climax. He went out into the living room, smoking a cigarette, and she went into the bathroom, then passed by Hamza's room to make sure that he was asleep. After she returned, she sat down next to Essam on the sofa and said, 'Darling, have you thought about it?'

'I have.'

'And have you made a decision?'

'I need to think about it some more.'

'Beloved, this is an opportunity that won't come again. You're an expert in cement. If we open a company to trade in cement, we'll make millions.'

'The problem is that it's not legal.'

'I told you, the company will be in my name.'

'You're my wife, which means that the law forbids you to trade in cement.'

'It's a common-law marriage.'

'It makes no difference.'

'No one knows I'm your wife.'

Essam smiled and said, 'There are lots of wonderful people about. As soon as we open a company, anyone could inform the Administrative Control Authority.'

'You're afraid of a man-made law? I acknowledge only the law of God.'

Sarcastically, Essam asked her, 'Did God really make a law for cement trading?'

Ignoring his sarcasm, she said seriously, 'I asked Sheikh Shamel and he said a company like that was acceptable religiously.'

'You must have taken him out for a good dinner.'

'Essam . . . please speak of our religious scholars with respect.'

He held his tongue. He would have liked to maintain the happy mood and was preparing himself for another bout of love, but Nourhan began a new manoeuvre. She snuggled up to him, kissed his neck, and whispered, 'Tell me frankly: are you going to form a company?'

'I'll think about it and let you know.'

'Give me a specific time.'

'In two weeks.'

'Promise?'

'Promise.'

She reached out and played with his white hair, then sighed and said coquettishly, 'Dearie me, I do love you, you old man, you!'

He felt the blood course through his veins at the touch of her soft, plump body. He kissed her slowly, his hands roaming. Suddenly the phone rang and he left her to answer it, uttering a few words that she didn't hear before ending the call. Then he kissed her on her forehead and said, 'Sorry, Nour. There's a big problem. I have to go back to the factory right away.'

8

Danya prayed the evening prayer plus the two supererogatory prostrations, put on her pyjamas, and stretched out on the bed. She pressed the button next to her and all the lights went out. Closing her eyes in the darkness, she went over what her father had said. She felt oppressed and her head filled with questions.

Wasn't Islam the religion of God, who was just and merciful? How could He allow people to be tortured, their dignity treated as though it were worth nothing? Had she done her father a wrong? Was she really a headstrong girl who acted on her emotions with no thought to the consequences?

The tragedy of Khaled Said had made a strong impression on her and she'd been keen to visit his mother, with no thought other than to console her. The impact of the visit on her father and her brothers was something she hadn't considered. She couldn't bear the idea that she'd been a cause of harm to them: they were the people she loved most in this world; there was nobody more tender or generous than her father. She prayed God one day to allow her to repay him for even a part of his kindness to her.

Was his reward to be that she caused problems for him in his work? Why had she begun sometimes to overreact and argue with him in an unbecoming way? When she remembered that her father was having her watched, her growing sense of guilt became mixed with anxiety. He must surely have found out about Khaled. It looked that way from his angry face. Hadn't he said that her riff-raff fellow students at the university had poisoned her ideas? Was that just a passing comment, or had he meant Khaled specifically?

Danya couldn't get to sleep, so she got out of bed and made herself a large glass of hot mint tea and lay down on the sofa. Despite her anxiety and exhaustion, a smile escaped her when she recalled that Khaled Madany stood accused of poisoning her ideas. How true was the charge? Khaled had been her fellow student since the medical prep year. His name began with the letter of the Arabic alphabet that came before hers, so they were together in every review group and in the practical and oral exams. She knew him by sight and would say hi when she saw him, as she would to any other colleague. She'd never thought about him much and her relationship with him might have remained as superficial as this till they graduated, but one day she'd read an article of his in the wall magazine where he said that morals without religion were better than religion without morals. At that time, she was an enthusiastic disciple of Sheikh Shamel. Khaled's article had provoked her so much that she'd thought of writing a rebuttal that would refute all the arguments he'd put forward. The following day, she'd seen him at the review group and hadn't been able to contain herself. Angrily, she'd asked him, 'Are you the one who wrote the article on religion and morals?'

'Yes.'

'It's a very bad article and you had no right to say any of it.'

He looked at her calmly from behind his black-rimmed spectacles, then smiled and said, 'You have the right to believe that.'

His calmness provoked her, so she said vehemently, 'How dare you say rude things about religion like that?'

'I didn't say anything rude about religion.'

'You said that morals are more important than religion.'

'I said that morals without religion are better than religion without morals.'

'You can't have morals without religion.'

'You can, and the proof is that lots of atheists have morals and a conscience.'

81

'If a person refuses to believe in God, God forbid, how can he have morals?'

'A person can put his morals into practice via his conscience rather than via religion.'

His immediate, confident answers confused her somewhat and she asked him, 'Are you a Muslim?'

'I am, thanks be to God.'

'God says, "The true religion in God's eyes is Islam" and He says, "If anyone seeks a religion other than Islam, it shall not be accepted of him" so all the ideas you wrote in your article are displeasing to God and His prophet.'

His smile grew broader and he said kindly, as though talking to a child of whom he was fond, 'Will you hear me out without interrupting?'

'Go ahead.'

'I pray and I fast and I perform my religious duties, but I believe that the true religion lies in what I do, not what I believe. Religion isn't an end in itself. It's a means to teach us virtue. Our Lord, Glorious and Mighty, isn't in need of our prayers and our fasting. We pray and fast to discipline ourselves. Islam isn't just a matter of outward form and acts of worship, as the Salafists believe, and it isn't just a means to gain power, as the Muslim Brothers believe. If Islam doesn't make us more humane, than neither it nor we are worth anything.'

She looked at him without answering. He continued excitedly, 'Why do we learn medicine? To treat people. In other words, there's no point to our studies unless we practise medicine. By the same logic, religion is an exercise in the doing of good. What is the point of performing its rites if they are not reflected in our morals?'

They talked a lot that day. Even though she fought him, deep down, she was impressed by his powers of analysis and his ability to express his views. He told her he was a poet. She asked, so he recited to her a poem of his called 'The Pharaoh'. When she asked him what some of the things in the poem meant, he said, 'You can't explain poetry.'

'Even if you're the one who wrote the poem?'

'I can't explain it precisely because it's my poem. Poetry has to explain itself.'

He spoke to her in a lovely, simple way. After that, they continued to meet often, and each time she discovered how meagre her store of knowledge was compared to his abundant supply of information. In each conversation, he would draw her attention to some new thing she'd never thought about before. Thanks to Khaled, her views on many things changed. He left such an impression on her that she could remember sentences he'd said word for word. Indeed, more than once she caught herself speaking just like him, and once she said to him, 'You know, when I listen to you, I can't believe that you're the same age as me.'

'I'm five months older than you.'

'Sometimes when we're talking I feel as though the soul of a sixty-year-old has passed into your body.'

He laughed loudly and said, 'So you think I'm possessed by a demon?'

She answered seriously, 'Really. Your ideas are far beyond your age.'

'I thank you, but they're not my ideas. They're all things I've read.'

'When did you read all these books?'

'The credit should go to my father, who noticed that I liked to read when I was small, so he gave me a subscription to the Palace of Culture. I began borrowing books, reading them and returning them. Imagine – that a simple, uneducated man could value reading so much!'

When he spoke of his father, a mixture of tenderness and pride appeared in his face. She respected this in him, that he wasn't at all embarrassed by the humbleness of his family. Once he told her, 'I've been very blessed. God gave me a father who was poor and honourable. I couldn't have borne it if my father had been rich and corrupt.'

She often wondered what the secret of this inner peace might be, which was always apparent on his face, as though he was completely certain as to the future. He took everything simply, even the class difference between them. Once he said to her mockingly, 'You know what? Sometimes I'm afraid of our friendship.'

'Why?'

'Your father could destroy me and my family in a second.'

'My father only goes after terrorists and spies.'

He laughed and said, 'Thank God I'm an upstanding citizen!'

Then he went on, jokingly, 'In any case, Madame Danya, I thank you for befriending someone like me who has exactly ten pounds and sixty piastres in his pocket and has to hop on a minibus every day to get to class.'

She appeared annoyed and said, 'Have you ever felt I lord it over my colleagues?'

'You're a modest person, but your modesty doesn't change the truth.'

'What truth?'

'That you are Danya, daughter of the aristocracy, and I'm Khaled, son of a driver.'

'Khaled, please . . . that kind of talk upsets me.'

He apologised and they spoke of something else. After this, she told her driver not to bring the Mercedes onto the college grounds and took to leaving on foot through the Qasr El Eini Street gate and getting into the car in the street. She even stopped wearing very expensive outfits and took to going to college in simple clothes, as far as possible. She tried to make friends with fellow students to whom she'd never spoken before and to divest herself of anything that might distinguish her from any ordinary female student. It upset her when he spoke of the social difference between them because it reminded her that their friendship had no future. Another year and they'd graduate. Inevitably, they'd go their separate ways. Her attachment to Khaled wasn't viable under any circumstances. Even if he graduated with top marks and was appointed a teaching assistant at the faculty, even if he got a contract to work in the Gulf and became rich, his father's job as a driver would remain an insuperable barrier. She couldn't even bring the matter up with her family. Despite all of this, from time to time, she was seized by an obscure hope that some unexpected event would occur (like in the movies) and that she'd marry Khaled and bear his children. She thought about it all the time. She went over him in her mind bit by bit: his clean, slender body that gave off a nice smell of soap; the thick hair on his chest that showed through the opening in his shirt; his beautiful, calm smile; his honest, trusting look from behind his spectacles; his smooth black hair, full lips, and even, shiny white teeth; his long, tapering fingers, like a pianist's. Often, she dreamed of him. She'd see herself sitting next to him on a sofa in a resplendent garden, surrounded by flowers more beautiful than any she'd seen before; she was whispering words that she couldn't hear to him and holding his hands. Then she'd embrace him and put his head on her breast and be shaken by an overwhelming pleasure, and the dream would end. In the morning, though, she'd feel guilty, and she'd shower, ask God for forgiveness, and pray.

Every day that passed brought her closer to Khaled. She told him everything she did, listened to his opinion, and asked him about everything that was on his mind. They spent long hours together at the faculty. She had asked him – to avoid gossip – that they not sit anywhere together, insisting that they talk while walking in the college grounds. Khaled made fun of her misgivings, saying, 'If being together is going to cause rumours, it won't make any difference whether we're walking or sitting.'

'There is a difference,' she said, seriously. 'If they see us when we're walking, we could be going to a lecture. If we're sitting on our own, though, we're proclaiming to everyone that we have something special.'

'Don't we have something special?'

'Of course, but it's not in our interest to announce it now.'

'Our friendship is honourable and respectable.'

She replied with affectionate sarcasm, 'Dr Khaled, we're living in Egypt, not Holland!'

'Meaning we have to submit to the rules of a backward society?'

'If I really matter to you, then you have to be concerned for my reputation.'

Khaled nodded and said, 'I'm not convinced, but I'll do whatever makes you comfortable.'

Every day they'd roam the Qasr El Eini grounds, talking. They called their meetings of this kind their 'strolls'. Despite her attachment to him, she felt no guilt. When she prayed, she stood before God with a clear conscience. She'd thank God that she hadn't committed any sin with Khaled (apart from the dreams, which happened involuntarily).

In two years, he had never touched her. He had never tried, and she wouldn't have let him.

Lying on the sofa now, she dozed off, waking the following morning with a headache and a pain in her neck. The moment she reached the college, she started looking for Khaled but couldn't find him. She rang him but found his phone was off. He appeared at the end of the day, and she asked him, 'Where were you?'

He said quietly, 'We'll talk on our stroll.'

Once they'd begun their daily round, she asked him angrily, 'Is it normal for you to hide all day?'

He smiled and said, 'I had a meeting at the National Association for Change.'

'Your phone was off.'

'During the meetings, we have to turn our phones off and put them somewhere else or they can be used to listen in on us.'

She thought of her conversation with her father about surveillance. Somewhat calmer now, she said, 'You ought to have told me, Khaled. I was worried about you.'

'Sorry.'

Silence reigned for a moment, then she said, 'I wanted to ask you about something.'

'Go ahead.'

'Does Islam permit torture?'

'Of course not. Islam forbids torture.'

'But Islam commands punishments such as flogging, stoning, and the cutting off of limbs. Aren't those all forms of torture?'

Khaled looked at her in amazement and asked, 'Who told you that nonsense?'

'A relative of mine who has read deeply on the subject of religion. He told me that there is a punishment in religious law called "castigation". It gives the ruler the right to imprison anyone and torture him if he considers him a danger to society.'

A whole minute passed, during which he walked beside her in silence. Then she said, 'Are you thinking about something else?'

'I'm ordering my thoughts so I can answer you.'

'Go ahead, professor,' she exclaimed in amusement. Then he said seriously, 'You know, Danya, in the days of the Roman Empire, the method of execution used was to throw the accused to the lions to devour. In those days, this punishment was so well accepted that people used to go and enjoy watching those horrendous scenes. What would you say if the Italian government was to revive the tradition and start throwing criminals to the lions again? Would that be acceptable?'

'No, of course not.'

'So we have to understand Islam in the same way. Primitive punishments, such as flogging and stoning, existed in a specific historical context which has now come to an end. By the way, the same punishments existed in Jewish law but were abolished. Islam has to be understood as consisting of general humane principles – justice, equality, freedom.'

'So you're against the application of religious law?'

'The law has to bring about justice. If we are to apply the punishments that were applied a thousand years ago, we'll never be able to realise justice.'

'If Sheikh Shamel heard you, he'd call you an infidel for sure.'

'Sheikh Shamel and his like are paid millions to spread Wahhabi thought and support the authorities. Frankly, I don't consider them men of religion to start with. They're businessmen.'

'But millions of Muslims want religious law to be applied.'

'Religious law is the rules of Our Lord, and jurisprudence is the method by which those rules are to be applied. The law is divine; jurisprudence is a human endeavour. It follows that one cannot apply the words of jurisprudents who lived centuries ago. We have to develop a new jurisprudence suited to the age. Islam permitted the purchase of girl slaves for sexual pleasure. Do you really think we should put girls on sale in Ataba Square, for example, and allow anyone who bought one to sleep with her? It is not acceptable, in the twenty-first century, to cut off someone's hand or flog him or throw him into a hole and stone him to death. "Castigation" may have been useful a thousand years ago but it cannot be applied now. If your relative is determined to implement the punishment of castigation, then we have the right to buy slave girls for sexual pleasure. You can't abandon one thing and apply another. If we're going to bring history back, we have to bring it all back.'

Khaled was quiet for a moment, then continued, 'Would you like me to tell you about a fixed principle that never changes? Everything that is foreign to justice and the truth is foreign to Islam. Everything that is against human dignity is against Islam.'

She said nothing for a while, so he asked, 'Are you convinced?'

'I'll have to think about it,' she replied lightly.

Suddenly, he stopped walking, looked at his watch and said, 'We have to go to Lecture Hall 95, quickly.'

'Why?'

'We have a meeting to prepare for Tuesday's demonstration.'

'Please take me to the gate first.'

'You don't want to come to the meeting?'

She was silent for a moment, as though plucking up her courage, then she said, 'I'm sorry, Khaled. I won't be able to take part in the demonstration.'

'You agreed.'

'I've changed my mind.'

He stopped walking and looked at her. Apparently on the verge of anger, he said, 'May I know the reason?'

'My participation in the demonstration could harm my family.'

'If everyone thought the way you do, no one would take part in the demonstration.'

'I don't think it's a shame or a sin to be afraid for my family.'

'Who told you I'm not afraid for my family? At least your family are important people. My family are poor. They wouldn't survive a single night at a police station.'

She smiled sadly and said, 'I was sure you wouldn't appreciate my situation.'

'No I do not appreciate your situation.'

Sharply she said, 'So you want me to bring harm to my family to make you happy?'

They had reached the gate. He looked at her and said, 'Danya, the issue is larger than our fear for our families. Many have sacrificed themselves for change, so that we can be decent citizens in a decent state. So that the police treat the lowest of citizens with respect. So that the law is applied to everybody. So that there won't be anyone in Egypt who can't find food to eat, who is without shelter, who cannot afford a doctor.'

She smiled and said, 'You mean that I, specifically, am going to make that change?'

Eagerly, he replied, 'Your participation in the demonstration is more important than mine. It's natural for me to demand change, because I'm poor, but when someone from a rich family demands change, it's something noble, because she's defending the truth disinterestedly.'

'There's bound to be rich people other than me in the demonstration.'

'You're waiting for others to do what has to be done in your place.'

She shook her head and said, 'There's no point in discussing this. I'm going. Bye.'

He tried to say something, but she turned her back and left, while he followed her with his gaze until she had gone through the gate. The driver leapt up and opened the door, she got in, and little by little the car took her away until it disappeared into the midst of the traffic.

9

Dear Mazen,

I thank you so much for agreeing to be my friend and I thank you too for describing me as beautiful, even though I think of myself as ordinary. My number is 0127 555 2518. You are welcome to phone me any time. I got home an hour ago, took a hot shower, made myself a cup of Nescafé, and thought, I have to talk to you.

I went to the interrogation at 10 a.m. as they asked me to on the summons. In its dirt and neglect, the Education Directorate building perfectly expresses the state of education in Egypt. I climbed the stairs to Legal Affairs, where the person in charge of the interrogation was a very fat man whose name, according to the wooden nameplate on his desk, was Muatazz Bahiy. Next to him was a secretary whose name I don't know. He wrote down my answers. After the standard questions about my name, age, and profession, he said, 'The headmaster accuses you of wearing inappropriate dress during work. What do you say?'

'My clothes are these, the ones I'm wearing in front of you, sir. Do you see anything inappropriate about them? I don't cover my hair but I don't believe that that contravenes the law. My problem with the headmaster isn't to do with my clothes.'

'What is the problem, then?' he asked.

'The problem,' I said, 'is that I don't give private classes and that I conscientiously explain everything in the classroom. The problem is that I'm a threat to the private classes network led by the headmaster in partnership with the chief teacher and most of the other teachers. All of them extort money from the girls by

forcing them to take private classes and attend "review groups".'

The investigator signalled to the secretary, who stopped writing. Then he said, 'Prof. Asmaa, I have to caution you. Every word you say will be recorded against you because these are official minutes.'

I replied, 'I stick to every word I have said. And I'm prepared to provide proof.'

He stopped the interrogation, ordered me a glass of lemonade, and embarked on a friendly chat with me. He told me about the English teacher who'd taught him when he was a student at Saidiya Secondary. I felt he was a nice man. After a little while, he smiled and said, 'I think your nerves have calmed down now.'

'Certainly.'

'Would you like to continue the interrogation?'

'By all means. I want to put on record that I teach English to three classes and not one of the girls failed the exam in my subject. Despite this, the headmaster, instead of thanking me, persecuted me and made a malicious complaint against me because I threaten his interests.'

He stopped the interrogation again and asked me in annoyance, 'What's the matter with you? I'm telling you that what you're saying will open the gates of Hell before you. Do you think the headmaster will keep his mouth closed when you accuse him of pressuring the students to take private classes – that he won't defend himself?'

I said, 'I swear before God it's the truth.'

In a low voice, he told me, 'I believe you. But do you think the headmaster is doing this on his own? Wouldn't he have to have backing from important people in the ministry?'

I said, 'I shall defend what is right no matter what the cost.'

'Are you a teacher or a lawyer?'

'It's up to everyone to fight the corruption that's around them.'

The interrogator laughed (at my naivety, perhaps) and said, 'Before you fight corruption you have to know your capabilities. Be very careful you don't take on an unequal fight or your future will be ruined for nothing.'

He gave me no opportunity to respond, but continued rapidly, 'Listen. We'll limit our interrogations to the charge. I'll question you and you'll say it's not true you wore inappropriate dress. Then I'll get an undertaking from you that you will wear appropriate dress. You'll sign the undertaking, and the subject, from the legal perspective, will be closed.'

'If I write an undertaking against myself,' I told him, 'it means I acknowledge the truth of the accusation.'

'Certainly not. It's just a formal procedure. If the charge were true, I'd sign off on a penalty against you. But I'm going to make do with the undertaking and suspend the complaint. What do you say?'

I said nothing. I wasn't sure what to do. What he said made sense, but my anger and sense of being unjustly treated were pushing me towards confrontation. The interrogator smiled and said, 'Very well. I'll write that you were taken ill and postpone the interrogation for a week so you can think about it at your leisure.'

I asked him, 'During that week, should I go to the school?'

He answered, 'From the legal perspective, no decision has been issued barring you from working, from which it follows that you ought to go to the school so that your absence isn't used against you.'

I thanked the interrogator and thought about it on the way home. I found his logic sound. For sure, the headmaster must have someone covering for him in the ministry. It followed that he could do as he liked. I'm not afraid of them and I don't care if they fire me, but I'm sad, Mazen. I don't believe I should be punished this way just because I carry out my duties conscientiously. Tell me what you think. Should I act according to the interrogator's logic and sign the undertaking so that the complaint can be suspended, or should I tell the whole truth and fight to the end? I'm sorry to bother you with all my problems.

Even though I'm depressed, I'm going to pull myself together, for your sake, and smile so you can see the dimples. See them?

Bye, my friend.

Asmaa

10

How did Ashraf Wissa manage to escape so quickly?

He was lying on top of Ikram, naked and stoned, when he heard the knocking on the door. Leaping off her and snatching up his dressing gown, which was lying on the floor, he ran into the bathroom, locked the door, turned on the shower, and stood there, panting, under the hot water. He could imagine what must have happened. His wife Magda had come home early for some reason, tried to open the door with her key, and found that it was locked from the inside. Obviously, she'd assumed he was having sex with Ikram: there was no other explanation and no matter what stories he might make up, she'd never believe him. She would certainly have discovered Ikram's nightdress, seen the cushions on the ground, and understood everything. She would, for sure, be punishing Ikram right now, before coming to him. He knew Magda and her penchant for drama. She'd yell and cry and slap her face and bewail the luck that had cast her into the clutches of a man like him, who'd betrayed her with the maid in her own house. She'd make his life hell. She was capable of keeping the screaming and wailing up for an entire day without getting tired, till his nerves were completely destroyed, and then, at the end, she'd take a hot bath and sleep as soundly as a child. Magda had been given an opportunity to play the victim. She'd make him an object of scandal everywhere and tell all their relatives and friends, starting with Butrus and Sarah. He'd never be able to look them in the eye again. They'd caught the respected, model father with the maid. He came out from under the shower, put on his dressing gown, and sat on the edge of the bathtub. He wished he had a joint to calm his nerves. He closed his eyes and recited the Lord's Prayer to himself, then prayed to Jesus Christ to save him from the scandal. Opening his eyes again, he felt somewhat better. He bowed his head and breathed deeply and little by little his fear turned to displeasure. What had he done that he should hide from his wife like a guilty child? No doubt, he'd made a mistake. But should the blame fall on him alone, or should Magda share the responsibility? If she'd been a good-natured, easy-going wife, would he ever have become involved with the maid?

Dear Madame Magda, you're not going to take everything! You're not going to neglect me and despise me and convince Butrus and Sarah to emigrate and leave me on my own! You're not going to live just for your work, as though you weren't responsible for a house and a husband, and end up with everyone's sympathy, as though you were the one who was hard done by! The role of the betrayed wife doesn't suit you, Magda. You're the cause of what happened. I had an affair with the maid because I found in her everything you were incapable of providing. Because she respects me, because she worries about me and takes care of me and believes me and thinks of me as her man. Because she doesn't despise me and doesn't remind me of my failure. Because, quite simply, she's a real woman and not artificial and false, like you.

Ashraf approached the locked door, put his hands in the pockets of the dressing gown, and decided to confront Magda, whatever the consequences. *You're going to expose me to scandal but I too am going to tell everyone the truth about you, one by one.* He plucked up his courage and summoned up the strongest phrases to direct at his wife. He heard footfalls drawing close, then a quiet knock on the bathroom door.

In a hoarse voice, he asked, 'Who's there?'

'Ikram, Ashraf Bey.'

96

He realised that Magda must be with her. She'd brought Ikram with her to confront her with her partner in crime. Very well. *Let today be the end of things between us, Magda.* He cleared his throat and slowly opened the door. Then, assuming the normal tone of a master speaking to the maid, he said, 'What is it, Ikram? Is something wrong?'

She was wearing her work dress, and he was amazed to find that she was alone. Looking embarrassed, she said, 'I'm very sorry. I don't know what to tell you, sir. Mansour, my husband, is waiting in the living room.'

Events were moving too fast for Ashraf to take them in. He looked at her as though he didn't understand. Then he said, 'Why is Mansour here?'

She replied in a low voice, 'He wants money.'

'So why doesn't he get it from you at home?'

'He asked but I refused.'

There was a silence. Then she sighed and said, 'He always does this. When I refuse to give him money, he comes to where I'm working and threatens me.'

'So what am I supposed to do?'

'Would you like to meet him, sir?'

'Why should I meet him?' Ashraf exclaimed in alarm.

Ikram said apologetically, 'I'd like to ask you for five hundred pounds, sir. I'll stuff them in his pocket and send him off, and I'll pay you back from my wages at the end of the month.'

He had no alternative. He had to get rid of Mansour by any means possible; he couldn't remain in his house a moment longer: Mansour was a thug and an addict, he might do anything, plus he was her legally married husband. He might assault him, or make a complaint at the police station and accuse him of adultery with his wife. The unsettling thoughts multiplied in his mind and he decided to act quickly. He went straight to the bedroom, Ikram following

97

behind, and gave her five hundred pounds. She left and he remained standing in the middle of the room, stunned, unable to concentrate. After a short while, Ikram returned, on her face an expression that fluctuated between embarrassment and amusement.

'It's done, sir,' she said. 'He's gone, thank God.'

Ashraf didn't respond, so she continued in a low voice, 'I don't know what to say to you, sir. Sorry, again.'

A fit of anger suddenly seized him and he said, 'All the same, I don't get it, Ikram. Even if Mansour wanted money, the normal thing for him to do would be to ask for it from Madame Magda, because she's the one who gives you your wages. Why would he come in the morning, when we're together?'

She didn't answer. He was still wearing the dressing gown over his naked body. He sat down on the bed and tucked his legs underneath him, then opened the drawer of the bedside table and took out a joint, which he lit. He took a deep drag and the joint glowed brightly, exuding the penetrating smell of hashish. He coughed and said, 'To be honest, Ikram, what happened is strange and suspicious.'

She gave him a look of something close to reproach, then moved nearer to him, so that he smelled the smell of perfumed soap, and whispered, 'I told you, sir, to think of the money as a loan till the first of the month.'

She pulled his head towards her breast, but he pushed her away with his hand and said, 'For heaven's sake, don't talk nonsense! You know I could never take money from you. Plus, do you think that settles the Mansour problem? Of course it doesn't. He's going to jump out at us every day and demand money. It's blackmail, and I won't stand for it. Really, it's appalling.'

As though trying to conciliate him, Ikram said, 'It's not my fault, Ashraf Bey.'

He took another deep drag and said, 'I swear I don't know. I can't believe that he just turned up by coincidence.'

Silence reigned. Then Ikram took a step back and said, 'You think I set this up with Mansour, sir?'

'Take it any way you like,' he said, turning his face away. She looked at him for a moment, said, 'Thank you, Ashraf Bey,' and went out, closing the door quietly behind her.

11

Dear Asmaa,

I hope you're well. It's 9 p.m. and I've been at the factory since morning. The workers have a general problem and I'm here to show solidarity with them. I'll tell you what happened later. Here's my short answer to your question: accept the interrogator's offer and write the undertaking. It's just a formality. Our battle isn't with the headmaster, it's with the corrupt system that produced him. That's my opinion and you're free, of course, to act as you think best. I'm going back to the workers now so we can decide what action to take with management. Thank you for your smile.

Bye, beautiful.

Mazen

12

Madany, the driver, was asleep in the car when he became aware of Eng. Essam's voice saying, as he opened the door and threw himself onto the back seat, 'Take me back to the factory, Madany!'

It took Madany a few moments to grasp what was happening, then he turned on the engine and the car set off. Essam took some gum from his pocket and began chewing it to get rid of the smell of the alcohol. He also put a few drops of Prisoline in his eyes to get rid of the redness. Then he started making telephone calls, to keep abreast of the situation. The traffic was light, so they reached the factory quickly. No sooner had Essam passed through the gates than he beheld a sight never seen before: the workers had turned on all the factory's spotlights and gathered in the brilliant illumination in front of the management building wearing their old, tattered, khaki-coloured work outfits. They were talking to one another excitedly but, as soon as Essam's car appeared, the angry cries grew louder, then quickly resolved themselves into a single cry: 'We want our rights! We want our rights!'

Eng. Essam ignored them and went upstairs to his office. A few minutes later, he emerged onto the balcony with a megaphone, through which he shouted, 'Everyone, choose someone to speak in your name so I can come to an understanding with you.'

A wave of commotion ran through the workers that went on for a few minutes. Then they chose Hagg Shirbini, the oldest of the workers, along with Mazen Saqqa, a member of the union committee. The men went up to Essam's office, where he invited them to sit, then lit a cigarette and asked in a calm voice, 'What happened?'

Mazen said excitedly, 'Management has taken away the workers' rights and they have decided to strike.'

'Uncle' Shirbini pressed Mazen's leg with his hand to make him calm down. Then he smiled and said in a friendly tone of voice, 'Essam Bey, we are confident that you will treat us fairly. When the Italian company bought the factory, it undertook to pay out a twenty-five-month workers' dividend annually. We went to get it and were taken aback to find that the dividend was only five months. We're all struggling to feed children. We have responsibilities and families, and every year we wait for these dividends. You could say our lives depend on them.'

Eng. Essam took a drag on his cigarette and said, 'You know, Shirbini, there's nobody who loves the workers or looks out for their interests more than me.'

Mazen made no comment but Shirbini exclaimed fervently, 'God preserve you, Essam Bey, so that you can go on helping us!'

Essam took a sip from his coffee cup and said, 'I'm well aware of your circumstances, but we have to be rational. The company gives you a twenty-five-month dividend when it's making a profit but when it's making a loss it can't do so.'

Shirbini said, 'The company committed itself to giving the workers a twenty-five-month dividend no matter what the situation, and whether the factory was making a profit or a loss. It's an article in the contract of sale for the factory, and the Italians agreed to it.'

Essam smiled and said, 'Logic is more important than any contract. Logic says that a loss-making company can't pay out dividends to its workers. Do you know how much the factory loses in a year?'

'The workers aren't responsible for the company's losses,' Mazen said.

'So who is responsible, my dear engineer?' Essam asked mockingly, to which Mazen responded, 'You want me to tell you something you're already very well aware of, my dear sir?'

'Speak respectfully!' Essam yelled.

Speaking calmly, Mazen answered, 'I am speaking respectfully. The Italian company has three factories that it owns outright. Our factory is owned 35 per cent by the Egyptian government. It follows that it's in the interest of the Italian company to lose money on our factory and make money on the factories it owns, so that it doesn't have to share its profits with the government.'

'So you're a conspiracy theorist!' Essam said sarcastically.

'You know it's the truth,' Mazen responded.

There was silence for a moment. Then Uncle Shirbini said, 'Essam Bey, the furnaces need maintenance, but the company left them till they stopped working. When the company took over the factory, seven were working. Now we have only two. Is that the workers' fault? The company moves the new spare parts to its own factories and gets us old, non-functioning spare parts. Is that the workers' fault? If the company wants to make the factory unprofitable so that it doesn't have to share its profits with the government, that's its business, but it has to give the workers their dividends.'

Mazen said, 'The company is obliged to implement the contract as signed.'

Essam looked at them both for a moment, then smiled and said, 'Very well. I promise you I will convey your demands to management.'

'God bless you, Essam Bey!' said Shirbini. Mazen, however, remained silent.

'All I ask is that the workers return to work,' Essam continued in a friendly voice.

'The workers will never halt the strike before the dividends are paid,' Mazen responded.

'Bringing the factory to a halt like this is unacceptable.'

'It's not in my hands or Uncle Shirbini's. The workers have decided to continue the strike till the dividends are paid in full.'

Essam suddenly rose, gestured to them to follow him, and went out onto the balcony, where he took hold of the megaphone and shouted, 'Everyone! I have understood your demands and will convey them to the owners' representative, Mr Fabio.'

Confusion reigned in the ranks of the workers, and there was a babble of voices. Then the cry returned: 'We want our rights! We want our rights!'

Essam shouted in a louder voice, 'Now that your message has been delivered, I think you can halt the strike and go back to work.'

The workers' voices rose in a babble, then resolved themselves into a single cry. 'Strike! Strike!'

Essam smiled and shouted, 'If you insist on striking, that's your right. Please take care of the factory because it's yours. I've given instructions to the kitchen to prepare a hot meal for you.'

Cheers and shouts arose, then the cry came back, stronger, 'We want our rights!'

Essam turned to Uncle Shirbini and said, kindly, 'Thank you, Shirbini. Goodnight. Will you be spending the night at the factory?'

Shirbini responded straight away, 'I can't leave the workers.'

Essam nodded understandingly, then turned to Mazen and said, 'Mazen, I need you with me for a vital mission. Uncle Madany, my driver, will return you to the factory at one o'clock.'

Essam didn't wait for a reply but grabbed Mazen's arm and walked with him to the car. As soon as Mazen was seated next to him, Essam smiled and said affectionately, 'I'm certain you haven't had dinner. You have to eat. The Struggle needs nourishment.'

They went to the Four Seasons hotel in Garden City, where Mazen noted that Eng. Essam was known to the staff. They entered the lift and Essam asked, 'You like Italian food?' but before Mazen could reply, Essam had pressed the button for the second floor. He was always like that. He'd ask you a question, then not listen to the answer and do what he wanted. Essam ordered food, a glass of whisky, and a bottle of beer for Mazen, who tried to object, but Essam said, jokingly, 'Shut up, boy! You have to drink, that's an order. I used to drink so often with your father, God rest his soul.'

Essam took a large sip of the whisky and appeared refreshed. He said to Mazen, 'As you know, your father was my best friend. Forget that I'm the manager of the factory. You're like a son to me.'

'Thank you, sir.'

'We don't need to say thank you to each other. I want to have a couple of words with you. Will you listen to me?'

'Go ahead.'

'Listen, Mazen. I make a large salary and I live my life without problems. The struggle between the workers and the company doesn't concern me in the least. The only thing I'm interested in is your welfare. Do you understand?'

'I understand.'

'Everything you're doing with the workers is, sadly, pointless.'

'I'm doing my duty.'

'Your duty is to work as an engineer.'

'The workers elected me to the union committee to defend their rights.'

'I see. You're at the slogan stage.'

Mazen responded angrily, 'Are you mocking me?'

Essam said, seriously, 'I could never mock you, Mazen. I respect your enthusiasm and your defence of the workers. It's a noble state of mind in which your father and I lived for many long years, but in the end I discovered that it was a delusion.'

Mazen began to object, but Essam said, 'We agreed you'd hear me out.'

Mazen fell silent and Essam continued, 'Do you really believe that if the workers strike, they'll get anything? Do you really believe that the Italian company works on its own? The company has backing from some of the highest officials in the state.

In Egypt, what the state wants goes, and no one can stand up to it. My advice to you is to drop this whole headache and start thinking about your future.'

'Thank you for the advice, but I can't take it.'

'My dear boy, try to understand! The workers whom you defend will sell you down the river at any moment in return for a raise or incentives. Thousands of communists were imprisoned and tortured for the sake of workers' rights. And what did the workers do to help them? Nothing! They don't even remember who they were.'

'To tell you the truth, I'm amazed to hear such words from you, sir.'

Essam smiled bitterly and said, 'On the contrary, I have to say these things because I don't want you to repeat our mistakes. Your father and I wasted our lives for delusions. I was one of the top students at the Faculty of Engineering. I could have concentrated on my work, made millions, raised a family, and lived a happy life. Your dear departed father was a genius at law. He could have become the most important lawyer in Egypt if it weren't for the politics that made him a homeless wanderer, sent him to prison, had him tortured, and saw him die young from the illnesses he contracted in detention. The one thing that's certain is that nothing in Egypt will ever change. Save yourself and look to your future before it's too late.'

Mazen continued to keep his gaze on Essam, who went on: 'Once, I was a romantic, like you. My understanding of reality was superficial and naive. You want to know the truth? Egyptians don't revolt, or if they do, their revolution is bound to fail because they're cowardly and submissive by nature. We're the only people in history who thought their kings were gods and worshipped them. Egyptian culture, which we inherited from the pharaohs, is the culture of obedience to the pharaohs. Until the nineteenth century, the Egyptian peasant was proud of his ability to endure a flogging so that he wouldn't have to pay taxes. Furthermore, Islamic culture makes one accepting of tyranny. Islam demands of you that you obey the Muslim ruler even if he whips your back and steals your money. The Egyptians love a dictatorial hero and feel safe when they submit to despotism. In Egypt, the only thing your struggle can lead to is your own destruction.'

Mazen interrupted him angrily: 'With all due respect, what you're saying isn't true. Islam was at base a revolution against injustice. Then it was transformed into an institution with interests tied to the ruling system. Dictatorships have arisen in Spain, Germany, Italy, Portugal, and Argentina, and none of those countries are Islamic or pharaonic. We can't judge the Egyptian people by its behaviour five thousand years ago. Your view is unjust.'

Essam laughed and said, 'I can almost see your late father in front of me. He used to regard the People as a holy entity and wouldn't hear a word against it. Fine, Mazen. Memorise these questions and get me the answers from the history books. Here goes: the Wafd was the party of the majority and it could have millions of Egyptians mobilised in the streets in a few hours. Why did the Wafd accept the formation of the 1923 Constitutional Committee by appointment and not by election? Why didn't it stand up to King Fuad when he was a tyrant? Why did Saad Zaghloul submit his resignation from the premiership when he was the leader of the nation, and why didn't he mobilise the Egyptians to confront the king and the British, and why did the Wafd allow Nasser to abolish democracy in 1954, when the Wafd at the time could have mobilised the people and forced the army back to its barracks? Why did the Egyptians tolerate the imprisonment of their beloved leader Muhammad Naguib, and why did they cling on to Nasser in 1967 after he'd brought about devastating defeat and the occupation of the country? After the slaying of Sadat, Hosni Mubarak freed the political prisoners, among them most of Egypt's intellectuals. Why did they make do with thanking Mubarak and not demand democratic reform? I could ask you lots more questions, and the answers would all lead to the same conclusion: our people never ever revolt, and if they do, they quickly abandon the revolution. Our people aren't ready to pay the price of freedom.' Essam drank off the rest of his glass at one go, then gestured to the waiter for another.

Mazen said, 'For every example you mention of the passivity of the Egyptians I could present more confirming the courage of the Egyptians.'

Essam made a gesture with his hand. 'Enough. You're stubborn and pig-headed. Do what you like.'

There was silence between them, then Essam took a sip from his glass and said, 'I have one question, just so my conscience is clear.'

'Go ahead.'

'If I got you a contract in the Gulf at a high salary, would you accept?'

'I could never leave Egypt.'

'It's your choice, but I want you to know that I've only with difficulty been able to prevent your detention.'

'My detention?'

'Naturally. Do you imagine National Security is ignorant of your activities? You're a member of the Enough! movement and you're inciting the workers to strike. It would be very easy for them to make up a case against you and put you in prison for at least ten years.'

'On what charge?'

'That question is meaningless in Egypt. Your father and I spent many years in prison. What was the charge against us? The Egyptian state imprisons you first, then begins looking for a charge.'

Mazen rose suddenly and said, 'I'm going back to the factory.'

Essam caught hold of his arm and said, 'Sit down. You have to taste the desserts they do here, they're really delicious.'

Mazen looked at his watch and said, 'Thank you, but I have to get back to the factory.'

'Stay for half an hour, my boy.'

'I can't.'

Essam pursed his lips and an expression of disappointment appeared on his face. 'Very well,' he said. 'On your way. Goodbye.'

'Could Uncle Madany take me?' Mazen asked.

'No, he couldn't.'

Mazen looked at Essam with annoyance. 'You told me, sir, that Uncle Madany would take me back to the factory.'

Essam bent his head and looked into the bottom of his glass, which he was rolling between his hands. Then he leant back against the chair and said, 'I've changed my mind. If you want to go to the factory, you can make your own way there.'

13

Ikram didn't get angry or pick a quarrel with Ashraf, but she began treating him in a formal manner. She controlled her smile, her tone of voice, and even her walk when she was in his sight, as though she was just a maid doing her job, no more, no less. She continued to take care of him as before but without enthusiasm, and simply as the performance of a duty, as though she'd taken a decision to cross out their relationship and behave as though it had never happened. Two days after this change, she went into the study (which had but recently witnessed so much happiness) and asked him in an unsmiling tone of voice, 'Would you like me to make you coffee, sir?'

He looked at her in silence but she ignored his gaze and repeated the question. He nodded affirmatively. He was sitting at his desk trying, fruitlessly, to write. His thoughts were scattered and a sense of gloom weighed on his chest. She returned with the coffee tray, placed it on the desk, and asked him, 'Do you want anything else, sir?'

He didn't reply, so she left quietly. He lit a joint and sat staring at the blue swirls of smoke as they ascended. He reflected that everything that Ikram was doing was just play-acting to cover up her despicable act. She was blackmailing him emotionally. She was pretending to be angry so that he'd take pity on her and forget that she'd plotted against him with her husband Mansour. Suddenly, he felt impotent and grief-stricken. He felt sorry for himself: was he turning, at the end of his days, into a miserable old man subject to the blackmail of his maid and her husband? His imagination took the bit in its teeth and his anxiety grew. What if Ikram had put a hidden camera somewhere in the study, as happens in films, and filmed him while having sex with her and given her husband the video? If that were the case, Mansour would go on blackmailing him for the rest of his life. He'd either have to pay whatever was demanded of him or face a horrible scandal. If that happened, he'd have only one solution: he'd have to run away immediately and abandon the whole kit and caboodle. He'd hide where no one could find him, not Mansour, not Ikram, not even Magda. He'd disappear into a little *pension* in Alexandria. He began going over in his mind the names of the *pensions* that he knew and comparing them. These uneasy thoughts continued to plague him for the rest of the day and in the evening he tried to distract himself by reading, without success. He felt tired and soon fell into a deep slumber. In the morning, he woke, had breakfast and, with the first cup of coffee and the first joint of the day, found himself in a new state of mind. His anger evaporated and his thoughts turned in another direction. Might he not have been unjust to Ikram? She'd never before been materialistic or greedy. She'd refused to accept his gifts of money even when he'd insisted. She'd always said, 'I don't want money. What matters is being with you.'

He'd believed her. Had she been lying to him? Had she been putting on a show for him all this time? It was possible, of course . . . but what clear proof was there that she'd been in cahoots with Mansour? Just because he'd come in the morning and not the evening? Mansour was addicted to pills and injections of Max and couldn't be expected to think straight. Plus, at the end of the day, he hadn't caught them red-handed and hadn't accused them of anything. He'd come to Ikram so she could give him the price of the drugs and hadn't been able to wait till she returned to the house because he couldn't delay the fix. Hashish wasn't to be considered a drug because it didn't cause addiction, or impair your judgment. But when someone was addicted to Max, or pills, like Mansour, he'd do anything to get his fix.

Ashraf decided to talk to Ikram. He had to give her a chance to defend herself. Either her innocence would be proven or her guilt confirmed. He drank his coffee, smoked another joint, then went to the kitchen, where he found her standing at the sink, as usual. He went up to her and said, 'Good morning.'

She mumbled a reply he couldn't make out, so he went on, in a friendly tone of voice, 'I'd like to talk to you, please.'

She turned towards him challengingly and said, 'You want me to do something for you, sir?'

He looked at her glowering face and, without realising what he was doing, touched her cheek, at which she pushed away his hand and said, 'Please. I just work here as a maid, that's all.'

She turned her back to him and resumed washing the glasses. He couldn't stand being so close to her beloved, soft backside, so he stuck himself against her, but she pushed him away, violently this time, and shouted, 'Ashraf Bey! Please let's be decent!'

Her tone brooked no refusal, so he withdrew to his study feeling angry and humiliated. He couldn't go on with these ridiculous theatricals. He couldn't do a thing. He couldn't write or read or think about anything except this problem. Even his little pleasures had lost their taste. He'd stopped watching a black-and-white film every night and no longer sat on the balcony at sunset to watch the people and the cars. He didn't even have an appetite for his morning clotted-cream-and-honey sandwich.

He spent the day in the dumps and an hour before Magda's return time, aware that this would be his last chance, he looked for Ikram and found her in the dining room ironing the household's clothes. 'Ikram,' he said. 'We have to talk.'

Quietly she replied, 'We don't have anything to talk about.'

'There's something important I have to tell you,' he responded heatedly.

Pressing the iron down on the pyjama jacket, she said, 'Ashraf Bey, please leave me alone to get on with my work.'

He stood there for a few moments, but she went on with her ironing without turning towards him, so he left, slamming the door. Guilty or maligned, it was inappropriate for her to treat him like that. How could she refuse even to talk to him? Who did she think she was? Whatever she was, she wasn't the Princess of Wales! At the end of the day, she was a maid, no more, no less. Madame Ikram could go to hell! He wouldn't die without her. He could easily find another better-looking maid who didn't come with problems or headaches. Along with the anger and humiliation there was another painful feeling that he didn't care to acknowledge. He missed her. He longed for her wonderful, smooth, delicious body. He remembered with yearning their beautiful post-lovemaking sessions. She'd kept him company. She'd made everything seem easy and consoled him when anything made him sad. He'd only realised how important she was to his life when their relationship had been broken.

All the same, in spite of how much he longed for her, he decided that he'd treat her the way she did him. He stopped trying to talk to her and began to ignore her completely. He'd ask her for whatever he wanted and thank her curtly, avoiding looking at her.

At the beginning of the month he was surprised to find on his desk an envelope with the words THANK YOU written on it in large, crooked letters. When he opened it, he found five hundred pounds inside. This was more than he could bear. He was seized by rage and for a few minutes couldn't think what to do. Then he decided he'd give her a severe rebuke. He was seized by the desire to humiliate her. It crossed his mind that he might slap her. He opened the door and called her in a loud voice, and when she came, gave her no opportunity to resist but took a firm grip of her hand, dragged her into the room, and closed the door. He went towards her until they were face to face, and the smell of scented soap stole into his nostrils. Suddenly, he found himself saying to her, 'I'm sorry, Ikram.' His voice sounded strange to him, as though it were coming from someone else. She remained where she was, seeming not to have heard. He whispered, 'I'm telling you I made a mistake. Please, accept my apology.'

She looked at him and opened her mouth to speak, but he didn't give her a chance. He swept her into his arms and clung to her as though afraid she would escape. He covered her in kisses, and when he felt the warmth of her body that he had missed so much, he whispered into her ear, 'I love you.'

She softened and went slack in his arms, as though she'd been waiting for him, and they surrendered to a wave of passion that threw them with joyful violence onto the shores of pleasure. They lay on the ground next to one another, naked. He closed his eyes, thrust his nose into her neck, and whispered, 'I've missed you so much,' then touched her face and realised that his fingers were wet. He opened his eyes and found that she was crying. Tenderly he whispered, 'That's enough, Ikram. Please.' She hugged him hard and whispered, 'I beg you, Ashraf Bey, don't do that again. Don't doubt me. I've always had bad luck with men. You're the only decent one to come my way. I couldn't bear it if I lost you.'

They put their clothes back on, before Magda could return, and got rid of any trace of their lovemaking, as usual. The next day, he tried to give her back the envelope with the money but she refused. Looking annoyed, she asked him, 'You want me to take the money?'

He nodded and she planted a quick kiss on his lips, then ran her hand through his smooth white hair and said gaily, 'How about we make a deal? You do something to make me happy and I'll take the money.'

He looked at her questioningly, and she went on, with childlike enthusiasm, 'I really want to go out with you, Ashraf Bey, even if it's only once. We can go anywhere. Then I'll take the money and I'll do anything you want me to.'

14

Dear Mazen,
    Are you back home or spending the night at the factory? I phone you but you don't answer. Please put my mind at rest. May the Lord protect you.
    Asmaa

15

On important occasions, Uncle Madany wore the smart outfit Essam Shaalan had bought for him – grey suit, white shirt, and a blue tie with a design on it. Despite his elegance, however, he somehow continued at such times to retain the appearance of a servant. This showed in his repeated bows and hurried steps, which made no sound; in his apologetic, expectant smile, the disciplined, submissive expression on his face and the subdued tone of his voice; and in the searching glances that he directed around him to see if there was anything he should be doing. This often happens with those who work in service, for the polite and submissive appearance that they affect at the beginning transforms itself with time into an inseparable part of their character. Madany's obedient and obliging mien was, however, simply a mask behind which hid a courageous warrior blessed with a will of steel and the persistence of an ant. From the time of the morning prayer, with which he began his day, till he went to bed at the end of the evening, Madany worked relentlessly, never tiring, never flagging, and not turning aside for even an instant, towards his one and only goal, that of earning his daily bread. He didn't sit in cafés, he had no friends, and he didn't spend a single pound on personal amusements. Even smoking, which he had been unable to give up, he practised within the strictest limits. He never took a day off from work and every year he asked Eng. Essam to convert his accumulated annual leave into cash.

Madany had attended school to the preparatory stage, then left to work and help his family. He had moved between numerous jobs before learning to drive while doing his military service, after which he'd worked for many years as a taxi driver until a police officer he knew pulled strings and got him a job as a driver at the cement factory. At first, he'd driven the cement lorries, then the factory's ambulances, and then one day Eng. Essam had seen him and chosen Madany to drive for him. At the beginning, Madany had treated his new boss with care, so as not to commit any mistakes, and was ill at ease with Essam's temperament. He had soon realised, however, that behind the stony face, the gruff voice, the mercurial temperament, and the dangerous bouts of irritability, an exceedingly good-hearted person was to be found – so much so, indeed, that it sometimes seemed to Madany that Eng. Essam put on that harsh exterior to hide his excessively delicate feelings, which might be inappropriate to the dignity of the manager of a factory.

Essam had given him everything that the factory's regulations allowed by way of raises, bonuses, and medical expenses, in addition to numerous cash gifts that he paid from his own pocket. When he gave him money, Essam didn't assume the air of either the generous master or the alms-giving, God-fearing believer. He behaved, rather, as one who had been poor himself and knew very well what it meant to love one's family and be unable to provide for their needs. Essam would come up to Madany, place his hand on his shoulder, and then thrust the money into his pocket and say in a low voice, 'Here, Madany. This is a little something towards the family's expenses,' or he'd smile affectionately and say, 'Your daughter Hind has entered university. I'm sure she needs a laptop. Go and buy her one and tell her, "Your uncle Essam says hi."'

Over time, a manly comradeship had grown up between Essam and Madany, a deep mutual understanding with regard to the essentials – an alternative, unspoken language of winks and glances which meant that Essam needed only a few words to convey his requests, to which Madany would respond immediately, like a private carrying out the orders of a general.

From Essam's perspective, Madany possessed positive qualities it would be difficult to find in any other driver: he was honest, active, and discreet, didn't complain if there was a lot of work or interfere in things that didn't concern him, and he spoke only when necessary. At the same time, his role went far beyond that of a driver. Madany was the only person who had the key to Essam's flat and could enter at any time. It was he who checked the maid's twice-weekly cleaning of it and he who agreed with the cook on what vegetables to buy and strictly checked their prices and quality. It was he who waited for the ironing man on Mondays, got the clothes that he was going to iron ready, and made him iron them again if he wasn't satisfied. It was he, too, who bought the whisky from Zamalek and presented it to Essam with the same respect with which he carried his briefcase, bulging with files from work. Madany's participation in such forbidden rites in no way offended his own religious sensibilities. It may be that he regarded them as a combat mission in his righteous war for his daily bread, or perhaps he found in them an opportunity to show his gratitude to his employer, as though he were saying to Essam, 'In return for your generosity to me, I shall serve you in sin without annoyance or extortion.'

When Essam went up to Nourhan's flat, it was Madany's job to stay in the street for a minimum of two hours. When these were up, he would park the car somewhere safe, get permission from the doorkeeper of Nourhan's building and enter the latter's room, where he would wash the plates and glasses that Essam used, then perform his ablutions and pray the evening prayer (at the stipulated time) and the sunset prayer (with retroactive effect). After this, he would go back to the car, push back the front seat and lie down to catch a bit of sleep until Essam left the love nest. Then he would drive him to Maadi, leave the car in the garage, and take a minibus to his home in Maasara.

Madany would push open the ancient iron gate, which would emit its familiar groan, then, in the darkness, climb the stairway, each of whose steps he knew by heart, and only then resume his natural rhythm and abandon his tense self-discipline, his face appearing relaxed and almost jolly, as though he were an actor who had played his part on the stage and gone back to his ordinary life, or a warrior who had put his weapons aside to enjoy a short rest.

This flat, which he'd been renting for a paltry sum for the past quarter of a century, held everything that mattered in his life: the members of his family, for whose sake he bore the exhausting work, resisted fatigue, and forced his ageing body to rise each morning, refusing to allow it to let him down; for whose sake he went to such lengths to please his employer, keep his head down, and put up with slights; and for whose sake his mind would transform itself into an implacable calculating machine that prescribed, with precision, what the boy and the girl needed, how to come up with the money for it, and the most appropriate place to shop for it. Nothing on this earth gave Madany greater pleasure than to sit in the middle of his family on the sofa in the main room, wearing his galabiya and sipping tea with mint while listening to Khaled and Hind and commenting on what they had to say with a sweetness of manner he never employed outside the house.

This deep loyalty to the family, which was almost a religious belief, had transferred itself from Madany to the other members of his family, making each feel responsible for the others.

When she entered secondary school, Hind had taken her first physics class and had understood nothing. She had come home from school feeling sad and burst into tears, but had refused her father's offer to pay for private lessons, saying, 'I might take the lessons and then get a low score on the exam, but Khaled's at medical college, so he deserves the money more than I do.'

In spite of this, Madany, with the help of a gift from Essam, was able to get her into the review classes at the neighbouring mosque, and she made a decent enough score to get her into commercial college.

For the past two years, the family had been missing one essential member. The mother had been stricken with breast cancer and soon died, as though she hadn't wanted to be a burden on them. Madany had mourned her and felt that a painful vacuum had been created by her absence, but had decided all the same not to remarry. He would never tolerate the existence of a stepmother who might hate, or be a source of harm to, his son and daughter, and at his age he no longer needed a woman the way he had when young. In addition, his daughter Hind had automatically, after her mother's death, trans-formed herself into the woman of the house. She'd started cooking, washing the clothes and ironing them, and had, in fact, manifested an amazing capacity to take care of the needs of the household out of the salary that her father turned over to her in its entirety, as he had done to her late mother.

It would be hard to describe the expression that appeared on Madany's face whenever he talked of his son, or the proud tone of voice in which he uttered his name, accompanied by his title – 'Dr Khaled.' He was Madany's pride and glory, his reward for the years of toil. Khaled had been such a quiet, obedient child that Madany had sometimes said to his colleagues, to make fun of him, 'The only one I raised was Hind. Khaled, God bless him, came out properly brought up all on his own.'

Madany couldn't remember ever having struck Khaled for being naughty, the way one does with small children. When he'd noticed his love of reading, he'd got him a subscription to the Palaces of Culture's Maasara branch, allowing him to borrow whatever books he liked and read them. At school, Khaled had been an untalk-ative, shy student who didn't make trouble or get into scrapes. He would sit quietly, always in the front row, and follow the teacher's explanations from behind his spectacles, always with the same look, focused and mixed with a slight amazement, as though fixing the lesson in his mind, once and for all. He had been top of the class in everything. He took first place in the district at the elementary and intermediate levels, and thirteenth in the whole country at the secondary level. His mother, God rest her soul, had been worried about the costs involved in studying medicine and suggested he should study something easier so that he could graduate faster and help with the family's expenses. She'd spoken in a low voice and short sentences as she folded the wash, while Madany sat on the sofa in the main room in the galabiya he wore at home. He'd looked at her for a second as though he didn't understand, then said, angrily, 'Shame on you! God has bestowed on us a clever son and you're going to begrudge what we spend on him? I'll get the money to send him to medical college even if I have to beg on the streets!'

Khaled continued to be top of his class and each year got a mark of Very Good and a paltry monthly sum from the college. Once, though, he'd said to his father, 'By the way, I deserve to get Outstanding, but of course that's reserved for the children of the big shots.'

Madany didn't understand, so Khaled had explained that the administration only gave Outstanding to the sons of professors and high officials, as that guaranteed their appointment as teaching assistants. 'But that's not fair!' Madany said angrily.

'Of course it's not fair.'

'You should file a complaint.'

Khaled laughed and said, 'What complaint, Hagg Madany? We're in Egypt. Injustice is the rule.'

Madany had grudgingly fallen silent but the next day he waited for an opportunity and described what was going on to Eng. Essam, who smiled politely as though listening to an old tale, and said,

'Don't waste your time on complaints and all those headaches. Tell Khaled to apply himself and graduate, and I'll get him a contract in the Gulf. He'll go there for a few years, make his nest egg, and come back and open a decent clinic.'

Madany was convinced by Essam's logic, and whenever Khaled complained about the state of the country, he'd criticise him and say, 'Why are you so upset, son? The country's theirs and they can do what they like with it. Concentrate on your studies and, as soon as you graduate, you can go abroad, God willing.'

Khaled had told his father about Khaled Said's murder and showed him a photograph of him, his head smashed up from the torture, and Madany had displayed mild, practically formal disgust, saying, 'God have mercy on him and grant his family patience.'

'We have to bring the criminals who killed him to trial!' Khaled said excitedly.

His father smiled affectionately and said, 'Our Lord will hold them to account. You work hard so that God is good to you.'

The day before, Madany had returned home at around 3 a.m. Noticing the light on in Khaled's room, he knocked on the door, opened it, and found his son sitting at his desk. Looking at him tenderly, he said, 'Still up?'

'I have to study.'

'Did you have supper?'

'Hind made me a sandwich.'

'Need money?'

'I have some, thanks be to God.'

'Goodnight.'

After Madany had closed the door, Khaled waited a little, then bent down and extracted from under the bed a number of posters, on which were written 'For Dignity's Sake, Take to the Streets on the 25th!', 'Down with Hosni Mubarak!', and 'Enough of Injustice and Corruption!'

He had hidden his political activism from his father. He thought he'd never understand what he was doing and never support him. If he were to find out, he'd live in a state of anxiety and tension that he could do nothing about. Khaled limited himself to talking about change with Hind, who shared his opinions. He'd urged her to record a video calling on everyone to demonstrate on 25 January, but she'd hesitated and asked, 'Why me specifically? Any of your female colleagues could make a video.'

In a serious tone, he'd answered, 'I chose you because you're beautiful and you look cheerful and normal. Any man who sees the video will feel like you're his sister or his daughter.'

Anxiously, she asked, 'What shall we do if Father sees the video?'

Khaled laughed and said, 'You think your father goes on Facebook?'

He then wrote out some words for her in large letters on a board, which he held up behind the camera, and he recorded her several times till she had overcome her embarrassment. He put the video up on Facebook, where it got wide exposure. Khaled was expecting a demonstration on the Tuesday and hoping that thousands of Egyptians would take to the streets to proclaim to the regime that there were people in Egypt who would defend freedom and dignity. He heard the call to prayer, made his ablutions, and prayed the morning prayer. He felt tired but checked the posters one last time and put them in his leather bag, then turned off the light, stretched out on the bed, and thought about Danya. He liked to think about her before he went to sleep.

16

Dear Asmaa,

Yesterday, I got back late. I didn't call you on the phone, so as not to disturb you, but I left you a message. What had happened, to be brief, was that the workers had gone on strike because management hadn't given them their dividends, so I went to show solidarity. Essam Shaalan invited me to dinner and then tried to persuade me to give up on the workers. I refused, of course, and when I decided to go back to the factory, he refused to give me a lift in his car, even though he'd promised to do so. I got a minibus on the Corniche and reached the factory at around 3 a.m. Then I noticed something unusual. There were people I'd never seen before standing around the factory. Uncle Idris, the security man, came out from his kiosk and caught up with me before I could reach the gates. He told me, 'The police have broken up the strike. They've arrested a lot of people and left goons everywhere. Go, quickly, or they'll arrest you.'

I thanked him and left. I crossed the street quickly and was lucky enough to find a minibus, so I got in and went back to the centre of the city. Then I understood what had happened. Essam Shaalan had deceived the workers. He'd let them continue striking and ordered them a hot meal. Then he'd left the factory, knowing that the police would attack them. He'd invited me to dinner to keep me away and had refused to give me a lift back to the factory because he was afraid I'd be arrested. My relationship with Essam Shaalan is one of the problems of my life. I've known him since I was a child and I love him because he was my father's best friend, not to mention that he used his contacts to get me a job at the factory. To be honest, he's been good to me, but in his capacity as the factory's manager, he's playing a very bad role on behalf of management. The workers hate him and call him an obscene name I can't write down. I'm confused by my contradictory feelings towards him. I can't reach a clear position on him and I can't understand the change that's come over him. Essam Shaalan was a warrior who made sacrifices and spent years in detention in defence of his principles. How did he come to be so transformed and to betray his history in such a way? If my father were alive, I'm certain he'd hold fast to his positions to the end.

When I got home, I was dying to get some sleep and I fell on the bed in my clothes. I woke up at noon and made some phone calls. It was then I found out that the police had detained twenty workers, who were interrogated by National Security and brought before the prosecutor, who ordered them held for four days pending investigation. The lawyers found signs of torture on the workers' bodies and made a police report recording these, but they aren't optimistic and believe the workers will be referred to the National Security prosecutor on a charge of incitement to strike. I went to the Enough! headquarters and, with my colleagues, issued a statement entitled 'New Crime by the Interior Ministry'. In it, we explained the workers' legitimate demands and stressed that striking is a constitutional right and that the Egyptian government has signed international agreements recognising that right. Then we demanded the workers' immediate release. We distributed the statement to the newspapers and then I went to the factory, where I found that the workers were angry and anxious about the fate of their friends. I gave them the statement and explained to them that the case was political and therefore the more fuss we made in the media, the greater the pressure we'd bring on the regime to release them.

The problem with the workers (and many other Egyptians) is that they think of professional rights as being separate from politics, meaning that they'll rise up to demand their rights to dividends, but they don't have much interest in electoral fraud or the Emergency Law. Our duty, Asmaa, is to explain to people that they can only live a decent life in a democratic state. What happened at the factory may be for the best. Lots of workers told me that they will take to the streets with us in the demonstrations on Tuesday. They've begun to understand that their struggle isn't with the Italian management but with the regime. Asmaa, I know that you'll take part in the demonstration. I want you to be with me. The routes for the demonstration we've announced could all change at any moment, to mislead the police. I'm going to start demonstrating with my colleagues on Tuesday at 4 p.m. in front of the Lawyers' Syndicate. Please come. I'd be so happy if you were at my side. Naturally, you won't be cruel to me and leave me without a smile. I need to see those dimples. Thank you for being in my life, Asmaa. Goodnight.

Mazen

P.S. My address is 6b Sharia El Sherifein, 5th Floor, Flat 20. Keep this. You may need it at any time.

17

Ashraf Wissa excluded the usual places. It would be impossible to take Ikram to the Four Seasons, or After Eight, or the Automobile Club. He wasn't ashamed to have her as a companion. The problem was that he had lots of friends who frequented them; Ikram's presence with him would pique their curiosity and the news would be passed around until it reached his wife. He had to find somewhere quiet and isolated. After extensive field research, he ended up with a small open-air restaurant tucked away in front of the old Qasr El Eini hospital and looking out over the Nile. He went once on an exploratory visit and found it completely empty but for a few courting couples too preoccupied with their passions to notice anything around them.

They decided on Tuesday for their rendezvous as it was Ikram's day off. At 3 p.m., Ashraf was waiting for her at the gates of the hospital, to make their meeting look ordinary and as though they were visiting a patient. He was wearing wide sunglasses and had placed a wide woollen scarf around his neck so that he could, if need be, cover his face and no one would recognise him. He waited a few minutes until Ikram arrived and then, for a moment, didn't recognise her. She had taken off her headscarf, tied her smooth black hair back in a ponytail, and covered her face with thick make-up. She was wearing a long blue dress more appropriate for a soiree than a daytime outing. It was a bit too large, so he realised she must have borrowed it. She'd made great efforts to appear worthy as his companion. There was something wrong about her crude, over-the-top appearance, but it was naive and moving, as though she were a little girl trying her mother's big shoes out on her little feet. She smiled and looked at him enquiringly, as though waiting for her new look to have its effect on him. He shook her hand and said, jokingly, 'How chic you look, Madame Ikram!'

She smiled gratefully and he felt the softness of her hand and guessed she must have rubbed it with cream. She snuggled up against his shoulder, put her hand under his arm, and then raised her head and walked along at his side, looking happy and proud. He led her across the street and they passed through the door of the restaurant together. Most of the tables were free and an aged, dark-skinned waiter wearing a white shirt and a worn white jacket with a crooked old black bowtie quickly appeared. He looked like a drawing of a character just emerged from the pages of a comic book. He smiled, his mouth seemingly empty of all but a few widely spaced teeth, then exclaimed jubilantly, 'Welcome to His Excellency the Bey!'

Ashraf replied with a friendly smile and advanced with Ikram till he arrived at a table on its own at the very end of the restaurant, looking directly over the Nile. Ikram ordered a glass of tea and Ashraf a cold beer. Then he said to her, 'What do you say to having a beer with me, when you've finished your tea?'

'I don't drink alcohol,' she replied.

'Because it's a sin?'

'No, I tried it a long time ago and hated the taste.'

'Beer is lovely, but you have to get to know it the proper way.'

In a dreamy tone, Ikram responded, 'I don't need beer. Don't people get drunk to be happy? When I'm with you, I'm happy without having to drink.'

Ashraf was moved and sent her a kiss through the air, and she whispered, 'My darling!'

A portentous silence hung between them, which ended when they heard a song coming from a boat on the Nile. The waiter brought the tea and the beer and left. Ashraf took a sip from the tall glass, then looked around him as though reconnoitring and lit a joint, the smell of hashish suddenly everywhere, and strong. 'Ashraf Bey!' Ikram cried out in terror. 'You can't smoke hashish here!'

'Don't worry.'

'How shouldn't I worry? If they catch us with hashish, we'll be in a terrible mess.'

He smiled and said confidently, 'Believe me, Ikram. It's not a problem. I came here on my own and smoked hashish and nothing happened. The smell gets lost in the air and we're sitting too far away for anyone to notice.'

She continued to look around anxiously, so he said, to change the subject, 'By the way, you're looking very beautiful today.'

She smiled and said, 'Oh come on! What am I next to the ladies you know?'

'You're the most beautiful woman in the world,' he whispered, taking her hand.

In joking tones she said, 'Listen, Ashraf Bey. While we're sitting here enjoying ourselves, I have some questions I want you to answer.'

'Fire away!'

She pursed her lips, making herself look like a little girl about to start an exciting game, and said, 'First question: what is it you like about me?'

Ashraf gazed at the expanse of the Nile as though gathering his thoughts, and said, 'To be frank, at first I liked your body. In other words, what I wanted was just sex. Later, when I got to know you, I found that you were a good and sensitive person and had self-respect. From then on, I loved you altogether.'

She laughed with pleasure and put her hand on his. Then she brought her head close to his and gazed into his eyes, so that they looked, at that moment, like any ordinary pair of lovers.

'Second question: Do you think you'll ever get sick of me?'

'What kind of silly questions are these, Ikram?'

'Give me an answer, for my sake.'

'That's impossible, of course.'

'Third question: you love me and I love you. What do you think that love will lead to?'

'I don't understand the question.'

'That's not true. You don't want to understand.'

'The weather's really lovely.'

'Please don't change the subject. I'm asking you, what will the love between us lead to?'

Ashraf lit his second joint and took such a deep drag that it made him cough hard. Then he said, 'Look, Ikram. I'm fifty-five years old. In other words, I don't have many years left on this earth. Most of what I have in my life are things I didn't choose. When I find something I really want, there's no way I'm going to part with it.'

'Explain, please?'

'In Egypt, a person's destiny is more or less determined at birth. The room for choice is extremely limited. If you, for example, had been born into a rich family, you would by now have finished your education and married a rich man, and you'd be living the best of lives. If I had been born poor, like you, I might by now have become a thief or a thug. In Egypt, a person inherits his circumstances and it's very difficult for him to change them. We don't even choose our own religion. You were born a Muslim and I was born a Copt, and if it had been the other way around, your name might be Teresa and mine might be Muhammad.'

She interrupted him laughingly and said, 'Teresa's a nice name, as it happens.'

He, however, went on seriously, 'After all these years, when I find a woman I really love, I think I have the right to hold on to her.'

130

Moved, she replied, 'I couldn't believe that I'd found you either and there's no way I can part with you, but sometimes the future scares me.'

He drank from his glass of beer and said, 'In our situation, it's wrong to think about the future. We know nothing. We don't know when we're going to die and we don't even know what's going to happen in an hour's time. How will worrying about the future help us? Let's enjoy our happiness, and what will be will be.'

She said nothing for a moment as though taking this in, then she said, 'You're right, but I'm still afraid.'

'Of what?'

'I'm afraid of Madame Magda finding out about our relationship.'

Ashraf smiled sadly and said, 'Don't worry. The only thing Madame Magda cares about is work. As far as she's concerned, I don't matter at all.'

'You mean she isn't jealous about her husband, like any other woman?'

'She'd be jealous for her reputation, not because she loves me.'

'So if she finds out, she'll make a big problem for us?'

'She won't find out. And even if she did, to be honest, I no longer care.'

There was silence again. Then Ashraf said, 'If you, Ikram, found out that Mansour loved another woman, what would you do?'

She pursed her lips and made a moue with them, indicating dis-appointment, then said, 'I wish! I'd thank her for ridding me of his mess-ups and the headaches he causes.'

'That's the difference between your class and mine,' Ashraf said. 'We have complexes that make us cling to appearances at any price. You have simplicity and directness.'

'You've known lots of women, right?'

'Right.'

'And how many did you love?'

'Would you believe me if I told you that this is the first time I've really been in love?'

She took hold of his hand and whispered, 'You know, if we weren't in a restaurant, I'd give you a hug!'

Ashraf smiled and lit a joint. She looked at him reproachfully and said, 'Ashraf Bey, that's your third hashish cigarette.'

He nodded and said, 'It's the last one, Ikram. I promise.'

She fell silent and sighed, looking ravishing to him. He took a deep drag and the soft, warm effect of the hashish overcame him. He decided to ignore anything that made him anxious and enjoy every moment he was with her. Suddenly, however, he noticed the aged waiter running towards him, a few people at his back. It crossed his mind that they might be hallucinations, caused by being high, and he shut his eyes hard, then opened them again, but the scene didn't change. The waiter and those with him were still advancing rapidly towards him. Ashraf said to Ikram, in an unsteady voice, 'There seems to be some kind of trouble in the restaurant.'

'Oh no!' Ikram exclaimed, but Ashraf forced a smile and said, 'Hold on, Ikram. Don't get rattled. Everything's going to be just fine.'

He threw the cigarette he'd been smoking into the Nile and was about to throw the piece of hashish that was squirreled away in his jacket pocket too, but then remembered how much it had cost him and decided to give the matter more reflection. Putting his hand into the pocket, he closed it over the hashish, and adopted a state of readiness: if he was sure that there was danger, he'd throw it into the Nile; if he survived, it would survive along with him. Suddenly, his thought processes came to a halt and his mind went as blank as if he'd lost consciousness. Then he became aware of the waiter's hoarse voice shouting, 'You there, sir!'

18

'By the way,' Khaled said, as he walked beside Danya, 'tomorrow's the demonstration.'

'I thought we'd discussed that,' Danya responded.

'I thought you might have changed your mind.'

'Khaled, I'm not going to take part in the demonstration. That's my final decision.'

She was upset. Silence reigned for a few moments and then she spoke about something else, and he responded curtly and seemed annoyed. Suddenly, she stopped and said, 'You don't want to talk to me? Fine. I'm going. Bye.'

He apologised, started joking with her, and soon she was laughing. She loved these manoeuvrings – anger, blame, reproach, and coquetry, always ending up with reconciliation. The usual lovers' cycle. Suddenly, he asked her, 'What do you intend to do after graduating?'

'It depends on my score in the finals.'

'I don't mean medicine. I want to know how you imagine our future.'

'All things are in God's hands.'

'To be honest, Danya, I want to know if you're going to keep our relationship up after graduation.'

The word 'relationship' rang in her ears with a happy sound, but she said nothing, so he went on, 'I'm waiting for an answer from you – yes or no?'

'To what?'

'Do you or don't you want to maintain our relationship after graduation?'

'It's the first time you've talked to me about the subject.'

'I think it's my right.'

'Can I give you my answer at the gate?'

'Why?'

'So I can give it and run!'

She laughed and he felt an irresistible desire to hug her. They suspended the conversation until they'd reached the gate. There, he stood in front of her and said, 'Please give me your answer.'

'Not today.'

'You promised.'

She remained silent, so he said, 'Yes or no?'

She looked at him and nodded her head in assent, then her face reddened and she turned quickly away towards the gate without saying a word. She knew he was following her with his eyes and decided that she wouldn't look back. On the luxurious back seat of the car, she relaxed, thought again of what he'd said, and smiled. What had made him open the subject today? Why hadn't he spoken of an engagement and just used the word 'relationship'? Perhaps, like her, their approaching graduation was making him anxious. Perhaps, like her, he knew that marriage was out of the question. She was suddenly overwhelmed by a wave of tenderness. She remembered his face and wished she'd put her hands on his cheeks and kissed him on his forehead. She felt, at that moment, that she loved him. She'd never be able to forget him, or imagine herself with another man. She knew their getting married was impossible, but might not a miracle happen? Might not her father, for example, admire Khaled's morals, overlook his circumstances, and welcome their marriage? If that happened, she'd be the happiest person in the world. An idea occurred to her, and the moment she reached the house, she changed her clothes, and went to her mother's room. Hagga Tahany was seated at her oak desk, in the spacious bedroom. She was wearing her spectacles and appeared to be reviewing some important papers. She smiled when she saw Danya, who kissed her on the cheek, and said jokingly, 'That's enough work! Come and talk to your daughter for a little.'

Her mother appeared to hesitate, then said, 'I'll talk to you for a little, but I really have to review the budget.'

Danya knew how to make her mother do what she wanted, and she pulled her by the hand, sat her down on the sofa, and said, 'I want to talk to you about something important. Nothing to do with business and religion.'

Her mother looked at her disapprovingly and said, 'God forgive you! There's nothing in the world that doesn't have to do with religion.'

Danya said jokingly, 'Didn't you tell me that your father was from a humble background?'

'God rest his soul.'

'Could you tell me something about him?'

'What's made you think of him?'

'I want to know more about him.'

Her mother hesitated, then said, with feeling, 'Your grandfather, God rest his soul, was a humble man but a great one. We were three girls. Your grandfather laboured honestly till he had raised us, given us the best possible education, and seen each of us settled in her own home.'

'What did he do?'

'Why does it matter to you?'

'Please, Mama. I want to know.'

'He was an usher at the court in Tanta. But we were never ashamed of his job. On the contrary, we were always proud of him.'

There was silence, then Danya put her arms around her and said in a dreamy voice, 'So no one can hold it against a young man who has morals and an excellent education that his father is from a humble background.'

135

The expression on Hagga Tahany's face changed. She pushed Danya away from her so she wouldn't be able to affect her so much and gave her a searching, suspicious look. Then she said, 'That was back then. Things were different for us than they are for you.'

'Different how?'

'Back then, people had morals. Everyone, rich or poor, had manners and was good-hearted. Now the poor bear grudges and have a bad attitude.'

'In every age, there are good people and bad.'

'In the old days, a bad person was rare. Now a good person is.'

'But you know lots of good people.'

'Why are you beating about the bush? If you have something to say, say it.'

'I'm just talking generally.'

Her mother gave her a stern look and said, 'I, however, am not talking generally. You, Danya, occupy a high position in society. You have to form an alliance with someone who is your equal in everything. That is the view of religion, and Sheikh Shamel has stressed it often.'

'I wasn't talking about alliances,' Danya said in a soft voice, but her mother went on in resolute tones, 'I'm going to tell you something and you need to "wear it like an earring" so you can spare us and yourself trouble: you must not form a relationship with anyone who is less than you. That can never happen. Religion forbids it, and your father and I will never agree to it.'

19

Dear Asmaa,

I shall forever remember that we witnessed the miracle together.

Where are you? I hope you're well. I phoned you but found your phone was turned off. I got home, half dead with exhaustion, of course, but very happy. There were the people they have so long accused of submissiveness and cowardice rising up like a giant to throw off the dictatorship that has humiliated them for thirty years! The thousands who gathered in Tahrir Square and all the other squares of Egypt, they're the real Egyptian people, the ones in whose name everyone claims to speak but whom no one actually knows. We have begun the battle for change and will be victorious, but the victory won't be easy. The regime will fight viciously to defend its existence and will have no compunction about committing every conceivable crime. Did you know that firing tear gas of that concentration is considered an act of homicide? Did you see how many fell to the ground, choking on the gas? Did you know that the regime has been shooting demonstrators dead in Alexandria, Suez, and other cities since the morning? We have reports of the disappearance of dozens of demonstrators in the various provinces who in all probability have been killed and buried in unknown graves.

You must have thought I was insane to declare my feelings in the middle of the demonstration. Believe me, I couldn't have found a more appropriate time than the moment of revolution to tell you that I love you. My relationship with you is bigger than the simple relationship of a man with a woman. You are my partner in the dream. Our affair has always been linked to the Egypt for whose *birth at our hands we struggle – the other Egypt, new, just, and free of corruption. I shall always remember your reaction when I told you 'I love you!': confusion and astonishment made your face very beautiful. If we hadn't been in the square, I would have kissed you on the spot. Even now, I don't understand how we were separated. When they started firing gas canisters, I ran, and I thought you were behind me. I saw the goons were arresting demonstrators on Talaat Harb Street, so I summoned up my courage and ran in the other direction. I went through the thick cloud of gas and came out on Champollion Street. I kept running until I stopped in front of Cinema Miami. It was about one in the morning. I found about twenty demonstrators around me, two of them girls. We looked at one another, panting, as though we couldn't believe we'd survived. We needed a while to organise our thoughts and talk. Suddenly we noticed, on the opposite pavement, a street sweeper, not less than sixty years of age. His appearance at that moment was bizarre. Have you ever heard of a street sweeper working at one in the morning? He was wearing a sweeper's orange uniform and pulled behind him a battered broom that I don't think could have swept up anything. He advanced with slow steps till he was facing us on the opposite pavement and shouted in a hoarse voice that echoed down the street, 'Children, you've begun! Keep going to the end! Mind you don't retreat!'*

His words were at odds with his appearance and his job. We remained silent, so he shouted in a louder voice, 'Mind you don't wound the snake and then leave it! You have to finish it off! If you don't kill the snake, it will kill you!'

It was a strange scene. I thought for a moment I was dreaming. The young people clapped warmly for the sweeper, who seemed to neither see nor hear them, as though he'd appeared just to say those words. He pulled on his broom and walked slowly off till he entered Abd El Khaleq Sarwat Street and disappeared. One of the young men who were standing there cried, 'What do we do now?'

A discussion began. Some colleagues wanted to go back to the square but I had a different idea. I said to them, 'We've had a victory over the regime and held a historic demonstration. In my opinion, we should go back to our houses and demonstrate again tomorrow somewhere security isn't expecting us.'

'Who says that if we go we'll be able to demonstrate again tomorrow?' a girl exclaimed.

'We'll fix the place on Facebook,' I told her.

Excitedly, she said, 'Firstly, the government could close Facebook down at any moment. Secondly, the demonstration didn't succeed thanks to the bloggers, it succeeded thanks to the ordinary people who don't even know what Facebook means. The people who came from Ard El Lewa, Embaba, and Nahya are the ones who supported us and they're waiting in the square now. We mustn't let them down.'

Voices were raised in support and I realised that most of the people there were against me. I confess their opposition annoyed me, so I said, 'Do you think we're going to arrest Hosni Mubarak this evening? Our battle against the regime needs stamina. If we go back to Tahrir Square now, we'll be seized immediately. What's the point of making a present of ourselves to the security forces?'

A youth came up to me and said angrily, 'Would you mind listening to me?'

'Go ahead.'

'My name is Hasan, from Ismailiya. I have a science degree and I've been without work for ten years. I have no hope of anything. I came tonight with two options – get rid of Hosni Mubarak or die. I'm not afraid of death. I might as well be dead anyway.'

Suddenly his voice trembled and he burst into tears. We were all moved and stopped talking. I told them, 'I'm with you whatever you decide to do.'

Their voices rose: 'Back to the square!' I went back with them and on the way, we found other groups of demonstrators who'd fled the gas and then decided to go back to the square like us. It's ten in the morning now. I left the square full of thousands of demonstrators. I'll sleep for a little, then go back. Please, tell me you're okay. Long live the revolution!

Mazen

Important PS: What I said to you in the square was from the heart. I really do love you.

20

That same morning, General Alwany woke his wife and said, 'Good morning. Pack me a change of underwear and some shirts. I'll send a private to get them at noon.'

Hagga Tahany struggled for a few moments to focus and emerge from the kingdom of sleep. When she saw that her husband was already dressed, she was astonished. Getting out of bed carefully to spare the pains in her knees, she said, 'Are you going away?'

The general replied brusquely, 'I shall spend the night at the office every day.'

She looked at him anxiously. 'Is everything alright?' she asked.

'Everything will be fine, God willing.'

In a smooth, feminine tone at odds with her amazing size, she whispered, 'Ahmad . . . please . . . set my heart at rest.'

He planted a quick kiss on her cheek and, struggling to keep control of his emotions, said, 'I can't tell you any details. Egypt is facing a conspiracy. Pray to Our Lord that He stand by us and save her!'

She uttered a heartfelt prayer, then placed his hand between her two plump ones, muttered a religiously approved charm, and exclaimed, with feeling, 'There is no god but God!'

'Muhammad is the prophet of God!' responded the general as he hurried out. It occurred to him to say goodbye to Danya. Gently, he opened the door to her room and found her sleeping. Going over to her, he contemplated her face, which looked exactly as it had when she was a child: when she slept, she would open her lips a little and look as innocent and beautiful as an angel. He went out, closing the door quietly. A few minutes later he was in his bulletproof car, his expression sharp and alert. On the road, he received reports from all the provinces. He issued his orders slowly, articulating each word as carefully as if aiming bullets, one after another, each of which had to hit its target. Instead of making its way to the Apparatus's building, however, the car followed another route until it came to a halt in front of a large villa in the district of Zamalek that looked out over the Nile.

The guards jumped from their cars and secured General Alwany's entry to the villa, then remained outside, their weapons at the ready, while two more accompanied him from the moment he passed through the door. General Alwany made his way to the back garden, where he went to see the other officers who were in position there with their weapons, greeting them and exchanging with them a few quick words, including expressions of encouragement. Then he went up to the roof of the villa where he found more officers armed with revolvers and automatic rifles, as well as seven snipers with modern rifles who had taken up positions covering each direction. He greeted them all, then went back downstairs to the first-floor room that had been set aside for him as an office, where screens had been suspended that transmitted the demonstrations in Cairo, Alexandria, Suez, and the other cities of Egypt. He asked for a cup of medium-sweet Turkish coffee, which he slowly sipped as he followed events. After approximately half an hour, the minister of the interior arrived. General Alwany shook his hand and the minister embraced him warmly. General Alwany smiled and said, playfully, 'So the country has to be turned upside down for me to see you?'

'I'm at your service, sir.'

'What do you say we talk outside?'

He didn't wait for an answer. He pulled out his mobile phone and placed it on the desk, and the minister did the same. Then he took the minister's arm under his and they went out to a distant corner of the garden, where there were a table and two seats, on which they sat. The guards understood what General Alwany wanted and withdrew to a distance that allowed them to monitor the place without being able to hear the conversation. In sharp tones General Alwany said, 'In response to circumstances, I've decided to move our activities outside of the Apparatus, as a precautionary measure.'

The minister said, 'We are preparing alternative headquarters, sir, and will move the important departments there today, or tomorrow at the latest.'

General Alwany waved to the distant private, who hurried to him. He ordered another cup of coffee and a bottle of water, and the minister asked for a glass of tea. General Alwany waited until the private was out of earshot, then said, 'I'm not going to talk about the developments. I'm sure you're in the picture. We are, unfortunately, paying the price for a delay in the political decision-making process. The service of which I have the honour to be the head has submitted two reports to His Excellency the President, one two months ago and one a week ago, in which we predicted the events that are taking place today, and we proposed a number of measures to abort them. Unfortunately, not one was taken.'

The minister nodded his head sadly, and General Alwany continued, saying, 'The provocateurs who are leading everyone in the squares today number no more than five hundred individuals, whose names and details we have presented in full and whose immediate detention we proposed, though, unfortunately, nothing happened.'

'Why, sir?'

General Alwany looked at the minister in what seemed like sorrow, and said, 'The furthest extent of my authority, politically speaking, is to present reports and offer proposals. Decisions are taken by His Excellency the President alone, based on considerations of which he is the best judge.'

'Would that His Excellency the President had acted on Your Excellency's proposals!'

'What's done is done,' General Alwany responded. 'Let's stick to what matters. I want to hear from you.'

The private brought the drinks. The minister sipped his tea and said, 'I had hoped to learn your assessment of the positions of the political forces.'

'Such as who?'

'The Brotherhood.'

'The Brothers have issued a statement condemning the demonstrations and they'll never run the risk of taking part in them, because the price will be exorbitant. For them, the most important thing is the safety of their organisation. However, if, God forbid, we were to lose control of the situation, the Brotherhood will for sure take to the streets to exploit the chaos. Have you detained some of their leaders?'

The minister nodded, and General Alwany said, 'Leave them in prison. They could be a useful card up our sleeve.'

'And what about the political parties?'

'The parties are all cooperating. They've all issued statements against the demonstrations.'

Nodding, the minister said, 'I sent Your Excellency Plan 2000.'

'I read it. You did well to send it via the secret email without the ministry's stamp. We're going through exceptional circumstances. We mustn't leave a paper trail.'

'I've taken a few measures outside the plan. I'd like to go over them with Your Excellency.'

'Please do.'

The minister extracted a small piece of paper and began reading in an official tone:

'Strengthening of the security details on vital installations and public figures loyal to the regime.

'Securing factories and workers' gatherings and impressing on our sources the importance of informing us of any attempt to incite the workers to action so that these may be dealt with immediately.

'Concerning schools and universities, these will be closed anyway because of the half-year holiday. Security details have been strengthened and any student who attempts to incite his colleagues to unrest will be arrested.

'Dozens of informers have been planted wherever demonstrators get together so as to get a clear picture of their lines of thought as they are adopted, accompanied by attempts to lure the lead elements out of the demonstrations and arrest them.'

General Alwany nodded his head and said, 'These are all sound measures.'

'Thank you, Your Excellency. Your Excellency has comments on the plan? I think of Your Excellency as my teacher.'

The general appeared to think, then shook his head slowly and said, 'The plan is excellent. What matters when it comes to implementation is the time factor. Every hour counts.'

'Absolutely, Your Excellency.'

'What matters to me is that the plan's philosophy should be clear to everyone who carries it out. Each officer must believe that he is in a real battle to defend Egypt. I want leaflets from the ministry distributed to every officer and every man in the ranks. They have to understand that the kids in Tahrir are a bunch of treacherous conspirators whose goal is to bring the country down.'

The minister nodded and, rising from his seat, General Alwany continued excitedly, 'Rebellion and demonstrations are something strange to the nature of Egyptians. They are an obedient people who have always respected their leadership even when angry with it. What is happening in Tahrir is something foreign to the Egyptian mentality. Our goal is to send a message to the Egyptians that the only outcome of the demonstrations will be chaos. Our goal is to tell the ordinary citizen, "Either you side with the demonstrations and lose your security, or you side with the state, in which case it will protect you."'

'I quite understand, Your Excellency,' the minister said in a low voice.

General Alwany sat down again, looked into the distance, and appeared to be organising his thoughts. Then he asked the minister, 'Are you going to cut telecommunications?'

'I gave instructions to cut telecommunications on Thursday, before the demonstrations on Friday. Cutting the mobile network and the internet will deny the saboteurs any means of communicating. Meanwhile, the ministry's communications network will continue to operate by code.'

General Alwany's face showed signs of approval. Then he leant close to the minister and said, their conversation now changing to a whisper, 'There are initiatives in the plan that are against the law. I agree to them, naturally. "Necessity makes the unlawful lawful." But we have to secure the officers against any legal consequences.'

'The officers have oral instructions,' the minister replied, 'to use live ammunition to control the demonstrations. There isn't a single piece of paper to prove that they have been issued with bullets. The issue recorded in the books is for cartridges and tear gas, that's all.'

'Does the plan allow for the opening of the prisons?' General Alwany asked.

'That will be done only in case of our failure, God forbid, to control the demonstrations.'

'Understood. How many prisons will you open and what will be the number of escapees?'

'We'll open about five and the number of escapees will be between twenty-five and thirty thousand. Of course, as set out in the plan, the goal is to create panic among the Egyptians, so they side with the state against the saboteurs.'

'Do you have legal cover?'

'It will be presented as an attempt at an uprising in the prisons to which the officers responded, but that there was an external power that helped the prisoners to escape.'

'Wonderful. But there's an important point to consider. The officer who all his life has believed that it's his duty to guard the prisons. How can you suddenly convince him that he should let the prisoners go?'

The minister smiled and whispered, 'I've formed a group of the most loyal officers inside the ministry. This group takes its orders from me personally and they exist everywhere, though their colleagues know nothing about them. Officers from this special group will open the prisons. The other officers will think that what's happening is an ordinary uprising.'

'Very well, but suppose that the ordinary officer actually opposes the opening of the prison and prevents it?'

'Your Excellency, if we are obliged to open the prisons, the prisons will be opened. My instructions to the special group officers will make it clear that they are not to allow anything to obstruct this, no matter what the reason.'

General Alwany said nothing and appeared to be weighing what he should say to the minister, who continued, in a serious tone of voice, 'Your Excellency, we are defending the Egyptian state; we are in a state of war. Even if there should be victims in any quarter, it will be the price of the survival of the state.'

'One final point,' General Alwany said. 'The media.'

'My instructions to state and private media are clear. They have to explain to the people the enormity of the plot. I've sent a supervising officer to control content on every channel, with the authority to stop any programme and arrest any person he sees fit.'

There was silence. Then the minister of the interior asked, 'Does Your Excellency have any further observations?'

General Alwany shook his head and said, 'No. Thank you.'

'Then, with Your Excellency's permission, I shall return to the ministry.'

General Alwany rose, shook the minister's hand warmly, and said, 'Stay in touch, and Godspeed!'

21

Panting, the waiter cried, 'We have to close the restaurant!'

'Why?' Ashraf Wissa asked in alarm.

'There are huge demonstrations in the street. The owner just phoned and ordered us to close immediately.'

Despite the surprise, Ashraf felt relieved. He removed his hand, leaving the piece of hashish in his pocket, safe and sound. Then he paid the bill, leaving the waiter a generous tip. He left the restaurant, Ikram with him. On the street, things were tense. It was jam-full of cars, pedestrians were hurrying in all directions, and shouted slogans could be heard echoing in the distance. In a low voice, Ikram said, 'Lord protect us! I'm afraid. Could you put me in a minibus, sir?'

'Minibuses won't be any use now,' Ashraf said, pulling her by the hand. He noticed a taxi close by, negotiated with the driver, and gave him the fare in advance. Then he put Ikram in the rear seat and said in a loud voice, 'As soon as you reach the house, let me know you're okay!'

She looked at him and squeezed his hand, as though to convey her gratitude. He took a photo of the taxi's rear number plate and kept his eyes on her, an encouraging smile on his face, until it had disappeared into the traffic. He decided he'd walk home, so he crossed the bridge leading to Qasr El Eini Street. He saw throngs of demonstrators calling for the fall of Mubarak, and, observing them with astonishment, asked himself, 'Who are these people? Where have they come from, and how did they take to the streets in such large numbers? What's going on in the country?' The demonstrations took him completely by surprise. He didn't use Facebook, which he considered a waste of time, and had stopped reading the papers or listening to news broadcasts years ago.

On reaching Tahrir Square, he found it crowded to the limit. They were ordinary Egyptians, from all the different classes: women with and without headscarves, young middle class people, plebeian types, and country people wearing traditional robes. They were standing in circles holding animated discussions. He wanted to hear what they were saying but it occurred to him that he might be searched at any moment and that he had a piece of hashish in his pocket large enough to guarantee that he'd be thrown into prison for years. He went home quickly and made himself a cup of coffee without sugar which he sipped, smoking a joint and following from the balcony what was going on in the square. He received a message from Ikram on his phone reassuring him that she had reached home. A little later, his wife Magda arrived. He greeted her unenthusiastically; her face was thunderous. She heated food and they sat down at the table. He sensed that she wanted to discuss the events and he was enjoying, to some degree, ignoring her. Minutes passed and then he said, chewing, and determined to provoke her, 'The food's delicious. Thank you, Magda.'

She replied with annoyance, 'Thank Ikram. She's the one who did the cooking.'

He continued to eat with appetite. Unable to bear his silence any longer, she said, angrily, 'Did you see the demonstrations?'

'I did.'

'I'm afraid for Egypt, Ashraf.'

'Afraid of what?'

'The chaos.'

'Could things be any more chaotic than they already are?'

She looked at him disapprovingly and said, 'You don't understand, or what?'

He replied sarcastically, 'Do help me!'

In an agitated voice, she replied, 'These demonstrations have been set up by the Brotherhood, and their aim is to take power.'

'Not true. The people I saw in the square aren't Brotherhood.'

Terrified, and as though she hadn't heard him, she cried, 'If Mubarak leaves power, there's no way we can stay in this country!'

He replied quietly, 'Speak for yourself. I will never leave Egypt.'

She gave him an angry stare and shouted, 'Go on living your delusions.'

'You're the one who's sick, with your fears.'

'You'll find out I was right when it's too late.'

He didn't reply. He knew it was pointless to argue with her. He got up from the table, patting his lips dry with the edge of the napkin. Then he said, 'Please excuse me. I have work I have to finish in the study.'

'It must be something urgent!' she responded.

She was mocking him. What she wanted to say was 'What work, when you're a failure and a dope-head?' He didn't have the energy or the desire for a quarrel. He felt that a great change was taking place around him and wanted to be free to watch and understand. He went into the study and then sat on the balcony and observed the square. The crowds kept increasing and armoured personnel carriers stood at the entrances, while hundreds of Central Security troops surrounded the square on all sides. He thought of Ikram and smiled as a feeling of tenderness swept over him. He recalled her childishly exaggerated attempt at elegance, her whispered words, the warmth of her hand, and her decency when she asked him to walk her to the minibus: she'd wanted to hail a taxi, but hadn't asked him to do so and had made do with expressing her fear. How could an uneducated woman, from an utterly deprived background, who had received no real upbringing, behave with such refinement? Were people born with their character traits or did they acquire them? How could Ikram, a girl from the streets, be more emotionally intelligent than Magda, graduate of the Mère de Dieu and the American University? He felt a sudden chill and returned to the bedroom, where he put on a heavy woollen dressing gown. Magda had gone to sleep, so he moved carefully so as not to wake her. He returned to the balcony and smoked a number of joints while he watched the square. He lost any awareness of time. The number of demonstrators continued to increase and about forty minutes after midnight, the gates of Hell were opened. The police let loose a hail of tear-gas shells. He saw demonstrators running in all directions. The thick smoke formed a cloud that made it impossible to see and that reached as far as the fourth floor, and he felt a burning in his eyes and nose and started coughing hard. He went in quickly, closed the balcony door, then hurried to the bathroom and began washing out his mouth and nose with warm water to get rid of the remains of the gas. He heard a sudden sound, as though the doorbell had been rung. He listened for a moment, and the bell rang again. Who could be visiting at this hour? He crossed the hall and went up to the door. Looking through the peephole, he saw before him a woman he didn't know.

22

Dear Mazen,

I'm going to tell you something you don't know about me. I suffer from a chest allergy that is so severe that when the dusty winds blow in spring, I have to use an inhaler to breathe. When they fired gas canisters at us with such intensity, I ran with all my strength and had to make an extraordinary effort not to lose consciousness. They struck from three sides, and the only direction that was open was Talaat Harb Street. I ran towards it and then discovered that they'd set up roadblocks in the street to catch demonstrators. The first was at the Diplomatic Club corner. From a distance, I caught sight of the police goons viciously beating a demonstrator and throwing him into a minivan. I found myself in a tight spot: if I went back, I'd choke on the gas, and if I went on, I was sure to be arrested. One of them noticed me and ran towards me. I quickly entered the first block of flats, next to the Crystal bakery. I ignored the lift and climbed the stairs as fast as I could till I found a flat whose lights were on, on the fourth floor. I had no other option, so I pressed the doorbell, and an old man came to the door. I said, 'I'm a demonstrator and the police are going to arrest me. Please take me in.'

It was a difficult moment. The man, poor chap, was overwhelmed by astonishment, but I didn't give him a chance. I entered and closed the door behind me. Then I showed him my ID card and said, 'My name is Asmaa and I'm a teacher,' and while he was examining my ID, I said to him, 'Please, let me stay here until the police leave.'

The man began to take in what was going on. He turned off the light in the living room and said in a low voice, 'Come. Please come with me to the study.'

He looked different. You'd think he was ancient, something of a relic – a pasha from the old days, for example, or a veteran actor who'd emerged from a black-and-white film. Slim and handsome, his face dark, with the wrinkles of age, and his hair smooth, completely white, and parted in the middle, like in the forties. He was wearing a woollen checked dressing gown with a roll-neck pullover under it. I knew that he was a Christian from the statuette of the Virgin at the entrance to the living room. Everything in the flat spoke of beautiful classical taste – the luxurious leather furniture set, the pictures hung on the walls, and the wooden, English-style desk. He shook my hand and said, 'I'm Ashraf Wissa.'

I said, 'I'm very grateful to you, sir, for saving me.'

He smiled, nodded, and avoided looking at me, as though my thanks had embarrassed him. He asked me what I would like to drink. I wanted to drink tea. He made two cups of tea and sat down at the desk. There was an elegant, aristocratic stamp to everything about him – his clothes, his walk, and his way of speaking. I felt that his face was known to me, so I said, 'I think I've seen you somewhere before, sir.'

He informed me that he was an actor and listed some of the small parts he'd played in a few TV serials. To be honest, I was amazed. The man seemed to be rich, so why would he play bit parts?

I said to him, 'I suppose you think of acting as a hobby, sir.'

He replied, 'To me, acting is both a hobby and a profession. I'm a graduate of the American University, Drama Department.'

'It must be nice to be able to combine talent and study.'

'That's true, in theory. But in Egypt, it isn't easy for an actor to get an opportunity, even if he deserves it.'

I noticed that he was a heavy smoker. After a little while, he seemed to get over the strangeness of the situation and he looked

154

at me in a friendly manner, smiled, and said, 'Pleased to meet you!'

'Me too, Mr Ashraf.'

'Allow me to call you Asmaa, without any title. You're about the same age as my daughter, Sarah.'

'Please do.'

'I'm going to be frank with you, Asmaa. You're a respectable teacher and you look as though you come from a good family. I don't understand why you'd expose yourself to all these troubles.'

'If everyone thinks about his own safety, the country will never get set to rights.'

'You mean you're ready to be arrested and go to prison?'

'Of course.'

'Why? For what?'

'For us to be a decent country, with justice and freedom.'

'You're an optimist, Asmaa.'

'Millions of Egyptians share my position.'

He didn't appear to be convinced. He said nothing for a while, then asked me, 'Could you explain to me the goal of the demonstrations?'

I told him, 'The goal is for us to force Mubarak to resign and then we'll elect a new president and build a new, democratic state.'

Hiding his sarcasm behind a polite smile, he said, 'That's all wonderful and we hope it comes about, but are you really sure that Hosni Mubarak can be made to resign by demonstrations?'

'Absolutely.'

'Mubarak has the army and the police. What do you have?'

'We have right on our side.'

'Right isn't always victorious.'

'Ben Ali was a terrible dictator, but the Tunisian people succeeded in overthrowing him through peaceful demonstrations.'

We had a long discussion. He wasn't convinced by the idea of revolution but I felt that he respected my enthusiasm, somewhat. You *know those nice characters who reject your point of view but never confront you with their rejection and beat about the bush and choose their words carefully so as not to upset you? Ashraf Wissa is one of those. He always behaves with sensitivity and grace. I liked him, not only because he saved me from being arrested but also because he always treated me with understanding and respect. Unfortunately, I made trouble for him with his wife. He kept looking out from the balcony to follow what was going on in the street and then suddenly I heard a woman's voice calling to him from inside the flat. He went inside and after a while I heard the sound of a heated discussion. I couldn't make out what was being said, but I realised that it was about me. Mr Ashraf came back after a while, looking angry.*

I told him, 'I'm sorry. If I'd known that I was going to cause you trouble, I'd never have knocked on your door.'

He said to me simply, 'First, you had no choice. Second, I'm happy to have made your acquaintance. Third, my wife and I are always at loggerheads and she's a constant cause of annoyance to me.'

I was amazed that he would speak so frankly. I got up and decided to leave. He blocked my way to the door of the study and said, 'I cannot possibly allow you to go down. The street is full of police.'

When I insisted, he threatened me, saying, 'If you leave, Asmaa, I shall go down with you so that they arrest us both. Would you be happy to see someone my age being arrested and abused?'

I will never forget that marvellous man so long as I live! What would make someone who didn't know me, and wasn't convinced in the first place of the value of the demonstrations, and who wasn't at all interested in the cause I was defending, behave that way? Imagine, he made me cheese sandwiches and eggs with pastrami and kept on at me till I ate. Can you believe that he didn't let me leave until six in the morning, after he'd gone down to the street on his own and made sure the goons were gone? Can you believe that he stopped a taxi for me and insisted on paying the fare in advance, and when I refused, he told me, 'My dear Asmaa, do as you're told! I'm old enough to be your father!'?

I almost cry every time I remember his conduct towards me, not just because I'm moved by his delicacy but because I feel so guilty. Today I discovered that I didn't understand the people. I feel embarrassed that I once said that the Egyptians were all either corrupt or cowards. I wish I could apologise to them one by one. Thank you, Mazen, for teaching me not to be in a hurry to judge people. I got home in the morning and found a big problem with my mother waiting for me that I'll tell you about later. The bottom line is, I'm fine, thank God. Please let me know how you are as soon as possible. I thank you for the beautiful feelings that you expressed in the square. I'm smiling now, so that you can see the two dimples that you like.

Goodbye, Mazen, my . . . friend (I was going to write something else but I was too shy).

Asmaa

23

Danya prayed the afternoon prayer, then got her medical bag ready and took a last look at herself in the mirror before going down in the lift. Her mother was sitting in the hall, talking on the phone. She seemed tense. Danya kissed her head and sat down next to her, waiting for her to finish the call. Her mother looked at her and said, excitedly, 'God protect Egypt, Danya! Your father phoned this morning. He's been sleeping at work for the last three days and he tells me he doesn't know when he'll be back. There's a big conspiracy against our country. They're trying to drive us into chaos, may God be their judge!'

Danya was in too dreamy a state to argue. She smiled, looked at her mother with affection, and said in an ordinary tone of voice, 'I'm going out.'

'Where are you going?'

'The medical faculty.'

'The faculty's open on a Friday?'

'Yes. The faculty has opened an emergency clinic to give first aid to the injured.'

Hagga Tahany's face took on an angry expression, and she said, 'You're going out to give first aid to those kids in the demonstrations? What have they got to do with you?'

Danya was confused for a moment. Then she said, 'As doctors, it's our duty to treat the sick, whoever they are.'

'Sheikh Shamel says that the kids in the demonstrations are "seekers of discord and sowers of corruption on the face of the land". Are you aware that the punishment for them in religious law is execution?'

'I have nothing to do with the demonstrations. I'm a final-year medical student and it's part of my training. The faculty sent out a call and told us to treat anyone who was wounded. It could be a demonstrator or it could be an officer or a police recruit.'

Hagga Tahany fell silent and Danya rushed to speak before she could, saying, in a tone of voice that she knew would make an impression on her, 'On the day of resurrection, when I stand in front of Our Lord, Glorious and Mighty, would you want me, Mother, to be carrying on my back the sin of having left an injured officer or recruit whom I could have saved to die?'

After a number of sentences of this kind, along with citations from the Koran and the Holy Traditions, her mother began to seem convinced and asked her daughter, 'Shouldn't we tell your father that you're going out?'

Sensing danger, Danya said, 'There's no need to make him anxious. There's nothing to it. I'm going to the faculty for two hours and will have the driver with me. He'll take a route that avoids the demonstrations.'

Her mother phoned the driver and gave him instructions, then recited a religiously acceptable spell over her head, gave her her usual goodbye kisses, and whispered, 'There is no god but God,' to which her daughter responded, 'Muhammad is the Messenger of God.'

Seated in the back of the car, Danya reflected that she hadn't lied to her mother, though she hadn't told the truth either. True, there was a field hospital to treat the injured, but it had been set up at the request of the students and some of the teachers, not by the faculty administration. And true, she was going to the faculty, as she had informed her mother, but she was going to transfer from there, with her colleagues, to Tahrir Square, where the field hospital was located. The thought that she was performing her professional duty protected her from feelings of guilt. She had given her father an undertaking that she would never do anything that would harm his position, but she was just going to give aid to the injured, no more, no less. It was her duty as a doctor to offer treatment to any who needed it. She smiled as she went over in her mind her long phone call with Khaled the day before. He'd told her, 'You refused to take part in the demonstrations. That's your right, but your duty as a doctor requires you to help the injured.' Had she been convinced because his logic was sound, or because she wanted to be with him?

The driver let her out in front of the Qasr El Eini gates, where she found Khaled, two of the professors, and around twenty of her fellow students, young women and men. They were wearing white coats. She knew them all and was reassured by their presence. She greeted them warmly. She noticed that Khaled looked haggard, so she asked him anxiously, 'What's wrong with you? You don't look well.'

Smiling, he said, 'I haven't slept since yesterday.'

He asked her to put on a white coat and told her that they were concerned about letting the security forces know that they were doctors doing their duty. Unthinkingly, she asked him, 'Would you like to come in the car with me?'

He laughed and said, 'My dear Madame Danya, no one goes to a demonstration in a Mercedes.'

She looked at him reproachfully, and he told her seriously, 'We're going to go to the square on foot.'

She asked the driver to wait where he was and set off with Khaled. They crossed the bridge and marched down Qasr El Eini Street. She exchanged laughing comments with her colleagues, in which he took no part. 'What's on your mind, Doctor?' she asked him.

He smiled and said, 'I'm not thinking about anything. I'm dreaming.'

'Is it a nice dream?'

'Very!'

'May I know what it is?'

'I'm dreaming that the revolution has been successful.'

Jokingly, she said, 'So when you dream, all you dream about is the revolution?'

'In the dream, I see you next to me.'

'I don't believe you. You dream about revolution and that's it,' she exclaimed coquettishly, but he moved closer to her and said, 'Danya, you will be with me forever, in my dreams and in real life. I'm lucky to have met you, and I'm lucky to have witnessed the revolution and taken part in it.'

She was too moved to speak. At that moment, she longed to hold him and take his head onto her breast. She wished she could tell him she loved him and would never leave him, that she could make it clear to him that she was prepared to fight the whole world to realise their dream of marriage. She wished she could imagine their home, and how many boys and girls they'd have and what their names would be. She turned her face to the side to hide her emotions. The demonstrators on the march began chanting 'Bread! Freedom! Social Justice!' People on their balconies and at their windows clapped and some of the women let out trills of joy that added an air of celebration to the demonstration, while the demonstrators began waving to those standing on the balconies and calling out, 'Countrymen, join us!' and 'Egyptians, to the streets!'

The march quickly began growing in size as it drew closer to Tahrir Square. Danya was gripped by what was happening around her: she felt she was dreaming, as though she'd entered a magical world she'd never known before. She looked at the faces of the demonstrators. They were ordinary people, like the ones she treated at Qasr El Eini. Where was the great conspiracy that her father had talked about? Had all these people taken money from abroad? Were the women making their trills of joy on the balconies CIA agents? Did religion permit the killing of these demonstrators, as Sheikh

Shamel had ruled? Did Islam permit the murder of those who called for justice?

The crowd of demonstrators had become so thick that it was hard to find a place to put one's feet. Danya was careful to stay next to Khaled. Being next to him made her feel safe. She looked back and found she could no longer see the end of the crowd. The slogans rang out like thunder: '*Bread! Freedom! Justice for All!*' '*The People . . . Demand . . . the Fall of the Regime!*' She didn't call out with them, not just because she was concerned for the welfare of her family but because she felt, in her heart of hearts, that it would be absurd and dishonest. Could the daughter of General Ahmad Alwany call for the ousting of a regime of which he was one of the most prominent pillars? When she found herself at the heart of the crush of demonstrators, she remembered her father's words about the security services that were watching her and was overtaken by a feeling of guilt, which she struggled to overcome. Even if they photographed her in the midst of the demonstrators, she was wearing her white coat, didn't join in with them in their slogans, and was performing her duty as a doctor – she clung to this comforting idea but, deep inside, wasn't convinced by it. She wasn't there just to help the injured but because she wanted to be with Khaled. Plus, there was something real and honest about the demonstration, which had begun, little by little, to affect her feelings. If she were from an ordinary rich family and her father and her brothers didn't hold important positions, would she have joined in the demonstrations? Probably, yes. The sense of justice has nothing to do with being rich or poor.

The organisers of the demonstration decided to put the doctors at the front, and the demonstrators fell back, so that the whole of the first row was made up of doctors, male and female, in white coats. They entered Tahrir Square, which was surging with the amazing throngs of demonstrators, who passed between heavy, broad pieces of metal with pointed projections like stakes that the demonstrators had put in the street to stop police vehicles from entering the square. Danya was advancing with her colleagues when suddenly she heard a terrible unceasing roar, after which the air quickly filled with thick gas. She felt a burning sensation in her eyes and nose and began to find it difficult to breathe. 'Hold steady!' shouted one of the demonstrators.

She felt afraid, coughed violently, and was soon completely unable to see through the thick smoke. Khaled took hold of her hand, pulled her towards him, and shouted, 'Come this way!'

They retreated far from the source of the gas. She kept choking. She found herself in the middle of a group of demonstrators who had been obliged to fall back because they couldn't take the thick gas. They stood all together by the wall of the American University, and her colleagues began handing out pieces of cotton soaked in vinegar and bottles they'd filled with a salt solution and on which they'd mounted spray heads. Danya inhaled the vinegar and then washed her face and nose with the solution, felt better, and began helping the demonstrators around her. After a little while, a police car appeared, moving fast towards the square, but it stopped in front of the pieces of metal that were scattered over the street. The officer was sitting next to the driver. He stuck his head through the window, looked angrily at the demonstrators, and shouted, 'Move the metal from the street!' None of them moved, and one of them shouted, 'We won't move it! You're going in there to kill our colleagues!'

24

That night, Ashraf tried to explain the Asmaa situation to his wife calmly, but she blew up, the traces of sleep making her face look bad-tempered and fierce.

'I don't want Muslim Brothers in my house!' she shouted.

'I told you, the girl isn't a Muslim Brother. She was in the demonstration, and the police were going to arrest her.'

'I don't give a damn!'

'Don't you have any pity? She's a respectable girl who works as a schoolteacher, and she's the same age as our daughter Sarah. How could I let her be arrested?'

'A respectable girl doesn't go on demonstrations in the first place.'

'Magda, the girl came to me for refuge and I couldn't give her up. Can't you understand that?'

She looked at him and realised that he'd never budge from his position, so she muttered something inaudible, returned to her room, and went back to sleep. For the next two days, Ashraf avoided her totally. She tried to talk to him about the demonstrations and to lure him into telling her what had happened with Asmaa but he'd answer her with curt, vague phrases, then withdraw. He was well aware that any conversation with her would cause problems and he didn't have the energy for a quarrel; he needed to be alone and to think. The succession of unexpected events had created within him an acute tension that he strove to overcome with hashish. He was now discovering that for years he'd been living in isolation and hadn't noticed that everything in Egypt had changed. He'd been hemmed in between his flat, which constituted his small, closed universe, and his pointless, bitter battles in the acting world, and now he suddenly found himself before a different kind of Egyptian. These Egyptians were, as Asmaa had said, entirely prepared to go to prison, and even to die, for the sake of justice. He contemplated them with a mixture of disbelief, admiration, and guilt. On Friday morning, he was surprised to find Magda entering his study carrying a small suitcase. In a loud voice and official tones, as though informing him of a judicial decree, she said, 'I've decided to go and stay at Mama's in Heliopolis.'

Making an effort to pull his thoughts, scattered by hashish, together, he cleared his throat and said, 'That's a strange idea.'

As though waiting for any word he might say so that she could explode, she yelled, 'No, it isn't strange or anything of the sort! The country's falling apart. Today, they cut off the internet and the mobile phone networks. After the prayers, the Brothers are going to hold demonstrations and God knows what will happen. It's dangerous for us to be so close to Tahrir Square. We have to go to Mama's for a couple of days till things quieten down.'

Ashraf smiled and said, 'Just so you know, Heliopolis has demonstrations, exactly like here.'

She gave him a furious look and shouted, 'I'd really like to know why you keep provoking me! Instead of trying to calm me down, you want to scare me even more?'

His smile widened and he said, 'I'm just telling the truth.'

'Even if there are demonstrations in Heliopolis, it's sure to be safer than here.'

'Fine. Go, and Godspeed!'

'I'm warning you, Ashraf. It's dangerous for you here. The Brothers could easily attack you sitting here in the flat. Aren't you afraid?'

'No.'

'Of course not. You rescued a Brotherhood girl, so now you're their darling.'

165

'I told you, that girl isn't with the Brothers and, to be honest, your fears are exaggerated. We haven't done anything that would make anyone attack us.'

'In the Brotherhood's eyes, just the fact that we're Copts makes us infidels whom they have to slaughter.'

Ashraf sighed and said, 'Are we going to go over all that again, Magda? Your panic is morbid. There's no point in talking about it.'

She took a step towards him and said, 'Are you coming with me?'

He shook his head, and she yelled furiously, 'Do as you like. I'll be at Mama's. If you want to come, you know the address.'

She turned and went out into the hall and delivered instructions to Ikram in a loud, sharp tone of voice. A little later, Ashraf heard the sound of the door closing and felt a sense of relief. He lit a joint, but Ikram soon arrived and asked him anxiously, 'Is Madame Magda upset?'

'No.'

'Okay, so why did she leave the house?'

Ashraf got up from behind the desk and took her hand. Then they sat next to one another on the couch. He planted a quick kiss on her cheek and said, 'Madame Magda is afraid to stay here because of the demonstrations. She's gone to her mother's house in Heliopolis.'

Ikram pouted her delectable lips and said, 'Can I tell you something, but you mustn't get angry?'

'By all means.'

'I really don't understand how your wife can run away and leave you when things get difficult.'

He looked at her and smiled, then took her in his arms. 'If I were your wife, I'd never leave you. We'd either live together or die together,' she whispered.

She had now become unbearably sexy. He hugged her and started

166

kissing her neck and ear. She whispered, 'Can I change out of my work things?'

He ignored the question and devoured her lips in a long, burning kiss. They were so aroused, they made love on the carpet without cushions. His performance was implacable, as though he wanted to rid himself of his anxieties in her body, as though he was using her to protect himself from his apprehensions, as though he was clinging to her to reassure himself that she was still with him. Her body received him with patience and understanding. She withstood his roughness and contained him with such overflowing maternal tenderness that he almost wept. After the lovemaking, he remained on his back, staring at the ceiling, his hand enfolding hers. He said nothing and didn't smoke his usual cigarette. He remained sunk in thought so long that she asked him, 'Who's the lucky girl?' He smiled and didn't reply. She planted a kiss on his cheek and whispered, 'Would you be so kind, sir, as to tell me what you're thinking about?'

'About what Asmaa said.'

She pretended to laugh and said, 'This Asmaa must be very pretty.'

He turned to look at her in astonishment. Then he embraced her and whispered, 'You're the only pretty one in the world.'

With frank anxiety, she said, 'You haven't talked about anything except Asmaa since the moment you saw her.'

His voice serious, he replied, 'Forget all this silly jealousy and understand what I'm trying to say. Asmaa represents to me a different generation and a new way of thinking. From the moment I had that discussion with her, I've been asking myself, "Who's right and who's wrong?"'

'I don't understand.'

'People my age have suffered all their lives from corruption and injustice but they never did anything to change the situation. I, for example, could have become a successful and famous actor if it weren't for the corruption in the field of the arts. What did I do to fight that corruption? Nothing!'

'What would you have liked to do, then?'

'Corruption in the arts is part of the corruption of the regime. The regime has to be changed first if everything is going to be put to rights. I knew that but I was afraid to get involved in politics.'

'You were right to be afraid. You're a respectable gentleman, sir, with a family and children, and anyone who tells the truth in this country disappears down a black hole.'

'That's exactly what I like about the young people like Asmaa. They aren't afraid like us. They're determined to put the country to rights and they're ready to pay the price. To be honest, they're braver than us.'

A wan smile appeared on Ikram's face; she still hadn't completely rid herself of the niggling feeling of jealousy, so she got up and pretended to be looking for her slippers. She walked past him, naked, and her full breasts, freed from all restraints, bounced, while her huge backside assumed a variety of pleasing positions. She knew that her naked body aroused him. He couldn't bear to see her naked without pouncing on her and initiating a new round of passion. This time, however, he remained wrapped in his silence. She bent over him, kissed him, and asked, 'Do you love me?'

'Of course.'

'Okay. If you love me, no more talk about the demonstrations.'

With an expert hand, she began playing around at the base of his belly, whispering, 'We're together and there's nothing to disturb us. Let's have fun and talk later.'

They lost themselves in a wild bout of love. Then she took a bath and came back, her hair up, wearing a blue housedress and looking as fresh as a newly watered rose. He suggested they have lunch in the dining room. They ate together and chatted. She made a point of telling him funny things about her neighbours in Hawamdiya. When he'd done eating, he told her, 'Thank you, Ikram.'

'For what?'

'For making me happy.'

She smiled gratefully, so he took heart and said, 'Please, make me a cup of coffee to drink on the balcony.'

In a tone of humorous complaint, she replied, 'It's no use! You still want to go on watching the demonstrations.'

He quickly crossed the hall, went into the study, opened the balcony door, and began following what was going on in the square. She removed the dishes from the table and washed them in the kitchen. While she was fixing her make-up in front of the large mirror in the living room, Ashraf's voice suddenly rang through the hall in a shriek.

'Come here, Ikram! They're killing them! They're shooting them dead!'

25

Dear Asmaa,

I hope you're well. I'm writing this letter quickly on a piece of paper because the internet has been cut off. I have no idea how I'll get it to you. I went back to the house to take a shower and change my clothes and I'm going back to the square even though I'm dying from lack of sleep. Today, after the afternoon prayer, I was in the middle of a demonstration heading for Tahrir Square, and when we reached the Shura Council building, we found the army blocking our way. An army officer with the rank of captain approached us and said, 'Listen up! There are Central Security forces trapped in the square and they want to get out. They're just poor lads and none of this is their fault. They haven't had a wink of sleep for three days. Will you let them cross to the other side so that they can get in the police vans and go back to camp? Then they can all go back to their villages.'

The appearance of the soldiers really was pitiful. They seemed to be exhausted and some of them were so tired they were sitting on the asphalt. I consulted with my colleagues and then told the officer, 'Tell them they can go through, sir, and we won't get in their way.'

The officer smiled and asked, 'Can I take that as a promise?'

We gave him our word and made a double human barrier, leaving a gap in the middle for the soldiers to go through, and began shouting, 'We are your brothers! We are your children!'

The scene was rapturous and moving. About forty soldiers went through, one after the other, to the next street and the Cairo Centre building, where a large police van was waiting, which they were sup-

posed to climb into. As soon as they reached the van, however, something happened that we could never have expected. A police general appeared. I shall never forget his face. He was thin and excitable. He distributed ammunition to the soldiers and gave them an order, and they began firing on us with live bullets. We tried to escape but discovered that they'd caught us in a pincer movement. The army had closed off Tahrir Square to give the police the chance to kill us. We ran towards the Shura Council, pursued by bullets. I saw more than one fellow demonstrator fall. Under the continuous hail of bullets, there was nothing we could do to help them. Imagine the horror! We were all running, and every moment another young person fell to a bullet aimed at them from behind. We entered the Shura Council and the workers there gestured to us to hide, but the soldiers followed us inside, shooting. Don't ask me how I managed to escape the slaughter, I don't know myself. Perhaps it was luck, because I ran to the Council's back door, on the Lycée side. I shall remember those terrible moments for as long as I live. I saw my fellows dying of gunshot wounds. I saw the martyrs' bodies scattered over the asphalt and I saw one fellow demonstrator die in front of me. He choked, and then his body shuddered and he died. I saw a soldier advance towards one martyr and rob his pockets, then remove the watch from his wrist and take it. This took place in front of his officer, who was shouting, 'Fire, private!'

The shooting kept up. I shall never forget the rancour and spite on the face of the police officer as he directed foul insults at us, examined the fallen, and, whenever he found someone who had only been wounded, kicked him with all his might where the wound was. I got out of that hell by a miracle. All day, I've been going over what happened and asking myself, 'How could the army officer permit himself to trick us? Doesn't he know the meaning of military honour? Plus, why such criminal behaviour from the police officer? How could he kill young Egyptians with such ease and deliberateness? What kind of pleasure was it that he felt when he kicked a wounded person in his injured foot? Why do they hate us so much?'

The martyrs will ascend to their Lord, who has promised them Paradise, but I'm sad, Asmaa, because the best of us are dying. Every one of those martyrs could have played a role in Egypt's rebirth, but Egypt killed them. I shall never forget what I lived through today. I shall never forget the martyrs who fell in front of me and I shall never rest until we have brought every murderer to trial, starting with Hosni Mubarak and his criminal minister of the interior and all the way down to the army officer who tricked us and the murderous police officer. I don't know why I'm telling you this. Perhaps to rid myself of the burden of the experience, perhaps to document the massacre. I don't know how I'm going to get this letter to you. Let me know that you're okay, by any means. Asmaa, death visited me today. The bullets passed me by and killed my fellows. I didn't die today, but I might at any instant, because the regime is becoming ever more criminal. If I die, remember that I love you.

Mazen

26

At fifty-nine, Muhammad Zanaty looked a decade older than his years. His body had grown so thin that his clothes, which were old, had become too large for it, and his hair had fallen out, with the exception of a few locks distributed on either side of his broad bald patch. His thick eyebrows had turned white and wrinkles had taken over his face. Even the skin of his hands was strewn with age spots. Why had Muhammad Zanaty's health declined so fast? Was it because of a quarter of a century of exile in Saudi Arabia? Or because of his debilitating work in accounts? Or because of the non-stop, vicious battles that he waged in defence of his livelihood, or the problems with his kidneys that afflicted him when he decided, despite the warnings of his friends, to save on the cost of mineral water and drink Saudi Arabia's tap water instead?

Whatever the reason, he was now an exhausted old man who gave the impression that his journey was nearly done. The one thing about him that hadn't changed was his smile. Whichever picture of him we look at, we find it unchanged – since the beginning, in a black-and-white picture in which he appears as a pupil at Talkha Secondary School for Boys, then in the pictures taken on the trip to the Barrages that he took when he was a student at the Faculty of Commerce, Cairo University, and again in the pictures with his colleagues at The Egyptian Contractors company, where he worked following his graduation, and up to the most recent pictures, which he took of himself, in his office at El Ghamidi and Co Importing, in Jeddah; throughout, Zanaty's smile had remained the same – innocent and modest, with an unusual stamp of tolerance and contentment. How often that smile had opened closed doors to him, how often saved him from tight spots! Zanaty didn't graduate with a good degree, and there were lots of accountants better than he, but none of his colleagues at work could hold out against him when there was any sort of competition. When it came to handling bosses, he was a creative artist of the highest calibre. He always knew how to influence his boss and win him to his side, how to put on a show of absolute obedience and bedazzlement by the man's genius, and how to go into ecstasies over everything he said, seemingly regarding it as the essence of wisdom and good business practice. In the presence of his chief, Zanaty was transformed into a different character: he altered, shrank, dwindled, bent his back, and spoke in a submissive, obedient tone of voice, because he considered that to show self-confidence before one's superior was an impertinence. And whatever the context or subject, Zanaty would draw close to his boss, bend over, and say in a voice that was low but audible to any who might be listening, 'Your Excellency only needs to direct me and I shall execute your instructions immediately. I am at Your Excellency's service.'

These submissive whispers would instil in the boss's soul a refreshingly manly feeling of control that would dispose him favourably towards Zanaty. Despite the fact that he had never in his life read anything but commentaries on the Koran, Bukhari's *Authentic Traditions of the Prophet*, and the *Al-Ahram* Friday edition (which he borrowed from one of his colleagues in the housing compound), Zanaty possessed an innate power of expression approaching the poetic. Who but he would say to his boss, 'Your Excellency – God bless you! – is like an ocean in knowledge! Every opinion Your Excellency expresses, I memorise word for word and then think about again at home, where I find I discover new meanings and learn beneficial lessons. God preserve you for us and bless you, sir!'

The last expressions he would modify when speaking to his Saudi sponsor, so that they came out as, 'God reward you well; may you live long! God have mercy on your parents and give to you as you have given to others and in keeping with your generosity to us!'

Like a champion sportsman glorying in his achievements, Mr Zanaty was proud of professional contests, in which he beat everyone. On one particularly difficult day that he would never forget, his proposed secondment to Saudi Arabia came close to being cancelled as the result of a rumour put about by a colleague who was angling to travel in his stead. Immediately, Zanaty went to the general director of The Egyptian Contractors and said to him, in a lachrymose, tremulous voice, 'Sir, Your Excellency, I have faith in Your Excellency's sense of justice. I have three children to support and their mother doesn't work and I'd like to go to Saudi Arabia so that I can cover their expenses. Should Your Excellency order the cancellation of my secondment, I shall gladly accept Your Excellency's decision, for I think of Your Excellency as my father, my model, and my ideal.'

This 'dose of medicine' was enough for the director to write, in green ink, the sign-off that changed Zanaty's life: 'Secondment approved.'

Should Mr Zanaty be regarded as a hypocrite? To be polite, we might say that he excelled at adapting to whatever circumstances he found himself in. Like millions of Egyptians, he didn't waste his energy on things unrelated to his three life goals: to make an honest living, to raise his children, and to be safe from scandal in this world and the next. He had made the pilgrimage to God's House twice and the lesser pilgrimage five times and he never skipped a religious obligation or forgot to follow the example of the Prophet, all of which are things that God, Mighty and Glorious, takes into account. When he spent the summer holidays with his family in Cairo, he was happy, indulging himself (to the extent that his age permitted) in legitimate pleasures with his wife, delighted to find himself amongst his children. Lately, however, he had noticed that his enjoyment of his Cairo holiday was less, and even that, on returning to his housing in Jeddah, he would feel that he had taken off his elegant summer suit and donned instead a wide, comfortable robe. He had become used to life in Saudi Arabia, and influenced by it, to the point that he had started to speak like the Saudis, saying 'Peace be upon you' on the telephone instead of 'Hello' and using Saudi expressions, such as *ratib* for salary, *dawam* for 'working hours', and *haris binaya* for 'doorkeeper'.

Mr Zanaty was good-hearted and religious, but he wasn't either an easy character or a weak one. On the contrary, he had sharp fangs, which he bared and applied ferociously when circumstances required. At the same time, earth and sky might be turned upside down but he wouldn't spend money for any but the most pressing of reasons. His sacred motto of 'My children first' drove him to scrutinise and examine in detail every transaction and even to carry out serious investigations before parting with a single pound or riyal. When he first began working in Saudi Arabia, he lived with two Egyptian colleagues, under an agreement whereby each bought his own tea, sugar, and coffee and used them exclusively for himself. In addition, they divided the rent and the electricity and water bills. They lived in peace and harmony until Zanaty discovered by accident that one of his colleagues was filching his own special spiced coffee mixture and drinking coffee at Zanaty's expense. Zanaty proceeded to mount war without quarter on the thief, quoting Koranic verses and prophetic traditions to confirm that betrayal of trust was one of the major sins and then threatening to expose the traitor to his Saudi sponsor, at which the former collapsed, apologised profusely, and agreed to buy coffee for Zanaty for six whole months as a sort of penance for his terrible deed. Another battle that Zanaty waged was against the Owners' Union of the block of flats in which he lived on Feisal Street. He refused absolutely to contribute towards the maintenance costs of the lift, and when the Owners'

Union went and made a padlock for the lift and gave keys only to residents who had paid maintenance costs, Mr Zanaty, unobserved, went and broke a small key inside the padlock on the lift, putting it out of commission. Furious, the officials of the Owners' Union carried out an investigation into the incident but failed to uncover the culprit and were obliged to provide a new lock, inside which Zanaty naturally broke another key. When the officials put on the third padlock, they increased surveillance of the lift, using the doorkeeper and some volunteer residents (the ones who had paid maintenance), but Mr Zanaty, who had now gained considerable experience, was able to outwit them and break another key in the lock as he was on his way down to pray the dawn prayer in the mosque. At this, the Owners' Union surrendered, cancelled the padlock idea, and opened the lift once more to all the residents. Nor was this his only battle with the Owners' Union, because he also refused to pay the water costs allocated to each flat, his argument in the matter being powerful and compelling and repeated by Zanaty calmly and with a smile to every resident he ran into: 'It's a matter of principle. Our Lord does not accept injustice. The water consumption of the ordinary resident does not exceed three litres a day. There are ten clinics belonging to doctors of various specialisations in the building. Each clinic is visited daily by between twenty and thirty patients. The dentist's clinic alone consumes four or five litres of water for every patient. It follows that the ordinary resident and the doctor cannot possibly pay the same.'

Zanaty succeeded in rallying public opinion to his side. Many of the residents refused to pay and he suffered punitive action by the Owners' Union, which submitted a police complaint against him. He was summoned to the police station, but by virtue of his polite manner and modest smile, Zanaty was able to win the sympathy of the interrogating officer, who shook him by the hand as he bade him farewell and said in a friendly tone, 'By the way, from the legal point of view, the Owners' Union can't do a thing. In other words, pay or don't pay, it's up to you.'

Zanaty shook the officer's hand warmly and called down blessings on his head with an eloquent expression that he had heard at the mosque: 'I pray God reward you with good and bring blessings to you, and upon you, and upon those around you!'

In the end, the Owners' Union decided to write off what Mr Zanaty owed and stopped asking him for it. Zanaty was careful (following his victory) to wipe out any ill feelings that might have built up in people's hearts and would greet his neighbours courteously when he saw them in the mosque, asking after their health and praying for their well-being, so as to leave them with a pleasant impression. God, may He be praised, had bestowed on him money and offspring, and Zanaty had been able, through His bounty, to raise, educate, marry, and find work for them in Saudi Arabia on lucrative contracts. Despite which God, Mighty and Sublime, often afflicts humankind with disasters to test their faith, and his daughter Asmaa was, without doubt, one of those afflictions. He could not comprehend how the beautiful, shy little girl had turned into the stubborn, quarrelsome young woman who brought him only problems and heartache. The root cause of the disaster was Karem, Asmaa's maternal grandfather, who had been a communist and a drinker of alcohol and who had poisoned her mind to the point of corrupting her. Asmaa had refused more than once to marry, had refused to cover her hair despite his pressuring her – sometimes by trying to convince her, other times by trying to scare her – and she had refused to work in Saudi Arabia. He no longer expected her to do anything but make his life miserable. He prayed she would find guidance, and his faith in the generosity of Our Lord – who has only to say of a thing, 'Let it be!' and it is – never wavered, but he could no longer stand the vexation she caused him. He was approaching sixty, suffered from high blood pressure and diabetes, and tension was dangerous to his health, as the doctor in Jeddah had told him. He'd left the problem of dealing with Asmaa to her mother, with whom she lived and who felt a degree of guilt because her father, Karem, God have mercy on his soul, was the reason for Asmaa's perverse ideas. Now, when Zanaty called (using the El Ghamidi Company phone) to check on his wife, he no longer asked about Asmaa, and the mother waged her battles with her daughter on her own. The day before, Asmaa had phoned her mother and informed her that she'd be spending the night at her friend Zeinab's to help her little sister with her English. Her mother hadn't felt comfortable with the story, but quietly brought the call to a close. At seven in the morning, Asmaa returned to the house and, on opening the door, found her mother waiting for her on the couch in the living room. She'd donned a green velvet dressing gown over a white flannel nightdress and put violet knitted bootees on her feet in hopes of getting warm. Asmaa was exhausted. In a low voice, she said, 'Good morning.' Her mother looked at her attentively, then yelled, as though embarking on the first movement of a raucous symphony that she would play to the end, 'Welcome home, Madame Asmaa! So how's Zeinab doing?'

27

'If a worker wants to demonstrate in Tahrir Square, I don't give a damn. But if a worker wants to demonstrate in the factory, I will have no mercy on him.' Essam Shaalan seemed in an excitable mood. He spoke vehemently, lighting one cigarette after another and sipping from two successive cups of unsweetened coffee.

The factory's managers and department heads sat facing him. One said, 'We can't allow any worker to stir up chaos,' another, 'Anyone who doesn't care about the bread on his table deserves what he gets.'

Essam ignored the comments and looked at them with a severe expression. Then he resumed, in his booming voice, saying 'Each of you has two pieces of paper in front of him. The first is a statement of support for and allegiance to President Hosni Mubarak, the second is an undertaking to report anyone who incites unrest at the factory. You must sign both papers. Any objections?'

They took refuge in silence. Essam went on, 'Each of you will write his name, position, and national ID number. The statement of support will be broadcast on the television and published in the newspapers. The security undertaking I shall submit to National Security.'

They busied themselves signing, then stood up, one after another, and handed him their papers. At the end, he said, in a threatening tone, as he arranged the papers in front of him, 'You have now become responsible for any incitement to unrest at the factory. Any slackness on your part will cost you dear. You may go.'

The first day passed without problems. On the second, it was reported to him that a worker named Shawqi in the furnaces division was calling on his colleagues to strike in solidarity with the demonstrators in Tahrir Square. He was arrested and a little later a procession consisting of Shawqi, his boss, who had reported him, and three factory security men arrived at Essam's office. The young man was dark-complexioned and thin and seemed steady and ready to take on any provocation. The security men pushed him into the middle of the room, continuing to hold him by the arms, but Essam yelled at them, 'Let go of him!'

Then he got up, approached the young man, and said in a commanding voice, 'What's your name, boy?' (Later, Essam would recall, in astonishment, that he'd used the same tone of voice with the worker that the officers had used on him when he was the one being interrogated in prison.)

'Shawqi Ahmad Abd El Barr.'

'Do you want to get yourself into deep trouble, Shawqi?'

Boldly, the young man responded, 'We want to fix this country.'

'Who's "we"?'

'All the millions of Egyptians.'

'My dear boy, take it from me,' Essam said, his tone now that of a kindly father, 'nothing you're doing will make any difference. You're getting yourself into trouble for nothing. National Security is at the factory gates. If they get hold of you, you'll be finished. Do you have children?'

The young man nodded, and Essam smiled and continued, 'What are their names?'

'Aya and Nasser,' the young man answered, in a low voice.

Essam put his hand on the young man's shoulder and said, 'Fine. Be sensible, Shawqi, for Aya and Nasser's sake.'

The young man looked at him in silence, and his boss yelled at him with a vehemence designed to curry Essam's favour, 'Engineer Essam is like your father and he wants what's best for you!'

The young man said, 'Engineer Essam wants what's best for him, not me.'

'And what's best for me?' Essam asked him, struggling to contain himself.

'You're worried about the millions you earn.'

Essam slapped him on the face, and the young man leapt at him, but the security men rained blows on him and dragged him outside, Essam's words ringing through the place: 'All I need is for some kid like you to try and go one better than Essam Shaalan. I was in prison before you were born, you little prick!'

They'd managed to get control of the young man by the time they got to the door but kept up their violent beating. 'Hand him over to National Security!' Essam said, gasping with anger. 'They can teach him some manners.'

The young man was taken away in the police van before the eyes of his colleagues. He was bleeding from his nose, his face was covered in bruises and scratches, and he wore a look of astonishment, as though he still couldn't believe what was happening. This was the factory's only example of unrest and it had been contained, but it had a bad effect on Essam. The youth's impertinence wasn't what disturbed him most. The very idea of a revolution happening was demolishing his theory about the submissiveness of Egyptians and their capacity to coexist with tyranny. He'd built his outlook on life on this theory, would defend it fiercely, and couldn't tolerate its being cast into doubt. His arrogant, coarse way with the managers, his slapping of the worker, his indiscriminate threats: all these were defence mechanisms that hid his panic at the idea that he might be wrong. He was like a fanatic facing someone trying to cast doubt on his religion. In the evening, he went home. He took a hot shower and put on his track suit, then drank three glasses of whisky one after the other. He felt the effect of the alcohol quickly and strongly and, all of a sudden, was seized by a desire to see Nourhan, whom he hadn't seen since the demonstrations began. He'd phoned her once, but she excused herself brusquely. She was living through a state of emergency at the TV station and behaving as though she were at war. The first day of the revolution, a colonel from State Security had come to the station, taken an office for himself in the security department, and met with the hosts and staff. He'd informed them that, from now on, and in view of the delicate conditions in which the country was embroiled, he'd be giving them daily instructions, the execution of which he would monitor personally. Everyone at the meeting enthusiastically agreed. Nourhan, for her part, waited until her colleagues had left and then asked the officer, in a low voice, if he would issue an order allowing her maid, Awatif, to enter the television building. When he asked her why, she replied with a warmth that was, despite her best efforts, mixed with a certain seductiveness, 'Sir, my religion doesn't permit me to sleep at home while my country burns. The maid will bring me my things from the house. I shall reside at the station until this affliction has departed the country.'

The officer wrote out the permit and thanked her for her patriotism, his face betraying his struggle to prevent himself from sliding into inappropriate thoughts. The same day, Nourhan phoned Sheikh Shamel to ask him for the perspective of religion on disseminating false news via the television. Sheikh Shamel was silent for a few moments and then told her, 'At present, we must regard ourselves as being in a state of war with saboteurs who wish to bring down the state. The True Religion makes allowable to Muslims at war things it does not allow them in times of peace, in accordance with the well-known principle that "necessity permits the prohibited".' Nourhan was reassured by this legal ruling and set about implementing the colonel's instructions with zeal and mastery. She didn't limit herself to giving airtime to callers selected by Security; she would even go over what they were to say with them, word for word, before going on air, and would lay out for them, like a seasoned professional director, a performance style. Egyptians are much affected by the scream of a woman. Every day, therefore, there would be a female caller begging for help because thugs wanted to rape her, along with her daughters. The officer had told her, 'Our goal is for each demonstrator to feel that his mother and wife are in danger, so he'd better leave the square and go home.'

Even this was not enough for Nourhan. She took it upon herself to phone well-known artists of stage and song and coordinate on-screen interventions in which they cursed the Tahrir demonstrators and accused them of being agents of foreign intelligence services. She invited Sheikh Shamel on air and asked him for the religious view of what was happening and the sheikh said, with incisive clarity, 'These demonstrations anger God and His messenger. Islam requires of us obedience to the Muslim ruler and to limit ourselves to offering him advice should he contravene the laws of religion.'

'Revered Sheikh,' Nourhan asked, 'what do you have to say to the demonstrators?'

Anger appeared on the sheikh's face and he yelled, 'I say to them that this is a Masonic plot devised by the Jews to divert the Muslims from their religion. I adjure my young sons in Tahrir Square – the sons of Zion have led you astray! Repent and avert a schism that will drown this country in blood! Young people, return to your homes, for this is not the path to change! You are simply destroying Egypt with your own hands. Return unto God! Return unto God!'

Nourhan ended the episode with Sheikh Shamel's appeal, after which patriotic songs were played until the next programme. That evening, Essam phoned her but she didn't answer. He drank another glass slowly. She then phoned back, sounding embarrassed.

'Sorry, Essam. I was on air.'

'I want to see you, Nour.'

'That will be very difficult. I have work to do at the television station.'

'Finish your work and come.'

'My work is never finished.'

'Ask their permission and come.'

'Where?'

'Here, to my house.'

She refused, but he insisted, then got angry and said, 'When I tell you I want to see you, it means I have to see you!'

His tone of voice was angry, and somehow threatening. Nourhan submitted, but she made it a condition that she wouldn't stay late. He didn't usually meet her at his flat, but that night he didn't want to go out. As soon as he opened the door and saw her, he realised that she was not in a normal state. She seemed tense. She had gathered her hair into a ponytail and her face, after she had removed her make-up, appeared pale, with rings of exhaustion visible beneath her eyes. She threw herself into the nearest chair in the living room. She didn't show her annoyance, as she usually did, at the fact that he was drinking alcohol. She appeared grave and somewhat preoccupied. He made her a cup of tea, and as soon as she'd taken a sip, she started talking fast: 'Essam, please don't be angry with me. I'm under a lot of pressure and my nerves are suffering. I stay at the station almost all the time. They may ask me to broadcast anything, at any time.'

Essam didn't answer. He took one sip from his glass, then kissed her hand and drew her into the bedroom. The sex was different this time. None of that bawdy, festive character remained. She was agitated and exhausted. He threw himself hurriedly into her arms, as though to squeeze out the remaining drops of joy before they disappeared. They were struggling to overcome something heavy in the air; they were resisting something funereal. They finished quickly and got up in silence. He went back to his seat in the living room and poured himself a glass. After a little while, Nourhan returned from the bathroom, having dressed in preparation for leaving. 'Are you leaving?' he asked her.

'I have to go back to the station immediately.'

He didn't respond. He sipped the whisky and lit a cigarette. She said, 'I want to ask you a question. What's your opinion of the demonstrations?'

'Nonsense.'

'What do you mean?'

'Nothing in Egypt is going to change.'

'Do you think the president will go?'

He let out a derisive laugh that seemed artificial.

'Are you an idiot, Nourhan? Since when could a few kids get rid of the president of the republic? Even if they keep it up for a year, nothing can possibly change.'

'I'm very worried.'

'About what?'

'I'm afraid the president will go and there'll be chaos.'

'That's because you don't understand the nature of the state in Egypt. "The state" means National Security, General Intelligence, Military Intelligence, the police, the army, the media, and the judiciary. Each of these is a strong institution whose only loyalty is to the president.'

'Every day we say the demonstrations are coming to an end and they get bigger.'

'Just be patient for a few days and you'll see. All those damned kids who are demonstrating will be arrested and tried before military courts.'

'That's speculation, not information.'

He smiled and said, 'It's my reading of history. Every struggle between the people and the state ends with the defeat of the people. In Egypt, the authorities are capable of failing at everything, except the subjugation of the Egyptians.'

28

Ashraf Wissa opened the door to the flat and rushed out onto the stairway. Ikram called out to him, then ran after him, closing the door behind her. In a few minutes, Ashraf and Ikram were in the middle of Tahrir Square. The scene was of sublime, mythic, and awe-inspiring proportions, as though some religious rite were being practised by thousands of believers. Everywhere throngs of demonstrators shouted and ran as death pursued them. Groups of snipers in civilian clothes were scattered over the roofs of the American University and other buildings overlooking the square, each group consisting of a small number of soldiers armed with recent-model sniper rifles, led by an officer. They had all placed white handkerchiefs on their heads, perhaps as protection from the sunlight, so that they could aim, or perhaps to hide their faces, in case anyone managed to take photos of them. Each sniper killed with the calmness and precision of a surgeon, squinting down the viewfinder of his rifle and then choosing his victim. At that point, a mixture of determination and hatred would appear on his face, after which he would squeeze the trigger and the bullet would be launched, to bury itself in the victim's head – one bullet, unequivocal, conclusive, putting an end to memories of childhood and parents' care, to the toils of study and the joys of academic success, to dreams of love and marriage. It all ended with a single squeeze of the trigger. The killing went on and the martyrs fell, one after another. The demonstrators refused to flee from death, as though challenging it. Instead of running away from the sources of fire, they surged towards them. None of them was afraid of dying any longer, as though they had become united in the will of one giant being that would not be still until it had realised the goal for which it had come out onto the streets. Every time a martyr fell, they picked up his corpse, shouting slogans and crying 'God is great!', and moved further forward in the direction of the Ministry of Interior. One young man fell next to Ashraf. He had been shouting slogans at his side and suddenly went silent and bent over as though looking at something on the ground, then fell. The demonstrators picked him up and Ashraf went towards him through the throng, Ikram tugging at his sleeve, her voice lost in the clamour. Ashraf kept on moving closer until he got to where the martyr was being carried on the shoulders of his colleagues. He looked into his face. It appeared so calm that Ashraf imagined he was about to smile. He was wearing trainers, jeans, and a shabby, cheap, black pullover. A strange, obscure desire seized Ashraf, and he went even closer, until he was up against the youth's body, then stretched out his hand and held the other's for a few moments, until the stream of demonstrators pushed him away. The boy's hand was cold to the touch and somehow familiar – the same feeling as a friend's handshake leaves on a cold day. Ashraf then distanced himself from the demonstrators and walked slowly till he reached the wall of the university, Ikram in tow. All of a sudden, he crouched down on the ground, put his head between his hands, and started gasping.

'Ashraf Bey, what's wrong?' Ikram yelled, but he didn't reply. His face was pale and he was breathing with difficulty. She said, 'Come on. Let's go home.'

They walked in silence. They passed through the lobby of the building and, as soon as they got into the flat, she seized his hand and pulled him along, and he yielded to her like a child. She opened the door of the bathroom and whispered tenderly, 'Have a shower and change your clothes while I make you a bite to eat.'

A little while later, he was sitting in the study, completely silent. Ikram came, sat down next to him, and put her arm around his body.

He took out a joint but she said, 'You're tired. No hashish, please, for my sake.'

Without looking at her, he said, 'Don't worry.'

He lit the cigarette and it glowed brightly. She brought sandwiches and went on at him until he began to eat. Trying to start an ordinary conversation, she said, 'By the way, when we're together, we should bolt the front door. Madame Magda might come back at any moment.'

Brusquely, he replied, 'As long as there are demonstrations, Magda will never come back.'

Silence took over once more, and Ashraf lit another joint. As though realising that there was no point in ignoring what had happened in the square, Ikram sighed and said, as though talking to herself, 'I would never have thought that Hosni Mubarak could be such a criminal.'

'It's a regime defending its interests.'

'What had the young man done wrong for them to kill him?'

'Mubarak and his men have wealth in the billions. If the regime falls, their fortunes will be confiscated and they'll be put on trial. The bastards are prepared to kill a million Egyptians to stay in power.'

'You mean they have no fear of God at all?' Ikram asked.

Her questions were those of a child, despite which her voice was not without a certain seductiveness. Under normal circumstances, he would have taken her in his arms and covered her with kisses, but he had changed. He was no longer as he had been. He was still preoccupied with the scenes of killing and could still feel the touch of the martyr's hand in his own. Suddenly, she hugged him and laid her head on his chest, as though she could feel instinctively that he needed her. She began kissing him, but, for the first time since she'd known him, he turned his head aside and pushed her gently away, saying, 'I can see the mother and father when they tell them that their son has been shot dead.'

189

'God grant them patience!'

'I feel as though the boy they killed in front of me could have been my son Butrus.'

'God forbid!'

'You know what, Ikram? I'm really angry with myself.'

'Why?'

'Because I've fallen short, so far short.'

29

Dear Mazen,

You can't imagine how happy I was to see you yesterday. You asked me about my problem with my mother. I told you that it all ended okay. That's not true. There are lots of things I can't say and that I prefer, as usual, to write. I have no idea why I'm that way. I know you're busy but I need to speak to you. You're the only one who understands me. I'm full of contradictions, Mazen. I can be normal, and then suddenly do something unexpected that I don't understand. Sometimes I feel that I'm two personalities. I live out one comprehensible personality whom everybody sees and, inside, another strange, hidden personality will suddenly appear. When I got home on Wednesday morning, I was very tired from the running, the smell of the gas, and the tension. I wanted to take a hot shower and sleep but I found my mother sitting in the living room waiting for me. I'd lied to her and told her I'd be spending the night at my girlfriend Zeinab's to help her sister with her English homework. I found my mother sitting in the living room. Sarcastically, she asked me, 'How's your friend Zeinab?'

I realised she didn't believe me. I think she would have been ready to go along with my story if I'd insisted on the lie. If I'd told her, for example, 'Zeinab's fine and says hello,' she would have said a couple of stupid things to me, as usual, and then left me in peace. But along comes my other personality, the one I don't understand, and I found myself saying, 'I wasn't at Zeinab's.'

Naturally, my mother was upset and asked, 'Where were you?'

I told her, 'I was at the demonstrations.'

'You lied to me, Asmaa?' she shrieked. 'Aren't you ashamed of yourself, you liar?'

A strange calm came over me, as though what was happening was happening to someone else, or I was witnessing what was going on through a sheet of protective glass. I told her, 'I lied to you on the phone so you wouldn't worry. Now that I'm home, I'm telling you the truth. I was at the demonstration and the police would have arrested me if I hadn't found a place to hide with some people.'

'What people were you with?' shrieked my mother.

I said, 'A kind man called Ashraf Wissa hid me in his house till the police had gone.'

Even now I don't know why I behaved that way – why I decided to push her to the limit and why I refused to go on lying. Was it because I'm so proud of the revolution? Or was it a desire to challenge my mother and reject everything she considers proper?

My mother shrieked, 'Shame on you! I'm sick and your father's getting old. He has diabetes and high blood pressure and he's still living in a strange place working like an ox on a waterwheel so he can support us. What am I to tell him? You want me to tell him, "Your daughter spent the night with people she doesn't know and the police are looking for her"?'

During confrontations like this, my mother just keeps shrieking and doesn't wait for an answer. I remained completely silent till her fit of temper had ended in bitter tears. Then suddenly I did something strange. Can you believe I hugged her? She laid her head on my shoulder and said, 'Go easy on us, Asmaa. We're old and tired.'

Those words pained me so much, Mazen. My run-ins with my mother are the worst thing in my life. She and I spend all our time alone in a closed flat endlessly clashing with one another, as though we were living out some divine punishment. She shrieks and cries, and

192

I take pity on her and console her. Then, in an instant, she provokes me, I respond, and we begin again. Quarrels and shrieking and lamentation. Imagine! In my heart of hearts, I totally sympathise with my mother! I can never take my confrontations with her to the limit. I always get to a point with her where I'm looking for a compromise to make her happy, but then I go back and stick to my position and she gets even angrier with me. It was because I wanted to avoid a confrontation with her that I agreed to meet all those suitors, and the same thing made me tell her I'd be spending the night at Zeinab's. Can you believe I have such a split personality? I'm convinced of all the positions I take. I believe absolutely in my choices. But I feel pity for my mother and understand how she thinks. This fluctuation between loving my mother and being at odds with her is painful. The worst thing in the world is to clash violently with someone you love, because at the very time that you're challenging her, you're feeling pity for her. I waited till my mother had calmed down and then said, 'I'm tired. I need to sleep.'

I withdrew and took a shower and when I came out, I found she'd made breakfast and put it in my room. This tenderness pains me more than the harshness. I knew that the big demonstration was on Friday, but she was aware that the mid-year break had begun, so I had no excuse to go out. I spent two days with her in the house. I tried every method I know to calm her down. I asked her to tell me about when she was young. How had she lived before she was married? Talking about that makes her happy. She tells me about the Saniya Secondary School for Girls and the Faculty of Commerce, where she met my father. He was in his final year and she in her first. He met her in the library and offered to help her with a research project she was doing. It's a story I've heard from her lots of times and each time she looks happy as she recalls it. On Thursday evening, I sat with her and we watched the Turkish serial. After the serial, my mother is at her best, and little by little her anger turned into loving, calm reproach. As she sipped her cup of milky tea, she said, 'I mean, if you were sensible, wouldn't you be sitting in your own house with your husband and children by now, instead of demonstrations and all that nonsense?'

'It's all fate.'

This is the best answer in such circumstances. She said, 'You're good-hearted, Asmaa, but you don't understand how the world works. This country of ours is broken and it'll never be fixed. Enough of wasting time. Think of yourself. A woman without her own household and children is in a wretched situation, no matter how successful she may be in any field.'

I didn't answer. Little by little, I steered the conversation to other subjects. On Friday, after the prayer, our street filled with demonstrators. I sat with my mother, following the demonstrations from the balcony. I felt she was a bit taken aback. Perhaps the size of the demonstration, which included thousands of people, surprised her. Watching them, she said, 'It's such a shame for them to waste themselves. I feel for their families.'

I said, 'It's because of thinking like that that we've reached rock bottom. If everyone opposed injustice and wasn't afraid, Egypt would be a decent country by now.'

My mother said nothing. She kept watching the demonstration and seemed moved. When the demonstrators began chanting 'Come and join us! Egyptians, come on out!' I couldn't stand it any longer. I stood in front of her and said, 'I have to go out.'

'Go out where?'

'I want to go with your blessing.'

'You want to kill me?' she shrieked.

'You've seen for yourself that the demonstration is peaceful, Mother.'

'Peaceful my foot! You're not going out, Asmaa.'

'I'm twenty-five years old. I have the right to decide for myself.'

'When you get married, your husband will be responsible for you. Now, your father and I are. If you're arrested or anything happens to you, it'll be us who suffer.'

'I'm the only person responsible for my conduct and if something happens to me, don't worry about it. I'll manage.'

I knew the conversation would go nowhere. I went out quickly, my mother's voice ringing in my ears as she called after me. Of course I felt guilty but I would have felt even more so if I hadn't taken part in the demonstration. It was a real battle. The officers were firing gas canisters at us like madmen. I had an onion, which I broke open and kept sniffing so I could resist the gas. It's something I learned from Facebook. I almost lost consciousness more than once. When we got to Giza Square, the shooting started. Martyrs fell before me. The officers were shooting randomly and the demonstrators were picking up the wounded on motorcycles which they got from God knows where. One of them told me they were using motorcycles because the ambulances were handing the injured over to the police. Like you, Mazen, since the Friday of Rage, I'm no longer the person I was. Like you, I feel that I owe the martyrs something. I watched our People reveal itself in its finest form, but I noticed too that many stood on balconies and at windows, observing what was going on, as though watching a film. They saw us die and took no action. I can't understand the position of these spectators. As usual, I await your explanation. Thank God, Mazen, that I got to know you! I don't know how I would have lived through these events without you at my side. I'll end my letter with a smile (do you still love the two dimples?).

Goodnight.

Asmaa

30

The officer looked grim and irritable. Gasping with anger, he shouted at the demonstrators, 'I'm telling you, move the metal from the street!'

They didn't move but stayed where they were, watching the officer warily and feeling a variety of emotions. They weren't going to let the car go in and kill their colleagues but at the same time they sensed the strangeness of the situation. They were addressing a police officer, standing in his way and blocking his path. Where had they found this strength? Every moment that passed took them further from retreat and added to their steadfastness. The officer shouted, 'I swear to Almighty God, if you don't move the metal right now, I'll show you what's what, you bastards!'

For a moment, silence reigned. Then Khaled Madany's voice was heard: 'You have no right to insult us, sir! You have to treat us with respect because we're Egyptian citizens, just like you. And you should reconsider your position. You should be standing with the people.'

This provoked the officer so much that he yelled, 'No way, sunshine! I'm defending Mubarak. Mubarak is your master, and you and everyone with you deserve to have your bottoms smacked!'

Shouts of protest arose from everyone standing there, but the officer turned his back on them, said something, and the back door of the car immediately opened and three privates jumped out, went over to the pieces of metal, and bent down to move them from the road. The demonstrators rushed forward and pushed the soldiers away, but they started beating them, the demonstrators responding with words and kicks. As the clash intensified, Khaled approached the car and shouted, 'Sir! Whatever you do, you will not enter the square!'

The officer's face darkened and he was about to say something but decided against it and looked at the ground for a moment. Then he pulled out his pistol and, without leaving the car, fired a shot. One shot, the sound of it ringing out and bursting like a jet of flame. Danya heard Khaled cry 'Aaah!' – a long scream that seemed to come from somewhere deep inside him and to be proclaiming some discovery. Khaled fell to the ground. Danya rushed to him and bent over him. His face was still, as though it had stiffened before its expression could form itself completely, as though he had been cut off in mid-sentence, as though he'd wanted to say something but had run out of time. The bullet had left a hole in the middle of his forehead from which blood was pouring. Did Danya scream and burst into tears? Did she shake Khaled and call on him to get up? Did she think that what was happening wasn't real? Did she think it was a nightmare from which she'd awake? Did she wait for Khaled to stand and wipe his forehead with his hand, the hole disappearing and the blood stopping while he spoke to her and laughed with her as he had been doing a few moments earlier? His body, prone on the asphalt, the hole in his forehead, and his staring eyes were the last things Danya remembered clearly. After that, the only things in her mind were shaky, distorted pictures, wrapped in a thick fog, like scenes ripped from a battered, out-of-focus copy of an old film. The soldiers hurried to get back in the car, which reversed and then moved off fast towards the Omar Makram mosque. Her colleagues were shouting, some of them trying to pursue the car and hang on to it to stop it. Danya was crying and screaming and hugging Khaled, and her white coat had become stained with blood. Her colleagues carried Khaled's body to a car that arrived from God knows where. They made way for her so she could get in next to him. She put his head on her legs and tried to staunch the wound with compresses, as though Khaled were a patient who could be given first aid: she and her colleagues couldn't believe what had happened, and it was as though they were waiting for a miracle, waiting for something suddenly to happen that would bring Khaled back the way he had been. As soon as they reached Qasr El Eini hospital, they placed him on a stretcher and ran with him till they found a teacher from the faculty. They didn't speak much. The scene was self-explanatory. The faculty member asked them to lift Khaled onto a bed. The man opened Khaled's eyes and stared into them, placed his hand on Khaled's wrist, then turned around calmly and said, 'Condolences.'

The shaky pictures followed one another in Danya's mind. She saw herself next to the bloodstained body, reading from a copy of the Koran that was open on her legs and stopping reading when the tears prevented her from seeing the letters. Along with the pictures, she recalled mingled sounds – screams and cries and wailing. Her voice, as she read from the Koran, seemed strange to her own ears, as though it was coming from someone else. Her colleagues kept coming in and out of the room and shouting and weeping and bending over Khaled and kissing him. After a little while, one of her colleagues approached her and said in a low voice, 'Khaled's father is here.'

31

Ashraf Wissa appeared, the next day, in Tahrir Square. His presence among the demonstrators seemed somewhat unusual and symbolic – an aristocrat in his fifties with smooth white hair parted in the middle and elegant, classic clothes (woollen suit, roll-neck pullover, English shoes). Ashraf looked a little as though he'd been resurrected from the past, a man of yesteryear, an actor of a past generation come to announce that he was joining the youth of the revolution. Ikram accompanied him. She'd dispensed with her headscarf and wore jeans and a black wool sweater. She had trainers on her feet, had gathered her smooth hair into a ponytail, and her beautiful face, without make-up apart from mascara and a touch of light-coloured lipstick, was plain to see. The odd thing was that her new look erased all traces of her social origins. Apart from a few letters that she pronounced in a low-class way, anyone who saw her would have thought she was a government employee or a university student. Ashraf circled the square time and again, listening to the speeches and debating with the demonstrators who had occupied it. He expressed his opinions with enthusiasm and in decisive tones: 'The revolution could have accepted compromise before the authorities started killing demonstrators. Our duty to the martyrs compels us to depose Mubarak and put him on trial.'

His appearance excited the curiosity of some. On such occasions, he'd look at them, smile, and say, 'Listen. First, I'm a Copt. Second, I was an ordinary citizen who had nothing to do with politics till I saw the killings. I saw a young man of my son's age killed in front of me.'

Everything in the square was organised. Committees of young men and women were scattered at the entry points to provide security for the square, and they searched those coming in, of either sex, and checked their IDs. Provisioning committees were in charge of providing food, which didn't stop hundreds of volunteers from bringing more with them; a volunteer would come in with hundreds of sandwiches and put them on the ground, invite those nearby to eat, and then disappear into the crowd. Media committees were in charge of contact with the press and with welcoming foreign journalists, and every now and then calls would be repeated over the loudspeakers asking for a doctor somewhere, or a volunteer to man one of the entrances. Tahrir Square had been transformed into a small independent republic – the first parcel of Egyptian land to be liberated from the dictator's rule. Each of those who had taken up residence in 'Tahrir' felt that he was realising some kind of ideal: each felt that the success of the revolution depended specifically on what he or she did. The main stage, where speakers made their speeches into a microphone provided with large loudspeakers whose echoes reached every part of the square, had been erected by their own efforts. On either side of it, the organisers had sat the mothers of the martyrs – pitiable middle-aged ladies in black over whom a mournful silence hung. Each had placed on her breast a large photograph of her martyred son and would gaze at those around them almost pleadingly, as though they might be able to bring their children back. Before anyone spoke into the microphone, the organisers would ask them to shake hands with the martyrs' mothers – a gesture perhaps intended to make the speaker understand that the revolution would never abandon the rights of those who had given their lives for it. The Mubarak regime sent groups of public figures one after the other to the square to convince the revolutionaries to end their sit-in and go home. The occupiers refused to listen to them and chased them away, despite which they didn't stop coming even for one day. At the corners of the square, day and night, there were speechmakers talking to groups of people. Once, Ashraf said to Ikram, 'You know, the square reminds me of Hyde Park.'

She looked at him questioningly, so he went on, 'Hyde Park is a park in London. Anyone who wants to say anything goes there and speaks and people listen.'

'Even if they speak against the government?'

'Even if they speak against the Queen, or Our Lord.'

'God forbid! You mean they're unbelievers?'

'It's their right.'

'And the government leaves them alone, as though it's normal?'

'What's it supposed to do? Kill them?' he asked her, laughing. Then he felt ashamed of his sarcasm and said seriously, 'In decent countries, the government protects the rights of its citizens to freedom of belief. Everyone chooses the religion they please, or becomes an atheist, but the point is, the citizen has rights.'

Those occupying the square were from all classes – aristocrats from the Gezira Club, Zamalek, and Garden City, low-class Cairenes and peasants from the Delta, Upper Egyptians, women both veiled and unveiled, bands of young football 'ultras' and other fans, the last two playing a decisive role in defending the revolution. They were organised and very fit and had a long experience of resisting the assaults of the security forces. Ashraf made their acquaintance and learned from them how the square was organised. They took him to the office of a travel agency that had been turned over to the revolution by its owner, where he met the head of the coordinating committee and the person primarily responsible for the organisation of the square, Dr Abd El Samad, a professor at the Faculty of Medicine who was over seventy. He was calm and extremely well-mannered and his face was friendly and peaceable. Ashraf introduced himself and said simply, 'I want to help the revolution.'

Dr Abd El Samad muttered a few words of welcome, then his face took on a practical expression and he and Ashraf exchanged phone numbers. As he said goodbye to him, Dr Abd El Samad said, 'Thank you again. I'll phone you soon.'

Thereafter, the square would witness, on a daily basis, the presence of Ashraf and Ikram, as they loaded hundreds of sandwiches and cartons of mineral water into the car and left them next to Qasr El Nil bridge, where the young people would take charge of distributing them to the occupiers. They brought everything that was needed by way of medical supplies, medicines, gauze, and cotton wool, as dictated to Ashraf by the doctor in charge of the field hospital in the Omar Makram mosque and which he would go with Ikram to buy from the medical supplies companies on Qasr El Eini Street or Giza Square. Ashraf also, at the request of the committee, welcomed the foreign journalists who flocked ceaselessly to the square and would take them around, explain to them what was going on, and answer their questions. They were impressed by his elegant appearance, broad, friendly smile, and command of English and French. The French newspaper *L'Observateur* even published a full-page article entitled 'The Rich Copt Who Joined the Revolution'. When the journalist took his photo, Ikram tried to move away, but Ashraf took hold of her hand and insisted that she remain by his side, and she appeared wherever the pictures were published. From the first day on, Ashraf had introduced himself, with fatherly affection, to the young Copts who had defied the warnings of the church and joined the revolution, among them a youthful priest who held mass in conjunction with the Friday prayer. The scene was awe-inspiring that day, the priest standing next to the sheikh on the main stage while thousands of Muslims and Copts, all carrying copies of the Koran or crosses, gathered. The sheikh gave the Friday sermon, then the priest gave his sermon and the prayer was held, followed by the mass. Finally, at the invitation of those on the stage, the occupiers in their thousands sang the national anthem 'My Country, My Country', many bursting into tears. Even the dozens of foreign correspondents standing behind their cameras were moved and looked serious and sincere, as though the spirit of the revolution had touched them as they conveyed to the world this 'unique human experience', as they described it. Once the mass was over, Ashraf took Ikram by the hand and they set off for the Zahret El Bustan café. On the way, she asked him, in a low voice, 'Do you think, Ashraf Bey, that Our Lord accepts the prayers of Muslims and Copts together?'

He stopped walking, gazed at her, and said, 'Our prayers here today, with one another, are better in the Lord's eyes than any prayers made by the sheikhs and priests who take their orders from National Security.'

She looked down and started walking again, an expression of re-assurance on her face. One word from him was enough to convince her of anything. To her, he was both her lover and her teacher, who always knew what was right. While they were crossing the square, Ashraf heard a voice calling to him, 'Mr Ashraf!' He thought the voice sounded familiar and turned and found Asmaa running towards him. Without thinking, he opened his arms to receive her, hugged her, and said with excitement, 'Asmaa, I'm so happy to see you!'

Panting, she replied, 'I'm happy, and proud to see that you're with us in the square.'

Ashraf laughed and said, 'You're the reason, Asmaa, because you convinced me.'

He now noticed a young man next to Asmaa whom she intro-duced with the words, 'Mazen Saqqa, engineer.'

Ashraf turned to Ikram and introduced her, saying, 'This is my friend, Ikram. And this is Asmaa, whom I told you about.'

The four made their way to the café, and Ashraf disappeared for a few moments, to return bearing bean and falafel sandwiches. They sat and ate and talked. The conversation between the two women began slowly and cautiously, as though they were animals sniffing each other curiously, but the tension soon disappeared and they talked as affectionately as two old friends. Asmaa's innocent appearance, and her clear attachment to Mazen, ensured that any trace of jealousy on Ikram's part was erased. At the same time, Asmaa's love for Ashraf extended to Ikram, as she could see that there was some bond between them. Mazen said to Ashraf, 'I'd like to thank you for rescuing Asmaa.'

Ashraf laughed and said, 'I'm the one who should thank her, for changing my life, as you can see.'

'The revolution has changed us all,' Mazen said, as though speaking to himself.

Mazen spoke to Ashraf about his struggle at the factory, saying apologetically, 'My circumstances don't allow me to be in the square. I have to be with the workers.'

'Your struggle at the factory is no less important than the struggle in the square,' Ashraf responded.

In his heart of hearts, Ashraf felt guilty. He told himself, 'Here's this young man who isn't yet thirty waging a serious struggle for workers' rights while, when I was his age, I was looking for fun and pleasure.' The following day, Ashraf, with Ikram's approval, opened the block's ground-floor flat and cleaned it out with the assistance of a group of young people from the square, and it became a base for the revolution. The last person to rent the flat had been the owner of an electrical appliance shop who used it as a storeroom. The young people got rid of the remains of wires and empty cardboard boxes and took a whole day to clean it, opening the windows, which had been closed for a long time. Ashraf put three beds for the injured in one room, stored medical supplies in another, and bought a large refrigerator for the food and medicine. Also, in the large room, he put a table and chairs for meetings of the coordinating committee, which Ashraf Wissa now attended at the invitation of its head, Dr Abd El Samad, and with the approval of its members. How proud he felt sitting with the members of the committee at the first meeting! There were representatives from the youth movements – Enough!, April 6, the National Association, the Revolutionary Socialists – and public figures. After the meeting, Ashraf left to give Dr Abd El Samad a lift and asked him, 'You've been kind enough to place great confidence in me, even though you've only known me for a couple of days. How come?'

Dr Abd El Samad smiled and said, 'Most of us didn't know one another. It was the revolution that brought us together.'

Then he fell silent and squeezed Ashraf's hand, as though embarrassed by his emotional speech.

Ashraf Wissa's life had changed to a degree that astonished him. He'd wake up at his usual time and, after the ordinary morning rituals, go down with Ikram to the square, from which they wouldn't return until night. The strange thing was that he'd lost his enthusiasm for the idea of writing a book and cut down on the amount of hashish he smoked – just two cigarettes to get going in the morning and a few before going to sleep, though sometimes, during the day, the desire for a joint would seize him and he'd sneak off to his flat and smoke one. He thought often about the change that had come over him. He had been drowning in a sense of frustration and lack of self-worth, and then he'd found himself in a real battle, waged by young people the age of his children, young people who believed in their cause to the point that they were prepared to die for it. He asked himself whether, if he hadn't been living in the vicinity of Tahrir Square and if Asmaa hadn't taken refuge in his flat and if he hadn't seen the killing with his own eyes, he would have sympathised with the revolution. He didn't know the answer. Magda, his wife, lived with him in the same place and she'd been hostile to the revolution since day one. After a week, she'd phoned him and

205

said with a sarcasm that was not without bitterness, 'I hear you've opened the ground-floor flat to the kids from the revolution.'

Angrily, he replied, 'They aren't "kids". They're respectable young people.'

'I can't believe that you'd bring the Brotherhood into our house.'

'I've told you a hundred times, the young people in the square aren't Brothers.'

'Even if they aren't, they want to destroy the country.'

'The country's already been destroyed and they're trying to fix it. Anyway, you left the house and went to your family, so it's none of your business.'

They exchanged more angry words, and then she ended the call, muttering. He was speaking to her from his study. When he left the room, he found Ikram in the living room. She looked at him with that enquiring, almost motherly glance that always allowed her to fathom what was going on in his mind.

'You looked annoyed,' she said, smiling.

'Not at all,' he said and lit a joint. She asked him quietly, 'Was that Madame Magda who phoned?'

He hesitated a little and then nodded. 'Is everything okay?' she asked.

'She's angry that I fixed up the ground-floor flat for the young people.'

'How did she find out?'

'The neighbours must have told her.'

'So now what?'

'Now nothing. We quarrelled.'

Ikram fell silent for a moment, then said in a low voice, 'You know what? You ought to visit Madame Magda and make sure she's okay.'

'I don't want to visit her.'

Ikram said nothing more, and he looked like an embarrassed child. Then he embraced her and said, 'My darling, Madame Magda doesn't care whether I visit her or not. We went on living together because we couldn't get divorced, no more, no less.'

In a tone that swung between coquetry and playfulness, Ikram said, 'It's none of my business, my dear sir. You're the one who doesn't want to visit his wife.'

He brought his head close and whispered in her ear, 'I suffered for years with Magda till Our Lord recompensed me with Ikram.'

Just before noon the next day, Ashraf and Ikram, along with some of the young men and women, were busy making lunch for the occupiers. Dozens of sandwiches had been placed on the table and they were putting each sandwich into a bag, after which they would add a banana and an orange and close the bag. One of the young people would take a hundred sandwiches and distribute them in the square. The atmosphere as they worked was enthusiastic and merry. Suddenly, the sound of repeated knocking on the window was heard, accompanied by shouts and insults. Ashraf advanced cautiously and looked through the slats of the closed shutters. He saw a group of not fewer than twenty individuals armed with machetes and crude, home-made revolvers and, behind them, a group of boys, who were throwing bricks at the window. One of the men, with a huge body, shouted, brandishing a long knife, 'Come out, Ashraf Wissa, you and the whore who's with you! Your master Mubarak's not good enough for you, you Coptic dog? I swear on your mother, I'm going to finish you off tonight!'

32

My darling Asmaa,

If you come to my small flat, you'll find four large speakers that
I've set up, one in each corner. I can't live without music. I have
learned, through experience, that the best speakers are the easiest
to wreck, because they pick up the most delicate sounds. Exactly the
same applies to you. You're a wonderful human being, but you're
too sensitive. The least word affects you and any passing situation
may hurt you greatly. You're not 'full of contradictions', as you say.
Everything you have done is entirely understandable, at least to
me. You have experienced the nobility of the revolution, so it's difficult for you to lie. Maybe you felt embarrassed about lying out
of fear for your mother, even though thousands of young people
have joined the revolution knowing they will never be the same. I
feel the same, Asmaa. The moment I witnessed the fall of the first
martyr was a turning point in my life. Neither I nor you will ever
be the same as we were before the revolution. Everyone who has
taken part in it has changed forever. You reproach those who watch
the demonstrations and do nothing? My friend, not everyone is the
same. In all of history, there has never been a revolution in which
the entire people took part. Somewhere I read that if 10 per cent of
the inhabitants of a country rise up, change is inevitable. Egypt has
offered up twice that number. We have paid the price of freedom
and will certainly achieve it. The regime has done everything in its
power to abort the revolution. It has shot demonstrators dead with
bullets. It hired thugs to kill them in the Battle of the Camel and
it opened the prisons and let out thousands of criminals to terrorise

the population. We face all the instruments of the regime. It wants to crush the revolution at any price. How did the thugs know where the field hospital was in the mosque and how did they know where Ashraf Wissa's flat was? Indeed, who gave them his name in the first place? They attacked specific targets based on information from the security services. When the thugs attacked the square, I found out about it from Twitter, so I left the factory and went there. With my own eyes, I saw bands of thugs on camels passing through the ranks of the army's forces, the officers clearing a way for them. And when we went to the colonel in charge and asked him to stop the thugs, he told us, 'You're against Mubarak and they love Mubarak. Aren't they Egyptian citizens just like you? They have the right to express their opinion. What about all this freedom of expression you're demanding?'

I told him, 'It's got nothing to do with freedom of expression. These men are armed thugs who have come to kill us, we are peaceful demonstrators, and it is the army's duty to protect us.'

The colonel looked angry. He said, 'I have no orders to intervene.'

Then he walked away, leaving us to face thousands of armed thugs. The only officer to disobey orders was called Maged Boulis. He fired in the air to protect the demonstrators but couldn't stop the thugs. Nevertheless, the people holding the square confronted the attack and it failed. Two weeks have gone by, and the revolution is still steadfast. Frankly, I didn't like your tone of voice yesterday when you asked me, 'If Mubarak falls, how long will the people continue to occupy the squares?' Mubarak will fall, Asmaa, and the revolution will be victorious. You want proof? Listen to what happened yesterday. Engineer Yehya Hesein, a member of the coordinating committee, had left one of the tents and was walking around in Tahrir Square when a poor man pulled out an old Nokia mobile phone and asked him, 'Do me a favour – will you buy this phone off me, or find me someone who will?'

Yehya questioned the man, found that he was from Sohag, of no fixed occupation, and concluded that he needed money. He offered to help him but the man refused absolutely, which compelled Yehya to buy the phone even though, of course, he didn't need it. It occurred to Yehya that thousands of the people occupying the square lived, like this man, from hand to mouth, were day-labourers or itinerant peddlers living from day to day, so when they joined the revolution, their livelihoods were cut off. Yehya put the matter to Dr Abd El Samad, chairman of the coordinating committee, who gave him a sum of fourteen thousand pounds from the contributions budget and asked him to use it to help any of the people occupying the square who needed it. Yehya put a wad of banknotes in the inside pocket of his coat and went to perform the evening prayer in the Omar Makram mosque. After the prayer he visited the tents in the square one by one. He spoke to the occupiers, to make sure that they were really in need, then offered them help. Yehya Hesein spent the whole night searching through the tents and finally went back to the head of the committee with the fourteen thousand pounds exactly as they were and not one pound less. Just think, Asmaa! People who might be shot dead at any moment, who have been prevented from working and cannot find food to feed themselves, but who still refuse any help from their colleagues! This principled position hasn't been taken by one, or two, but by thousands of the poorer occupiers. How can we be defeated, Asmaa, when these noble people are among us? How can we be defeated when a million men and women are living together in Tahrir Square without a single incident of sexual harassment or of theft, and when they take part together in everything as though they were members of a single family, dividing the food and drink and facing the bullets and cartridges and gas canisters and thugs' knives together? I will never forget the man who entered Tahrir Square from Qasr El Nil bridge riding a bicycle on which he was carrying a large bag. He was old and poor and wearing a tattered galabiya and had flip-flops on his feet (in winter), which could only be because he didn't have the money to buy shoes. As soon as he entered the square, he parked the bicycle, unloaded the bag, opened it, and began distributing sandwiches to the people there. I will never forget all of that and I will never betray it, Asmaa. I will never betray the martyrs who fell beside me or the wounded whom I carried on my shoulders. I will never betray the simple people who faced the attacks of the thugs at the Battle of the Camel and who asked us, the educated, to move to the rear, saying simply, 'Get back! If we die there are plenty more like us, but you're educated. Egypt needs you more than it needs us.'

I will never betray those people, not ever.

All this nobility was hidden under layers of frustration and injustice. Then the Egyptians rose up and produced the best that was in them. Never doubt for one instant that we shall be victorious!

I love you very much.

Mazen

33

The meeting was held in the atrium of the villa to which the Apparatus had moved, a large chamber into which daylight penetrated via the tall windows made of coloured glass and the cupola in the glass ceiling. The villa had belonged to an aristocratic family and had been confiscated during the Nasser era, remaining thereafter in the keeping of the Apparatus. Anyone seeing it from the inside could imagine how it had been in the past. Balls had been held in this room. Beneath a staircase that led to the upper floor was a raised stage on which had sat the musicians with their instruments, while the guests danced in the open space and the servants, with their striped caftans, cummerbunds, and red tarbushes circulated with trays full of drinks. The villa's historical character lent an atmosphere of drama to the meeting that was to be held at such a critical point in Egypt's history. The time had been set for twelve noon and the invitees had been asked to arrive at least an hour before that. They had passed through the electronic security gates and their mobile phones and the ladies' bags had been taken from them (one actress had objected, but a stern look from the officer in charge made her submit). The guests had been warned to use the toilets in advance as, from the moment the meeting began, no one would be allowed to leave the room for any reason whatsoever. Thus it was that, in a rare scene, the stars of Egyptian society, men and women, were to be found standing in a long queue in front of the lavatories so that they could empty their bladders. Once this was accomplished, officers accompanied the guests to their specified seats at round tables covered with white cloths in the middle of each of which stood a small silver vase containing a single rose, the precision of the arrangements having a somewhat military air. The number of invitees was one hundred, all of whom attended, since it was unthinkable that anyone would excuse themselves under such circumstances. In addition to the well-known media figures, there were the major Salafist sheikhs with their white robes made of the most expensive materials, their Saudi head cloths, and their elegant shoes, each holding a small string of prayer beads formed of precious stones. There were the football stars, idols of the Egyptian masses. The cinema stars were the most talkative and fidgety. The front row of tables was set aside in its entirety for the big businessmen. The older ones among these wore three-piece suits and ties, the younger 'casual' clothes – shirts and pullovers and slacks bearing the signatures of celebrated fashion houses (the rich often resort to this kind of *négligé* look, either because, perhaps, they're sick of formal clothes or, equally possibly, to assert their superiority, since they feel that despite their ordinary clothes they are still distinguished, well-received, and objects of interest to all). The waiters passed between the tables to take the orders of those present, most of whom asked for coffee or Nescafé. An atmosphere of tension and anticipation filled the hall. Everyone talked in whispers about the events the country was witnessing, with the exception of some of the actors, who never stopped trying to attract attention. One famous actress even let out a lascivious feminine laugh that rang through the place, causing a certain embarrassment; many directed towards her looks of disapproval, as if to say, 'This is no time for levity!' At twelve o'clock precisely, the door opened and General Alwany entered with his office manager, a young major. They were surrounded by four other officers wearing civilian clothes. General Alwany was elegantly dressed, as usual, wearing a light grey suit, white shirt, and blue tie. The guests all stood to show their respect, and he smiled and said, 'Good morning!'

Men's and women's voices mingled as they responded, 'Good morning, sir!'

He made a gesture and they sat, and he did the same, on the seat prepared for him behind a small table on the stage, and held a whispered conversation with the officers, as though going over the details with them for the last time. He tried to give the impression that morale was high, even letting out a histrionic and artificial-sounding laugh, but his face expressed an anxiety he could not conceal. Approaching the microphone, he said in amiable tones, 'Thank you all for coming, though we would not have expected otherwise of you, as patriotic Egyptians.'

The general began presenting his officers – a brigadier and three colonels. Then he took a sip from his cup of coffee and said, 'Our time is short, events are moving fast, and we have many tasks before us, in difficult circumstances. I will get straight to the point. Today, at six o'clock, it will be announced that President Mubarak has stepped down.'

Despite himself, his voice quavered. He took another sip of coffee and gazed sadly at those present, who were uttering loud cries of protest.

One sheikh exclaimed, 'There is no might and no power but with God!', another, 'This, I swear, is that schism than which murder is not worse!'

An actress, whose face had still not recovered completely from the cosmetic surgery that had left her cheeks puffed up into two little balls, shouted, 'I'm angry with the Egyptian people. Instead of honouring President Mubarak, it does this to him? It's shameful! I swear it's shameful!'

A muscle-bound young actor who specialised in action films exclaimed, 'Even if he has stepped aside, Mubarak is still my president!'

The football players stood up where they were and let out cries of protest, waving their arms about. A famous player known for his rocket-like, long-distance goal shots said, 'Sir, with all due respect, who in this country has the right to make the president step aside? A few kids who take money from America and Israel to sabotage the country are going to kick out the president? No way will we accept his resignation!'

The goalkeeper for the national team shouted, 'Sir, we should have a march to demand that His Excellency the President stays in his post!'

General Alwany remained silent for several minutes. Then, moved, he said, 'The resignation is a final decision, taken by President Mubarak himself to preserve Egypt from harm. Authority will shift to the Supreme Council of the Armed Forces and President Mubarak will continue to be treated with honour and respect. No one will be allowed to do him any harm.'

The uproar quietened down a little and the sound of crying from the actresses' table faltered. General Alwany continued, 'I appreciate your noble sentiments. However, this is not a time for weeping but for work. Egypt – whose name is mentioned in the Koran! – will remain well, God willing, until the Day of Resurrection. All the saboteurs who have taken part in the demonstrations do not number more than 10 per cent of Egyptians. The rest of the people have nothing to do with what is happening. This is according to an accurate study. We have in the Apparatus a department for gauging public opinion that gives us the results of its studies as they come in. Everything that is happening is foreign to Egyptian culture. Our authentic Egyptian values raise us to respect our elders and obey our leaders.'

A well-known star of comedy rose and shouted, 'Sir, what happened in Tahrir is a despicable plot.'

Then the man turned towards the seated audience and said, 'I'd like to know why the army hasn't killed these kids. Bomb them from the air and rid us of them!'

General Alwany raised his hand to show that he didn't mean to interrupt him. Then he said, 'Naturally, there is a conspiracy against the Egyptian state. We have the names of the conspirators and know how much money they've received. We shall reveal everything at the appropriate time and bring them to trial. But we have to acknowledge that some young people have imported ideas that are foreign to our values, our religion, and our society. These young people on Facebook and Twitter have appeared from nowhere, like foreign plants in our good soil.'

'Who invented Facebook? The Zionists and the Masons, God curse them! They want to destroy the nation of Islam,' cried a Salafist sheikh, while General Alwany nodded his head as though in agreement. Then he resumed, 'We have put in place a plan to save the country from chaos, and I have invited you so you can join us. Each one of you will carry out his mission in his own field. Egypt, today, is in need of you all.'

'We are all at your command, sir!' cried out a celebrated footballer, known as the Rock of the Defence.

A variety of enthusiastic voices around the room responded with approval. General Alwany said, fervently, 'This is what we expected of you. I came to welcome you and explain your mission. Meetings with the officers will follow. Each group of you has a designated officer who will assign you your specific tasks and review the group's performance.'

'May we know the nature of the tasks that are asked of us?' enquired a well-known businessman who was over seventy. The general looked grave.

'The tasks are varied but all of them need money and effort. We face a true war, intended to destroy Egypt from within. Wars of this kind are called "fourth-generation wars". Under these circumstances, we cannot abandon the minds of the Egyptians to the tendentious rumours spread on Facebook. What is asked of our patriotic businessmen is that they play a role in protecting people's awareness.'

The general fell silent, as though arranging his thoughts. Then he looked at the businessman and continued, 'We will task you, and your colleagues, to open media outlets in all their forms – television and radio stations and newspapers and internet sites. We have to regain the initiative. Our duty is to spread awareness among Egyptians so that they are empowered to scotch the conspiracy. These projects will cost you a great deal of money and will bring you no financial gain. They will, however, save the country. I'm certain you won't hang back.'

'Naturally, sir,' the businessman said, 'each of us will take part, according to his capacity.'

General Alwany was alive to the hidden meaning in the man's words, so he asked him earnestly, 'What do you mean?'

'I mean we shall do what we can. "God does not charge a soul with more than it can bear."'

'It seems you didn't understand what I said,' General Alwany said. 'I'm telling you this is a national duty and we can't waste time.'

The businessman responded, 'I only said, each according to his means.'

The general's face darkened and he said in decisive tones, 'We know everything about your means. We have complete data on every one of you. You will carry out what we ask of you in full. There is no room for refusal. Egypt is your country and she's been good to you and given you all your wealth. If the Egyptian state falls and the saboteurs take power, your wealth will be confiscated and you'll be thrown in prison.'

The audience uttered phrases of enthusiastic agreement and General Alwany rose, saying, 'I apologise but I have to leave. I wanted to explain things to you myself. You will now be divided into groups – media people and performers, sportspeople, men of religion, and

217

businessmen. Each group will sit with the officer in charge. I hope the results are positive. My fellow officers will submit reports to me and I shall follow everything and meet with you regularly. Goodbye.'

Everyone stood to bid him farewell and he left, a blend of satisfaction and enthusiasm on his face. Things were going as planned. The conspirators would celebrate Mubarak's resignation today, but it was the last thing they'd ever celebrate. His office director approached him and whispered, 'The Supreme Guide of the Muslim Brotherhood is waiting for Your Excellency in the office.'

General Alwany looked at his watch. The Supreme Guide had arrived, as was his wont, ten minutes early for his appointment. General Alwany ascertained, with a single glance, that he had heard of the resignation, and perhaps even knew what was required of him. He knew from long experience how efficient the Brothers were at information-gathering. The Supreme Guide was a thin, bald man, around seventy years of age, with a white, trimmed beard. He smiled and asked, 'Has Your Excellency prayed the noon prayer?'

The general smiled and said, 'Not yet.'

'Then let us pray it together, God willing.'

There were five of them – the general, his office manager, the Supreme Guide, and the latter's two young assistants. They took off their shoes and made their way to the space set aside for prayer, which consisted of a large fine carpet with the Kaaba woven into it which had been laid down in the corner of the room and oriented to the direction of prayer. The general did not, by nature, like to lead the worshippers but for him to pray behind the Supreme Guide of the Muslim Brotherhood and take him as imam would have had an unacceptable symbolic significance. He led the worshippers in four prostrations and made sure to get up quickly so that the others would understand that time didn't allow performance of the non-obligatory additional prostrations. In a loud voice he said to his office manager, 'I wish to speak with the respected Guide alone.'

The officer left immediately, and the Supreme Guide nodded to his assistants to go. The general sat down behind his desk, and the Supreme Guide sat in front of it, in an armchair. Now they were face to face. Their relationship was simultaneously friendly and guarded, as though they were two sportsmen who had competed against one another in a number of events and learned each other's abilities, a situation that produced, despite their opposition, a kind of mutual professional respect. The general began by saying, 'You are perhaps aware that President Mubarak will be stepping aside.'

'Rule belongs to God. He gives it to whomever He pleases and takes it from whomever He pleases, and there is no might and no power but in God,' responded the Supreme Guide.

'The Muslim Brothers have always been a model of the sort of patriotic opposition that places the national interest above political gain.'

'Praise God for that!'

'Bear in mind that I have summoned you previously in critical circumstances and that we have cooperated for the sake of the country.'

'The Brothers have never been, and will never be, slow to respond to the interests of religion and the nation.'

'Can we depend on you this time?'

'We have always, through God's grace, observed any agreements we have made with you.'

'The country is in a state of unrest. Following Mubarak's resignation there will be demands for a new constitution. Such a thing will open the doors to a conflict in society whose end only God knows. We will put the matter to the people in a referendum. We want your support so that the Egyptians agree to modify certain articles of the old constitution rather than writing a new one.'

'We shall cooperate with you for the common good, God willing.'

'If you prove that you can cooperate well, we will remove any obstacles that may face you in the parliamentary elections.'

'God reward you!'

Silence reigned for a moment. Then the Supreme Guide smiled and said, 'If you don't mind, Your Excellency, I'd like to know the names of the members of the committee charged with amending the constitution.'

'We shall leave the choice of the committee members to you.'

'God reward you!'

The major gave him a searching look, as though testing his intentions, and the Supreme Guide smiled and said, 'Your Excellency knows that we have kept our side of every agreement we have made with you.'

Suddenly, the door opened and the major who managed the office appeared. The general gave him an angry look but the young man ignored it, hurrying up to him and then bending over him and whispering, 'Dr Danya is here and wants to see Your Excellency.'

34

The spacious living room was furnished in the arabesque style, the balcony was embellished with pots of roses, and the view of the Nile filled all the windows of the façade. Essam Shaalan wasn't used to seeing his flat during the daylight hours. It was his custom to wake early, breakfast quickly, go to the factory, and not return until evening. Even on Fridays, the day off, he'd sleep on until the late afternoon, under the influence of the late hours that he kept on Thursdays. Now he had time to contemplate the details of the flat at his leisure. He recalled the voice of the officer who had phoned him from National Security: 'Listen, Essam. The president has decided to step aside. The announcement will be made this afternoon.'

'What! How can that be?'

'It's just the way it is.'

'And who will take control of the country?'

'The Supreme Council of the Armed Forces.'

'I can't believe it.'

'God protect Egypt! Naturally, there'll be agitation and chaos, and we're going to need some time before we can get control of the situation.'

'Fine. So what am I supposed to do?'

'It would be better if you don't go to the factory for the next couple of days.'

'Would you like me to submit my resignation, sir?'

'As of now, we have no instructions. Stay home till I phone you.'

He drank off what remained in the glass at one go. Finding the bottle empty, he got up to get another. If he hadn't bought two boxes of whisky before the demonstrations broke out, he would have had nothing to drink. The off-licence in Zamalek had closed its doors and his driver, Madany, had stopped coming to work following the disaster that had befallen his son. He opened the new bottle and poured himself the first glass. He always liked to drink it straight up. He'd tell his friends, jokingly, 'A bottle of whisky is like a woman. It has a hymen. The first glass is like the first act of sex with a virgin. It has a delicious, unique taste that can never be repeated.'

He'd spent a whole week in the house, during which he'd tried to see Nourhan. He'd phoned her three times but she always made the excuse that she was too busy at the television station. In that soft voice of hers that always aroused him, she said, 'Essam. Darling. Please understand my situation. I can't leave the station for a second.'

If this had happened under ordinary circumstances, he would have quarrelled with her, but now he accepted it in a silence that was not without bitterness – if Nourhan wouldn't stand by her husband at such a time, then when would she support him? But was she really his wife anyway? What value did the marriage have under any circumstances? He'd gone with her to the lawyer's and signed the customary marriage paper in front of witnesses. Did God need a piece of paper stamped by a lawyer's office? What an absurdity! He'd put up with all this silly play-acting to satisfy Nourhan, nothing more, nothing less. This morning he'd looked at his face in the mirror and been astonished. Little white hairs were growing in his beard, day after day, and gave him an odd look, as though he were an escapee or a prisoner. The amazing thing was that he'd got used to his isolation. He no longer found it trying. He didn't feel bored and didn't long to go out. In fact, in his heart of hearts, strangely enough, he felt the relief that despair engenders. The worst that he could imagine had happened, so he no longer feared anything. It was as though the match had ended with his losing so there was nothing left to worry over. It was time for him to take a rest. It was time for him to drink, chew over events and contemplate them. Each morning, he awoke as usual at seven thirty, took a shower, then put on his track suit, made himself breakfast and coffee, and read the newspaper all the way through. Then he'd turn on the television and open his laptop so that he could follow what was going on blow by blow, on the TV channels and on the net. At noon, he began drinking and would send the doorkeeper out to get something for him to eat. The cook had stopped coming and he could no longer order food over the phone because the security situation prevented the delivery of orders from restaurants. What was going on in Egypt? When would 'The End' appear on this wretched film? Sometimes he'd fantasise about a telephone call from the National Security officer informing him that they'd regained control of the country and telling him to go back to the factory. He realised, though, that things were more complicated. What devil had whispered in the Egyptians' ear and driven them to behave completely contrary to their nature? Egyptians knew nothing about revolution. They didn't understand it and if they got caught up in it, they quickly deserted it and came to hate it. When he saw on the television people dancing in the streets out of joy at the toppling of Mubarak, he was possessed by rage. He was less upset at losing his position than he was at the self-deception of the Egyptians. He would have liked to write an article in which he'd say, 'O Egyptians, read the history of your country and the history of revolutions around the world before you begin driving your youth to their deaths to no avail! There are peoples who are revolutionary by nature, but you, O Egyptians, were not created for revolution and it was not created for you. Not one revolution in your modern history has succeeded. Every revolt of yours against authority has failed and things have got worse.'

It was a truth he'd learned at great cost. He poured himself a new glass, lay down on the couch, and stared at the ceiling. Suddenly, the peep show began and memories appeared before him in order. Was he drinking to forget, or to remember? Why did these events come back to him now? They'd been buried for so many years that he'd thought they were dead. Why were they being resurrected now, as living witnesses, with the same colours and voices and even the same smells? He beheld the main hall of Cairo University as it had been forty years ago, and saw himself with the leaders of the student movement agreeing with the police generals to break up the sit-in and hand themselves over, along with their colleagues. The early hours of a cold, wintry morning, the surroundings of Cairo University looking like part of a cloudy dream shrouded in fog. The huge police lorries standing in a long line in front of the main gate. The students, men and women, emerging in groups, surrounded by silence, their young faces tense and exhausted. They climbed one by one, in accordance with the agreement, into the police vehicles. Suddenly, a colleague of his at the Faculty of Engineering raised his voice and began singing, 'My country, my country, to you my love and my heart.' His voice was sweet and sad. Little by little, the other students joined him until thousands of throats were roaring out the anthem, which sounded like a mighty hymn sung by a sad giant, as though it were the voice of Egypt itself as it mourned for its children, who defended its freedom even as they went to prison. Many students wept and he had seen with his own eyes officers and soldiers averting their faces or looking at the ground to hide their tears.

His alias in the party had been Comrade Hamdi. The day he was elected to the Central Committee, his friends had thrown him a party at Gamal Saqqa's house, and they'd drunk until dawn. As he said goodbye to him at the door, the party secretary had told him, 'Comrade Hamdi, you bear a great responsibility. Don't let us down.' Then he'd embraced him and hugged him with a genuine affection made all the warmer by the alcohol. He didn't think he'd disappointed his comrades. He'd carried out his party responsibilities efficiently and sincerely and hadn't underperformed in any task allotted to him. He'd been arrested often, sentenced three times, and spent a total of ten years in prison. Imprisonment came with its own traditions, which he'd learned by experience. The first day in detention, there was the 'reception party' or 'investiture'. The line of prisoners passed between two rows of soldiers, each of whom struck the prisoner in front of him with all his strength, either setting his skin on fire with the leather strap or punching him or kicking him with his army boots. The blow would fall on the prisoner's head or his belly or his face or his testicles. He'd learned from experience never to stop moving during the investiture. He would receive the blows, pick himself up, and keep running. If he were to stop or fall, they would beat him to death, the blows then being focused and inescapable. His last imprisonment had been his worst. After the usual beating and torture, luck had placed him in the hands of Mohsen El Gazzar, director of Abu Zaabal prison. El Gazzar ('the Butcher') wasn't his real name but a nickname that had attached itself to him because of his cruelty. Terrible stories were associated with him of prisoners who lost their minds or died as a result of torture at his hands. Essam was chosen from among his colleagues because he was responsible for the communists in the prison, and when the treatment became too bad, his comrades went on hunger strike. Their demands were clear and just – application of the prison regulations. When the warders entered with the trays of food, Essam said to them, 'Take it back. No one is going to eat it.'

'Why?' he was asked, and Essam shouted, in his gruff voice, so as to let the comrades in the neighbouring cells hear, 'Go tell the director that I and my comrades are on hunger strike.'

The warders returned after a little while and led him to the director's office. Mohsen El Gazzar was in his forties and looked a lot like a film star – handsome and extremely elegant with, like all great executioners, a soft, gentle voice and a calm face that hid his reactions. He asked Essam in a seemingly friendly way, 'Your name?'

'Essam Abd El Men'em Shaalan.'

'Your profession?'

'Engineer.'

'You've called a hunger strike?'

'I and all those accused in the Secret Communist Organisation case have decided to go on hunger strike. In accordance with the law, I respectfully ask you to notify the prosecutor general.'

'You want the prosecutor general, just like that, mummy's boy?'

'Kindly speak to me with respect.'

'Upset because I mentioned your whore of a mother?'

'My mother has more honour than you.'

Essam uttered the last words in a challenging tone that came over as a little forced. A faint expression of surprise passed rapidly over the Butcher's face. He may have raised his eyebrows slightly, or moved his lips. Then he gestured to the goons. Those moments came back to Essam now with all their colours and sounds and even the smell of wood and new paint in the Butcher's office. The goons stripped him of his prison clothes and stood him up in front of them in his underpants. Suddenly the gates of Hell opened. Violent blows rained down on him. There were four of them and they beat him with their hands and feet. At first, he tried to resist the torrent of punches and kicks, but he quickly realised that resistance was pointless and began to protect his head with his hands, which allowed the goons to direct their painful blows at his body. As the beating continued, the office lights began to shake violently before his eyes and he wished he'd faint, if only for a few seconds, from the pain. The beating stopped as suddenly as it had started and Essam tasted the blood from his nose and the wounds on his face. The director laughed and said, as though joking with a friend, 'Tell me, Mr Engineer, are you a real man?'

Essam didn't reply, so the Butcher continued, 'If you don't mind, we'll have to examine you.'

This was code, and the goons pounced on him all together, seemingly acting out a scene they had acted out many times. They pulled off his pants and threw him down on his stomach, spreading his legs, while he struggled with all the strength that was left to him, but in vain. Then they began to insert something solid and thick (which, as he learned later, was a thick wooden stick known as 'the basha's rod') into his backside. He'd never experienced a pain like it – a terrible, mounting pain that made him cry out at the top of his lungs. Later, he could never forgive himself for having moaned and given voice to his pain in long, high-pitched screams. He started to beg and plead. He had never forgiven himself for having cried out, 'Please, enough, Mohsen Bey! Let me go! I kiss your feet, but let me go!'

The memory of those words would pain him more than anything else that happened. His abject pleading to the Butcher had left inside him a feeling of shame that was with him even now. Afterwards, he'd often asked himself, had it really been impossible for him to bear the pain with courage? Why had he screamed and begged the officer for mercy in such a humiliating way? Was he underlining that he was broken, out of abject hope for the Butcher's pity? He would blame himself for his ignominious breakdown during the torture, and sometimes he'd blame himself for blaming himself: it wasn't right to blame the victim; that day he had suffered pain no human could bear.

He couldn't return to the block on his own feet. The goons carried him, the blood dripping from his anus and leaving a string of spots along the corridor floor. They threw him down onto the concrete floor of the cell, closed the door, and left. The comrades gathered round him and tried to give him aid, using the simple means available. One was a recently graduated doctor and he tried hard to stop the bleeding using cotton wool, gauze, and tincture of iodine that he'd managed to smuggle into the cell. Essam couldn't sleep on his back or his side, he was in such pain. He lay on his stomach and remained completely silent. His companions tried to talk to him but he didn't reply, as though what had happened had destroyed his ability to speak, or there was no point in his saying anything. He stayed lying on his stomach and gazing at the dozens of cockroaches that ceaselessly entered and exited the cracks scattered over the wall of the cell. At night, his comrades would sleep, and the familiar sound of their snoring would ring out. Gamal Saqqa approached him, placed his hand on his shoulder, and whispered, 'Hang in there, Essam! We are stronger than them.'

When he saw Gamal's loving, pitying face, he could not contain himself and burst into tears, repeating in a low voice, 'I'm done, Gamal. I was so terribly humiliated. Who are we suffering such humiliation for, Gamal?'

He would repeat the question often thereafter. After they'd both left prison, they would spend nights in endless discussion. They would smoke and drink and each would stick to his opinion. Gamal still believed in the cause, but Essam's view was unequivocal: 'You cannot help a people who do not want to help themselves. I've been imprisoned and tortured and my self-respect has been demeaned, for what? How many Egyptians remember the sacrifices of the socialists?'

One night, they had drunk a lot and the discussion between them had become so heated it had turned into a quarrel. At that point, Essam stood in the middle of the room and said to Gamal, 'Have you heard of Vera Zasulich?'

'No.'

'Vera was a young socialist in Russia in 1879. When she heard that General Trepov, the governor general of the city of St Petersburg, tortured prisoners, she went to his office and shot him. However, she wounded him and didn't kill him. They arrested her, and when they asked her at the investigation if there was any enmity between her and Trepov, she said, "I don't know Trepov, but I know that he tortures prisoners and I decided to kill him because no one should be able to mistreat people with such deep confidence in their ability to escape punishment."

'With this sentence, Vera was transformed into a national hero. Tens of thousands of Russians demonstrated in support of her every day. Can you believe it? Even children demonstrated in their thousands in front of the courthouse, carrying a large banner on which was written 'Thank You, Vera, For Defending Our Dignity!'

'Faced with such extreme pressure from Russian public opinion, the court found her innocent, even though she'd confessed. After she was released, the police tried to re-arrest her, but the masses defended her and prevented her from being taken into custody.'

Gamal listened in silence, while Essam continued excitedly, 'Do we have anyone in Egypt like Vera Zasulich? Do we have a public opinion that protects political activists? Do we have any awareness of the importance of the dignity of man? We have nothing. It follows that no amount of activism can lead to any outcome but the loss of our dignity and of our future.'

Gamal tried to respond but Essam was too carried away, and he yelled in his friend's face, 'Listen to what Vera said: "I decided to kill him because no one should be able to mistreat people with such deep confidence in their ability to escape punishment."'

Essam bowed his head in silence for a moment, then said in a trembling voice, 'I was tortured and my honour was demeaned and every one of those who tortured me has escaped punishment and not one person has defended me.'

Why was Essam remembering all this now? What drove him to drag up the past? The revolution that he hadn't expected, or the worrying situation he was living through, or because he had drunk too much? He was recalling these painful scenes at leisure, as though he found some pleasure in torturing himself. It occurred to him that he was reliving the events of his life because the mistake he'd made was being repeated. Here were the same young people, like Mazen Saqqa, demonstrating and holding sit-ins and being arrested for the sake of a people that couldn't care less about what they did. What a waste! Here was poor Madany, losing his son who was his pride and joy and his only hope in life. He drank what was left in his glass and suddenly felt dizzy. He remembered that he suffered from diabetes. The doctor had warned him about drinking too much alcohol because he might end up going into a coma. He loved life and wanted to live a long time. If he had to die, he'd prefer to drink, so that he could die quietly, with no pain, no pity, no impotence, and no burdens to be borne by those he loved. Suddenly, the doorbell rang. He got up with difficulty. He was completely drunk. Who could be calling? He remembered the security collapse. It could be one of those prisoners who had escaped from gaol. He thought of a newspaper headline: 'Bellini Cement Factory Manager Murdered by Persons Unknown'. He tried to stop himself from staggering and cautiously approached the door, then looked through the peephole and saw Fabio, the owners' representative, standing outside. Quickly, he opened the door and said in English, 'Hello, Mr Fabio!'

Fabio smiled and said, 'Sorry to come without an appointment. I phoned you many times but you didn't answer.'

Essam welcomed him, apologised for being inappropriately dressed, and then poured him a glass. Fabio sat in the armchair facing the couch, took a sip of his whisky, and said, 'When was the last time you were at the factory?'

'A week ago.'

'Have you heard what happened?'

Essam was trying hard to recover his concentration from the muddle of his intoxication. He stared at Fabio's face, which had darkened. Fabio went on in an angry voice, 'There's a big problem at the factory. I've come so we can find a solution.'

35

My darling Mazen,

Yes, I love you. I'm no longer embarrassed by my feelings. I feel liberated. I've become a new person. I shall never forget the moment when they announced Mubarak's resignation and you hugged me in front of everybody. I wasn't embarrassed. I felt your body shaking with excitement, and your tears wet my face. I shall never forget the millions of people shouting and singing and crying with joy, all over Egypt. I shall never forget how, the day following Mubarak's fall, the young men and women swept the streets and repainted the pavements. See how smart and civilised our revolution is! Did it ever happen before in history that the people rose up, overthrew the dictator, and then swept the streets? I spoke with a lot of the young people who were doing the sweeping and they told me, 'Egypt is our country now, and it has to be clean.'

I shall never forget those tremendous moments, Mazen. How lucky I am, in you and in the revolution! Can you believe I even found my mother was happy? She kissed me and said, 'Mubarak was a tyrant. He went too far and got what was coming to him. Enough said.'

Even my father, who used to avoid me altogether so that we wouldn't quarrel, phoned me from Saudi Arabia and said, 'Congratulations, Asmaa! It's over, right, and Mubarak's fallen? Please, think about your future now.'

The big surprise was at the school. Do you remember the journalist, Hisham, who did an interview with us at the Enough! movement building and published it in Al-Ahram? They'd read the interview at the school and seen my picture with our colleagues. On the first day after the half-term holiday, I went to the school and was amazed at the excitement and joy. The moment I entered the classroom, more than one of the girls said, 'Congratulations, Miss Asmaa!'

I started explaining the lesson, as usual, but I felt that there was something new about the girls, as though they were taking in what I said in a different way, as though they'd been weighed down by chains and were now free, as though they wanted to talk about what had happened but were waiting for me to start. I found myself asking them, 'What do you think about the revolution?'

They began calling out and competing with one another to tell me how glad they were that Mubarak had fallen. Then I asked them, 'Which of you took part in the revolution?'

A quarter of the girls raised their hands, exactly the same percentage as the revolutionaries among the rest of the people.

I told them, 'Each one of you who took part in the revolution should be proud and tell their children that they shared in the building of a decent, clean, new Egypt.'

The moment the first class finished, the janitor came to summon me to the headmaster's office. There I found Mrs Manal, who hugged me and kissed me, while Mr Abd El Zaher welcomed me warmly, saying, 'If it weren't a sin, I'd kiss you, Asmaa! I'm so proud of you and of all the young people of your generation.'

I was slow to react, I was so surprised. How could Mr Abd El Zaher, who had referred me for investigation and treated me insultingly and unfairly, have changed so fast? 'Thank you,' I said. 'I didn't do anything. The credit should go to the Egyptian people.'

Mr Abd El Zaher smiled and said, 'No, the credit (once, of course, God, Glorious and Mighty, has received His) should go to your generation. You have done what my generation could not. You are wonderful, fearless young people for whom nothing is impossible.'

I looked at Mrs Manal and found her smiling at me affectionately.

233

I didn't know what to say. I was very moved. I made an effort not to cry. Mr Abd El Zaher invited me to sit down, ordered me a cup of tea, and said, 'I asked you to come so that I could tell you something. In the past, we have had our problems with one another. Please understand me. I'm not afraid of my superiors. I'm not afraid of the undersecretary at the ministry or even the minister. I fear only Our Lord, Glorious and Mighty, whom I take into account in everything I do. It is this sense of responsibility that sometimes makes me overly strict in my dealings with the teachers.'

'I did nothing wrong, Headmaster,' I said.

He smiled affectionately and said, 'May God forgive the past, Asmaa! I want us to start a new page.'

Before I could reply, Mrs Manal said, 'I too would like to open a new page with you, Asmaa. Our Lord alone knows how much I love you and think of you as my daughter.'

Naturally, I thanked them, saying, 'All of Egypt is opening a new page.'

Everything really has changed. The dictator was stifling Egypt. When he was overthrown, all Egyptians were liberated. I'm writing to you from home, having just come back from the school, and I have lots of questions begging for an answer. How could the headmaster's and Mrs Manal's attitude towards me have changed so amazingly? Is the revolution changing people's natures? Is it giving them back their confidence in themselves and causing them to review their mistakes? While waiting for your answer,

All my love, Asmaa

P.S. I know of course that you're busy at the factory. I want to see you at the earliest opportunity. Phone me an hour ahead and I'll wait for you at the Zahret El Bustan café.

36

The workers gathered in the courtyard of the factory at 8 a.m., when the first shift changed, and began congratulating one another on the fall of Mubarak. Then they elected a four-man committee, one of whose members was Mazen Saqqa, and charged it with full supervision of the factory and negotiation with the Italian management to fulfil the workers' demands. The day passed normally, and the second shift changed, and then the third. At four in the morning, Essam Shaalan arrived unexpectedly at the factory. The car didn't enter by the main gate but by Gate 4, at the back, then went round behind the trees and only then arrived at the administration building. There was a man in the front seat of the car, next to the driver, while in the back seat sat Essam, with another person, who was sitting next to a large metal box resembling an air-conditioning unit. The moment the car stopped, Essam jumped out, opened the office with his key, and went in quickly, while the two men got down, pulled out the black metal machine, and carried it into the office. The driver then drove off. Essam turned on the lights, bolted the office door, and the two men got to work. They set the machine in the middle of the large room and connected it to the electricity. It was a large paper shredder. Essam took off his jacket and began putting documents into the machine, which shredded them fast, expelling them in little bits at the bottom, where the two men had placed a large black rubbish bag. Essam started taking papers out of the drawers of his desk, out of the glass-fronted cupboard, and from a small desk located in the corridor. He knew the documents by heart. He had only to glance at one to decide its fate. An hour passed and he was still shredding documents. His attention was attracted by shouting and noise outside. He told the two men, 'Keep working whatever happens.'

He fed the machine a new file but shortly after received a telephone call and then went towards the door and looked cautiously through the peephole. Then he pulled back the bolt and opened the door a little, and Mazen Saqqa walked slowly into the middle of the room. He looked exhausted. Essam shook his hand and said, 'How are you, Mazen? Congratulations on the success of the revolution. God willing, things in the country will go better with you people in charge.'

Mazen didn't reply. He observed the shredding of the papers, then looked at Essam anxiously and said, 'The workers phoned me and asked me to meet with you, sir.'

Essam smiled irritably and said sarcastically, 'All's well, I hope?'

'The workers are opposed to the shredding of the papers.'

'I have the right to do what I want with my own papers.'

'These aren't personal papers. They're official papers and they concern the workers.'

'Concern the factory, you mean. I have instructions from the owners' representative to shred the papers.'

Suddenly, outside, a cry arose, and Mazen said anxiously, 'The workers are in revolt and things could get dangerous.'

Essam smiled and shouted in a voice that made Mazen think he might be drunk, 'No one threatens Essam Shaalan, Mazen! Understand?'

Outside, the workers' cries grew louder: 'Essam! Shaalan! You're a coward!' and 'If you're a man, come out and face us!'

Suddenly, he heard the sound of breaking glass and a brick fell onto the floor of the office. Some workers had left the night shift, leaving their colleagues working so that the factory wouldn't come to a halt, and many workers had been summoned from their homes.

236

All the spotlights had been turned on and they emitted a brilliant light. The workers had surrounded the administrative building and started chanting slogans against Essam Shaalan, after which they had begun throwing bricks and the glass in all the windows had shattered. Mazen went out to them, and they gathered around him, shouting excitedly, 'We saw him take a paper shredder in. We can't let him get rid of the documents.'

'Those papers are sure to have stuff that management doesn't want us to see.'

'Of course. The proof is he came at four in the morning.'

In a loud voice, Mazen said, 'Everyone! The papers have been shredded, it's over. We can't get them back, and there are lots of papers we prevented him from shredding and saved. Please, no more brick-throwing. The things that are getting broken are your property.'

Voices rose in opposition, so Mazen said, 'What do you want Essam Shaalan for?'

A worker shouted, 'We want to keep him prisoner in the office till the administration fulfils our demands.'

Mazen replied calmly, 'That's a bad idea. You workers aren't thugs. The country has changed and the factory is in your hands.'

Excitedly, the worker replied, 'If we keep Essam a prisoner in the office, management will do what we want.'

'First, Essam Shaalan is no longer of any importance to management, and second, if we do what you say, we will have committed the crime of illegally detaining a citizen. Plus, what's the point of holding him? The factory is under our control and we shall take our rights in full.'

With these words, Mazen left the workers to their discussions and returned to the office, where he found the two men who had accompanied Essam in a state of panic. One of them cried to him in a tearful voice, 'Please, Mazen Bey. I've got nothing to do with all of this. I came to help Essam Bey and I want to leave right now.'

'You're afraid of a few kids?' Essam shouted at him. 'Be a man!'

Then he paced to the other side of the room and returned and shouted, looking at Mazen, 'My name is Essam Shaalan. With my history, I cannot accept being taken prisoner by a bunch of rabble.'

He turned to the door to leave, but Mazen held him by the shoulder and said, 'Essam, sir, if you hold me responsible for your safety, please don't go out there. The workers are angry and anything could happen.'

The warning had its effect on Essam, and he sat down on the couch and lit a cigarette. Then he picked up his telephone and said in a low voice, 'I'm going to contact the army.'

In a short while, the factory had filled with military police. They spread out, with their well-muscled bodies, military uniforms, and distinctive red berets. The workers' chanting grew louder, as though they were taking the soldiers as witnesses to their demands. An officer with the rank of captain entered the office. He shook hands with everyone and apparently grasped the situation, because he didn't ask for any explanation. He just smiled and asked Essam, 'Where have you parked the car, sir?'

'Behind the building,' Essam said.

The officer contacted someone and informed him where the car was, and after a few minutes he received a phone call, opened the door, and poked his head through it as though to make double sure that his men were in place outside. Then he made a sweeping gesture with his arm and said, 'Please. Come with me.'

The privates formed a cordon around Essam and the two men, and the officer walked ahead of them, with Mazen behind. Soldiers formed a line the whole way, facing the workers and creating a safe passage, though the scene looked almost like a religious rite for the punishment of sinners. Essam looked challengingly at the workers as he walked and the latter hurled insulting comments at him, such as 'Bye, thief!' and 'If we see you in the factory again, we'll break your legs,' and 'Say hello to your master Fabio, you Italian lapdog!'

Essam grew even angrier and, raising his hand, made an obscene gesture at the workers, who went berserk and started directing ugly insults at him. One of them got so angry that he held up one of his shoes to throw at him, but the soldier in front of him stopped him. When Essam reached the car, he shook the officer's hand and thanked him warmly, the officer replying in earnest tones, 'I'm just doing my duty. This private will ride with Your Excellency until you get to the road.'

The car set off at speed and disappeared from view. Mazen smiled and said to the officer, 'Excuse me. I have to get back to the workers.'

Calmly, the officer responded, 'No. You stay with us. We'd like a few words with you.'

37

Over the past few weeks, General Alwany had slept at home on only a few occasions, when he would go at night to make sure his wife and daughter were alright and return early in the morning to the villa in Zamalek. During his meeting with the Supreme Guide, he was surprised to find his office manager approaching and whispering to him, 'Dr Danya is here.'

His face darkened and he asked in alarm, 'Who told her about this place?'

'Sir, she phoned me half an hour ago and said she wanted to see Your Excellency on a subject that couldn't wait.'

'This is a mistake,' General Alwany muttered. He thought quickly, then said, 'Have her wait till I've finished.'

The general finished his meeting with the Supreme Guide, saw him to the front door, and returned to find her in the waiting room. He hugged her and kissed her, noting that she was pale and seemed exhausted.

'What's wrong, Danya?' he asked.

She burst into tears and told him what had happened. He remained silent for a few moments, then pulled himself together and said, 'Danya, please, think of my situation. The country is going through a difficult period and I bear a heavy responsibility which I could never forgive myself for failing to fulfil.'

'I want just one word from you.'

The general interrupted her decisively, saying, 'Please go home and rest and at the end of the day we can sit and talk.'

She seemed unsure but affected a smile. He called his office manager to accompany her to the car, then phoned his two sons, and finally buried himself completely in work. At 7 p.m., while the rest of Egypt was celebrating the victory of the revolution and the fall of Mubarak, a family council was convened in the large living room. The mother sat on the couch wearing the black robe in which she had performed the evening prayer, the Koran open in front of her, holding a string of amber prayer beads and repeatedly whispering 'I seek refuge with God' and other prayers. Danya sat next to her and facing the two of them sat her two brothers – Abd El Rahman, the judge, in three-piece suit, tie, and spectacles, and Bilal, the officer in the Republican Guard, with trim body and bulging muscles, wearing a blue jacket and yellow shirt without a tie, his smooth black hair carefully parted and anointed with gel. An atmosphere of gloom and tension hung over the assembly, even though none of them had mentioned recent events. General Alwany was sitting in an armchair next to the window. He took a sip of the coffee brought to him by their Indonesian maid and said, in the same decisive tones he used to run meetings of the Apparatus, 'You are aware, of course, of the difficult circumstances through which the country is passing. President Mubarak resigned to preserve Egypt. It is our duty to take our country back from the traitors. I have to be back in the office in half an hour. Your sister has a problem. Tell them, Danya.'

In a low, exhausted voice, Danya told them what had happened to Khaled Madany, doing all she could to prevent herself from crying. Then she said, 'My colleagues obtained the name of the officer who murdered the martyr Khaled and filed a report and I want to testify in court.'

Silence reigned for a few moments, and those sitting there seemed to be making an effort to absorb the surprise. Then Bilal, the officer, said sharply, 'Testify to what?'

'To the crime of murder.'

'What made you join the demonstrations in the first place?'

Quickly, Danya responded, 'I was with my fellow students at the field hospital organised by the faculty.'

General Alwany smiled sadly and said calmly, 'That's incorrect. The faculty administration has nothing to do with the field hospital.'

Danya said, 'You know everything about it, sir. My fellow students set up the hospital to provide first aid to the injured, and it was my duty as a doctor to take part.'

Bilal, who seemed to be the angriest, shouted, 'I can't believe you've joined the traitors.'

With equal vehemence, Danya responded, 'My fellow students who went on the demonstrations aren't traitors.'

'No! They're traitors and they've taken money to destroy your country.'

'You don't know them. I do, and they love the country and want it reformed.'

'Did they brainwash you or what?' Bilal exclaimed sarcastically, looking at the others as though calling on them to be witnesses.

Danya was silent for a moment, then said quietly, 'Can we talk about the subject at hand?'

'What subject?'

'My testifying against the officer who murdered my colleague Khaled in front of my eyes.'

Abd El Rahman, the judge, cleared his throat and said quietly, 'In which prosecutorial district did you present the report?'

'Qasr El Nil.'

'Who presented the report?'

'The martyr Khaled's father.'

'Do you know the name of the officer?'

'Heisam Ezzat El Meligi, of Central Security.'

'And who confirmed to you he was the killer?'

'He killed him in front of our eyes. We all know what he looks like. We couldn't mistake him for anyone else.'

There was silence for a moment, then General Alwany said regretfully, 'I can't understand how you could treat your family with such contempt,' which Hagga Tahany followed heatedly with, 'Danya has always loved her family more than anything in the world' (an intervention calculated to affect her). Danya, however, avoiding her mother's eyes, responded, 'I saw a murder take place before my eyes. Neither my religion nor my conscience permit me to stay silent.'

Bilal suddenly stood, went up to Danya, and shouted, 'You're aiding the traitors with this behaviour of yours. They stirred up the demonstrations and got rid of President Mubarak. Their only goal is to destroy the country and get into power.'

'I saw an act of murder take place before my eyes and I must testify against the killer.'

'The officer you want to testify against is a hero, because he was defending us both.'

'Anyone who shoots a young man dead for expressing his opinion is a criminal and must be tried.'

'If I'd been in his place, I'd have done the same.'

'Then you would have been a criminal like him.'

'Shut your mouth!' Bilal shouted.

He stared into Danya's face, and she looked back at him defiantly. Abd El Rahman rose and pulled his brother away, returning him to his seat. Then he sat down again and said, 'Everyone, please, let's talk calmly.'

'There is no god but God!' the mother exclaimed. 'What else have You in store for us, O Lord?'

Judge Abd El Rahman looked at Danya and asked her, 'How many are willing to bear witness to the incident?'

'Six.'

'Fine. So make it five.'

'You want me to suppress my testimony, Abd El Rahman? Do

243

you know the punishment for suppression of testimony in Our Lord's eyes?'

Everyone kept quiet, as though awaiting the result of Abd El Rahman's attempt to answer. Then he smiled and said, 'God forbid! I would never ask you to do something forbidden by religion. As you know, I fear God, Glorious and Mighty, in everything I do. I want you to calm down and listen to me. Given that there are five other witnesses to the incident and given your family's situation, you could make do with your colleagues' testimony.'

'It's my duty to testify, regardless of the number of witnesses.'

'I can assure you, based on my experience, that the judge will never hear more than four witnesses for the prosecution.'

'Even if the judge will hear only four, I have to be one of them.'

General Alwany had been following the conversation in silence. Now he said, 'Danya. I've been silent from the beginning and let you speak. Will you listen to my opinion now?'

'Please.'

'First, you were wrong to go out into the streets with those little saboteurs, and your argument that you were giving aid to the injured is unacceptable because your family's situation should have prevented you from putting us and yourself in that position. Second, your not testifying will have no impact on the trial. Third, and most importantly, from the religious perspective, you will have committed no sin: so long as there are other witnesses you are not obliged to testify.'

'We could phone Sheikh Shamel and ask him,' the mother said.

'Sheikh Shamel will say whatever is asked of him, as always,' Danya said.

'Be respectful when you speak about Sheikh Shamel!' General Alwany said angrily.

'It's the truth!' Danya responded defiantly. 'That Sheikh Shamel of yours isn't a man of religion. He's a businessman.'

This was something Khaled had said, and she uttered it proudly, the words ringing in her ears and moving her. There was silence for a moment, during which General Alwany appeared to be making an effort to master his irritation. Then he said, 'Danya, I have every sympathy for your sorrow over your colleague but please try to think without emotion. Your testimony will add nothing to the case but it will certainly harm Bilal and Abd El Rahman.'

'If I don't testify, I'll live the rest of my life with the guilt.'

'What is it you want, girl?' Bilal shouted angrily, and she raised her head, looked at him, and shouted back, 'Talk to me politely!'

'You will do as your father tells you!'

'I won't go against my conscience.'

'Just you try testifying!'

'Just you watch!'

Bilal rushed at her to hit her, but their mother threw herself at him, wailing, 'Enough! Shame on you all!'

General Alwany took a stance in the middle of the room and said, 'Bilal, I'm warning you, do nothing to hurt Danya in any way! Do you understand? Danya, do what your conscience tells you. Don't think for a moment that the Egyptian state is finished. President Mubarak gave up power to save the state. The security services are unchanged, and everything is as it was. The Supreme Council of the Armed Forces will take power and you have a father who holds an important position in the state, a brother who is an officer in the Republican Guard, and another who is a judge. Your testimony will have no impact on the case but will certainly hurt your family. If your conscience allows you to do us harm, go ahead. If we've done something to deserve injury at your hands, go ahead and testify. I swear by God Almighty I won't stop you.'

38

An aura of mystery surrounds Hagg Muhammad Shanawany, above and beyond the distant, uncommunicative, glassy presence that characterises millionaires in general. He wears a fixed, minimal smile that never broadens and never disappears. He fastens on those around him a strong, enquiring gaze from his wide blue eyes but speaks only when necessary and generally uses only expressions capable of more than one interpretation. His overall appearance harks back to the seventies of the last century – three-piece suits in summer as well as winter, ties patterned in the same colour as the handkerchief that he places in his breast pocket, gold cufflinks fastened in the wide, rigid, old-fashioned cuffs. Shanawany still uses a blow-drier, making his black, dyed hair stand up so that it conceals the bald patch in the middle of his scalp, which two hair implants have failed to cover to the desired degree. Who is Muhammad Shanawany? No one knows anything about his childhood or boyhood beyond the fact that he was born in Alexandria, obtained an industrial diploma, and went to Italy where he spent thirty years, returning with immense riches. The stories are many and there is no way to check them. They say that, with his slickness and good looks, he was able to seduce a rich Italian lady, the widow of an Italian businessman from whom she had inherited a ceramic tile factory; that he married her so as to obtain Italian nationality, acquired from her a large sum of money with which he set up a tile factory in Egypt, and then divorced her. Sometimes they say that he joined the Mafia and used ceramic powder to smuggle drugs. Be that as it may, within a few years of his return he'd become one of the pillars of

Egyptian industry. Shanawany became intimate with the family of the president of the republic and partnered with the president's son on a number of projects, which it is said he initiated specifically as cover for the vast wealth that he bestowed on the president's family. Similarly, he donated vast sums to the charities presided over by the president's lady wife. Thanks to the good offices of the presidential family, he was able to acquire thousands of acres of state-owned land at low prices, which he then resold at the market price, making him profits of mythical proportions. He also used some of the land as collateral for loans in the millions that he secured from banks and that he repaid only irregularly (but what bank employee could hold a man close to the president to account?). At the meeting called by General Alwany the day the president stepped aside, Shanawany was one of those most affected by emotion: he waited in the hallway after the meeting and, the moment he caught sight of Alwany, said to him enthusiastically, 'Allow me to assure Your Excellency that I am prepared to give up all my wealth to save the country.'

The general smiled and said, 'Just what I'd expect from a patriot such as yourself. Spend time with the assigned officer and keep him up to date with every step.'

Shanawany met with the officer and they agreed to set up a major television channel, which Shanawany suggested be called Authentic Egypt. Over the next few weeks, four flats in a luxury block overlooking the Nile in Garden City were bought to serve as the channel's administrative offices, and a huge studio was equipped in Egyptian Media Production City. Work on the new channel proceeded apace, officers from National Security and the intelligence services taking charge of the appointment of all broadcasters and performers who worked there. Hagg Shanawany was careful to attend all interviews with the candidates, which was how he met Nourhan for the first time. The morning of the interview, Nourhan had stood in front of the mirror and hesitated only slightly before deciding to adopt a natural look. She put on a green silk dress, long and modest, that covered her body completely, arranged her hair in a bouffant, and applied light make-up appropriate to the workplace. As soon as she came through the door, she smiled and uttered the Islamic greeting: 'Peace be upon you!'

The interviewing team was a trio – the channel's director, his assistant, and, seated between them, Hagg Shanawany, whose eyes gleamed for an instant, as though an idea had suddenly crossed his mind. Resuming his normal smile, he said, 'And peace be upon you, and God's mercy, and His blessings! Welcome, Mrs Nourhan!'

Nourhan let out a shy, low laugh, but then her mascara-ed eyes widened in surprise and she said, in comic disbelief, 'Don't tell me you remember my name, sir!'

'Of course I do. You're a celebrated broadcaster.'

'A thousand thanks, Hagg!'

'What for?'

'Well of course, Hagg. You, sir, God aid you, have taken it upon yourself, with your mega-projects, to take care of thousands of people who could never otherwise have set up homes . . . so when you remember a simple person like Nourhan, obviously I have to thank you.'

'Well and good. But what would you say if were to tell you I watch you every night and love your programme?'

Nourhan released a medium-modest laugh and said, 'In that case, I could only say that God had been more than kind to me.'

At this moment, the channel's director suddenly recalled an urgent matter that he had to take care of and excused himself, and his assistant likewise, the hagg giving them permission to leave without even turning to look at them. Then he extracted from his pocket a piece of the imported gum he'd taken to chewing after the doctor, in the wake of the hagg's recent heart operation, had forbidden him to smoke cigars, and repeated his welcome to Nourhan, who responded, in a soft voice, 'Go easy on me, Hagg, please! I still can't believe that I'm sitting here with you, just like that.'

The way Nourhan pronounced 'go easy' and 'just like that' – or, to be more precise, the breathy way she pronounced, specifically, the heavy letter *h* that occurs in both phrases – seemed to have a noticeably heating effect on the hagg, evidenced by a widening of his smile and a change in his expression, and he required a few moments to recover his former self. He asked her what her goal would be in working for the new channel, and she said enthusiastically, 'My goal would be to expose the conspiracy, so that every Egyptian understands that they have been duped and that they committed a terrible crime when they allowed President Mubarak to step aside.'

'Excellent.'

'I obey God and His prophet, God bless him and give him peace. Our Lord has commanded us to obey the ruler and forbidden us to indulge in schisms. Learned Sheikh Shamel has ruled that Islam forbids us to demonstrate or go on strike. These are all forms of schism that the Jews and Freemasons have foisted on us by stealth in order to break apart the Islamic community.'

An expression of satisfaction appeared on Hagg Shanawany's face. He passed his fingers over the corners of his mouth, a habit of his when thinking, and said, 'Congratulations on your new job. I shall ask legal affairs to draw up the contract and am prepared to comply with all your requests.'

'I have only one request, and have every confidence in your generosity, sir.'

The hagg's eyes widened and he said, 'I'm sure we can come to an understanding. Just state the salary you're asking for.'

Nourhan looked down for a moment. Then she slowly raised her head, looked at him almost in sorrow, and said, 'Material things have never concerned me. I shall be happy to accept whatever salary you set for me, sir.'

'In that case,' the hagg said warily, surprise appearing on his face, 'what is it you want?'

Nourhan sighed and said, 'My only request is that you allow me to appear on screen with my hair covered, sir. I was obliged to uncover it when state television banned the headscarf.'

'But you don't normally cover your hair!'

'I have a problem that you, sir, are perhaps the person most likely to appreciate. If I were to wear the head covering in ordinary life and take it off in front of the camera, I would not be able to bear the feeling of guilt. My greatest hope is that Our Lord will be kind to me and allow me to wear the head covering till the day I die.'

'God forbid! God grant you good health!' muttered the hagg.

Nourhan pursed her lips, looked at him almost merrily, and, like a child asking if she can go out and play, said, 'So you're going to let me wear the head covering on screen, Your Excellency?'

'God forbid I should ban what God has declared lawful!'

'Thank you, Hagg! I'll mention you every time I pray, I swear! And you should know, my prayers get answered.'

The hagg laughed for the first time and said, 'Thank you very much in that case, really. I could certainly use your prayers.'

A little later, Nourhan asked leave to go. The hagg almost told her to stay but he suppressed his desire and stood up to say goodbye to her. As she rose in haste, her dress, despite her best efforts, was pulled tight, revealing the shape of her breasts and a part of her backside. It all happened quickly, but the hagg took note. In a low voice, Nourhan said, 'I don't know how to thank Your Excellency. Please excuse me, but I don't shake hands with men, following the example of the Noblest of Creation . . .'

The hagg interrupted her by saying, 'The best of prayers and blessing be upon him! I'm very happy with you, Nourhan. I hope we can become good friends.'

Such was their first meeting. Had Nourhan tried to seduce Hagg Shanawany? The answer must be, 'Absolutely not!' Nourhan was a married Muslim lady who feared Our Lord and maintained her husband's honour whether he was present or absent. Similarly, when he met her, Shanawany had abided by the One True Religion and been modest in his speech; indeed, he hadn't even shaken her hand, in accord with the opinion of the great majority of Sunni scholars on the matter. True, she had sat in the office with him with no one else present, which might be considered 'seclusion with a stranger', forbidden by religion, but when she entered the office the director and his assistant had been there, and they had left on urgent business. It follows that she was not responsible for finding herself alone with the hagg. Nourhan had made absolutely no effort to seduce Hagg Shanawany, who would, anyway, have been hard to seduce as he was surrounded by women: the most beautiful women of Egypt would have loved to catch his fancy, which in turn would have resulted in much good fortune. Not to mention that he had two wives – the hagga, who was the mother of his children, and the actress Salwa Hamdan, who, following their marriage, had found guidance at his hands and taken to covering her hair and appearing only in religious dramas. Nourhan signed the contract and was happily surprised to see the large amount awarded her by the hagg as salary, along with a healthy percentage of the income from the advertisements that would be run during her show. What mattered to her most, though, was the deep psychological relief that she felt at the fact that she would, for the first time, appear in front of the cameras with her hair covered. She was content, expected great things from her new job, and spared no effort in preparing for the programme, even though certain problems began to manifest themselves in her relationship with her husband, Essam Shaalan. From one perspective, she had neither the time nor the energy to go to see him as she had been accustomed to in the past. He phoned her and pressed her to do so, and she made numerous excuses; in the end, though, what obliged her to go was her fear of offending God, since a woman who refuses to give her husband his conjugal rights will pass the night cursed by the angels. That day, she had passed by his flat after work. She was exhausted and in a hurry, and Essam was drunk as usual and kept going on about how the Egyptians had failed in all their revolutions. She'd heard his opinions on the matter many times and was in no state to discuss them with him, so she took him by the hand and led him into the bedroom, where she gave him his due and then went into the bathroom. On coming out, she was surprised to find that he'd fallen asleep from fatigue and intoxication. She gathered her things together and left. And the second time, she'd found him drunk again, so she'd given him his legal due, but when she came out of the bathroom, she'd found him in the living room, drinking. In a sudden rage, she said to him heatedly, 'By the way, you're drinking too much. It's your business, of course, but I want you to know that alcohol is a major sin, and God has cursed anyone who drinks it, serves it, or transports it.'

'What is it you want?' Essam said, looking at her disapprovingly.

'I want you to fear God!'

'Fear God yourself and leave me be.'

'Our Lord has commanded me to counsel you. It's the duty of a Muslim wife. Alcohol is forbidden by religion, Essam.'

'The alcohol's got nothing to do with you. Stick to Shanawany.'

She began collecting her things together, preparing to leave, but Essam burst out, 'I know that that boss of yours Shanawany is a big-time crook.'

Angrily, she responded, 'Please, Essam! It's forbidden to speak ill of anyone when he isn't there.'

'And the land and the bank loans he's purloined, they're considered permissible by religion?'

She took refuge in silence, stood up, bag in hand, and went over to the mirror to take one last look at herself. Essam, however, came up behind her and shouted, 'It's the dirty types like Shanawany who caused the fall of Mubarak.'

Calmly, she said, 'I'm going. Bye.'

'Stay with me for a little!' Essam cried out, unexpectedly.

Nourhan yelled, 'You're sitting here drinking and you don't have any work you have to do. I work all day long and I want to get up early tomorrow.'

Essam, who at this moment appeared to be totally drunk, said, 'So why do you come, then?'

'So that Our Lord won't be angry with me.'

'If you come here for Our Lord and not for me, then you'd better not come again.'

She left, slamming the door behind her, but the following day, when he phoned to apologise, he was amazed to hear her say, 'I've forgotten all about it. But I do want to see you.'

He said she'd be welcome, and she could sense the happiness in his voice on the telephone. She came at the appointed time. He was drinking, as usual, but she made no comment. She shook his hand, sat down in front of him in the living room, and said, 'Essam, thank you for everything you've done for me.'

'Don't mention it!' he said, good-humouredly.

Then she looked at him and said calmly, 'This is as far as we go.'

'Meaning what?'

'Meaning that just as we came together as friends, we should part as friends.'

He stared at her as though he couldn't understand. She smiled and said affectionately, 'Essam, you're a decent man, and I'll never forget the time we spent together, but our time is up. I'm asking for a divorce.'

He lit a cigarette. He had sobered up a little, and he placed his hand on her shoulder, but she pushed him away with gentle determination. Softly he said, 'Please, Nour, think. We can't destroy our life just like that.'

'It's all up to fate.'

'When I spoke to you so rudely, I was drunk, and I apologised.'

'Look, Essam. I have done nothing in my life, thank God, that I haven't first made sure is in accordance with religion. If a Muslim woman seeks a divorce, she is not obliged to give her reasons, and there's more than one Tradition to that effect. Our Lord, great and glorious, has said, "A woman must be retained honourably or released with kindness."'

'Fine. I suggest that you take a while to think it over.'

'I've thought and I've decided.'

He looked down for a while, then said, angrily, 'Listen, Nour, I know why you're asking for a divorce.'

'The reason doesn't matter. Please, divorce me.'

As though he hadn't heard her, he went on, 'You grabbed on to me when I was useful. Now I've become a burden to you.'

'May the Almighty forgive you!'

'Drop the humbug! You make yourself out to be the Grand Lady Sheikh of Islam but you're a liar and an opportunist.'

'May Our Lord forgive you!'

His anger suddenly swelled and he said in a loud voice, 'Listen, sunshine. My name is Essam Shaalan and no one ever put one over on me. I'm not someone you can take what you want from and leave.'

'Religion gives me the right to ask for divorce.'

'I don't give a damn about religion.'

'Fear God, Essam!'

'I'm not going to divorce you, Nour. I look forward to seeing what you're going to do about it.'

39

My darling Asmaa,

Egypt has awoken. The revolution has brought out the best in the Egyptians, just as tyranny brought out the worst. I completely understand why the headmaster and teachers support the revolution, but the real test will be whether they can change their behaviour. We have been victorious in the first battle, but the war will be long. We have overthrown the dictator, but the corrupt regime remains in power. The alliance of thieving capitalists remains in place. No one has touched it and now it's changing its colours like a chameleon in order to stay in power. As you notice, I keep my telephone conversations short. Obviously, we are still under surveillance. The security services remain as they were even if they've changed their headquarters. These are confirmed facts. This is why I keep any important details to myself and then put them in writing for you, as we agreed.

After Essam Shaalan got into his car and left, the military police officer accompanied me to the commanding officer's office.

'Am I under arrest?' I asked, as I followed him.

He laughed and said, 'God forbid! The commanding officer just wants to make your acquaintance.'

We made our way to a small building behind the factory that had belonged to the Ministry of Supply and that the army had subsequently taken as its headquarters, following the withdrawal of the police. It was after 6 a.m. when the commander received me welcomingly – a colonel in his forties. The surprise waiting for me in his office was Fabio, the owners' representative. I was astonished to find him there at that early hour. He'd brought an interpreter with him, which is something he does only for important meetings. There was also a young man in civilian clothes, whom the commander introduced as Major Tamer (I think he must be National Security). I shook hands with everybody, and when the commanding officer asked me what I'd drink, I ordered Nescafé. I was tired and needed to concentrate. I realised that every word I said at this meeting would have an impact on what happened at the factory. The colonel started the conversation, saying, 'Welcome to the leader of the workers!'

'I'm not a leader. I just represent the workers because they elected me to the union committee and the four-man committee.'

'Could you explain to us what this "four-man committee" is?'

'It's a committee elected by the workers to manage the factory in place of Engineer Essam Shaalan.'

'So you decided to nationalise the factory?'

'That is not correct. The dismissal of Engineer Essam was a fundamental demand of the workers. The factory will not halt production for even an instant. The profits will be delivered in full to the owners of the factory after deducting what is owed to the workers.'

Fabio was listening to a simultaneous translation as I said this. He interrupted me angrily and the interpreter translated what he said into Arabic, as follows: 'This is wrong and I will not permit it to happen. The workers do not have the right to dismiss the manager. Such things are the prerogative of management. Plus, what are these profits that you're demanding, when the factory is losing money?'

I looked at the colonel and said, 'If Your Excellency will permit me, I would like to speak without anyone interrupting.'

The colonel looked at Fabio and said, 'Kindly allow him to finish what he has to say.'

I explained to the colonel why the Italian company was deliberately running our factory at a loss while it made all its profits at the three other factories that it owned outright. The colonel asked for clarification on certain points, and I gave him detailed answers. He began taking notes and I felt that he sympathised with me, unlike Major Tamer, who didn't utter a word and whom I noticed more than once looking at me with contempt and hatred. The colonel then gave the floor to Fabio, who spoke angrily and arrogantly, repeating what he'd said before about the prerogatives of the board. The colonel let him speak until he'd finished, then asked me for my opinion, so I said, 'Mr Fabio speaks as though we hadn't had a revolution and hadn't deposed Hosni Mubarak. From now on, the workers will impose their management and the board will not be able to repress them the way it did before.'

Fabio said, 'I'm warning you and your colleagues, because what you're doing is against the law.'

I said, 'The revolution imposes its own laws.'

'I'll bring cases against you in Egypt and in Italy.'

'You won't be able to, because the workers will manage the factory and give your company what it is owed and will give the Egyptian government what it is owed, but after we have given the workers all their delayed dividends, as specified in the contract. You're the ones who violated the contract and denied the workers the dividends you'd undertaken to pay.'

'We will never pay dividends to the workers of a factory that is losing money!'

'Mr Fabio, I'm not going to repeat what I've said. Nothing you say now will make any difference. The factory is under the control of the workers.'

At this, Fabio looked at the colonel and shouted, 'How can the Egyptian army permit such anarchy?'

'That question would better be addressed to all of you,' the colonel said. 'The army is currently carrying out a patriotic mission in keeping the country safe following the disappearance of the police.'

I responded, 'The withdrawal of the police was deliberate, sir. The police decided to punish the people for the revolution by withdrawing and creating chaos in the country.'

The colonel looked annoyed and said, 'That's not what we're here to talk about, Mazen. My mission is to keep the entire Turah area safe. It follows that I shall prevent any problems anywhere and I have complete authority to do so.'

We all fell silent, and the colonel went on calmly, 'Look, Mazen, will you undertake before me to preserve the factory's installations and production?'

I replied, 'Sir, the workers will never permit acts of destruction in the factory, and they have given an undertaking that production won't stop even for an instant. I and my colleagues on the four-man committee are prepared to write any undertaking management may request, be it for the integrity of the factory or a guarantee of the profits.'

The colonel appeared relieved and he looked at Fabio. Then he said slowly, allowing time for translation, 'Mr Fabio, write any undertaking and I will have them sign it in front of me.'

Grudgingly, Fabio acceded to this. I thanked the colonel, shook hands with them all, and left. While I was walking back to the factory, I saw Major Tamer riding next to Fabio in his Hummer. Day had come and I was surprised to see that the workers on the night shift hadn't left but had joined the workers on the morning shift. Large numbers of workers had come from their homes to join their colleagues. In view of the growing number of workers, we decided to meet on the football pitch. I spoke over a sound system and told the workers what had happened, and they cheered and shouted, 'God is great!' and repeated their slogans:

'Long Live the Revolution!
Long Live the Workers' Struggle!
Bread! Freedom! Justice for All!'

The strange thing is that I was very moved by the workers' joy and their slogans. Will you believe, Asmaa, that I cried? I don't know why. Perhaps because I remembered my father, who spent years in detention and suffered torture and banishment all for the sake of a moment like this. We are victorious, Asmaa! The revolution is scoring one victory after another but we still have a lot of work ahead of us. My time is totally taken up by the factory, so forgive me if I've been bad at contacting you. I love you.

Mazen

40

The corridors of Qasr El Eini Hospital are long and dim. Madany traversed them with rapid steps that turned, at the end, into as much of a run as his ageing and exhausted body would allow. He entered the room panting. Khaled lay on the bed, his white coat splattered with blood. His eyes were closed and his features had relaxed, as though he were on the point of smiling, while in the middle of his forehead was a round hole that looked, at first glance, as though it had been drawn on and wasn't real. Khaled's colleagues hurried to receive 'Uncle' Madany. Some were crying. They surrounded him for a moment, then fell silent, as though unable to think of what to say. Madany ignored them and rushed towards the bed, an expression on his face that indicated that what he was seeing was disturbing indeed, but quite familiar. In a worried voice, he said, 'Khaled! What's up?'

One of Khaled's colleagues tried to drag him away, but Madany pushed his hand aside roughly and raised his voice again.

'Answer me, Khaled! Get up and speak to me, son!'

Silence reigned for a moment, then Madany cried out, 'Why don't you answer me, Khaled?'

His voice sounded strangely hoarse and he turned around suddenly to face the door, as though he'd decided to leave. After a few steps, however, he stopped and suddenly fell to his knees, screaming, 'Khaled! My son!' and began sobbing loudly, his body shaking hard. Khaled's colleagues gathered round him offering their condolences, and some embraced him. Madany then stopped weeping, and his face took on a hard expression that never again left it, as though what had happened had taken him beyond the range of any expression, as though he'd retreated to a mysterious inner world that absorbed him totally. Hind now arrived and screamed and beat her face, and those present gathered around her and the nurses pulled her aside and, when she began to scratch her face with her nails, held on tight to her hands. Khaled's colleagues took care of everything. They obtained the forensic doctor's report and the burial permit and brought in the undertaker, with whom they settled up, and prepared everything for the funeral. Madany attended the washing of the body and its wrapping in a shroud but remained silent, neither weeping nor saying a word, though from time to time he would bend over Khaled's body and stroke it, running his hands gently over his chest and hands and feet. His look remained unfocused, as though he was unaware of what was going on.

Once the formalities had been completed, the funeral procession exited the Salah El Din mosque next to Qasr El Eini, attended by tens of thousands of the youth of the revolution, the cries ringing out like thunder:

'Sleep, Martyr, and Rest! We'll Do the Rest!'

'Revenge or We Die Like Them!'

Madany hugged the bier hard as they lowered it into the grave, then took a step back and said, in a loud voice, 'Goodbye, Khaled! I'll see you again soon, son.'

Madany failed to turn up for work for about a month, and when he came back Essam Shaalan had been fired and the four-man committee had taken over the running of the factory, so he presented it with a request to be transferred back to the ambulance department, after which he sat in the garage continuously reading the Koran and neither looking around him nor speaking to anyone, totally absorbed in his inner world until such time as a call should come, when he would get into the ambulance and take care of it. Every attempt by his fellows to involve him in conversation failed. He would answer them curtly, or sometimes just look at the person who spoke to him and not reply. Khaled's colleagues took him to the public notary, where he gave power of attorney to the lawyer who would follow up on the complaint against the officer implicated in the murder until it reached the courts. On the eve of the trial, Uncle Madany didn't sleep. He took a day off from the factory and went to the Sayeda Zeinab mosque, where he prayed the dawn prayer, and then to the courthouse, which hadn't yet opened its doors. He sat in the café next door and began drinking coffee and smoking until the lawyer came, along with Hind, Danya, and Khaled's other colleagues, and they took him into the hearing. Madany insisted on sitting next to the prisoners' dock and asked Khaled's colleagues to point out his son's murderer when he arrived. The officers accused of killing demonstrators entered the courtroom and the guards escorted them to the dock. Madany then devoted himself to gazing at the officer who had killed his son. He was young, not more than thirty, and smartly dressed. He had placed sunglasses over his eyes, was well-built, and had a small patch at the front of his head where the hair was thinning. Madany was gripped by a strange urge that made him stare at the killer's right hand. He couldn't tear his eyes away from it. It was a plump hand, its fingers short and stubby. This was the hand that had killed Khaled. This finger was the one that had pulled the trigger, releasing the bullet that had lodged in his head. Couldn't the officer have arrested Khaled instead of killing him? Couldn't the officer's hand have misaimed? Couldn't Khaled have bent forward, so that the bullet struck him in the shoulder or the arm and didn't kill him? Madany continued to gaze at the officer until the hearing ended and the lawyers told him that the case had been postponed. Madany left the courthouse with Hind and shook the hands of the lawyers and his son's colleagues, but Danya insisted on taking him home in her car, saying to Madany in a low voice, 'I need to talk to you about something important.'

Madany got in next to the driver and Danya and Hind sat in the back seat. They didn't exchange a word throughout the trip. Madany had met Danya with the rest of Khaled's colleagues after he was killed. He loved them all, and whenever he saw them, an affectionate expression would appear on his face, though it would soon fade and make way once more for the hard expression that so rarely left it. Once, it occurred to him that Danya's sorrow over Khaled was different. His thoughts took him no further than that, as he'd lost the ability to concentrate on anything. Thoughts crossed his mind like broken fragments, only for him to be brought up sharply against the same fact: his son Khaled was dead. He would never see him again. He'd never rejoice at his graduation, never need the money that he'd saved up to buy him a practice. Khaled would never marry and he'd never rejoice in his children as Madany had so often dreamed of doing. Danya's driver took on a somewhat displeased look as he asked Madany for directions through the lanes of Maasara. Hind answered the driver and in the end they arrived. It was the first time Danya had seen Khaled's house. She looked about her and was swept by such a rush of affection that she almost smiled. This was where Khaled had come from, this poor neighbourhood where small children played barefoot. From this crumbling staircase, from this flat painted with peeling whitewash, Khaled had come to her at Qasr El Eini, full of confidence. How had he put up with all this poverty without being broken or despairing or hating the world? How had he kept up his confident smile and enquiring glances from behind his spectacles when he was leaving such misery behind him? Danya remembered how he'd talked about his father and recalled the humour in his voice as he said, 'Our Lord loves me, Danya. He gave me a poor, decent father instead of a rich, corrupt one.'

Utterly absorbed by her thoughts, she gazed around the flat once again till she heard Uncle Madany saying 'I seek the forgiveness of

God!' He'd finished the noon prayer and now sat down in front of her on the couch, running his long prayer beads through his fingers as though waiting for her to begin.

In a low voice, she said, 'I'm sure you know, sir, that the late Khaled was close to us all. He was very dear to me, specifically.'

Something like a smile appeared on Madany's face, breaking out and then vanishing immediately. Danya told him everything. Strangely, she wasn't embarrassed and she left nothing out. She told him in detail what had occurred at her confrontation with her family and how guilty she would feel whether she testified or not. Madany lit a cigarette and said in decisive tones, 'Of course you shouldn't testify.'

She looked at him in amazement and then he said, 'Khaled wouldn't want you to lose your family. We have enough witnesses. All the lawyers confirmed that we have enough witnesses.'

Hesitantly, she said, 'So you mean, sir . . .'

Uncle Madany interrupted her. 'Don't testify, my dear. I'm Khaled's father and I'm telling you not to testify.'

Danya didn't raise the matter again, but in her heart of hearts was embarrassed that she'd felt relief. She took her leave, and when she asked Uncle Madany if he needed anything, he looked at her, hesitated for a moment, and then pulled her to him and hugged her. To his amazement, she threw herself into his embrace and he felt her arms encircling his back, then became aware that her body was shaking as she wept. He led her to the door of the house and Hind accompanied her to the car, then went back in and asked her father if she should make him lunch. Entering his room, he said he wasn't hungry but would sleep for a little. He threw his body down onto the bed and quickly surrendered to a deep sleep from which he awoke to find himself being gently shaken. Opening his eyes, he found Hind whispering softly, 'There are some people outside who want to see you.'

He took an instant to gather his thoughts, then asked her in a low voice, 'What people?'

'I've never seen them before,' she answered. 'They say they want to see you about Khaled.'

41

Testimony of Saida Ahmad

I was arrested at the 9 March sit-in. As soon as I arrived at the museum, I was met by an officer whose identity I don't know. He told me, 'Hello, Saida! Finally made it? I've been waiting for you.'

The first thing he did was give electric shocks to my belly. They said, talking about us, 'We got them from a brothel.' They poured water over us and gave us electric shocks and cursed us with very disgusting words. Imagine – people spitting on you and cursing you and hitting you on the face with their shoes! They wanted us to be sorry for 25 January. They wanted us to be sorry we'd done the revolution. Then they took us to the place called S28. I thought they'd interrogate us and then send us home. What more could they do to us? They'd done what they'd done at the museum, and it was over.

They put us on buses. Of course, our hands were tied, and they didn't beat us, they dragged us over the ground. When they got us inside S28, they made us stand in a line and fetched empty bottles that really did look like Molotov cocktails and set them all out in front of us. They photographed us with them as though they belonged to us and we girls were prostitutes and the boys were thugs. Imagine – after that they put us on the bus and left us in it till morning. All this happened without anyone interrogating us. It was just them talking dirty. They kept cursing us and saying, 'You're the ones who ruined the country – what do you expect back from the country?'

This was how they started, with different shifts taking over from one another all through the night. Like, four soldiers would go and four more come and beat us. All night long we were beaten. As soon as they brought us in, they said, 'If anyone opens her mouth or says a word in here, we'll bury her in the sand. There's no one to see and no one to hear.' They treated us so badly that all of us left prison messed up psychologically, physically, and in our morale. In the end we got to the military prison. They took us and made us stand in a line. They said, 'Anyone who's got anything on her, hand it in.' They'd taken my bag and my things, but I had my ID card in my pocket, and I had fifty pounds on me for expenses. I handed in my ID and stuff. They'd taken my bag and everything, but it wasn't a problem, I didn't care. Any girl who was wearing anything, anyone who was wearing a gold ring, had to take it off. We handed our mobiles in to them. We handed our ID cards in. We were standing in this line and I swear to God I saw a new picture of deposed president Hosni Mubarak hanging there. I asked the officer, 'Excuse me, sir. What's Mubarak's picture doing here?' and he told me, 'What's it got to do with you?' with insults, of course. He said, 'We love him. You don't want him to be your president any longer but he's our president. What have you got to do with him?'

The officer told us, 'Let's go. You're going to be examined. Which of you has any injuries?' I told him, 'All of us have injuries, sir, from all the beating and the slapping.' They took the first in line, then the second, then the third till it was my turn. I went into a room, a kind of chamber, with a window a metre and a half long on each side – a large window, and the door was open, and the soldiers could see you from the other side. There was a woman there whose job was to search me. I thought she was just going to search me the way we get searched at the airport, like the way they do when they do an ordinary search. I heard her say, 'Take off your clothes.' I took my jacket off. I heard her say, 'Take off all your clothes.' I said, 'Okay but if you don't mind, ma'am, could you close the window and close the door and then I'll be with you.' She told me no and brought someone in who kept hitting me. I was forced to undress against my will.

Of course, the soldiers who were standing at the window were laughing and winking and I was naked, and the people at the door could see me, the ones coming and going and the officers. In other words, they were coming and going and taking a look at me and I was naked. Seriously, I wanted to die that day and I kept saying to myself, 'Some people get heart attacks, why can't I have a heart attack like them and die the same way?' It doesn't matter what I tell you about what happened that day . . . I wish that had been enough for them and we'd been finished with. They took us out. I sat on the ground and they divided us into two groups. One group went into a kind of cell and the other into another cell. They humiliated us. You know what I mean? You wanted to die. I mean you started saying to yourself, 'All those people died, how come my turn never came, how come I didn't die?' A little while after that, the officer came in and he had a master sergeant with him, the one called Ibrahim who was with us at the beginning and gave us the electric shocks. They started cursing us using very foul language, like they were show-ing off, seeing who could curse better. The officer said, 'The married ladies stand on their own and the girls on their own.' I stood on the side where the girls were. The officer said, 'So we can see if you're prostitutes or not.' A girl would get up and go out, first girl, second girl, third, fourth. My turn came. I didn't talk to anyone. I didn't object and I couldn't speak anyway. I heard her tell me, 'Lie down on your back and open your legs so the bey can examine you.' This 'bey' was a lieutenant wearing an olive-green uniform. I took off all my clothes in front of them. It was like a wedding party. A bunch of officers and soldiers were watching us. I said to her, 'Okay, please, if you don't mind, close the window.' The private began giving me electric shocks to my belly and cursing me with disgusting words so I

268

gave in and lay down and opened my legs. A doctor spent about five minutes examining me. What for? How should I know? I was lying down naked with my legs open and the lady was standing at my head. Can you believe it? The doctor left me like that and picked up his mobile phone and started playing with it. I mean, see how humiliating it was? See how far they'll go to humiliate you? They'll break your soul just so you won't think of saying, 'I want this country to have its rights,' so you won't think of going out on a demonstration again or protest against any injustice. After his examination, I heard him saying, 'Get up, then, so you can sign the report that you're a virgin.' It's lucky perhaps that I hadn't got married. If I'd been married, I'd have faced a charge of prostitution. Now, you know, they didn't have the right to do anything, but you couldn't say a word. You just did what you were told to and that was it. I saw that he'd left a large space under the report, and he wanted me to sign leaving, like, several lines. I told him, 'No, if you don't mind, sir, I'll sign right underneath the report.' Right then, it was like, 'Over my dead body!' meaning I felt that if I signed a few lines lower down, something might happen, and I might face a charge. I signed. After this, they put us into two cells. After they'd finished the examinations, they took us in groups, returning each person to her cell. I was sitting there in shock. I couldn't believe they'd do such things. It never occurred to me that they would do that. The shocking thing I want to tell you is that these were commandos who were being trained on us. So the girls who left and went home and didn't say anything were right to do so, given what they'd suffered at their hands. Personally, after what I saw them do, I wouldn't be surprised at anything they did. Listen to the charges they brought against me – attempted aggression against officers of the army during the performance of their duty; second, possession of ten Molotov cocktails; third, possession of knives; four, breaking the curfew. The curfew at that time was two o'clock at night and I was arrested at three thirty in the afternoon. The traffic jams, the cameras, and everyone knew that the traffic was coming and going just like normal. Those were the charges. When I went to the public prosecutor, I said to him, 'Please, sir, I'm a virgin, really. None of that's true.' The public prosecutor was supposed – I expected from him, that he'd ask me, 'Who did all that to you?' He's the one who's supposed to defend me. The public prosecutor came to me and he cursed me and made fun of me and had someone give me an electric shock right in front of him. I really didn't expect anything like that from them. I never expected anything like that would happen. I'd hoped that the public prosecutor would get me my rights. Instead I found he was just like them, and he told me, 'This is a document from the Supreme Council of the Armed Forces accusing all of you of such and such.' Then we went downstairs to the judge. They brought in a few lawyers of their own, just to make a show, you know what I mean? The judge began by reading all the charges and at the end, he said, 'You must have been part of the sit-in at Tahrir because you look so beat up.' I thought, 'Good, in a moment I'll be able to speak and tell him it was the officers from the army who did this to us.' I found myself being pulled out. I held back. The army officers dragged me before the judge. At the same hearing as me, there were boys thrown on the ground who couldn't speak – the public prosecutor would say, 'So-and-so!' and the boy would just about be able to kind of wave his hand because he couldn't speak because he'd been beaten and thrown on the ground. There were people who couldn't walk from the torture who they carried in and put down on the ground so they could appear at the hearing. I personally say to the Egyptian people, 'Save me from their hands! Save me from them!' It's the Egyptian people who will save me from them, it's them who will get me my rights, not a court case, not a judge, not a public prosecutor. None of those will confess or give me my rights. The ones who will give me my rights are the Egyptian people.

Testimony of Nashwa Abd El Aziz

A master sergeant asks me, 'Are you pregnant, girl?'

I told him, 'No, I'm a virgin.' He said, 'Whatever. We'll soon find out whether you are or not.'

We went to the military prison at Hykestep. The first snapshot, as it were, that you see when you get out, inside the prison, is a picture of Mubarak staring at you, just like that, recently hung and brand new. We started going in for examination. They were using two rooms which opened onto one another. One room you went into and waited your turn to be examined, and in the other room there was a woman warder called Azza, who wore a black head-to-toe covering. It had a door that was ajar, not shut. What did the examination consist of, ma'am? It consisted of you undressing completely and standing without any clothes. Just imagine yourself standing stripped of your clothes and every bit of your body in full view and then they ask you, if you have some injury, 'How did you get this injury?' and then you sit down and have to do sit-ups and the window's open and the doors are open and the soldiers are coming and going looking at you – how do you feel? I can tell you it was a terrible feeling. Even up till today I haven't been able to get rid of it. Up till today I'm still really suffering from the whole thing.

The head of the police station came and spoke to me. At that moment there were girls inside, being inspected. He says to me, 'What's the matter?'

I tell him, 'Sir, women aren't supposed to see one another's private parts. They're not supposed to be exposed, in Islam. Anyway, I don't know why you think I'd do something like that.' He told me, 'If you won't let Madame Azza examine you, I'll get a private to do it.'

I went in and I was forced to let her examine me, which at least was better than some man coming and doing it. What would it have been like if a private soldier had come and examined me? Azza examined us so thoroughly she even took our hair down. She took out the pins in our headscarves. But one thing was special. She called out to the soldier when I was naked – can you believe it, I was inside naked and she asked the soldier and the soldier was standing there and we were all naked? – 'Should I take this hairgrip out or not?' The woman really had no feelings. Seriously, she's not human if she brings in a soldier when I'm naked and asks him something or other. She wouldn't even agree to have him wait outside. No, she made him come inside when we were all naked and wearing no clothes. No matter how much I talk about it or describe it, I can't tell you how I felt. I can't describe that feeling but there was fury and huge anger, seriously. I don't understand how they can treat humans worse than they treat animals. I can't put words to it.

After that a doctor came in to see us. He had some sort of blank list in his hand in which he entered each of us and if she was a Miss or a Mrs and everyone went and put her thumbprint to it. After that, the master sergeant called Ibrahim came in and said, 'If any of you says she's a virgin and she isn't, I'll give her an electric shock and beat her,' and he said something else that meant that he'd have sex with her. In those terms, but a bit uglier and I can't say it. We said to him, 'No. Why are you saying that?' And he said, 'Because there's going to be a doctor's examination.' We objected, 'How can anyone do that?' He said, 'It's orders.' After a little while, the private came and took us. He took us into the second room, the one where there were thirteen girls when we were together. He told us, 'The girls go to one side and the married ladies to the other.' There were seven of us young girls on one side. The married ladies were sitting down.

We refused the doctor's examination, but it was done against our will and in the most disrespectful way. I want you to understand. If you weren't examined, you'd be beaten and given electric shocks and they'd still examine you. I went out and saw they were bringing a *bed into the corridor between the two rooms. My turn was number five on the list. The people there were the master sergeant Ibrahim, the doctor, and the female warder. I was afraid, terrified of what was going to happen. Why were they doing this? Of course, the door to the prison was open, so there was nothing to stop anyone coming in when you were like that. Of course, I began to undress, and I got onto the bed and the doctor examined me. After he'd examined me and seen and confirmed that I was a virgin, he wrote a statement that I was a virgin and untouched and intact and I followed him. Put yourself in my place or your children in my place and imagine how you'd react. Think of your sister or yourself or any mother or decent woman who's sitting at home and ask, 'Why do you go down into Tahrir Square?' Imagine your daughter in that situation and ask yourself what you'd do.*

Testimony of Lubna Asaad Muhammad Gad

I am Lubna Asaad Muhammad Gad. I was part of the sit-in in Tahrir Square and then there was the shooting on Wednesday, and I went back to see what was going on and defend my colleagues and try to get them out because I was afraid for them. Suddenly I heard shooting and people trying to shoot anybody who was around. The army used live ammunition. To be honest, I've no idea where I found the courage, but I stood up in front of them and I said, 'Either you shoot me or you bring me my friends!'

Of course, no one paid any attention to me. After the shooting died down, I was going back, and I still hadn't got to in front of the museum when I found I'd been arrested. Some member of the public told me 'The army wants you' and there wasn't just one, there were about fifteen standing round me. One was holding my hands like this, as though he was holding on to a thief or a thug. So I was walking in the middle of a group of men and they took me and delivered me to the general. I really don't know what to say about that general, except God forgive him. Really, I don't know what to say. When he first saw me, he told me, 'Calm down, calm down.' I thought he must be a kind, good man but then I found him suddenly raining slaps on my face, saying, 'See, you're the prostitutes who've filled the country and got the people to march behind you and made out that you aren't scared even though you're really cowards. Look at you, frantic as a chicken now you're in front of us!'

I asked him, 'Why have I been arrested, sir? On what charge? What have I done to you?' Bottom line, I was under arrest. Of course, the electric shocks began on my legs – something called 'the electrics', meaning electric shocks to my legs. Girls, by the way, they'd give electric shocks to on their breasts and on their legs. Something very improper and extremely impolite and with bad words no one ought to have to put up with. I was in a state of nervous collapse at that point and then one of our colleagues, as soon as he saw me, came in and said to the officers, 'Guys, this is my fiancée!', so they took him and beat him up. One of his arms was already broken so they broke the other for him and kept giving him electric shocks and then they took him and put him with the men. When me and the girls went to the military prison, we went into a room with two doors and a window. The doors opened onto one another. We kept pleading with this lady to close the doors and the window, but she wouldn't. The girls would take off all their clothes and get examined and there were cameras outside that were photographing us so that prostitution files could be drawn up against us, but nobody knew about all that, nobody noticed. Not all the girls noticed the cameras outside that were photographing us, so that prostitution files could be drawn up against us, while we were taking off all our clothes. The girls who said they were virgins were examined by someone, we had no idea if he was a doctor or a private or which one of the people they have.

274

42

When Ashraf Wissa recalls what happened that day, he feels astounded. He was in the ground-floor flat with Ikram, two of the boys, and three girls. They were totally surrounded. Outside were more than twenty thugs armed with knives and crude, home-made guns who had actually begun to break into the flat, after first pelting it with stones and breaking the windowpanes. How had he managed to maintain his poise during those critical moments? The only thing that had mattered to him was to protect Ikram and the girls, so he made them go into an inner room while the two boys phoned their colleagues, who quickly arrived from the square, and a terrible battle with the thugs began in which some of the young men were injured and taken to the field hospital. Faced by such fierce resistance, the thugs took to their heels. Three of them were seized and disarmed and then filmed on video as they confessed that they had received money from businessmen to attack the revolutionaries and evict them from the square. They also stated that officers from National Security had given them detailed instructions and a plan of attack for certain identified locations, among them Ashraf Wissa's home, where the revolutionaries held their meetings. During the thugs' confessions, Ashraf had to intervene to prevent the young people from assaulting them. One young man objected, shouting, 'Mr Ashraf, let us teach them a lesson! The bastards came to kill us.'

Ashraf replied firmly, 'You arrested them, so you're responsible for them. To harm them would be dishonourable.'

Ashraf smiled bitterly when he remembered that they'd handed the thugs and the videos of the confessions over to a lieutenant colonel in the military police; they would discover later that he'd let the thugs go. At that point, they still believed that the army supported the revolution, though its true intentions were soon to appear. How did Ashraf survive all these battles? Where did he find such strength and courage? Being an only child, he hadn't even done military service. Now, he found himself in a strange and astonishing world. Sometimes it seemed to him that he was dreaming, or that the original life that he'd known had come to an end and he'd now begun a new one. How had he plunged into all those clashes and faced death without fear when he'd never till then taken part in a single fight? At the Lycée, he'd been a model student, and he couldn't remember causing a single problem or taking part in any hooliganism. Being a Copt, his position had always been delicate. He'd learned to follow the rules and resort to good manners to overcome the aggression of others through friendliness. He'd learned to prefer peace to justice in a society that discriminated on the basis of religion. And being the son of an aristocratic family, he'd always been a polite, well-dressed student who'd arrive with well-ironed clothes and shining shoes. Then he'd graduated from the Lycée and entered the American University, where he lived in a well-off, closed society with little interest in what went on in Egypt. This isolation had left its stamp on his life. With the frustration of his hopes as an actor and the failure of his marriage, feelings of depression and bitterness had grown within him, making him take refuge in hashish. Now, it was as though he'd broken through the shell within which he'd been imprisoned all his life and had launched himself into a new, real life. He felt he'd begun to think, move, and walk in a different way. Even his voice became warmer and more confident. His life was now freighted with missions to fulfil – preparing food and drink, and organising the meetings of the coordinating committee, which were held on the ground floor. He'd never forget the moment he'd experienced on the square when the fall of Mubarak had been announced. He'd never imagined that he'd live to see a million people cheer and shout and weep for joy. He'd hugged Ikram, burst into tears, and begun crying out, 'The martyrs have taken their first rights, Ikram!'

He kept repeating this sentence at the top of his voice, though no one could hear it because the cheering was so loud. Hundreds of thousands were chanting, 'Hold Your Head Up High, You're Egyptian!'

That night, he'd insisted that Ikram drink a bottle of beer in celebration of the victory of the revolution. She danced for him and the two of them passed a night he'd never forget. Mubarak's resignation was, however, swiftly followed by other events. It had been Ashraf's opinion, as well as that of some of the revolutionaries, that they should continue the sit-ins in the squares and elect a Higher Committee from among themselves to oversee the implementation of all the revolution's demands. However, the dominant opinion was that everyone should withdraw and cede authority to the Military Council. Ashraf Wissa and those with him did, however, succeed in having the committee meet weekly at least, in addition to any emergency meetings that Dr Abd El Samad, its head, or three of its members, might call. The morning after Mubarak stepped aside, Magda phoned him and said sarcastically, 'I thought I'd congratulate you on the president's resignation.'

'Thank you!' Ashraf responded.

'I suppose you'll be going back to your normal life now.'

'My life is normal, Magda.'

'I meant, you'll give up the revolution and all that stuff.'

'Once the revolution has realised its goals.'

'What else do you people want?'

'The goal wasn't just to overthrow Mubarak. The whole regime has to change.'

'So you don't want me to come home.'

'You're welcome any time you want to come.'

'I can't possibly come until the house is back to the way it was.'

'It'll never be the way it was.'

'Why?'

'Because the revolution has changed everything.'

Magda was silent for a moment, then said, angrily, 'You've really lost your mind, Ashraf. Goodbye.'

She ended the call but kept up the pressure by various means. A few days later, Butrus and Sarah phoned him. They'd phoned him during the first days of the revolution, and he'd informed them of his participation in the demonstrations. At the time, he'd felt that they hadn't really completely taken things in, but he'd reassured them without going into details. This time, he sensed a certain disapproval in their voices, after the polite expressions of affection. He realised that their mother must have phoned them. She'd always known how to influence them and make them do what she wanted. He had an affectionate conversation with them, then said, in a serious tone of voice, 'Don't worry about me, I'm doing fine. I have to go now because I have a meeting of the coordinating committee.'

After the call, Ashraf felt sad. Why were Butrus and Sarah never convinced by his logic? Why was their mother capable of planting any idea she wanted in their minds? Was it because their mother was the successful model, he the unsuccessful? The thought pained him. Sometimes he sought to excuse them, on the grounds that she was their mother, but then he'd say to himself again, 'Even if their mother's influence over them was once so absolute, aren't they supposed to think independently once they became mature young people?'

A week later, he was surprised to receive a visit from Marina, Magda's niece, who brought with her a large, empty suitcase. Magda had sent her to get her clothes from the house. Naturally, Marina was expecting a scene of high drama befitting the sad occasion on which a wife abandons the home and sends someone to fetch her clothes. She was amazed to find that he accepted the matter straightforwardly and talked to her with affection, as though they were at a picnic. Magda stayed on the phone with her while Marina gathered the clothes, and he noticed that she didn't take all of them. He knew Magda would continue to try to exert influence over him, and he watched what went on calmly. Why didn't Magda bring up the subject of Ikram at all? She fought with him over the revolution but made no reference to Ikram whatsoever. He was living on his own in the flat with her. Wouldn't that make any wife jealous? But he knew her. She was ignoring the subject of Ikram because she considered herself far too superior to compete with a maid, and because talking about Ikram would stir up a lot of gossip in her family, which would be embarrassing for her, and also because she didn't love him enough to be jealous or, to be honest, didn't love him at all. He didn't love her either and couldn't care less about her, as though he'd been freed from her forever, as though she belonged to a past that was behind him and he'd made the decision never to look back. Now he was doing what he wanted and he felt, perhaps for the first time, that his life was useful. Now he had an icon in which he could find solace. Whenever he felt tired or was seized by doubts as to the value of what he was doing, he'd recall the young man who'd fallen before his eyes on the Friday of Rage. He remembered his body stretched out on the shoulders of the demonstrators and his ordinary, cheap clothes. He remembered the jeans, trainers, and shabby black pullover. He remembered his fixed stare into nothingness, as though he'd seen in death something we can't in life. When the army began its attacks on the demonstrators and the violation of girls through the virginity tests occurred, Ashraf had said at the meeting, 'I've always thought that all those generals were Mubarak's children and we shouldn't trust them.'

Then he proposed the formation of a committee to bring a case against the army. Some members threw doubt on the possibility of the idea succeeding, saying, 'The case will be heard by the military

279

courts. Do you really expect the army to condemn itself?'

At this point, Karim, a lawyer, intervened, stressing that it was possible to bring a case before the administrative courts. Ashraf waited until they'd finished, then said, 'The aim of the virginity tests was to break the girls' will and to humiliate them. Unfortunately, the backward traditions of our society make that easier. The point of the case isn't to win it before the military courts but to focus the spotlight on the virginity tests. We have to encourage the girls to talk and rid them of their feelings of shame. If we realise one of these two aims, we will have achieved something.'

The proposal was voted on and won by a large majority. Dear Lord Jesus, who would make proposals to expose the crimes of the Military Council? Ashraf Wissa, hashish-smoker and bit player, who withdrew from the world years ago? In his old life, it would not have been in his power to do, or even to imagine doing, any of the things he was doing now. How had he changed so much? What had made a new man of him? The answer consisted of one word: revolution.

He went on at Ikram until she gave in and took one thousand pounds and gave them to her husband Mansour, telling him that she'd take Shahd to stay with her at Ashraf Bey's because the security situation was bad and she was afraid for herself and her daughter, and that she'd pay him the same sum at the beginning of each month. Ikram told Ashraf that Mansour had snatched the money and looked at it in amazement, saying, 'Thank you very much. Mind you don't forget about me. You know there's no work.'

Ikram would always remember the day she took Shahd with her to Ashraf's. She'd given her little body a hot bath, done her hair in two plaits, and dressed her in the shiny shoes and dress that she'd bought for the Feast, with knee-length white socks, and she carried the case that contained her few clothes and changes of underwear. When she opened the door of the flat, she found a surprise she'd never forget. Ashraf had hung up coloured balloons and bought Shahd chocolate and ice cream and a big, beautiful plastic doll. As soon as he saw Shahd, he hugged her and kissed her. The strange thing is that the child, who wasn't four yet, hung onto his neck even though she'd never seen him before. The sight of the two of them was so moving, Ikram could barely contain herself. It was like a dream. Her family life had become complete in a house where she had started as a maid. That night, when they made love, she gave Ashraf her body without restraint, generously, almost gratefully. And when they were entwined and naked in the dark, she whispered, 'Do you know, I was frightened today?'

'Why?'

'It's true that I've suffered a lot of injustice in my life, but who'd believe that Our Lord would compensate me with so much? You're too much for me, Ashraf Bey. I'm afraid Our Lord will take all this happiness from me and I'll go back to being miserable. You know, if that happens, I'd rather die.'

He was about to say something but instead hugged her and kissed her. He no longer needed to say anything, and the heat of his body confirmed to her that he'd always be with her. Each night, they went to sleep holding one another. She would wake at seven and slip quietly out of bed. She'd wake Shahd, give her her breakfast, and then take her to the nearby nursery school and come back to clean up the centre on the ground floor, and then the flat. She'd bought two pairs of gloves, at Ashraf's request, to protect her hands from getting wrinkled when she was cleaning. And after cleaning up, she'd go upstairs to the flat, take a bath, and then get dressed and wake him. She'd look at him as he was sleeping, then touch his forehead and lips and kiss him gently, and he'd open his eyes and smile. He'd go into the bathroom while she made breakfast. After coffee and his morning joint, he'd go down with her to the centre and busy himself all day with the affairs of the square.

She'd withdraw at noon to get Shahd from the nursery school and bring her back home, and he'd come back in the evening and find her waiting for him, with Shahd asleep in her room. They'd have dinner and perhaps watch television. She took pleasure in making herself up for him – putting mascara on her eyelashes because he loved mascara and rubbing cream into her feet and hands because he loved her to be smooth. They'd sleep together like a married couple. Now, he made love to her in a different way. The tense, sinful stealth was gone, to be replaced by the peace of mind of a man and wife who slept together without embarrassment or fear, with sure deliberation, tasting the pleasure slowly and with absorption.

One day, when Ikram had gone to fetch Shahd from the nursery school and Ashraf was on his own on the ground floor, he heard a sudden knocking on the door. He opened it and found two of his neighbours who lived in his block of flats – an elderly Copt called Nessim who lived alone, following the death of his wife, and the emigration of his children to America, on the top floor, and a Muslim in his fifties called Ahmad Dendarawi who worked for the Exhibitions Organisation. They exchanged the usual greetings, and then the men began gazing at the revolutionary posters on the wall and the beds and the oxygen cylinders and the medical equipment. In the tone of one who has prepared what he is going to say beforehand, Dendarawi said, 'Ashraf Bey, we've known one another all our lives, and we all love and respect you.'

Ashraf smiled and said, 'Thank you very much. I too have always held you in the highest regard.'

With an unctuous smile, Nessim now said, 'Ashraf Bey Wissa is the scion of noble parents. He's always been taken as an example of taste and morals.'

There was silence for a few moments, and Nessim looked at Dendarawi as though to urge him on. 'As Your Excellency knows,' the latter then said, 'we left the building because of the demonstrations, the gas, the beatings, and the general mess. We went to stay with our relatives. Some of us stayed in hotels. More nuisance. Now we've come back and we want to relax.'

In support, Nessim added, 'To be able to relax in his own home is the least of a man's rights.'

Ashraf nodded in understanding, having now begun to guess the purpose of the visit. Dendarawi went on, 'Your Excellency has, of course, the right to be against President Mubarak, even if lots of people think he didn't deserve what we did to him.'

'Which reminds me, Ashraf Bey,' Nessim interrupted, 'did President Mubarak harm Your Excellency in any way?'

Ashraf replied vehemently, 'Mubarak harmed the whole country and even now hasn't been brought to account. He has to be tried for the crimes he committed against the people.'

Dendarawi faked a smile and said, 'You mean to say President Mubarak committed crimes?'

Ashraf made an effort to control himself and said, furiously, 'You want me to tell you Mubarak's crimes?'

'Whatever he did,' Nessim said, 'we ought to thank him for keeping our country safe and protecting it from war.'

Suddenly, Ashraf became aware of the absurdity of the conversation. In a loud voice, he said, 'Look, Mubarak isn't what we're talking about. Is there any service I can do you?'

Dendarawi smiled in annoyance, then looked at his companion as though making sure of his support and said, 'Your Excellency has opened the ground floor to the young people from Tahrir. Naturally, that exposes us all to danger. A battle could take place at any moment inside the building. Gas could be thrown or bullets fired. I have my son living with me and he has children. I don't believe Your Excellency would be happy to see any of us harmed.'

'My situation is difficult too, Ashraf Bey,' Nessim said, in emotional tones, 'as Your Excellency knows. I'm an old man and sick and living on my own. In other words, I'm expecting the angel of death at any moment,' which Dendarawi followed with, 'God give you health, Uncle Nessim!'

Ashraf suddenly felt distaste for the two men. Silence reigned, but Dendarawi went on in a low voice, to impress upon him the seriousness of the situation, 'Anyway, it's not just the residents who are affected. The shop owners are very upset and wanted to meet you, but when they learned we were going to talk to Your Excellency, they said, "We'll leave it to you."'

'There are shop owners who've been affected?'

'All of them, Ashraf Bey. The owners of the bakery and the furniture showroom, even the news vendor can't work. The poor chaps' livelihood is at a standstill. And of course, the presence of the young people from Tahrir exposes both them and us to danger. To be honest, the shop owners had made up their minds to stop the young people from entering the building but, thank God, we were able to persuade them to behave sensibly.'

'Don't persuade anyone!' Ashraf said angrily. 'Let anyone who wants to stop the young people try and see what's coming to him!'

There was silence again. Then Ashraf resumed and said, trying to master his anger, 'Look, fellows. You've been my neighbours and friends for ages. But the fact is, I'm the owner of the building and I have the right to do with it as I want.'

'So long as no harm results to the residents,' said Dendarawi, while Nessim took refuge in silence. Ashraf responded by saying, 'So you're concerned about harm to the residents but not about harm to the whole country? I have a question, Dendarawi. Didn't the young people who were killed by bullets in the square have parents who were as afraid for them as you are for your children?'

'God have mercy on the people who were killed in the square, but nobody told them to demonstrate.'

'The young people died defending my rights and yours.'

'I never asked anyone to demonstrate.'

'You have a right to your opinion, of course, but unfortunately I won't be able to comply with your request.'

'Meaning what?'

'Meaning that this centre belongs to the young people of the revolution and no one can keep them out.'

'In that case, Your Excellency must bear responsibility for any harm that befalls the residents,' Dendarawi said, angrily.

Ashraf stood, signalling the end of the meeting, and said, 'Thank you for coming.'

Dendarawi asked, 'So what are we to tell the shop owners?'

'Tell them what I told you,' replied Ashraf, decisively.

The two residents stood up, looking furious, and made their way towards the door. Suddenly, Dendarawi said in a loud voice, 'By the way, give our best to Mrs Ikram.'

His tone carried an impertinent connotation, so Ashraf responded contemptuously, holding the door open as he did so, as though to hurry them out, 'I shall do that. I shall convey your greetings to Mrs Ikram. She's getting the girl from the nursery school and then she'll make food for the young people in the square.'

Ashraf remained upset by this visit for the rest of the day and, at night, when he finally found refuge in bed with Ikram, he told her what had happened. She listened and said, 'What are you going to do?'

'Nothing at all. I'm the owner of the building. Let them do their worst.'

'You think they're acting alone?'

'No, of course not. Magda is with them and for sure they tell her everything.'

'I'm afraid,' she whispered.

Ashraf said, 'Ikram, please. I told you not to be afraid. I'm with the revolution and I'm living with you in the sight of everyone. If anyone doesn't like that, they can go to hell.'

She wiggled her body over in the bed and clung to him so that he could feel her warmth, then hugged him in the dark and whispered, 'Okay. Don't get upset. I won't be afraid.'

The next day, they resumed their life as normal. Ikram woke him, he took a bath, dressed, and ate breakfast. Then, as he sat in his study smoking his morning joint over a cup of coffee, Ikram entered, looking flustered. He looked at her smilingly and asked, 'What's up, Ikram? Is there something going on?'

'There's a priest outside to see you,' she said, in a low voice.

43

Dear Mazen,

I haven't seen you for a whole week, but you've been with me all the time. When I heard about the hideous crime the army committed against those girls, I couldn't believe it at first, but then, unfortunately, it was confirmed. Can you believe it? Seventeen girls stripped completely naked in front of officers and soldiers? Each one of them forced to open her legs so that the officer – the 'Bey' – could examine them while the soldiers looked at her naked body and exchanged comments and jokes? All that humiliation as punishment for the girls' asking for justice and freedom for Egyptians? I cried for a long time, Mazen, as I imagined myself in the same place as any one of them. Then I remembered your words. I remembered the revolutionary covenant that we took upon ourselves in the name of the martyrs. I remembered that the old regime wouldn't give up easily and that it would go to extremes in committing hideous crimes. They want to break us but they will not succeed. The following day, I went to the school after not having slept all night. I finished my classes and set off for the centre, at Mr Ashraf's house, where we held an expanded meeting that included our colleagues from Enough!, April 6, the Alliance, the National Association, and the Revolutionary Socialists, as well as Mr Ashraf, naturally. The man constantly dazzles us with his courage, wisdom, and devotion to the revolution. He's the one who proposed bringing a case against the army, an idea that was carried by a large majority. A committee was formed, and I was chosen as a member, at my request. There are three of us on the committee – me, Asmahan Ali, and the lawyer Karim Ahmad. Our task was to meet with the virginity test victims and convince them to bring a case against the army. We were able to get hold of the telephone numbers of ten out of the seventeen girls and we're still trying to get the numbers of the rest. The sad surprise was that the girls, once their honour had been violated, no longer wanted anything. Most of them refused to take part in the case. One of them, when I suggested the idea of bringing a case, gave the receiver to her mother, who asked me, 'What do you want with her? Isn't it enough that she went along with you till what happened happened! You want to make her more of an object of scandal than she already is? Don't ever phone here again!'

All the girls more or less gave the same answer: 'We will not bring a case. The country belongs to the army and no one will ever win us back our rights.'

I lost my temper with one of them and told her, 'What happened to you could have happened to me or any girl from the revolution. By withdrawing, you're giving them what they want.'

When I heard her crying over the phone, I controlled myself and apologised.

Only one girl, called Saida, was responsive to us and another, Nashwa, asked for time to think, which means that she may join us. Saida said her father had encouraged her to bring a case for restitution. The lawyer, Karim, believed if we brought one case, for this one girl, we could get restitution for all the girls, and they would probably join us in the case later on. The next day, the four of us – Asmahan, Karim, Saida, and I – met. We went to the public notary's office and Saida gave Karim power of attorney. After that, we had no choice but to go to the Military Court building, S28, to file an official report. Imagine! Saida collapsed at the last minute and was unable to enter the building. Imagine, that a woman can be so abused as to be literally incapable of entering the building in which the abuse took place, even though she had come with us to present a complaint! We *left her outside with Asmahan and I went in with Karim. We were met by a captain. When Karim presented him with the complaint, he asked to see Karim's lawyer's ID and he gave it to him. The captain read the complaint, then said, sarcastically, 'This Miss Saida has a great imagination. She'd make a good writer of soap operas. It's inconceivable that such things could have happened here.'*

I told him, 'These things didn't happen just to Saida. They happened to seventeen girls, and their honour was violated here and at the military prison.'

The officer looked and me and said, 'Who are you?'

'I'm Saida's friend.'

'You don't have the standing to speak.'

I tried to object, but he said, 'Silence, girl!'

'Don't call me "girl"!'

'I can have you imprisoned immediately on a charge of being disrespectful to the office of the prosecutor. Explain it to her, Mr Lawyer.'

Karim persuaded me to stay silent so that things wouldn't get out of hand and the officer insisted on my leaving the room, so I left. The officer officially received the complaint from Karim and in a few days we'll know the date for the opening of the investigation. We left and met up with Saida and Asmahan. Now we have a new problem, on which the fate of the whole case will depend. We have to have witnesses. When we thought about it, we found that those who witnessed the incident were either military personnel, and they of course wouldn't testify for us, or the girls themselves, and most of them were, as I told you, broken psychologically and refusing even to speak of what happened. I will not despair, though, as you have taught me, Mazen. I'll keep working with the girls to convince them to testify. Our aim in this case isn't to hold the criminals who violated the girls' honour to account. We're not so naive as to believe that the military courts will condemn the army. Our goal, as Mr Ashraf said, is to turn the spotlight on the case and, at the same time, raise the morale of the girls and free them of their feelings of shame. Our revolution continues and will prevail, as you have taught me. I love you.

    Asmaa

44

Uncle Madany went into the living room and found visitors – Sheikh Shamel accompanied by a fiftyish man, bald apart from a circular ring of hair that had been dyed black, who was carrying a medium-sized Samsonite case. He was wearing a smart black suit and a black tie (in sign of mourning) over a white shirt. Madany recognised Sheikh Shamel from the television and had listened to his lessons on the Right Path channel more than once. Madany shook hands with them and invited them into the guest parlour, where Hind asked them what they would like to drink and Sheikh Shamel asked for hot mint tea while the other man asked for a cup of coffee. The parlour was a cramped little room that was kept locked except for special occasions, and it contained a suite consisting of four armchairs and a sofa in feeble imitation of Louis Seize style. In the middle of the room was a table topped with white fake marble on which stood a blue porcelain *bonbonnière*. On the walls were Koranic verses, sayings of the Prophet, and a photograph of the Noble Kaaba. Madany's reception of the two guests wasn't effusive. He still hadn't woken up completely and his mind was exhausted from the trip to the courthouse. At the same time, he found the visit strange, and this feeling was converted into a kind of stand-offishness and indifference. He welcomed them brusquely, then fell silent, gazing at them as though demanding an explanation for their visit. Sheikh Shamel apologised that the visit was so sudden. Madany muttered something curt. The sheikh looked at the man who was with him as though seeking his permission, then said to Madany, 'Hagg Madany, let me introduce you to our worthy friend Colonel Hassan Bazaraa from public relations at the Ministry of Interior, one of the most knowledgeable and observant of our officers when it comes to our religion (we give precedence over God to none!).'

The colonel looked at the floor, as though the praise embarrassed him, while Madany continued to look at them without comment. Silence reigned for a moment, then Sheikh Shamel began to speak, thanking God and praising Him, calling for blessings on God's prophet, most noble of creatures, and then saying that he had come first to perform his duty of offering condolences on the death of the late Khaled, who he thought must be a martyr in God's eyes, God willing. Hind brought the coffee and the mint tea but Madany gave her a look that she understood, and she left the room. The colonel set about drinking his coffee, never removing his powerful gaze from Madany's face, while Sheikh Shamel uttered the words 'In the Name of God, the Merciful, the Compassionate,' took a sip of mint tea, and then resumed, saying that he knew that nothing in this world hurt so much as the loss of a son and cited the example of the noble prophet (God bless him and grant him peace), who, even though he was the best of God's creation and the most patient of them in adversity, had wept when his only son, Ibrahim, had died.

Madany continued to stare silently at Sheikh Shamel, until the latter said, 'You are now, Brother Madany, the one who seeks vengeance in a blood feud, and religion allows you the right of reprisal, if the killing was deliberate.'

'The killing was deliberate,' Madany said.

'Have you ascertained that for sure?'

'The companions of the late Khaled will all testify in court that the officer killed him deliberately.'

'How do you know that the officer charged is the killer?'

'All of them recognised him and affirmed that the officer Heisam El Meligi killed Khaled in front of their eyes.'

Sheikh Shamel looked down, uttered the words 'I ask God for His forgiveness' in apparent regret, and then raised his head and said, 'Brother Madany, the one true religion allows you the right of retribution but God, Glorious and Mighty, has commanded us to grant pardon whenever possible.'

Madany was about to say something, but Sheikh Shamel, smiling, raised his voice and said, 'Praise the noblest of creatures!'

Madany muttered the formula of praise, and Sheikh Shamel continued in a calm voice, 'Hear me out, then either accept or reject what I say, as you wish. By God, who has my soul in His hand, I mean only good! I have undertaken this initiative of my own accord and I have spoken with the leading officials of the state, and our goal, God willing, is to defuse the discord into which we, as brother Muslims, have fallen. Thanks be to God, He has blessed my humble efforts and I have convinced those officials to set aside a large sum of money for the families of the victims as legal blood money. I am now, as you see, visiting the victims' families, one by one, with my brother Colonel Hassan, my sole goal in making this effort being to acquire the approval of God, Glorious and Mighty, and of his noble messenger.'

Madany remained unchanged, staring at the two of them with a hard expression and a vacant look. The sheikh resumed, 'Think well, Brother Madany. Your son has met his end and he would in any case have died, even if he had taken no part in this discord. Has not Our Lord, Great and Glorious, said, in the chapter of the Koran titled "The Ramparts", "To every nation a time; when their time comes they shall not delay it by a single hour nor advance it"? (God has spoken truly!)

'Your late son went to his maker at his determined time, at the instant at which his term came to an end. Neither you nor I nor any mortal whosoever is capable of keeping death from a person once his ordained time has come. If the late Khaled hadn't been killed, he would have died in an accident, or he would have contracted a fatal disease, or even died in his bed. You, Brother Madany, are a believer, and the believer is astute and intelligent. I see you have a daughter, a beautiful young woman who will marry, God willing, and need money for expenses, and you owe her the duty of assuring her future, God willing.'

Madany remained silent, and Sheikh Shamel said once more, 'Accept the blood money, Brother Madany! Be merciful, that God may be merciful to you on the Day of Resurrection, God willing.'

'What blood money?' said Madany.

'Blood money is a sum set by the One True Religion to be paid by the family of the killer to the family of the one killed in return for their exempting them from retribution.'

Madany looked at the two men and asked in a low voice, 'And how much is the sum?'

Relief appeared on Sheikh Shamel's face and he said, 'In the days of the Prophet (God bless him and grant him peace!) the blood money set by law was a hundred camels. We calculate that to be – God willing – at today's prices, the equivalent of half a million pounds.'

Madany looked at the colonel and asked him, 'And what is required of me in return for the blood money?'

In his powerful voice, the colonel replied, 'You are required to withdraw the complaint made in your name. You can leave the rest to us.'

Madany said nothing, and the colonel continued, fervently, 'Listen to what I say, Hagg Madany. The living last longer than the dead. Your son is with Our Lord in Heaven, God willing. What will you gain if the officer is condemned to death or life in prison? Common sense says you should take the blood money.'

Sheikh Shamel said, 'By accepting the blood money, Brother Madany, you will become a winner in this world and the next, God willing. You will have been merciful, and God loves mercy, and you will have acquired a goodly sum of money that will be of help to you in bearing the burdens of this life.'

Madany kept looking at him and was about to say something but thought better of it and returned to his silence. At this point, the colonel lifted the case off the ground and placed it on his knees. Then he opened it and said, in a loud voice, 'Let's get it over with. We come prepared, Brother Madany, and "the best acts of piety are those that are done swiftly", as the Prophet said. Take the money and take as much time as you like to count it. When you're sure it's correct, I'll give you the complaint withdrawal to sign.'

45

The phone call was unexpected, curt, and strange. It didn't come from one of the National Security officers, who were known to Essam Shaalan. It came from the Apparatus. The officer introduced himself, told Essam that he wanted to see him, and gave him the address of a villa in Zamalek. Then, in a tone of finality, he said, 'I shall be waiting for you tomorrow at 10 a.m.'

Essam spent that night sitting on the balcony, drinking and thinking. Why would Apparatus officials want to meet with him? He knew that the Apparatus was more important than National Security. A junior officer in the Apparatus wielded greater influence than many a general. But wasn't that before Mubarak's fall? Did the Apparatus still enjoy its old influence? And, in addition, what did they want from him? They must surely be in need of him in these difficult circumstances. Would they bestow a new position on him? Naturally, he'd accept any position they offered, though his preference would be to return to his job at the factory. He'd like them to make him manager again, if only for a week, so that he could take revenge on the workers who'd insulted him and would have beaten him up if it weren't for the protection of the army. He knew each of them by name and would wreak vengeance on them all. Though even if his new position were far from the factory, he'd still be able, using the influence of the Apparatus, to take revenge on that rabble. An idea occurred to him that amazed him at first but that he quickly put into action. He set about writing down on a piece of paper the names of the workers who'd insulted him. There were eight of them. It hadn't been enough for them just to shout slogans against him; they'd insulted him to his face. He'd preserved their names on the piece of paper. Under the influence of the liquor, he felt his anger rising. 'I'll show you what you get for humiliating me, you slaves and sons of slaves! You'll understand in the end, after you've paid a heavy price, that revolution isn't made for you and you aren't made for revolution. Your fate is the whip, as it has been for your ancestors for centuries.' He didn't try to sleep as he knew he wouldn't be able to. As soon as the sun rose, he took a quick shower, shaved carefully, ate a quick breakfast, then drank a number of cups of coffee laced with a little whisky, a few drops of which cleared his mind and relaxed him. His new driver was a young man in his twenties whom the doorkeeper of his building had found for him. He found the address of the villa in Zamalek easily. At the gate, he was subjected to a minute inspection, for which the young officer apologised after he finished by saying, 'Please excuse the inconvenience. You'll take the circumstances into consideration, I'm sure, sir.'

Essam nodded understandingly. They led him to an office in which sat a man of roughly his age whom he guessed to be a general. He was aware that, in the Apparatus, they didn't display signs with the officers' names on and that they most probably used assumed names. The general received him affably, shook his hand with a smile, invited him to sit, and said jovially, 'What will you drink, Essam Bey?'

Essam asked for Turkish coffee without sugar, amazed to find that the general seemed to be in such a good mood, as though the state of the country was quite normal. A friendly silence prevailed, the general giving the impression that he was preparing himself to speak, though it was Essam who said, suddenly, 'God protect Egypt, sir!'

The general looked at him with a friendly expression and said, 'Thank God, the Lord has extended His protection.'

'The credit is all yours, sir!'

'Everything is according to God's will.'

'I would dearly hope, sir, that you will bring all the conspirators who have got the people involved in this to trial!'

The general smiled and said, 'Look, we know them by name. Every one of them will get his turn. I swear to God Almighty, not one will escape!'

The general leant back in his armchair, seemingly having decided to end this conversation and to turn to another topic.

'Listen, Essam Bey,' he said. 'All of us in the Apparatus are aware of your patriotism and your loyalty. Unfortunately, the current situation required you to leave your position, but don't let that worry you. Soon, God willing, we'll have need of your help in another appropriate position.'

'I am at the service of the state at any time, sir.'

'That's just what we'd expect of you, Chief Engineer Essam.'

Essam felt confused. Things suddenly seemed unclear. The general was talking about a post in the future. So why had they summoned him? He remembered the piece of paper in his pocket and the names of the workers whom he wished to punish. He had a headache from lack of sleep, alcohol, and tension. The general gazed at the ceiling for a few moments and seemed to be arranging his thoughts. Then he said, in friendly tones, 'The fact is, I invited you because I want to talk to you about a certain subject.'

'At your service, sir.'

'By the way, we're almost the same age. I'd like you to think of me as your younger brother.'

'That would be an honour, sir.'

'The subject is Madame Nourhan. She's asked you for a divorce and waived all her material rights. I'd like the divorce to take place quietly and respectably, and at the earliest opportunity.'

Essam stared at the officer's face and it took a few moments for the surprise to sink in. Then, trying to hide his anger, he said, 'Did Nourhan contact you, sir?'

'No.'

Essam smiled with irritation and said, 'I imagine you will agree with me, sir, that my divorce from Nourhan is a personal matter.'

'I have orders from the head of the Apparatus to see the divorce goes through. His Excellency has asked me to talk to you friend to friend. Tomorrow morning, God willing, you will honour me with your presence here and bring with you the common-law marriage contract. Madame Nourhan will be present. You will swear before her that she's divorced, we will tear up the contract, and everyone will go their own way.'

'What does His Excellency the head of the Apparatus have to do with divorces and marriages?'

'My job is to carry out His Excellency's orders, not discuss them.'

'I reject this intervention in my personal life.'

'Look, Essam. If you really think of me as a brother, I'd advise you to divorce Nourhan so as to avoid difficulties you don't need,' said the general, his face taking on a grim expression, as though the earlier friendliness had been nothing but a mask.

In a loud voice, Essam said, 'If Your Excellency is threatening me, I refuse to accept your threats.'

Angrily, the general shouted, 'Drop the commie talk because it'll only hurt you. We protect you and we can take that protection away at any time.'

'You protect me from what?'

The general sighed, as though his patience had run out, took hold of a file bulging with papers that was on his desk, and held it out to Essam, saying, 'It seems the drink has affected your memory.'

'I object to Your Excellency's choice of words!' said Essam, in a low voice, but the general went on as though he hadn't heard him. 'Read! These are copies of the reports on you by the Office of the

Administrative Auditor and the Central Accounts Apparatus. We can send them to the prosecutor general's office tomorrow morning and you will be tried and imprisoned. If that happens, you will have no one to blame but yourself.'

46

Dear Asmaa,

The criminal virginity tests caused me sadness beyond description. How could an Egyptian officer, or soldier, do that to the girls? How could he violate them with such brutality and then return with a clear conscience to his home and children? I understand that the generals are defending the interests of the regime of which they are a part and I understand that the military regime forces people to carry out orders, but why make such a vicious example of girls who were utterly helpless? A friend, whose brother is an officer, told me that the army command feeds the troops and the officers the idea that the revolution is a conspiracy and that the revolutionaries are agents who take money to cause chaos and destroy the country. The generals of the Military Council denied having carried out this crime, and then one of them admitted to CNN that virginity tests are a tradition in the army when any girl is arrested so that she can't claim afterwards that anyone assaulted her. A stupid and illogical thing to say. I don't want to hate the army because it's the people's army, not the dictator's. I always remember the image of Captain Maged from the police who defended the young people of the revolution when the thugs attacked them at the Battle of the Camel. We no longer have a choice, Asmaa. All we can do is keep up the battle out of respect for the thousands who sacrificed themselves for the revolution – the ones who died and the ones who lost an eye or were crippled.

The workers threw Essam Shaalan out. I regard his expulsion as a true victory for them but I can't rejoice over it as they do. My relationship with Essam is complicated, as I told you. I'm against him as a manager but I love him because he was my father's friend. We have taken over the entire management of the factory and written the undertaking; we, the members of the four-man committee, signed it and deposited it with the military police. We have undertaken to keep the factory safe and to manage it and deliver the profits to the owners after deduction of the workers' dividends. Do you remember your question about the people who would watch the revolution from the balconies without joining in? We have people like them in the factory too – a group of the workers and administrative staff that is by no means, unfortunately, small. They watched events without getting involved on either side. They were sure the Italian administration would win. When we did, they were completely confused. Many of them stayed away from the factory, waiting to see how things turned out. After about a week, they delegated one of the staff to come to me. He's called Uncle Fahmi and he's one of the factory's longest-standing employees. He said to me, 'Listen to me, Engineer Mazen, sir. I and lots of my colleagues don't understand who the factory belongs to now.'

I explained to him what he already knew very well about the new situation, and he said, 'Look, you're my son's age. To be honest, we don't care for the revolution and all that stuff. We just want to earn a living and raise our children.'

'The revolution came about so that you could earn a living and raise your children.'

'Listen to what I'm saying. Suppose we meet with you now as the new management and after a month or two the owner of the factory returns and takes it back and throws us out. If that happens, nobody will be able to do anything for us.'

I was going to argue with him but when I looked at his fearful face, I realised that there was no point in talking. I told him, 'Okay, Uncle Fahmi. I'll sort the matter out.'

I went back to the military police commander and asked him for a written statement from Fabio, the owners' representative, recognising the four-man committee. I told him, 'It won't be possible for us to carry out our undertaking without a clear statement from the owners' representative, to reassure the workers and staff, so that they go back to work.'

He asked me to give him a day's delay and, indeed, I went to his office the next day and found a statement in Arabic announcing that the owners' representative recognised the four-man committee as the management of the factory. I felt moved as I read the statement. It was a moment when I could see the victory of the revolution. I went back to the factory and made lots of copies and put them up everywhere. At that moment, the hesitaters and the doubters joined us. Some of the revolutionary workers directed harsh comments at them but I stopped them from doing them any harm. The revolution has to take from each according to his capacity – my father, God rest his soul, often used to say this in front of me, and here I am, alive, and understanding its importance. My father is always with me. I wish he could have lived to see the victory of the revolution, so that he could be sure that the sacrifices that he made during his life weren't in vain. We have taken the factory over completely. It's impossible for me to describe to you the workers' discipline and their enthusiasm. They're wonderful. The shifts change at precisely the right time. We are going to take over sales and will give the workers their dividends as specified in the contract and then send the revenue to the owners. The engineers have made detailed suggestions for putting the non-operational furnaces back into service and, according to studies, if we keep going this way, the factory will realise profits never seen during the period of Italian management. I regard the factory as a small-scale model of Egypt as a whole. Everything has changed with the revolution and it can't go back to being what it was. The factory has never been in better condition. Of course, there are a few problems.

Yesterday, a lorry carrying cement was attacked after it left the factory. Thugs stopped it and fired in the air, made the driver and his mate get out, and took the lorry with its load somewhere unknown. I told one of the lawyers from Legal Affairs to draw up a police report on the incident. The detective became enthusiastic and promised to work hard to arrest the thieves. When I phoned the officer to thank him, he told me, 'Just doing my duty. Egypt belongs to all of us and we won't permit chaos.'

I apologise, Asmaa, for not being with you. I live at the factory. I sleep in an empty rest house that the Italian management used to use to put up its foreign experts. I only go to my flat in the centre of town every two or three days. I want to see you, of course, but you understand the situation better than anyone. You too are waging a battle in defence of the revolution. My greetings and good wishes to all the colleagues. I miss you very much. I will see you soon, God willing.

Smile, my darling. When I see your smile (even in my imagination), I feel certain that we shall win.

Goodbye, most beautiful of people.

Mazen

47

Ashraf knew Priest Matthias and liked him. He was a slight, energetic man whose age was impossible to fix precisely because he had preserved an extraordinary liveliness. Ashraf went up to him and greeted him, Ikram vanishing into the interior of the flat, and opened the door to the reception room for him, inviting him to sit down. The priest smiled and said, 'Thank you, but I don't have time.'

Ashraf looked at him in surprise as the man continued, 'I know you're fond of me and I'm fond of you. Do you trust me, Ashraf?'

'Of course.'

'In other words, if I were to ask something of you, you'd trust that it was for the best?'

'For sure.'

Father Matthias smiled and said, 'Then you have to get dressed and come with me.'

'Where?'

'If you trust me, don't ask. We are going to do good.'

Ashraf stood there hesitating, but Father Matthias shoved him with childish good humour, saying, 'Go and get dressed and don't hold us up!'

Ashraf went in and found Ikram making the bed in his room. He felt that she was waiting for him. While he was changing his clothes, he said, 'I'm going on an errand with Father Matthias.'

'Do you know him?'

Ashraf said, as he dressed, 'I've known him for ages. There are lots of priests I wouldn't trust, but Matthias is different. To be honest, I like him and trust him.'

'That's why they sent him,' she said simply.

He looked at her and asked, 'Who?'

'Don't you understand why he's here?'

'He refused to tell me.'

'He's going to try and reconcile you with Madame Magda.'

Ashraf didn't reply. In his heart, he knew Ikram was right. She was always amazing him with her ability to read a situation. A single word would pop out from her, and the truth would be laid bare at one go. He brushed his hair and put on his favourite perfume, Pino Silvestre, while Ikram continued to stand next to the door. Feeling she was a bit sad, he hugged her and whispered in her ear, 'You have to remember that I love you and can't do without you. Okay?'

She tried to smile and her beautiful face took on a miserable and affecting expression. He gave her a quick kiss on her lips, then quickly left. He got into the car with Matthias and they spoke of general matters. Ashraf was not surprised when Matthias steered the car onto Salah Salem Road, going in the direction of Heliopolis, then parked it in front of the block of flats where Magda's family lived in Triomphe Square. They entered the building and got into the lift without speaking. Ashraf was driven by an insistent desire to take things to their conclusion. He wanted to face Magda and her family once and for all. What annoyed him most was the way Magda continued to conspire behind his back and mobilise people against him while playing the role of the victim. 'I'm ready for the show-down, Madame Magda,' he thought to himself. 'Do your worst!'

In the spacious living room, he found three people sitting, as in a court. In the armchair next to the window sat his mother-in-law, Madame Wasima, with Magda to her right and Magda's brother Amir to her left. Ashraf rushed over to his mother-in-law and shook and kissed her hand. He liked her, despite his problems with her daughter – an aristocratic lady of over eighty, good-natured, refined, and mild-mannered. When she got angry, she would give vent to her ire in French. Amir, as usual, was as smartly dressed as a film star; his hair was dyed black apart from a few white streaks left at the sides, and he wore a diaphanous patterned silk shirt and a chain of pure gold that disappeared beneath the thick white hair of his chest, while a diamond ring perched on his small hand. Amir was Magda's only brother and owned the Barsoum jewellery shop on Mosque Square. He was a year younger than Ashraf and they'd never liked one another. To Ashraf, he was a boorish, arrogant character who made an ostentatious show of his wealth, and he was on the list of those to whom Ashraf was going to send a copy of his book, to shock him out of his complacency and show him the truth. At that moment, Ashraf wished he had a joint on him to calm his nerves. He didn't shake hands with Amir and Magda but greeted them with a nod of the head. Amir responded with a gesture of his hand, and Magda ignored his greeting altogether. Ashraf noticed that she'd put on a white silk dress that she'd bought in Paris and had done her hair in ringlets, one of which she'd left dangling over her forehead, and painted her fingernails and toenails deep red. She was in full make-up but had adopted the look of the estranged wife whose dignity has been cruelly abused and who expects to have her proper standing restored immediately. Ashraf ignored her and began talking with Madame Wasima, who seemed to be caught between her genuine desire to welcome him and her sense of duty towards her daughter. Ashraf asked after her health. This was a favourite topic on which she liked to talk at length, reviewing first her medical condition and the types of medicine she was taking, then drawing comparisons between the bone-setters of yore and medicine these days, now that it had been turned into a business. An angry look appeared on Magda's face and she shot her mother a glance full of significance, so the latter cut her speech short and said, 'We must thank Father Matthias for bringing Ashraf to us. Have you decided not to talk to us, Ashraf?'

This was the signal to begin, and Amir now said, to stake out a place on the battlefield, 'To be honest, Ashraf, Magda's very angry with you.'

Ashraf decided not to lose his temper. He lit a cigarette and said, calmly, 'The truth of the matter, Amir, is that I'm not the cause of the problem. Magda left the house and didn't come back. It was her decision.'

'It never occurred to you to come and make up with her?'

'I'd make up with her if it was I who'd upset her.'

Magda spoke for the first time and said, 'Of course you upset me, Ashraf.'

'I did not,' Ashraf replied firmly. 'You left the house because you were afraid of the demonstrations.'

'Then I got upset by your strange behaviour.'

'My behaviour is normal. I explained it to you and you refused to understand my point of view.'

'I'm not the only one who's upset by your behaviour,' Magda responded sharply. 'All the neighbours and the shop owners have spoken to me more than once and complained about the kids you bring to the ground floor.'

In a loud voice, Ashraf replied, 'First, I've already told you not to call the young people in Tahrir "kids". We have to respect them, because they have done what our generation couldn't. Second, I'm the owner of the building and I have the right to do anything on the ground floor so long as I don't break the law. Third, I've taken part in the revolution like millions of other Egyptians. What's the problem?'

'If you don't mind, Ashraf,' Priest Matthias said, 'I'd like to say a word.'

'By all means.'

'I think what Madame Magda means is that, as Copts, we have a special place in Egypt. Common sense says we should support the country's president even if he's a tyrant, in return for his providing us with security. Even Our Lord the Pope has warned his flock against taking part in the demonstrations.'

'Our Lord the Pope announced his support for the revolution, once it had succeeded, and many Copts have taken part in the revolution. The truth is that Our Lord the Pope's authority is spiritual, not political. If we are going to reproach the Islamists for mixing religion with politics, the church should stay out of politics too.'

Priest Matthias smiled and said calmly, 'The Pope never engages in politics. He gives us advice as children of the church and never imposes anything on us. Our Lord the Pope always sees further than us, based on his wisdom and his knowledge of the Holy Bible.'

Unexpectedly, Ashraf asked, 'Does the Holy Bible tell us to support injustice?'

The priest emitted a tut-tutting sound with his lips, indicating displeasure, while Magda cried out, 'Please, speak of the Holy Bible with respect!'

'You're not going to teach me how to respect my own religion,' Ashraf responded sharply, and a tense silence descended. Then Amir's voice rose again to further provoke him, saying, 'I, as a Copt, supported Mubarak, and was sorry when he stepped down. It was enough that he protected the Copts.'

Ashraf replied, sarcastically, 'Can you give me the number of massacres that took place during the era of Mubarak, this man who "protected" us? Starting with the massacre at Kosheh and ending with the Saints Church massacre.'

Amir yelled, 'And you like it now? After Mubarak left, how many churches have been burned down? Every Copt in Egypt is living under threat.'

'Everyone, let's use our heads a little,' Ashraf said. 'During the revolution, the police vanished completely, and despite that, there wasn't a single attack on a single church from Alexandria to Aswan.

How are we to explain that the assaults all happened after Mubarak's downfall?'

Amir said, sarcastically, 'Do explain to us, Ashraf, so we can benefit from your wisdom!'

Ashraf replied challengingly, 'To be honest, Amir, if you could understand me, you would indeed benefit. All the assaults on churches were organised by the security apparatuses. We have lots of evidence. All the churches were set on fire using the same method, the same scenario: the military police are withdrawn from in front of the church, the electricity is cut, and then the thugs arrive and set fire to the church at their leisure. They disappear and the military police reappear. The old regime intends to terrify the Copts so as to make them hate the revolution and throw themselves on the mercy of the Military Council.'

'Frankly,' said Magda, 'I'm not interested in your theories, Ashraf. Because of this revolution of yours, we, as Copts, have lost our security and are in a terrible state. That is the truth.'

'The revolution didn't take power so that you could hold it to account.'

'The fact is, you're sitting with your friends from the revolution and don't know what's going on. Our churches are being burned every day, the Salafist groups attack us in our houses, and there's no one to protect us.'

'Egypt is changing,' Ashraf said calmly, 'and every change has its price. Lots of people have paid the price of freedom. The Copts have to pay like everyone else.'

At this, Amir's voice rose and mingled with Magda's in a blend of angry words, but the priest made a sign to them and they fell silent. Then he said to Ashraf, 'It's hard to persuade people to put up with attacks on their churches and their children for the sake of change.'

'And why do we forget that thousands of Egyptians were killed during the revolution? Why do we only think about our woes as

Copts? Why don't we think about the young people who lost their eyes to shotgun pellets or received injuries that left them helpless?'

Amir said, 'Enough empty slogans! All those people who demonstrated took money to destroy the country.'

'No one takes money so that he can die.'

Magda shook her head and said disapprovingly, 'I can't believe that you're thinking like this now, Ashraf.'

Ashraf smiled and said, 'You never did know how I thought, or care to find out. Everyone, let's talk frankly. Are you upset with the revolution because of the burning of the churches or because business has come to a halt?'

'What do you mean?'

'What I mean, Amir, is that your jewellery business has certainly been affected by the revolution, and you, Magda, your accounting firm has surely been affected too.'

'When someone is afraid for his work, he's wrong?' asked Amir, disdainfully, while Magda muttered, in a low but audible voice, 'Work was never something Ashraf cared about.'

Ashraf looked at her angrily and said, 'I will not permit you to treat me with disrespect. No one has spent a single pound on me to give him the right to say that.'

The priest intervened, saying, 'Ashraf, she didn't mean to upset you.'

Amir, however, decided to get in another blow. Smiling calmly, he said, 'Anyway, if Magda and I are successful at our work and worried about it, it's something for us to be proud of, and you should be proud of it too.'

Ashraf looked down for a moment, then said, 'Success is a relative thing. For example, if I'm a jeweller who gets stolen gold and melts it down and sells it and I get taken to court and pay a bribe so as not to go to prison, can one call that success? And if I'm an accountant whose job is to make fake budgets so that big companies can evade taxes, should one call that success, or fraud?'

Everyone cried out in protest. Even the mother objected, saying, 'That's a very unkind thing to say, Ashraf. What's got into you? *Tu es devenu fou.*'

'See how the truth hurts?' said Ashraf. 'I just wanted to tell you that I'm not a failure. I have rejected false, faked success. No one has the right to read me lessons. People who live in glass houses . . .'

'Apologise immediately for what you said!' Amir shouted.

Ashraf said, 'Apologise for the truth? It isn't true you were charged with stealing gold?'

Amir leapt up and rushed at him, but Father Matthias held him back. Turning towards the door, Ashraf said, 'Before I go, I want to tell you that I'm with the revolution. I will remain with the revolution till I die. Your home is at your disposal, Madame Magda. Whenever you come, you're welcome. Those "young people from the revolution" would be happy to see you. They're happy to see anyone, provided that person isn't corrupt and can understand what they're trying to do. Goodbye.'

The priest hurried after him, but Ashraf, breathing heavily, said, 'Stay with them, Father. I'll take a taxi.'

48

Anyone who'd been at the meeting would have felt sure that Uncle Madany had agreed to accept the blood money. True, he hadn't actually said, 'I accept', but he hadn't objected either. He'd gone on watching the sheikh and the colonel with complete calm, listening to them attentively as though what they were saying was expected and acceptable. He'd even asked how much he was to receive. However, just at the moment when the colonel opened the case and began taking out bundles of banknotes to give to Uncle Madany to count before signing the waiver, and at that moment only, Uncle Madany abandoned his silence, jumped up from his seat, and rushed out of the parlour to the front door of the flat, which he opened, shouting in a hoarse, strange-sounding voice, 'Get out of here, the two of you!'

A moment elapsed before the sheikh and the colonel grasped what was happening, but Uncle Madany, who at this point was looking upwards as though calling on some higher being to witness what he was doing, grasped the doorknob and began waving his other hand, shouting, 'Get out, immediately!'

The sheikh exclaimed, 'God forgive us! Brother Madany, spite the Devil!'

'You're offering me money for my son's life? Get out!'

'It's the legal blood money, as set by Our Lord,' the sheikh said.

'You think you know anything about Our Lord, you impostor?' Uncle Madany yelled.

Sheikh Shamel could sense the gravity of the situation, so he made straight for the door. The colonel first carefully closed the case, then picked it up and stood, looking at Uncle Madany for a moment. Then he issued an angry roar and yelled, 'You think you can throw us out, you good-for-nothing son of a bitch?'

The colonel rushed at Uncle Madany, intending to strike him, but Sheikh Shamel threw himself on him and pulled him with difficulty out of the flat. Madany slammed the door, the colonel's ugly curses continuing to reach his ears. He returned calmly to the couch in the living room and sat down, tucking his legs under him, as though nothing had happened. Hind, who'd been listening to the conversation from the kitchen, quickly appeared and threw herself into her father's arms, weeping. He hugged her and stroked her hair, without saying a word. The next day, when he went to the factory, he spoke to no one. He spent his time, as usual, absorbed in his inner world, sitting silently in the garage, a fixed, grim expression on his face. He would read the Koran until a job came up, then drive off in the ambulance, take care of it, and return to where he'd been sitting before. From time to time, he'd break his taciturnity with a comment or a word, or maybe behave in some sudden, violent way, as he had done with the sheikh and the officer, then revert as quickly to his deep, angry calm.

As usual, he didn't sleep on the night before the court session. He prayed the morning prayer at the mosque of Sayeda Zeinab, then went to the café opposite the courthouse and started avidly drinking coffee and chain-smoking. When Khaled's colleagues and friends arrived, he shook hands with them warmly. These were the only people for whom he could raise a smile. They reminded him of Khaled – they had the same innocent looks and enthusiasm, and the deep, honest awareness of his sorrows was present in their voices, their loving, embarrassed faces, and their constantly asking him if there was anything they could do for him. Uncle Madany sat, as usual, next to the dock and kept his eyes on the officer Heisam, who had hired a well-known lawyer who, in his elegance and conceit, resembled a film star, while the lawyers for the late Khaled were three young volunteers, whose competence, nevertheless, embarrassed the masterful jurist more than once. The judge heard all the witnesses and all of Khaled's colleagues confirmed that they had seen the officer Heisam El Meligi kill Khaled with a bullet that he'd fired from his government-issue revolver from the police car. The celebrated lawyer tried to catch the witnesses out and show up contradictions in their testimonies, but the young lawyers raised objections and compelled him to be silent, at the request of the judge. Then the lawyers clashed with him again when they refused the long postponement he requested. All of a sudden, during the turmoil of the arguments, Uncle Madany emerged from his private world and started shouting, leading to uproar in the hall, and the presiding judge, his face registering distress, began banging on the dais with his wooden gavel, saying, 'Silence! If anyone makes noise, I'll have him imprisoned!'

Uncle Madany, however, had got started and could no longer restrain himself. At the top of his voice, he yelled, 'Your Honour, I have a few words I have to say to you right now.'

49

When Nourhan appeared on screen with her hair covered, her popularity increased. Millions of women viewers who wore the headscarf felt a kind of pride when they saw her doing so too, as though they'd scored a victory in an important war. Over and above this symbolic triumph for Islam, Nourhan provided a model of elegance for the Muslim woman. Her dresses were designed to cover the body completely but bore the labels of the biggest global fashion houses, though usually Nourhan (who'd mastered the art of sewing during her days in Mansoura) would make certain modifications as required by religious law. Her headscarves, on the other hand, were brightly coloured and original.

One of the nicest things Sheikh Shamel had said to her was, 'I pray that God, Great and Sublime, grant you blessings commensurate with your good influence!' What the Reverend Sheikh had in mind was that Nourhan's Islamic chic would drive many girls to imitate her by covering their hair. However, Nourhan's brilliance extended beyond her clothes to her face, so that when she put on her headscarf, it was as though she were simply completing the picture. She moved through the world like a full moon, the serenity brought by faith visible on her face, along with the tranquil smile of a female believer who has tasted the sweetness of obedience and by so doing pleased both her Lord and herself. Nourhan became one of the most prominent broadcasters on all the channels and her daily show, 'With Nourhan', registered unprecedented ratings, according to the ratings organisation and the statistics of specialised companies. Each night, the Egyptians watched Nourhan host academics, intellectuals, and strategic experts who asserted, unanimously, and basing their assertions on scientific evidence, that the revolution that had taken place in Egypt had been no more than a conspiracy funded and planned by the CIA with the participation of Israel's Mossad. And each time, concern would appear on Nourhan's lovely face and she'd bring the episode to an end by repeating the following prayer, uttered in a voice full of reverence as the camera held the closing shot: 'O Lord, make Egypt a secure land, and save her from the evil-doers and the traitors!'

Sometimes, a tear would find its way into one of her beautiful eyes, and she'd take out her coloured handkerchief and wipe it away as the programme titles appeared on the screen. All the guests were nominated by the security apparatuses, but Nourhan had her additional touches. In one celebrated episode – the one that had perhaps the greatest impact on public opinion – Nourhan began with a little speech that she had written herself and that she read with her face composed into an expression of elegant distaste. She said, 'In the name of God, the Merciful, the Compassionate. Dear viewers, we are accustomed, in this programme of yours, to transparency and openness. We are accustomed to speaking the whole truth, however painful it may be. We have hosted the greatest minds in Egypt, and all of them agree that what is called 'the revolution' is nothing but a despicable conspiracy to destroy our country. Tonight I shall host a strange character, someone who herself asked to appear with us, on condition that she remain unidentified.'

Nourhan now stood up and moved, followed by the camera, to where the guest was sitting. The director had blurred out the girl's face so that no one could recognise her. Nourhan sat down in front of her and said, 'Of course, we're not going to give your name, as per your request.'

'Thank you, Madame Nourhan.'

'Why do you prefer to remain unidentified?'

317

'Because I feel so ashamed,' said the girl, in a troubled voice.

'And why did you ask to appear on this programme?' Nourhan asked her.

'My conscience has been troubling me. I want to make the people understand the magnitude of the plan that I took part in against Egypt.'

'That is a grave thing to say. Kindly proceed.'

'I and all the young people in Tahrir have taken money from foreign sources.'

'From whom precisely did you take money? Be specific.'

'We took money from foreigners whose identity we don't know, but they were probably from Western intelligence services.'

'How much did you receive?'

'Each one of us received one thousand dollars for every day he spent in Tahrir.'

'Are you really saying that the thousands of protesters all took money?'

'All the young people who organised the others took money. But there were people who believed us and followed us.'

'You're saying that every one of the young people involved in the revolution got a thousand dollars a day?'

'A thousand dollars a day plus travel costs.'

Extreme distress appeared on Nourhan's face and she said, 'Please, you have to explain to us about the travel costs.'

'We went to Serbia and Israel and were trained in how to demonstrate so as to bring down the regime and we got large sums of money for the training.'

'How much did you get?'

'I, for example, went to Israel. I got fifty thousand dollars and was trained in stuff there for three months.'

'Where?'

'In a camp on the outskirts of Tel Aviv.'

'What exactly were you trained in?'

'In stirring up public opinion on Facebook and Twitter, organising demonstrations, wearing down the security forces, and a bunch of activities that would inevitably lead in the end to the downfall of the state.'

'And the rest of the young people in Tahrir?'

'Listen. There are about five thousand of us, boys and girls, from all the provinces of Egypt. We all got training and we all took money. Some people got trained in Israel and some in Serbia, in Qatar, and in Turkey. The trainer would usually be Israeli or American, though. The people believed us and rushed out to demonstrate but we were carrying out the instructions of the organisations that had trained us.'

Here the conversation was suddenly interrupted, and the camera moved in close to Nourhan's face, on which an expression of revulsion could be seen.

'You mean to say that you and others like you are traitors and took money to reduce Egypt to ruin? And that the good-hearted Egyptians believed you and followed you? Shame on you! You'd betray and destroy Egypt, your own country?'

'Enough!' the girl cried. 'I despise myself!' Then she burst into tears, her face still hidden.

The camera now turned back to Nourhan, whose face had taken on the look of one shocked by a vile betrayal, and she said, 'To be honest, I cannot find words to describe what these traitors did. Egyptians, be on your guard against them! They are traitors. O Lord, preserve Egypt from their evil!'

Nourhan left the set and conducted the girl to the supervising officer, who looked pleased and said, 'Bravo, Muna! You were great!'

She was a petite girl with a headscarf and smart clothes and she nodded her head gratefully while breathing heavily, like an actress worked up at the end of a performance.

319

'Thank you, Madame Nourhan,' said the officer, 'for your patriotism.'

The supervising officer at the station treated Nourhan with special consideration, firstly because she was the best of the broadcasters and the one with the most impact and secondly because he was aware of how close she was to Hagg Shanawany. And here we must stress, once more, that Nourhan did nothing to make Shanawany fall into her clutches. Nourhan, an observant Muslim woman, could never have attempted to seduce Shanawany or anyone else. Everything, however, is fate, and no son of Adam takes a step that God has not commanded. All that happened was that her problems with the drunkard Essam grew worse; she asked for an appointment with Hagg Shanawany, via his office manager; he gave her an appointment for the following day (a rarity, considering how busy the hagg was); Nourhan went to Shanawany and told him about Essam and, unable to control herself, wept bitterly. Shanawany, moved, said, 'Nourhan, I have a question which I want you to answer frankly.'

She looked at him with her tear-filled, mascara-ed eyes (she used an imported brand that didn't run) and said in a quivering voice, 'I'm at your service, Hagg.'

'Has your life with Essam truly become impossible?'

Fervently, she replied, 'I cannot live with someone who drinks alcohol night and day and has weird ideas about religion.'

'Could you elaborate on that?'

'He has no religious convictions!'

Anger appeared on the hagg's smooth face, made shiny by the masques that his private hairdresser applied to it weekly. Then he said, 'If you are certain that he is not a Muslim, it follows that you must separate.'

In broken tones, Nourhan replied, 'He told me that he's not a Muslim, and when I asked for a divorce, he refused and threatened me. I'm afraid he'll do something to my son, Hagg. I'm very afraid.'

Nourhan used, once again, the tone of voice that caused the Hagg's face to take on a livid hue, while his eyes briefly glazed over. Then he controlled himself and said, 'Don't you worry. Leave the matter to me. He'll divorce you whether he wants to or not.'

'Really, Hagg, would you do that? If he divorces me, you'll be in my prayers for the rest of my life, and I'll never forget the favour you've done me.'

Shanawany smiled and said, 'He'll divorce you and then – who knows? – maybe Our Lord will put a better man in your path.'

The sentence rang loud in Nourhan's ears though she pretended to pay it no attention. An expression of satisfaction did, however, cross her face like a sudden flash of light.

This was how Essam came to divorce her, under pressure from the Apparatus. She went to the villa in Zamalek and refused to speak to him or even look at him until the customary marriage contract had been torn up and he'd sworn the oath of divorce before her. She thanked the general, then went to Shanawany to thank him, and he looked at her for a while before smiling and saying, 'Listen, my dear lady (bless the Prophet!).'

'May God bless him and grant him peace!'

'I, praise the Lord, live and die in obedience to God and His messenger. I am asking you to marry me. I have two wives. The mother of my children, and another wife whom you may know – Salwa Hamdan, the actress – so you'll be the third. God willing, I shall treat you all equally.'

Hagg Shanawany wasn't saying anything she didn't already know and she looked at him for a moment and almost said something, but then became very confused. A kind of regal distress seemed to affect Hagg Shanawany and he asked her, 'What's the matter, Nourhan?'

In a voice broken by emotion, she answered, 'It's too much for me. I can't believe it. Who am I to marry Your Excellency?'

'You are the best of women!' replied Shanawany, contemplating her lovely face, which suddenly changed, as will the colour of the sea. 'May God's blessings upon you, Hagg,' she said, 'be equal to the righteousness with which you have treated me!'

When he asked her what she would ask for, she said in a submissive voice, 'I swear, Hagg, if my bride price were nothing but a few dates, I would be the happiest woman in the world!'

She'd heard the sentence at a class given by Sheikh Shamel. It had been said by a woman to one of the companions of the Prophet when he asked her to marry him. 'God bless you!' said Hagg Shanawany, startled and clearly moved.

Shanawany married her the day after the mandatory waiting period was over. He threw a small party in the villa that he'd bought for her in the Fifth Settlement that was attended by Nourhan's brothers and sisters, her aunt, who was her proxy at the writing of the contract, and a few close friends of Hagg Shanawany's (among them two generals from the ruling Military Council). Shanawany didn't announce his marriage to everyone at the channel. 'By the way,' he told the director when the latter was in his office and as though mentioning something mundane and of merely passing interest, 'I've married Nourhan, according to the rules established by God and His messenger.'

The director of the channel congratulated him in an embarrassed way and the news spread with the speed of lightning. No one, however, dared to congratulate him publicly, as ordinary people would do. Perhaps one or two plucked up their courage, waited for an opportunity, and whispered, 'A thousand congratulations, Hagg! A happy home and children, God willing!'

To be fair, Hagg Shanawany was the best of all the men Nourhan had taken as husbands. Her two previous husbands couldn't hold a candle to him, perhaps because he was seventy-four (as she learned from the marriage contract) and that made him look after her with the paternal affection she'd lost with the premature death of her father, or perhaps because his wealth made him more able to provide her with a comfortable life than her two earlier husbands, or perhaps because he was very generous by nature and saw, in spending money on his wife, a way of drawing closer to God. Suffice it to say that he made a formal marriage contract with her, because common-law marriage was, in his view, of dubious validity, or so at least a number of legal scholars believed. Nourhan welcomed the marriage even though she knew that getting married formally would lead to the termination of the pension she received as a result of her marriage to her first husband, the late Hani El Aasar (Shanawany's wealth made her protectiveness of her pension seem far-fetched and silly). All this aside, the basic reason why Nourhan got on so well with Shanawany was their shared faith that fear of God was more important than this world and all that was in it. Hagg Shanawany was an admirer of Sheikh Shamel's and frequently invited him to give a lesson at one of his mansions. Sheikh Shamel attended the wedding party, congratulated the bride and groom, then taught Nourhan a prayer that she was to say each day after the evening prayer to prevent the envy that is mentioned in the Koran. As well as the villa in the Fifth Settlement, which he registered in her name, Shanawany bought her a Mercedes of the latest model, paid a bride price much larger than that specified in the marriage contract, set aside five million pounds as the payment to be made in the eventuality of their divorce, and gave her a collection of jewellery that Nourhan hesitated to show her girlfriends for fear of envy. He also furnished a private wing in the villa for her son to live in and when she asked him, in a pitiful voice, whether her son's living with them would bother him, he smiled and said, 'First, you won't be at ease psychologically unless your son is with you, and second, do you want to deprive me of the heavenly reward that goes with raising a fatherless child?' Weeping, Nourhan called down fervent blessings on his head.

And so things were settled. Nourhan moved her son Hamza to the American School in the Settlement and he lived with her during the week; then on Friday and Saturday, she sent him to her uncle in Mansoura so she could be free to attend to her husband. Shanawany, in keeping with the custom of the Prophet (God bless him and grant him peace), spent two days with each wife, then rested for one day in his private mansion on the Maryoutiya Canal. If he bought one wife a present, he bought something similar for the other two. Nourhan, naturally, investigated how things stood with her two co-wives. The first, the mother of Shanawany's children, was out of the competition: she was old and being treated for a number of medical conditions. The second wife was Salwa Hamdan, an actress whom the hagg had married some five years before, after which she'd adopted the headscarf and ceased playing anything but religious roles. Nourhan watched her in a number of roles in serials that had been shown recently, inspected her minutely, and discovered that she had had, at the very least, two cosmetic operations on her face: she had had her lips plumped out, she had had the wrinkles removed, and her cheeks had definitely been injected with something (they looked puffy when the camera came too close). Nourhan felt a deep relief and waited for a moment when the hagg was in bed and in a good mood to say, as though the thought had just occurred to her, 'Just imagine, cosmetic surgery is everywhere in Egypt these days. Really, it's disgusting.'

Shanawany looked at her in amazement, and she continued, 'First, the Reverend Sheikh Shamel has stated clearly that it's a sin, because it changes the work of the Creator, Mighty and Glorious. Second, why should a woman refuse to acknowledge that she's grown old? And third, frankly, I can't understand how a man can bear to be close to his wife when her face is all blown up like a balloon.'

At this point, Shanawany finally got what she was aiming at and deftly shifted the conversation to another subject. As was her custom, Nourhan satisfied her husband's sexual needs so well that, had religion not required that he have sex with his two other wives, he might have found the pleasure he enjoyed with her enough: he left Nourhan's with no energy left. Not only was he of an advanced age, but Shanawany had recently had open-heart surgery and each morning took a variety of pills and capsules. Nourhan realised that she would have to apply with Shanawany an abbreviated form of the sexual programme she had used with her two previous husbands. She cut out the belly dancing number and likewise the one where she played with the 'seven spots' of the man's body. She focused her energy on sucking the hagg's penis, which rose only with difficulty because of the blood pressure medicine and the widening of the arteries. Once it was up, she had to put on a show of ecstasy because the hagg was also, unfortunately, given to premature ejaculation. Sometimes, when she was giving it her all but the erection was slow in coming, Shanawany would stretch out his hand, raise his head, and whisper in embarrassment, 'I seem to be worn out this evening.'

At this, she would hug him and whisper, 'Don't you mind. The only thing that matters to me is being in your arms.'

Nourhan was neither crude nor demanding. On the contrary, she treated her intimate encounters with the hagg as a task requiring a certain technical precision and one that she strove to carry out correctly. In musical terms, their encounters were more like concertos than symphonies, in that Nourhan would have to play on her own and wait for a long while before the hagg's ancient instruments, with their frayed strings, responded. It follows that she bears no responsibility for what happened on a certain Friday.

Shanawany had come to her after the prayer, as usual. She'd made him the dish of macaroni with bechamel sauce that he loved. The hagg had begun with a passionate kiss and a fondling of her breasts, and Nourhan, faking arousal, had let out a passionate moan to excite him, lowered her head to perform the usual task, and his penis had responded, its stiffness gradually increasing. Then suddenly Nour-han had felt the hagg's body tremble. Raising her eyes, she saw that he was extremely pale and, abandoning his penis, she exclaimed with concern, 'What's the matter, Hagg?'

He was panting and sweating, and a strange, absent look had appeared on his face, as though he couldn't make out what he was seeing. He opened his mouth and tried to say something but emitted instead a single gasp, after which his head fell back onto the pillow.

50

At the appointed time, a little before the afternoon prayer, a black BMW halted in front of the villa and two assistants and three armed guards descended and formed a circle around the Supreme Guide of the Muslim Brotherhood. Naturally, the Apparatus's security people wouldn't let the Guide's guards bring their weapons in with them; the guards handed their weapons over as soon as the Guide had passed through the gate.

The meeting began with the prayer. General Alwany led his office manager, the Guide, his assistants, and his guards in the prayer, and then everyone withdrew, leaving the general and the Guide on their own together. Meetings between the two men were normally quick and focused due to General Alwany's lack of time. After the customary greetings, the general said to the Guide, 'On behalf of the members of the Supreme Council of the Armed Forces, I thank you and your brothers for keeping your word.'

'Don't mention it, my dear sir. Does God not say, in "The Night Journey", "Keep your promises; you will be called to account for every promise you have made"?'

'The Brotherhood's stand with us against the writing of a new constitution has saved Egypt from confusion and chaos.'

'God preserve Egypt! I have a request to make of Your Excellency.'

'Please tell me.'

'I would like to meet with the honourable members of the Supreme Council of the Armed Forces. I wish to convey to them in person the allegiance and support of the Brotherhood.'

The general smiled and said, 'Rest assured, I shall convey your messages without delay, but circumstances don't permit a meeting now. Following the resignation of His Excellency President Mubarak, the press has been acting like a wild animal. If you were to be seen entering army command headquarters, it would open the doors to the kind of gossip mongering that we can do without.'

The Guide nodded understandingly and said, 'The media are, indeed, out of control.'

'The patriotic businessmen did their duty and opened television channels to raise the Egyptians' awareness, but a large part of the media is still calling for chaos.'

'Among the wonders of the Koran is that there is no matter, great or small, regarding the life of the Muslims for which it does not provide a rule. Our Lord, Mighty and Sublime, says, in "The Apartments", "Believers, if an evil-doer brings you news, ascertain the correctness of the report fully, lest you unwittingly harm others, and then regret what you have done" (God has spoken truly!). Should this verse not be considered a charter for the media?'

'How very true!'

Silence briefly reigned, then General Alwany said, 'I asked you to come today to talk to you about an important matter.'

'There's nothing wrong, I hope?'

'You are aware of the magnitude of the responsibility shouldered by both myself and the members of the Military Council.'

'May God help you and bless you for your efforts!'

'In the coming period, we shall be forced to employ certain harsh measures to ensure security and restore respect for the state. We will not allow sit-ins or demonstrations in the streets.'

'And we shall support you in that, God willing, till things are back to normal and the state is functioning again.'

General Alwany smiled and said, 'I'm asking you – from the perspective of religious law, does not the ruler have the right, in

Islam, to "strike the hands" of those who stir up civil strife?'

'That is not merely his right but his duty. The scholars of religion are in agreement that the punishment for one who stirs up civil strife is imprisonment and flogging, and some scholars go so far as to call for his execution.'

General Alwany said nothing. Then he looked at the Guide and said, 'We don't want the Brotherhood to take part in any sit-in or demonstration.'

'I give Your Excellency my word that not one member of the Brotherhood will take part in any civil disobedience. We have previously announced that the sit-ins are contrary to God's law because they allow young people of both sexes to mingle in a way that could encourage sinful acts, God forbid!'

'I don't want to hear any criticism from any leader or even from any individual member of the Brotherhood of any harsh measures we may take.'

'We shall not simply refrain from criticising them, we shall, God willing, back them and support them.'

General Alwany gave him an enquiring look, as though probing his hidden depths, and said slowly, 'The elections for the People's Assembly are growing close, and I have promised you that we will allow the Brotherhood this opportunity to win as many seats as they wish without interference from us. If any member of the Brotherhood should happen to object to any measure we take against the saboteurs, our agreement concerning the People's Assembly will be cancelled.'

The Guide smiled and said, 'The Brotherhood's support for you will be complete, God willing.'

General Alwany smiled once more and said, 'Let us read "The Opening".'

The two men reverently bowed their heads and murmured the opening chapter of the Koran.

'To work, then,' murmured General Alwany, who wanted to bring the meeting to a close, but the Guide smiled and said, 'I know that Your Excellency is very busy, but I have a request.'

'Nothing serious, I hope, Your Reverence,' said General Alwany in a none too welcoming tone.

The Guide said, 'As Your Excellency knows, our first and last goal is to call people to God. We would like to open new centres for the Brotherhood and we have, God be thanked, the locations and the necessary funds. However, the security forces are making things difficult for us.'

General Alwany frowned as though in denial and asked, 'In what way are the security forces making things difficult for you?'

As though the general had made a joke, the Guide smiled and said, 'Your Excellency knows better than I, naturally. The security forces have numerous ways of preventing the opening of the new centres.'

'And what is it you want?'

'One word from Your Excellency would see the Brotherhood's new centres opened.'

'Very well.'

The Guide kept up a stream of thanks until he was gone, and a pleased expression appeared on General Alwany's face. Everything was going to plan. He looked like a director who has succeeded in having all the actors learn their parts and now awaits the beginning of the performance with confidence. Calling in his office manager, he said to him, 'Tell the colonel in charge at the Military Council that the Brothers have agreed. Use the cipher. No writing and no telephone.'

The director nodded understandingly, and General Alwany said as he got up, 'I'm going home and I'll be back tonight.'

In the car on his way home, his anxieties returned. In the thick of the battle that he was waging to retain control of the country, he'd forgotten about his other battle, at home. When he arrived, he found his wife Tahany in a terrible state, and the moment he asked her what was wrong, she shouted, through her tears, 'Do I have ten daughters, Ahmad? My only daughter is slipping away before my eyes and I can't do anything.'

General Alwany set off in the direction of Danya's room, but her mother rushed after him, grabbed him, and said, 'I beg you, don't put pressure on her, Ahmad. She's been through enough already.'

The general nodded and tapped with his fingers on the door of Danya's room, but she didn't answer. Opening the door gently, he found her sitting on the couch. She looked tired. It appeared she hadn't slept, and he realised that she had been crying. He smiled and told her, 'I came home early from work. I thought I'd say hello. I've missed you, Danya.'

She looked at him, nodded, and tried to smile but couldn't.

He sat next to her on the couch and it occurred to him that sitting with her like this had once provided some of the most pleasant moments of his life. Recalling Tahany's warning, he said to her in a calm, affectionate tone, 'Danya, you've always been an intelligent person and I've always been proud of the way you think. Do you think the way you're behaving will solve any problems?'

She didn't reply, so he resumed, affectionately, 'Do you think the solution is to stay away from your classes?'

'I can't go to the faculty,' Danya responded in a low voice, as though talking to herself.

'Danya, none of what you're doing will change a thing. You're destroying yourself.'

'I can't forget Khaled being murdered in front of my eyes.'

'You believe in God and you know that every life has a fated end.'

'We can't murder people and then say that the life God decreed for them came to an end.'

'What are you trying to say?'

331

'I'm trying to say that Khaled wasn't the only one who died. Lots of young people died during the revolution.'

'Please, Danya. I've made up my mind not to argue with you. What you call a revolution was a conspiracy and we have all the details.'

'Khaled wasn't a conspirator.'

'Of course, there were people who were taken in and followed the conspirators. The ones who paid them to demonstrate are the ones who should be blamed.'

'You forbade me to testify.'

'All your colleagues testified and after hearing the submissions, the judge will postpone the case until the sentencing. If the officer was the one who killed your friend, he will get his punishment according to religion and the law.'

'You're keeping an eye on the case?'

'Of course, and I'm also keeping an eye on the fact that you visit his family every day.'

'Yes. I visit them.'

General Alwany was trying to keep control of his feelings. Danya went on, in a low voice, 'The least I can do for Khaled is make sure that his father and sister are alright.'

The general rose and gently pulled her up by the hand, at which she suddenly threw herself into his arms and burst into tears. He stroked her head, whispering, 'Danya, I beg you, fight this mood you're in. Bear in mind that your mother's health has declined because of you. Promise me you'll go back to the faculty.'

51

Testimony of Lamya Hassanein

I don't need to introduce myself to those who already know me but for those who don't, my name's Lamya Hassanein, twenty-five years old.

I'm going to give testimony about the events of 9 October in front of Maspero, because when I went home that day and saw the TV, I felt they must be talking about some other country.

On Sunday, I went to Shubra to go on the march which was going to Maspero from there. The march was supposed to get moving at three o'clock and join the silent candlelit vigil in front of Maspero, in mourning for the army's violence against peaceful demonstrators the week before, at five. Obviously, it's the right of every Egyptian, whatever his religion, to enjoy security of life, home, and place of worship, especially after the events at the Marinab church in Aswan.

I got there at 3 p.m. The demonstration was gathering. Very large numbers, lots of entire families – children, fathers, and grandfathers all together. Crosses raised, young men and women wearing aprons with 'Martyr Available' written on them and bitter cries asking why can't an Egyptian, if he's Christian, feel that his church is safe? Why aren't the police and the army protecting the churches from sabotage? And why, after the revolution, is the regime still using the same methods as in the days of Mubarak?

I liked some of the slogans but not others, and whenever I heard someone complain that some slogans were religious, I'd ask him to join the demonstration to make it clear that we were in solidarity with and concerned for every Egyptian, without discrimination, and from then on, the slogans would change.

At 4.30 p.m., I sent a Twitter message saying, 'The priest who's acting as spokesperson has confirmed that the march is peaceful and welcomed the Muslims who have joined in.' A little later, the slogan was 'Tantawi, where's your army? They burned the houses of the Christians! They burned the churches of the Egyptians!'

We were chanting, 'Sons of Shubra, come on down! There's a million Mubaraks still around!' and 'Egyptians, come on down!' and the numbers were in fact growing, with Christians and Muslims joining the march. Most of the Muslims who passed us in Shubra showed their solidarity. They smiled, joined in the slogans – there wasn't even the smallest communal clash in Shubra. The first problem occurred beneath the Shubra flyover. We passed beneath the flyover without any problem and as soon as we got out the other side, we found that bricks and bottles were being thrown at us by young kids on top of the flyover and from inside the Abdin area. I personally didn't see who was doing the throwing. There was also a sound of stun grenades and tasers coming from the same direction. The man next to me shouted at me, 'Run and hide!' The lady who was next to me began praying and calling on Our Lord to take care of us.

This is what I sent out on Twitter:

5.35: 'The march is being pelted with bricks from on top of the flyover.'

5.43: 'The stone throwing has stopped from on top of the flyover and it's started from the street.'

6.00: 'Bricks and bottles being thrown from inside Abdin. The march keeps going.'

The battle went on for perhaps a quarter of an hour. They were throwing bricks and bottles and we were responding with a few bricks. Then the march made it to Maspero.

Under the Galaa Street flyover, the marchers' morale was high. Strong slogans. Most of the religious slogans disappeared and personally I was happy but anxious. I was afraid of what might happen when we reached Maspero. At 6.40 I wrote, 'The demonstration is full of old people and children, if anything happens, it'll be a tragedy.' We were chanting, 'Enough, enough of soldiers as boss – we're the line you cannot cross!' and 'Egypt for every Egyptian – every sect and every religion!' and 'Why did the church burn down? Is Adly back in town?' At that time, I learned from a friend on Twitter that there were around ten Central Security lorries loaded with soldiers parked in the Abd El Men'em Reyad car park. At the time, there were about twenty-five thousand of us and we were close to Maspero. The atmosphere on the march was great and for a moment I began to feel reassured. I thought, 'Okay, the army and Central Security might beat us up at night but they aren't crazy enough to beat us up when the march is full of children and there's no call to.' When we'd almost reached the turn-off to Maspero, I decided to go look from somewhere else to see what the situation was.

The moment I got to the area of the Maspero Building and before the march could reach it from the other side of the street, I found the people from the demonstration chanting, 'Muslims, Christians, one hand!' and about thirty seconds later I saw ranks of Central Security men running at us and firing in the air. Everyone ran to get away from the shooting and the shooting that had been into the air started to be at the level of our bodies. I ran to the first street and turned to see what was going on and to look for my friends on the other side of the street from Maspero, next to the Nile. I found that the shooting was continuous and everyone was running. Soldiers from the army and Central Security had us surrounded from every direction – on top of the flyover, underneath the flyover, Ramses Hilton Street, and Abd El Men'em Reyad Square. People with children and old people began running in every direction trying to get out of danger. Everyone was really stunned. No one was prepared for such violence.

At 6.26 I said on Twitter: 'The bastards are firing on a march full of children' and at 6.32: 'Another round of shooting.'

At the time, I was at the Ramses Hilton on the Nile, and most of the people who were left were with me. I was standing in the middle of the road trying to work out what had happened. Suddenly, we heard people shouting at us to get up onto the pavement. We ran and saw two armoured army personnel carriers driving at crazy speed down the middle of the road, which was full of people. At first, I thought they were just stupid soldiers and were going to kill us with their stupidity but then the carriers started driving at this crazy speed this way and that along the street. They were driving in zigzags. They'd see a group trying to escape and drive after them. They'd drive up onto the pavement and run over people. They'd see people on the other side and they'd turn and crush them. I was terrified. Then the first two carriers were switched for two others, which did the same – driving crazily, running people over, everyone running in all directions to get out of the way of their attempts to run them over. One group of people, among them two very young girls, fourteen to fifteen years old, were hiding behind a private car that was parked there. I saw the carrier drive in their direction, ride up over the car and smash it, and crush one of the people who were hiding. The rest ran in the direction of the Central Security forces to save themselves.

The two carriers drove off and quickly disappeared but one slowed down and everyone gathered together and ran behind it and pelted it with stones as it was moving and they stopped it and threw at it the remains of a broken traffic light that was on fire. The carrier caught fire and the stones continued. Most of the people started chanting, 'Stop the stones,' and kept shouting at the soldier, 'Get out! Get out! Get out!' so that he wouldn't be afraid. They were afraid he'd be *burned inside. Eventually, the soldier climbed out and jumped and some people started hitting him, but most tried to save him. That soldier had just killed our brothers and sisters, he'd just been charging us with a heart of stone, but the people decided not to stain their hands with blood. I saw him running away under the protection of two elderly men.*

I now moved towards a building in front of which there was a group of people. I found myself coming to a halt with a corpse at my feet. His chest was full of bullet holes, his shirt was torn from the blood and the bullets. I froze. Then a boy shoved me and told me not to just stand there like that and I helped him move the body into the entrance of the building. I went into the entrance of the building and found lots of people there and two doctors helping lots of wounded people and there were two bodies in front of me. We put the man riddled with bullets next to them. Another man had taken a shot to the chest, and the doctor was trying to find a pulse and failing. Next to them was a boy whose head had been squashed and chest flattened from being run over by the personnel carrier. All the injured and the bodies that I saw were wearing civilian clothing. I tried to help out at the 'hospital' in the stairwell of the building, but I was in such a state of shock I couldn't do anything, so I went out. Everyone outside was stunned. It felt like we were at war.

After a few minutes, I wrote on Twitter, 'According to what I saw and reliable witness statements, three died.' I couldn't imagine things could be so bad.

I went looking for my girlfriend near the Ramses Hilton. There were lots of people, especially ladies of my mother's age, standing and praying in the middle of the street, asking God to have mercy on us, and suddenly I found a hail of bullets being fired at us from on top of the flyover. There was a long line of soldiers from the army firing at us. Everyone ran and then a few came back and courageously faced the bullets with bricks. In the middle of the confusion, I saw a man fall to a bullet.

The shooting went on for a while and then stopped and the tear gas began. It caused severe choking and burned the skin more than usual. I went into a side street to buy a Pepsi for the gas. I saw a woman screaming and saying, 'O Lord, is there no place for us in our own country, O Lord? O Lord, are You trying to tell us that theirs is the true religion, O Lord? Have mercy on us, O Lord!' I went and hugged her and saw that she was standing with her husband, who had been hit by a bullet, at her feet. We tried to move him so we could get him to the first aid station. He was dying and making frightening rattling noises and the blood was coming out of his chest in spurts. The rattling and the blood stopped before we reached the first aid station, and the first aid man told us he was dead and that we'd have to wait for another ambulance as the priority was for the critically injured. I was sitting on the ground, holding the lady in my arms, she was screaming, and her husband was next to us, dead. Till now I haven't been able to find out his name so I can go and offer my condolences.

Horror-stricken, I went out onto the main street. The shooting at people and the gas was continuing, and from our side, the throwing of bricks was continuing. I sat on the pavement and cried for a little till a friend of mine called Muhammad pulled me by the hands and got me away from a gas canister that had exploded next to me. I thought of the slogan 'Muslims, Christians, One Hand!' that I'd been hearing through all of this.

The situation went on this way for hours. Then suddenly a group of young men wearing cheap clothes and holding machetes appeared behind us, chanting racist slogans against Christians. Later, when we talked to them, we found out that they were from Bulaq. They'd heard on the TV that the Christians had armed themselves and were attacking the army, so they'd gone out onto the street to defend the army. One of them kept asking, 'Where are the Christians' weapons?'

It was a long night. We continued to be shot at at Maspero and into the centre of town for hours. Vile people shouting 'Islamic' slogans appeared and insulted the Christians. One of my friends saw them getting down from a Central Security lorry. We'd gone back to the same old dirty work.

I can't go on now.

What happened on Sunday had nothing to do with confrontations between Muslims and Christians and it wasn't communal conflict. It was simply violence by the authorities against peaceful demonstrators, the same as used to happen in the days of Mubarak. And not just that, but the authorities were prepared to use the media to make Egyptians fight one another on the basis of lies. They were prepared to set the country on fire.

But what is clear to me is that Sunday overturned all our preconceptions. Sunday proved that the Military Council is prepared to sacrifice us all, Muslims and Christians, create communal strife out of nothing, and ask Egyptians to go out onto the streets and beat up other Egyptians just like themselves, just so they can keep the regime we wanted to get rid of the way it was.

That day a still unknown number of demonstrators was martyred. The lowest number given by the Ministry of Health was twenty-five. I personally saw seventeen bodies. One of them was a boy I knew called Mina Danyal. Mina was someone I'd met in Tahrir. We weren't friends but I knew him. Mina was a brave young man: on the day of the Battle of the Camel he was hit by a bullet and survived. This time, though, the bullet, which struck his chest and went out through his back, killed him.

Brave Mina, whom I used to see at the demonstrations, I saw dead. It didn't look like him.

Testimony of Shenouda Assad

The beginning

*Today's march was different from the two other marches held before
this to condemn the demolition of the church of St George in the
village of Marinab.*

The numbers were huge compared to before.

*Shubra Street was closed off starting at the Shubra roundabout
and all the way to Masarra.*

That whole stretch of the street was packed with people.

Muslims and Copts.

*They weren't happy with the way the last sit-in in front of Maspero
had been broken up using force. And they weren't happy with the
churches being burned down – acts of injustice and no punishment
or deterrence. So they went out onto the streets chanting 'Muslims,
Christians, One Hand!'*

*Most of the chants were directed against Tantawi and the Military
Council, and we had more Muslims with us than the times before.*

We went down Shubra Street as normal as could be.

A few minor clashes and harassments as usual.

*Still, because the numbers were huge and everyone was furious,
no one dared to insult us or spit on us like the two times before.*

The calm before the storm.

We reached the beginning of Shubra safely.

*As we were going through the Shubra underpass, under the Sab-
tiya flyover, we met with a downpour of stones and bricks falling on
us from on top of the flyover.*

*A few people suffered minor injuries and they were given first aid
on the spot.*

*We waited under the flyover till the young men from the Maspero
Union went up on top of it.*

As soon as they saw them, the people who'd been throwing bricks ran away.

We satisfied ourselves that it was just a minor exchange and those types were just local people who hadn't liked the sight of the crosses in the march so they'd decided to say good morning in their own special way.

We kept going till we reached Qulali.

We got to a building there belonging to the local council and heard very heavy firing.

Everyone split up and began running in different directions.

There was a priest standing in the back of one of the trucks that had the chanters who were leading the demonstration.

As soon as he saw that there was trouble, he took hold of the microphone and began calming people down.

He said, exactly, 'Everyone, our demonstration is peaceful. Whatever provocations or harassments occur, it will remain peaceful. And, please, we don't want anyone getting angry or losing control. We don't want to spoil the look of the march with insults or abuse.'

Everyone calmed down a little and the chants against the Council and Tantawi and Enan began to heat up.

The massacre

We reached the Ramses Hilton, and, before we could go on to Maspero, there was a priest who got up into the truck that was leading the demonstration and said, 'Everyone, we've come here to deliver a message and then we'll leave right away. Whatever happens, our march is going to stay peaceful. We haven't come to pick quarrels or fight. We're saying, "O Lord, kyrie eleison!" If anything happens to anyone or anyone gets injured or dies, I assure you they will be regarded by Our Lord as martyrs for Christ.'

341

It was as though the priest could feel what was going to happen. Half an hour later, everyone understood why the priest had said that, and their enthusiasm was rekindled, and we continued the march.

I stopped to buy a can of Pepsi from a kiosk in front of the Ramses Hilton, and I phoned my mother and sister to tell them I was okay.

The important thing is, I was held up for about ten minutes.

The group that I'd set out with had got far ahead of me and I was now at the back of the march.

As soon as we entered the Corniche, we heard a sudden very intense burst of gunfire and all at once we saw that everyone in front of us was turning and running towards us, shouting, 'Run! They're shooting!'

I thought the army must be trying to scare us as usual with a few shots in the air.

All at once, all the streetlights went out and I heard the sound of screeching tyres.

I looked and saw an army personnel carrier coming from the distance at an insane speed and with a soldier at the gun that was mounted on it spraying bullets in all directions.

The carrier was running over everyone in its path.

The light was very poor and nobody could really see what was happening in front of him. All we could hear was the screams and the sound of the glass in the building before the Maspero Building shattering from the bullets.

I ran to take cover between two parked cars till the carrier had passed and I thought, 'It's over.'

I looked and saw two more personnel carriers coming fast and doing the same.

They too were running over everyone in their path.

They got to the end of the street, turned around, and came back, repeating what they'd done but on the other side.

Imagine what everyone looked like in their panic, especially given that most of the march was made up of ladies and youngsters.

We ran towards an alley that leads to the parallel street.

It was black as pitch.

Sounds of crying and screams everywhere.

I kept running till I reached the Ramses Hilton.

I stopped and tried to take in the scene that I saw. I was stunned by the army's reaction because no one had expected it would be so violent.

I was stunned at the sight of the body parts that filled the place, and the sound of the weeping and of people screaming 'O Lord! O Virgin! O Jesus!' After about ten minutes, the young people began to try to move the injured and take them away.

No matter what I write or say, I'll never be able to describe the horror of the bloody scene that I saw.

I saw two of them carrying someone the lower half of whose body was missing.

I looked at his face and found it was the person who'd been chanting in front of me. Before we entered, I'd been walking next to him, from where I joined the march to where I stopped and bought a Pepsi. In other words, if I hadn't bought a Pepsi and been held up, I would have been where he was.

I saw several people who'd taken bullets all over their bodies and whose blood was all over the street.

Everyone had gone berserk.

Some of them tried to remove the bodies and take them into the Ramses Hilton, but the security personnel prevented them and assaulted them, so everyone went insane and began knocking and banging on the glass.

As I walked, I saw around ten Central Security lorries going into the Maspero area.

I don't know what happened after that because I didn't know what I was doing.

I stood in the street for around half an hour unaware of what was going on around me, I was in such a state of shock.

When I got home, I found my family was of course looking for me everywhere.

I also found Egyptian state TV, which I cannot find words filthy enough to describe, saying a lot of very weird nonsense, such as 'Two soldiers die martyrs' deaths at hands of Coptic demonstrators' and how Coptic demonstrators had tried to storm the Maspero Building and fired live rounds at the army's forces.

That was bad enough, but those sons of bastards the talk show hosts with their provocative language were something else.

The bottom line is I want to make a few things clear, so everyone understands what really happened.

First: There were Muslims with us on the march, maybe not many, but more than on the two previous marches. They even joined in some of the Christian chants.

Second: When we came under fire at the beginning of Shubra, all we did was run. If we'd had weapons on us, as the media says, the least we'd have done was respond to the attacks.

Three: Throughout the march, we kept repeating that it was peaceful, and the priest warned us more than once against any provocation or harassment that might lead to violence.

Four: The number of people who were run over or killed by bullets was many times the number the media has reported so far (thirty-nine martyrs).

Five: As I said before, some people had a very strong reaction to the sight of the blood and the body parts everywhere. So any incidents of violence or assault after this between the demonstrators and the army or the police would be a very natural consequence of what happened (same scenario as the incidents that took place during the revolution).

Now, I beg of you, don't believe a word of what is being said on

Egyptian TV, no matter how respected or trusted the person who says it. That filthy place . . . There isn't a millimetre of space in the Maspero Building that isn't under the control of the soldiery. There isn't a word said there that isn't planned and calculated.

Don't believe any rumours or anything that's said about strife between Christians and Muslims until you've checked out the source because it's a dirty game now and you can't take anything for granted. The Council of Shame has been transformed from criminal to victim and gained the sympathy of most Muslims who don't know the truth of what happened. It's also gained the sympathy of many Christians who opposed the march and thought it was a mistake and that the types that went on it deserve what they got!

Publish any information or stuff from the media that can make it clear to everyone what really happened. And pray that this nightmare of the soldiery comes to an end before Egypt is destroyed.

Don't make things worse and fight with one another, for the sake of the people who died today chanting 'In Peace! In Peace!'

May God have mercy on the soul of every hero who became a martyr today and protect our blessed country from ruin!

Testimony of Mahmoud El Sayyed

First, let me offer my condolences to the families of the martyrs and mourn all our Egyptian martyrs. I think of them as martyrs in God's eyes.

Second: This is a testimony, not an analysis, meaning that I'm telling only what I saw, without analyses or inferences.

Testimony
The day of the march I was at work and following the march on Twitter from the moment it moved out of Shubra. At the Shubra

flyover, they were attacked by thugs and Our Lord protected them and they kept going and while all this was going on I was following on Twitter. They told people to cross over to the Al-Ahram building on Galaa Street and that everyone should join up with them. I thought, Shame on you, you ought to take part in this march, I'll go down and meet up with them at Abd El Men'em Reyad Square. I thought, it's unacceptable for me to be in solidarity with their cause and always making a fuss while just sitting at my computer. My conscience told me, Go, kiddo, even if it's only for half an hour and you just put in an appearance; at least I'll be in sync with myself and my principles. So, I went down and got a taxi. I left my car behind and didn't even have my wallet on me. I wasn't going to Tahrir or setting off on some big demonstration.

Anyway, I went down and got to Ramses Hilton and saw the numbers were large and that they'd reached the TV building. And as I'd expected – after all, it was Christians who were demonstrating – everyone was super well behaved and carrying signs and crosses and candles. I took a candle and walked for a little in the middle of the demonstration to have a look. The demonstration was full of Muslims and people banging drums and girls and ladies and women wearing headscarves. I got as far as the Corniche at the shop that sells spectacles next to RadioShack and someone took my right hand, just like that. I looked and found a young man smiling the 'We're All One Hand' smile at me, so I smiled back and walked with him. The kid was walking and holding my hand as though to proclaim a position. I mean, he didn't ask me who are you and I didn't ask him and he didn't ask me are you a Muslim or a Christian and I didn't ask him. There was a priest on a truck that was full of sandwiches. He kept saying Kyrie eleison and we kept repeating after him Kyrie eleison – Lord, have mercy upon us!

Suddenly I heard a lot of shots and the voice of a woman screaming and there was turmoil around me. The kid pulled me towards the pavement because everyone was running in panic and I couldn't understand what was going on and I was terrified because the sound of the shots was coming from every direction. All of a sudden I found that my hand was being pulled downwards. I looked at the kid and saw his leg was giving way and there was a bullet in the right side of his head. It had almost come out the other side and the kid started to stagger and fell in a heap on the ground and he looked up at me with a look of incomprehension at what was happening, a look like, Okay, so I'm dying, but why and how? A look of incomprehension at death itself. At first I thought he was looking at me but when I went over it in my mind later I discovered that he was looking up at Our Lord. I was just in his way. His look didn't contain any anger or sadness. It was just incomprehension and astonishment and questioning and half of a smile. I swear to God, I have no idea whether the kid was a Christian or a Muslim. I hadn't found an opportunity to ask him. He wasn't wearing a cross and I didn't notice whether there was a cross tattooed on his hand or not because I wasn't focusing on that. All the time, he was holding my hand. Then he calmly let go of my hand and collapsed completely onto the ground with his eyes open. I was so stunned, I knelt down next to him and kept shaking him and saying, Snap out of it! Snap out of it! A few people came and looked at me and said, What are you talking about, snap out of it? Just help us carry him. We carried him over the ground and when I looked to the left in the direction of the television building, I saw people milling around everywhere like ants and scattering. Why? Because an armoured personnel carrier was coming at us like a mad thing or like the driver was drunk and not in control of his movements. This carrier was coming towards us so fast that, after we'd all lifted the boy off the ground, without thinking we put him down again and ran. Have you ever seen anything less dignified than that? Do you know what a man feels when he runs and leaves behind someone who's dead or injured? Runs for his life because he's afraid for his

347

life? It's demeaning, and real men will understand what I mean.

I was one of those who ran towards the Nile. Gas had filled the air and I was crying, I don't know if it was from the gas or because of the kid who'd died or for myself or for the whole thing. When I think over it again, I can see with my own eyes the quantity of body parts that the carrier left behind it – intestines and brains and a pair of legs and half of a human being. I saw all those. But what was more horrible was that I saw people running and stepping on those remains in their panic. No one was thinking. Everyone was trying to save his own life. Do you know what it means to see the corpse of a martyr in front of you that keeps being subjected to indignity and trodden on and turning and moving because people are running over it and stepping on it and no one is thinking about looking down?

I kept moving back till I got to the National Party headquarters and saw people on top of the October bridge throwing bricks at the people beneath. It looked like a war zone with people screaming and people running back underneath, and I noticed people running after the personnel carrier which had been crushing us a little while before as it came back after it had finished its round.

I was running in the other direction and I went back to my workplace. I want to say that if I'd been killed that day, no one would have known, and I wouldn't have shown up because I went out without my ID. I might even have ended up as one of those martyrs that they bury without a name in the common charity graves. My question is the same as that of the kid who died and who became my dearest friend even though I don't know his name to begin with: Why did it happen? If anyone knows the answer, kindly be so good as to inform me, and thank you.

End of testimony

52

How was Nourhan able to keep a cool head in this difficult situation? The only explanation is that, as a reward for her piety, Our Lord, Great and Glorious, inspired her with wisdom and steadied her heart. Hagg Shanawany was naked and she was naked. She quickly put on a dress and flat-heeled shoes, did her hair in a rush, then brought fresh underwear and clean pyjamas for Shanawany, exerting considerable effort to get him into them. His body was stiff, the muscles rigid. She moved his legs, lifting them with difficulty, and it took a further effort to lift his body and rest it against the headboard. About half an hour was needed to make Hagg Shanawany look like a man sleeping normally in his pyjamas on his bed. After this, she opened the wall safe and took out the contract of marriage and thirty-two pieces of jewellery with which she was thoroughly familiar. She counted them one by one and put them in a large Boy Chanel handbag. God inspired her to take these precautionary measures for an important reason: Hagg Shanawany was married to two other women and had grown children who exercised significant influence within the state, and she was aware that her marriage to him had displeased many. It was perfectly possible that someone would steal the marriage certificate or the jewellery (of which twenty pieces had been bought by Hagg Shanawany alone). Once she'd set her mind at rest by placing the certificate and the jewellery in her bag, which would never thereafter leave her side, she moved on to the next step and phoned Shanawany's private doctor, screaming, 'The hagg came back from work, had lunch, and told me, "I'm going to sleep a little." When I woke him I found he was . . .'

Nourhan couldn't finish the sentence because she was weeping and screaming, 'Hagg, get up! Answer me, Hagg!'

After a few minutes, the ambulance arrived and with it the doctor (who lived close to them in the Settlement). The doctor forced Nourhan to swallow a tranquilliser because she wouldn't stop screaming and crying and trying to slap her face, which the servants and paramedics tried to prevent her from doing so that she wouldn't hurt herself. The doctor gave Shanawany a thorough examination, then drew the curtains, and announced happily, 'The hagg is alive, thank God!'

She approached and exclaimed, 'Doctor, I beg you, do something for him! I kiss your hands! I have no one in the world but him!'

The hagg was transported in a specially equipped ambulance to a military airport about a quarter of an hour from the villa, where there awaited him an army helicopter equipped for emergency medical assistance that had been sent by the head of the armed forces when his office informed him of what had happened. This took him to the Army Hospital, the most efficient and the best equipped in Egypt. In the helicopter, Hagg Shanawany had responded to first aid, opening his eyes and saying 'Aaah!' in a weak voice. Much moved, Nourhan exclaimed joyfully, 'God save you from any more "aahs", my darling!'

Following exhaustive tests, which took place immediately upon his arrival, the doctor stated to Nourhan that the hagg had been exposed to some extreme exertion. Then he asked, in a low voice and with a tentative smile, 'When you found him, Madame, had he fallen ill on his own?'

Nourhan ignored the doctor's sceptical look and said in a loud voice, 'Yes. I went into the room and found him, poor thing, just the way you saw him.'

The doctor made no comment and simply assured her that the hagg needed a week's rest in the hospital. Nourhan now conducted herself as a Muslim wife should: she asked the doctor to inform his first wife and his children while she withdrew to her house after having instructed the doctor to summon her at the appropriate time. News of Hagg Shanawany's presence in the hospital spread, and his room, and the corridor leading to it, filled with bouquets of expensive imported flowers, while such large numbers of people came to pay him visits that the doctor was forced to forbid all visits whatsoever, except, of course, those by important personages. Thus, the supreme commander of the armed forces was pleased to make Hagg Shanawany a personal visit, after which General Ahmad Alwany, the members of the Military Council, and the ministers of the cabinet all did so too. Likewise, the Supreme Guide of the Muslim Brotherhood visited him, with two members of its Guidance Office. A week later, as predicted by the doctor, Shanawany's condition had improved, though his face was still pale and his movements difficult and restricted. All the same, he insisted on attending, even in this state, the meeting called by General Alwany for the media group. Shanawany was accompanied by his doctor, whom he asked to remain outside the meeting room as a precaution should he be overcome by fatigue. The meeting was in the same large room in which the meeting on the president's resignation had been held. What a difference there was between this day and the day of Mubarak's resignation! Today, General Alwany seemed calm and confident. All the prominent media personalities, owners of private channels, and high state media officials had been invited. About fifty people had been seated at the round table, while General Alwany sat alone on the dais with, at his side, the major who directed his office, who stood throughout the meeting and left the room from time to time, returning to whisper news to His Excellency the General or receive instructions. Turning to Hagg Shanawany, General Alwany said affectionately, 'First, I'd like to congratulate Hagg Shanawany on his recovery.'

Friendly whispers ran through the room and Hagg Shanawany smiled and weakly raised his hand to acknowledge the people sitting at the table. General Alwany went on, looking at Nourhan, who was seated next to her husband, 'Second, I must acknowledge you, Nourhan, for your mighty efforts at the Authentic Egypt channel. Are you aware that the monitoring services say your programme now comes first in the whole republic in number of viewers?'

Nourhan smiled shyly and nodded but the general continued enthusiastically, 'The fact is, everyone, Nourhan is an example. It isn't enough for her just to carry out instructions, she comes up with her own ideas for raising people's awareness. You ought to be director of programming.'

Whispers and laughter ran around the room and Nourhan said, in meaningful tones, 'For that job you need a backer, sir.'

Everyone burst out laughing and the general, looking at Shanawany, said, 'I'll be your backer. See to it, Hagg Shanawany.'

'Most willingly.'

'So that's it. Congratulations, Nourhan. You're now director of programming.'

Laughing comments rose, some of those present congratulated Nourhan, and an atmosphere of bonhomie filled the place. General Alwany continued in his good mood, beginning his speech by saying, 'Before I tell you the reason for this meeting, I'd like to talk to you about the apparatus of which I have the honour of being the head. Officers of the Apparatus are not simply security men. All of us have studied psychology and sociology and many officers have degrees from major universities. We are all patriotic Egyptians, and here let me be frank. Our people are ignorant and backward. Most Egyptians have no idea how to think for themselves. The Egyptian People is like a child: if you leave it to decide for itself, it will do itself harm. The media in Egypt has a different role to play than in developed countries. Your task as media specialists is to think for the people. Your task is to mould the brain of the Egyptian and form his opinions. After a period of effective media influence, the people have come to regard whatever the media says as the truth. If you say so-and-so is a thief, he is a thief. If you say so-and-so is a hero, people believe he is a hero. I do not belittle the people. I am a son of that people. I am talking to you about the formation of the Egyptian character. The ordinary Egyptian is a simple man who keeps himself to himself. His only desires in life are to eat, raise his children, watch football, and, on Thursdays, smoke a couple of puffs of hashish or drink a beer and have sex with his wife.'

Laughter broke out around the room and General Alwany laughed too, but he went on to say, 'Isn't that how it is? The Egyptian never thinks about anything more than that. Food, family, football, and sex. The ruler of Egypt has an aura of respect and a position that is unlike that of any other ruler in the world. The Egyptian will never rebel against his ruler. Do you know why the January conspiracy succeeded at first? Because some kids created their own media. All the issues that got people excited began on Facebook and Twitter. That was our mistake as a state, and we've learned our lesson and rectified our errors. What I'm trying to say is that the task that has been placed on your shoulders is large. You are shaping how Egyptians think during a difficult period. Imagine: if you hadn't covered the Maspero incidents so well, what might have happened to the country? You are leading the defence of the Egyptian state. You are like the artillery in a war: it has to soften things up with a heavy bombardment before the infantry moves forward. I could have all those kids who betrayed the country and created the January conspiracy arrested in a single night, but the media has to discover them first. They have to lose any support among the people. The people has to hate them and, when I seize them, the people has to rejoice. I have called you together today to tell you that, in the coming period, the Egyptian state will enter into violent confrontations with the saboteurs. What happened at Maspero was just a beginning. All our options are open and we will need your support more than ever.'

53

Dear Mazen,

If it weren't for your words, which I recall whenever I need to feel hope, I wouldn't have been able to bear one hour of what I went through yesterday. I'd spent the day with the families of the Maspero martyrs at the Coptic Hospital. I smelled death. I became aware, yesterday, that death has a smell. I can't describe it but I've come to know it – a heavy, black, gloomy smell. I saw the martyrs whom the Egyptian army's personnel carriers had run over. I saw a girl hugging her fiancé, whose head had been crushed, extruding the brains. I saw a mother bending over the body of her son, whose upper body the carrier had totally flattened. Can you believe that Mr Ashraf, despite his experience of life, collapsed and wept like a child? He was unconscious until the doctors revived him. Despite that, he refused to go home and insisted on staying with us until the martyrs were buried. How can the Military Council have become such criminals that they would issue orders to run over Copts with personnel carriers? Why wasn't it good enough for them to kill them using bullets? Did they do that deliberately to terrorise the Copts? Many questions posed themselves in the midst of the hell that I experienced yesterday. To make the tragedy complete, there were Muslim citizens massed in front of the hospital chanting slogans against the Copts and threatening them with death. They believed that the Copts were the ones who had attacked the army, as the television keeps saying (that despicable talk show host Nourhan and her like). The families of the martyrs told me about Muslims who had shown solidarity with them and tried to protect them from the massacre, but also about Muslims who had assaulted them and were happy that the army had killed them. Yesterday I beheld the ugly Egypt against which we rose up – the religious fanaticism, the injustice, the criminality of the authorities, the killing of innocents, the falsification of forensic medical evidence, the submissiveness of the public prosecutor's office to the will of the security forces. Everything dirty in this country I saw yesterday. Can you believe that I and my colleagues and with us Mr Ashraf had to wage a long battle to get permission for autopsies to be performed on the martyrs' bodies? Who was our battle with? With the public prosecutor, of course, who had received instructions from National Security officers and refused to allow the autopsy because it would provide incontrovertible evidence of the crime. Unfortunately, our battle wasn't just with the public prosecutor but with the families of the martyrs themselves.

Imagine – because the priests had convinced them that there was no call for autopsies as those would mean the dismemberment of their dear ones, while a speedy burial would allow 'Our Lord the Pope' to pray over them before he returned to the seclusion of his cell! Can religion influence a person so much that he waives his rights? I don't blame the families. They are simple and poor. I ask myself, why does death reap only the poor in Egypt? After we'd convinced the families and the priests of the necessity and importance of autopsies, the public prosecutor's office asked us for a written undertaking that we would be responsible for protecting the forensic doctors who would carry out the dissection of the bodies. Another attempt by the prosecutor to terrorise the families and prevent the autopsies. Imagine – in a country with a police force and an army, unarmed citizens are asked to protect the doctors who will dissect the bodies of their children, who were killed by the army! Mr Ashraf went into the prosecutor's office and said, 'My name is Ashraf Wissa. I am a Copt and the oldest of those present, and I undertake to protect the forensic doctors.'

Tragedy turned into absurdity. Instead of ordering that they be guarded, the public prosecutor placed responsibility for protection of the doctors on the shoulders of Ashraf Wissa. Mr Ashraf signed the undertaking and we all signed after him. In the end the reports came out and we stayed with the families until the prayers for the martyrs had been performed in the church. I shall never forget these sorrows, Mazen. I shall never forget the cries of the mothers and the wives. I shall never forget the bodies piled on the biers. We left the church and I went home. I have three hours left before the meeting. I won't be able to sleep, of course. I shall take a shower and drink a coffee and go to the meeting. I had to talk to you. I love you, Mazen, just as I love our revolution, which will be victorious.

Asmaa

54

The moment Madany yelled, 'Your Honour, I want to say something,' the courtroom erupted in turmoil. The guards rushed forward and surrounded Madany, who had surrendered totally to the fit that had come over him and continued yelling, face glowering, eyes shining, and kept waving his arms at the judge. The latter, looking alarmed, said in a loud voice, 'Who's that?'

'Your Honour,' said Madany, 'I am the father of Khaled, the student who was killed.'

An expression of relief appeared on the judge's face, and he said, 'Very well. Approach.'

Madany strode towards the dais and the judge, clearly sympathetic, asked, 'What's your name, Hagg?'

'Madany Said Abd El Wares.'

'Do you have an ID card?'

It took Madany a few minutes to get the card out of his pocket and present it to the judge, who asked him again, in the same sympathetic voice, 'What is it you want, Hagg Madany?'

'I want to tell Your Honour a couple of things.'

'Please go ahead.'

The officer's lawyer fidgeted and tried to object, but the judge raised his hand and said in a determined voice, 'Kindly allow him to speak, Counselor.'

Madany's face showed a degree of calm and he cleared his throat, giving the impression that he was sorting out in his mind what he was going to say. Now, he was before the dais, even if he was still surrounded by guards who were prepared to seize him at any moment, and his young lawyers who were worried that the judge would become angry if he went too far. The assistant judges looked at him in a friendly fashion, as though affected by the sympathy of the president, who leant forward and rested his chin on his hands to listen to Madany. Madany said, 'I raised my son Khaled well. I'm a simple man and I work as a driver. In other words, I toiled so that Khaled could receive an education and enter the faculty of medicine and then Officer Heisam killed him and all the witnesses have confirmed to Your Honour that he killed him. I want Our Lord's justice.'

In compassionate tones the judge replied, 'You will get your rights, Hagg. We're here to see justice done. The court is adjourned.'

The judges rose and left, and Khaled's lawyers and colleagues surrounded Uncle Madany, who didn't seem to have taken in what had happened. Once they had left the courtroom for the lobby, the lawyers tried to explain to Madany: 'The judge adjourned the session because if he'd uttered any word indicating sympathy for you, the officer's lawyer would have had the right to have the court revoked.'

'What do you mean, "revoked"?'

'It means that he could request that what he said be set aside and that they bring another judge.'

'Why?'

'Because the law says that if the judge expresses his opinion on the case before the sentencing, he has to step aside.'

Uncle Madany didn't appear to understand. He'd throw out questions and not listen to the answers. He seemed nervous and kept looking at the people with him and then at the passers-by in the street, after which he'd light a cigarette and repeat his question: 'Why did the judge go away?'

The lawyers shook his hand and left, and Danya insisted, as usual, on taking him home in her car. On reaching the house, she noticed that he was still nervous and wasn't responding to her questions, so she said to Hind, 'Your father needs to rest.'

Danya left, and it occurred to her on the way home that the driver must certainly be reporting all her movements to her father, though it also occurred to her that she'd told her father of her visits to Khaled's family and that no one could stop her from making them. She returned to the house, greeted her mother, and went to her room, where she took a shower and switched off the lights. She was exhausted and yearned to sleep a little, but the moment she closed her eyes, the telephone rang, and Hind's voice came to her over the line, weeping, as she said, 'Danya. Father's very sick. He keeps talking to himself and walking around the flat. Please help me.'

55

It was a big meeting. Representatives of the Enough! movement, April 6, the National Association, the Revolutionary Socialists, and some independent personalities who had committed themselves to the revolution attended. There were about twenty of them, and Ikram had to bring two extra chairs from the flat on the fourth floor. She had made tea and coffee for everyone and sat down next to the members of the meeting in silence, as was her custom, ready to see to anything they might ask for. Dr Abd El Samad began by saying, 'I'm happy that you're here, in keeping with your unwavering commitment to your responsibilities. When we began this revolution, we were under no illusion that the battle would be easy. We knew that the road would be full of sacrifices. The old regime didn't surrender, it sacrificed Mubarak so that it could itself survive. Our battle now, quite clearly, is with the Military Council and its allies, the Muslim Brotherhood. The counter-revolution's plan was obvious – the withdrawal of the police followed by a security breakdown, the opening of the prisons and the release of the criminals to terrify the Egyptians and, at the same time, the defamation of the revolution via a gigantic media machine. Every day, the television broadcasts phone calls, videos, and forged reports accusing us of treason and of being agents of Western intelligence services. Naturally, we have submitted complaints to the public prosecutor accusing them of defamation and slander and we have requested that the telephone calls and videos be examined, to prove that they are fakes, but every one of these complaints has been set aside. Once the ground had been prepared, it was time for the massacres. The Maspero massacre targeted Copts who supported the revolution. Having them run over by armoured personnel carriers in front of the cameras was intended to terrify the Copts collectively, so that the revolutionary spirit wouldn't spread to them. In my estimation, these massacres will continue. The Military Council will target every sector that took part in the revolution, one after another.'

A young man from the Revolutionary Socialists shouted, 'Listen, Doctor, we know all that already. We're here to find out what to do.'

The doctor looked displeased, but he kept his temper and told the young man, 'Even if you do know it all, please hear me out. I'm getting to an idea that I want to present to you.'

The young man apologised and fell silent, and Dr Abd El Samad continued, 'We need media for the revolution. We cannot abandon the masses to the lies of the counter-revolutionary media. Of course, we don't have the same money as Shanawany and the big thieves who have inaugurated TV channels to defame the revolution, but we do possess the truth and the capacity to think rationally. My idea is simple: can you make a video that collects all the crimes of the Military Council, starting with the arrests of 9 March and continuing with the virginity tests and Maspero? Then we can publish such a video through a large social media campaign.'

A young man from April 6 said, 'Technically speaking, we could make the video because all these crimes were filmed. But why should we show it only on social media? We want to reach the ordinary people on the street.'

Dr Abd El Samad smiled and asked, 'How, in your opinion, should we reach those people?'

The young man said, 'We should organise a campaign on the street to show the Military Council's crimes to everyone. We should go from place to place, from street to street, all over Egypt.'

Murmurs spread, and a young woman said, 'Do you really think the Military Council will let you mount a campaign against it?'

'Since when did we need the permission of the Military Council?' a young man responded immediately, and another said, 'If we'd waited for permission, we wouldn't have started the revolution.'

Dr Abd El Samad said, 'If we mount a campaign, it must have strong security.'

A young man said, 'We at April 6 can, God willing, guarantee security and perhaps we can ask the ultras for help. After all, they have plenty of experience of standing up to the security forces.'

Dr Abd El Samad said, 'Great! So the idea's on the table – recording the Military Council's crimes on videos and showing them anywhere we can. Does anyone want to say anything more about the idea?'

No one responded, so Dr Abd El Samad went on, 'So let's put it to a vote. Those in agreement with the idea raise their hands, please.'

The proposal won by a large majority, only three of those present objecting.

Dr Abd El Samad, who had voted for the idea, smiled and said calmly, 'Now, to the details. What do you need to implement the idea?'

A young man said, 'We need to buy lots of stuff. We have to buy tent material to make marquees, and chairs for the audience. We need to hire a small truck. What we need most is large screens, and at least three good-quality laptops.'

Ashraf Wissa now spoke for the first time. 'Please write down on a piece of paper everything you need,' he said, 'give me an estimate of the cost, and I'll pay for it all immediately. We don't want to waste time.'

56

My beautiful Asmaa,

It is our fate to wage battle against a vast criminal regime that owns the media, the army, and the police, while all we possess are our dedication, our dreams, and our readiness to make sacrifices for the revolution. I sometimes watch television and I'm appalled at the terrible deceptions it practises on the People. Every day, new lies are invented to persuade everyone that the revolution is a conspiracy. Were you aware that the private channels that have been opened by businessmen are losing millions? Why would a businessman open a television channel that he knows will lose money? To abort the revolution, because if it reaches power, he will lose all his wealth and probably be tried for his crimes and thrown into gaol! The old regime is fighting its last fight. Our problems at the factory remain unchanged. Attacks on the lorries carrying cement continue, following the same pattern: the lorry leaves, loaded with tons of cement, then masked thugs hold it up, open fire, and force the driver and his mate down; the thugs then drive the lorry and its load off to some unknown place. We have made numerous complaints to the police but unfortunately the police officer who showed such enthusiasm at first has done nothing. I met with the commander of the police station and apprised him of the magnitude of these attacks and asked him to guarantee the safety of the factory. I was surprised to hear him say, 'Didn't you mount a revolution, bring down the president and set fire to the police stations? Guard the factory yourselves!'

I told him, 'First, we regard it as an honour to have mounted the revolution. Second, we didn't burn down the police stations, and you know who did, and who opened the prisons and released the criminals to terrify people. Third, I am a member of the factory's management committee and I'm telling you that thugs are hijacking the cement lorries. If the police can't provide security for the factory, then what is their job?'

I shall never forget the look of hatred, and the vengeful smile, on his face as he said, 'We shall just have to hope for the best. We shall make our enquiries and when we get somewhere, we'll let you know.'

I left the police station certain, of course, that the police would do nothing to protect us. I went to the military police and they asked me for a detailed written complaint, which I wrote and submitted formally to the colonel, who promised me that everything would be okay. But the attacks continued and increased, to the point that yesterday three lorries and their loads were hijacked. At the factory, we have a few badly trained security guards and about ten old registered pistols. We thought of having an armed security person go with each lorry but then it occurred to us that so far the thugs had made do with chasing away the driver and his mate and taking possession of the vehicle. According to witnesses, these thugs are armed with automatic rifles. If a security person fired even one shot from his ancient pistol, they'd return fire and kill everybody. So we dropped the idea. We have a real problem. The factory loses the price of every load that is hijacked, plus the cost of the vehicle. Even worse, a state of tension has begun to grip the drivers and mates as they leave with each load, and of course, if these attacks continue, the merchants with whom we deal will stop trading with the factory and buy cement from other factories. We're going to hold a meeting today with the department and division heads – we have to find a solution, and fast. Sorry, Asmaa, for spending the whole email talking about the factory. You're the person closest to me so I have to tell you.

I love you.
Mazen

57

As soon as Nourhan took over as director of programming, she revealed her amazing administrative capabilities. It's not easy to control twenty-five presenters, male and female, in addition to the directors, back-up staff, and artists. Nourhan would review the programme scripts one by one, then take recordings of the shows home with her to watch and the next day call in the director or presenter and offer him her observations with a sweet smile and a resolute and final tone of voice. Within less than two months, the Authentic Egypt channel had made it to the top and become the most watched in Egypt, according to the ratings agencies. Each night, Egyptians watched as confirmed and diverse evidence indicated that the revolution was merely a conspiracy to drag Egypt down into chaos. Each night, Nourhan would broadcast recorded phone calls between foreign officials and young people from the revolution as proof of their treachery. Each night, she allowed the viewers to read reports from official sources confirming the links between the young people of the revolution and foreign embassies, alongside spots on revolutions in other parts of the world that had been planned by the CIA. There were interviews with ordinary citizens who cursed the revolution because it had led to a downturn in the economy and others who believed the people had treated President Mubarak very badly by dismissing him and putting him on trial. Each such spot was technically accomplished, and Nourhan kept her eye on every minute detail, such as lighting, sound, and camera angles. Even though she had never studied media, she could discuss any technician's work with him, silence his arguments, and, if need be, take him to task. Nourhan always kept the most important of these many successful spots for herself, the advertisements for her own spot running throughout the day until she finally appeared at 10 p.m. Some of Nourhan's episodes were unforgettable and had such a strong impact that the next day people would be discussing them everywhere. In more than one episode, she hosted young people, their faces obscured, who all confirmed that they had taken part in the revolution and confessed that they had received money and been trained in Israel. In another celebrated episode she presented, she showed a video of young revolutionaries celebrating one of their birthdays and drinking beer. In this episode, she hosted Sheikh Shamel, who lashed out right and left at those who drank alcohol, asserting that such a person was less than a man and that his testimony could not be legally accepted by a judge. The camera moved to Nourhan's face, which expressed extreme distaste. She asked the sheikh, 'Revered Sheikh, can we place any trust in those who call themselves "revolutionary youth" now that we have seen them drinking alcohol and mocking our religion?'

'By God, we cannot!' the sheikh answered, in loud and emphatic tones. 'By Him who holds my soul in His hand, I cannot trust such people, now that I have seen them angering God and His messenger! And I call on all Muslims to boycott these evildoers who have given themselves up to alcohol. Do not listen to them, for these are traitors! They have betrayed God and His messenger and they have betrayed Egypt, our precious motherland.'

This was the episode that had the most impact. So much so, in fact, that a high official of the Apparatus phoned Nourhan afterwards via an unlisted number and told her, 'I have been tasked by His Excellency, the Head of the Apparatus, to congratulate you on this splendid episode. He thanks you for your sincere devotion to the state and assures you that the Apparatus stands ready to obey your every wish.' Nourhan sighed and said that she thanked His

Excellency the General, Head of the Apparatus, but that she had no need, praise God, of anything.

Using her total control and professional superiority, Nourhan imposed what one might call 'precautionary measures' at the channel: from the time she assumed the directorship onwards, not one presenter, male or female, managed to see Hagg Shanawany alone. They could now see him only at meetings, where Nourhan, as director of programming, sat next to him and ran things. Hagg Shanawany objected to this measure only once, when he said to her with an apologetic smile, 'It seems there are some presenters who wanted to see me, but you said no?'

It was while they were sitting in the garden of the villa. Regardless of the presence of the servants around them, Nourhan rose from her seat, sat down next to Shanawany, and clung to him, then reached out her hand, put it on his knee, and whispered, 'Were they male or female presenters who wanted to see you, my darling?'

Hagg Shanawany became confused and a kind of struggle appeared on his face between his objective opinion and his desire for the overwhelming pleasure that Nourhan knew how to give him. Nourhan rose, took hold of his hand, and said, 'Come on. Let's go inside and rest.'

Shanawany never returned to the subject and the rule became fixed: anyone who wanted something from Hagg Shanawany had to deliver their message via Madame Nourhan, while she monitored everything via the spies she had scattered throughout the channel, such as the office messenger Abd El Sattar, the director Hasan Marei, the hairdresser Esh-Esh, and others. This espionage network fed Nourhan with information largely without going to her office but through phone calls or messages. The only person who made her feel uneasy was a presenter called Basant who had come to the channel on the recommendation of a National Security general, whose mistress she was rumoured to be – a situation that caused her to behave with a certain confidence at odds with the conduct of the other workers at the channel. To be fair, Basant was beautiful, though her beauty was a great deal less than Nourhan's. The problem lay in the tight, revealing clothes that Basant wore and that attracted the looks of the men. At first, Nourhan followed the rules. She called Basant into her office and said, with affectionate frankness, 'Listen, darling. You are, of course, free to go around half naked if you wish. That's something only Our Lord can hold you to account for. But we, as presenters, enter the homes of millions of people and we have to set a good example.'

Basant fixed her with as much of a stare as her contact lenses would allow and said, 'Madame, I do not cover my hair.'

'I didn't say anything about covering your hair. I'm talking about the clothes in which any respectable female presenter is supposed to appear.'

A silence, charged with aversion and wariness, reigned between the two women. Then Nourhan looked at the papers in front of her on the desk, gestured at Basant, and said, 'That's it, thank you. Please go and see to your work.'

The following day, Nourhan issued a decree that was distributed to all the female presenters in which she defined the dress code in detail. Deep cleavages and all see-through or tight clothing were forbidden; furthermore, the decree stated that any presenter who contravened these instructions would be subject to sanctions ranging from not being allowed to appear on air to being expelled from the channel. All the presenters undertook to wear the prescribed clothing and it seemed the problem had been solved. Basant's games did not, however, stop. She took to wearing the required clothing in front of the cameras but on days on which she didn't appear on screen she would turn up in her normal scandalous dress and roam around the channel as though challenging Nourhan. She also told her colleagues offensive things about Nourhan that reached the latter, down to the last detail. Then came the big battle, on the day when Nourhan was on air and she received a message on her phone from one of her spies warning her that Basant was on her way to Hagg Shanawany's office. By luck, she received the message while broadcasting a report, so she ordered the director to move to a long advertising break and hurried as fast as her high heels permitted to the corridor that led to Shanawany's office. The luxurious red carpet muffled the sound of Nourhan's shoes, so she was able to fall on Basant as she strutted along in a very short turquoise dress that revealed her thighs and that was so open at the chest that her breasts (nipples excepted) could be seen bouncing up and down with complete freedom. Words cannot describe the transformation of Nourhan's beautiful, demure face into the hideous mask of a savage tigress, as she yelled, 'And where do you think you're off to, sweetie-pie?'

Basant was taken aback for a moment, but, having decided to join battle, she replied in a loud voice, 'I want to see Hagg Shanawany, the owner of the channel. I believe that that is my right as a presenter.'

'No, it isn't your right, because you have a director, and it won't do for you to go behind her back.'

'Suppose I want to see him on personal business?'

'Meaning what?'

'Meaning something that's between him and me.'

Unable to take any more of this, Nourhan dragged Basant away by the arm, her voice resounding down the corridor: 'You want to see him on a personal matter, or you want to show him your tits, sunshine?'

58

My dear Mazen,

*I write to you in a strange situation, one in which I never im-
agined I'd find myself. Yesterday, I went to Muhammad Mahmoud
Street before going to the school. Yet another massacre, perpetrated
by the soldiery against the youth of the revolution, was going on
there. What Dr Abd El Samad said is right. We've been dragged
into a carefully prepared plan for the dissolution of the revolution.
After the breakdown in security and the terrorisation of the Egyptians, followed by intensified propaganda via the media to the effect
that we are agents of foreign powers, they have begun carrying out
massacres against us, one after another. Yesterday, army and police
forces attacked the families of those who had given their lives for
or been injured in the revolution, who were holding a sit-in in the
square. The number was small, not more than a hundred individuals, many of them disabled. Suddenly, without prior warning,
they were attacked by men from the army, who beat them viciously. Imagine the soldiers beating a cripple in a wheelchair, or an old
lady, or the mother of a martyr who'd come to demand her son's
rights! They were the bait. The soldiers knew the revolutionary
youth would never tolerate seeing the injured and the families of the
martyrs being beaten. And indeed the young people came out onto
the square to find the Central Security and military police forces
waiting for them. The demonstrators chanted 'No to Rule by Soldiers!' and demanded the Military Council step aside in favour of a
temporary civilian government that would take over until elections
can be held. And the response was a true massacre, as I saw with*

my own eyes; a massacre in which everything was permitted, begin-
ning with killing demonstrators with live ammunition and ending
with firing shotgun pellets right into the young people's eyes. Do you
know Ahmad Harara? The doctor who lost an eye on the Friday of
Rage? Yesterday, he lost his other eye. Malek Mustafa lost an eye.
Lots of young people lost their eyes because that's what the officers
were aiming at. One scene will dog the army with shame until these
criminals are put on trial – soldiers tossing the bodies of young peo-
ple the army had shot and killed down next to rubbish skips. The
scene is on YouTube but I saw it with my own eyes, Mazen. What's
left, after our bodies have been thrown into the rubbish, Mazen? I
can't stop crying as I write. With each body thrown into the rubbish,
I imagine the joy felt by his family when he was born. I imagine
him as a child. I imagine him at university and I imagine his joy at
the revolution. And now I see him murdered and thrown into the
rubbish. Our colleagues are collecting all these videos to put them
together for a campaign that will travel round and expose the crimes
of the soldiery to the Egyptians. As you know, the Muslim Brother-
hood betrayed the revolution from the start, and they didn't take
part in the Muhammad Mahmoud demonstrations and didn't utter
a word of comment on the massacre. The Brotherhood wants power,
even at the price of all of us dying. The biggest disaster, though, is
the impact of the mighty media machine. Watch TV and you'll see so
many of the lies being promoted by the Military Council. They keep
repeating that the young demonstrators on Muhammad Mahmoud
Street are hired thugs who want to attack the Ministry of Interior so
that they can set it on fire so that chaos becomes general. Naturally,
no one mentions that Muhammad Mahmoud Street doesn't lead to
the Ministry of Interior in the first place. It seems we were wrong
when we underestimated the huge impact of the media on people.
We were wrong when we thought that the revolutionaries in Tahrir
Square represented all Egyptians.

Time came for school, so I walked from Muhammad Mahmoud Street to the Corniche and took a taxi to the school. The moment I got in, the driver asked me apprehensively, 'Are you one of the Tahrir people?'

I shook my head and he said, 'I thought not. You look like a respectable person, Madame.'

This was followed by an aria abusing the revolution and the young people who supported it, who wanted to destroy the country. Word for word, he repeated sentences from 'With Nourhan' and other programmes. He was totally convinced we were agents who'd been trained in Israel. I was still suffering from the sight of the martyrs whom they'd thrown into the rubbish. I let him insult the revolution as he wished. I wasn't ready, psychologically, to debate with him. I thought to myself, 'Even if I convince this man, what about the millions of other Egyptians who have believed the media and begun talking like him?' Imagine, the person insulting the revolution isn't a millionaire or a general in the police, he's just a taxi driver! In other words, he's a simple man of the kind whose rights the revolution came to defend in the first place. I found it very hard to take, that the young people should die defending his rights while he cursed them and accused them of betraying the country.

That was the first scene. The second took place at school. I've stopped talking about the revolution at school because the atmosphere has turned hostile and I can't stand the quarrels and the arguments that go nowhere any longer. Today, I was going down the corridor and there was Mrs Manal, the head teacher, standing at the door of the classroom. I smiled and said hello but was taken aback to hear her say in a loud voice, 'Enough! Have some mercy on Egypt! What do you want with her? Shame on you!'

I approached her and asked, 'Are you talking to me, Mrs Manal?'

In a rude tone of voice, she replied, 'Yes, you! Aren't you for the

373

revolution? Enough! Why do you want to set fire to the Ministry of Interior and bring down the state?'

I tried to explain to her the demands of the revolutionaries who were in Muhammad Mahmoud Street and that they were far from the Ministry of Interior, but she used every word I said to attack the revolution. Her voice echoed so loudly that the teachers came out. I withdrew and heard with my own ears accusations from the teachers that I was a traitor and an agent. They said the young people in Tahrir had taken money and been through training exercises in Israel and all the rest of the nonsense they see and hear on TV. Remember, Mazen, when you were amazed that the teachers were supporting the revolution following the fall of Mubarak? You told me then that the future would reveal if their joy was genuine or fake. It is now absolutely clear to me that it was fake. They are totally corrupt, and their profession has taught them to fawn and bend with the wind. I believe they congratulated me because they thought that the revolution would take over and they wanted to reserve their seats with the new authorities. Then, when they became sure that the Military Council was hostile to the revolution, they showed their true colours.

I had intended to go by Muhammad Mahmoud Street again after school, but I was depressed and decided to go home. The moment I opened the door, though, I found the real surprise waiting for me. I saw my father sitting in the living room. I don't think I welcomed him as I should have, and he too greeted me rather stiffly. It wasn't possible to meet him like that, after a whole year of absence. I hugged him hard and kissed him but there was still something keeping us apart, something that I could see in my mother's face. We talked about general topics, as though avoiding the confrontation, which wasn't long in coming. After we finished lunch and while I was helping my mother remove the dishes, my father said to me, 'Asmaa, come into the parlour. I want to talk to you.'

*I'm not going to narrate to you the whole conversation in detail,
Mazen, because it hurts me every time I think about it. My father
thinks I have been the reason for his problems in life, because I refuse
to wear the headscarf and I refuse to get married and I refuse to
work in the Gulf; I refuse everything that's normal and do abnormal
things. He thinks it was my grandfather Karem who corrupted my
way of thinking because he was a communist who drank alcohol. In
his opinion, I am the undutiful daughter God has afflicted him with
in order to test his patience and his faith. He said that, because of
the pain I cause him, he'd decided to ignore me entirely because he's
sick and the doctor had warned him against stress, and because I'll
be no use to him if anything should happen to him; he also said that
guidance comes from God (it being a given that I've gone astray).
Nevertheless, when he saw that I'd broken all bounds, he'd decided
to come from Saudi Arabia specially because someone needed to put
a stop to it. He told me my decisions didn't concern just me, because I
was living in his house, and until I went to the house of my husband,
my father would be the final decision-maker on everything concerning me. And he assured me that above all he would never shut up
about my participation in the revolution, because that was the straw
that broke the camel's back. You'll be astounded to know, Mazen,
that he thinks the country was better before the revolution. Imagine
– he said, 'I was happy when Mubarak resigned, but now I wish he
was still president.'*

*Can you believe he asked me, 'Of course, I know all about your
morals and your upbringing, Asmaa, but how could you all sleep in
Tahrir, girls and boys together?'*

*He has been influenced, unfortunately, by the disgusting things
the media has been repeating about sexual relations among the
young people of the revolution. He even hinted more than once,
when he was talking to me, that some of the young men were funded by intelligence services. When it got to this point, I shut up. I felt*

there was no point in arguing. It was then that my father made the offer that he'd come to make. In fact, it isn't an offer, it's a paternal diktat that must be carried out and that rules as follows: first, that I refrain from taking part in demonstrations, meetings, or any other revolutionary activity; second, my father has made an arrangement with a private driver to take me in his car to the school and bring me home, the aim being, of course, to be sure that I do not take part in the demonstrations . . .

At this point, I couldn't control myself and I said, 'That, I refuse.'

My father said, 'Why, if you don't mind telling me?'

'I can't abandon my fellow revolutionaries.'

Here, my mother yelled, as though she'd been waiting her turn to take the stage, 'Your fellows who want to destroy the country?'

I said, 'My colleagues are the most decent people in the country. They mounted a revolution and died and are being killed right now and their bodies are being thrown into the rubbish because they're defending our dignity.'

I was speaking heatedly, of course, but my father said to me with a strange calm, 'Listen, Asmaa. You've cost me a huge amount of money. This trip is at my own expense and the sponsor didn't want to give me permission. I'm not going back till I'm sure you've come to your senses.'

'I refuse your offer, Father.'

'I was wrong to offer you anything,' he screamed in my face. 'The offer is withdrawn. I'm your father and you are legally obliged to obey my orders. There'll be no more going out or demonstrations and you're going nowhere without the driver. If you leave the house at any time other than school hours, your mother will be with you. If that's okay with you, it's okay. If not, go to hell.'

My mother of course added some mood music, screaming in my face, 'Shame on you! Are you trying to kill your father?'

I left them, went to my room, closed the door, and haven't been out since yesterday. I'm in a fix, Mazen. I didn't go to school today. I refuse to abandon the revolution and I refuse to be placed under surveillance, but my father put me in this trap and I don't know what to do. Mazen, I have to end this email because my father is calling me. God preserve us!

59

Ashraf gave the money to the young people, who went that morning and bought all the required equipment – three laptops, two projector screens, large spotlights, lots of cables, the sizes and types of which had been precisely calculated, and four dozen chairs, plus the necessary equipment for the marquee. Finally, they came to an arrangement with a small truck, which hauled the equipment from Abd El Aziz Street to Talaat Harb Street. Once the equipment had been brought into the headquarters, the young people worked hard for two whole days, during which Ikram kept them supplied with sandwiches, coffee, and soft drinks and emptied the ashtrays of the butts of dozens of cigarettes. Finally, the work was done and the young people invited Ashraf to see the video. They turned out the lights and the show started. There were beautiful words from the army command affirming that the army never had attacked and never would attack Egyptians, followed by the testimonies of the girls who'd been abused while undergoing virginity tests. This was followed by scenes of armed personnel carriers running demonstrators over at Maspero and of demonstrators being shot and their bodies thrown into the rubbish on Muhammad Mahmoud Street. During the showing, Ashraf appeared moved. Ikram sensed this in him and took his hand, but he went out into the hall and smoked till he had regained control of himself, after which he returned to the room. The video continued for about twenty minutes and then the lights were turned back on. The young people started making their remarks to the director, who was a student at the Cinema Institute. Ashraf said nothing until the director asked him for his opinion, when he said calmly, 'I think that the video is clear and accurate. Anyone who sees it is bound to call for the trial of everyone responsible for these crimes.'

Once they were happy with the video, they started to discuss the details of the campaign. A young man from April 6 pulled out a map and said, 'We can begin with Dar El Salam, then move to Maasara, then Turah.'

Another young man said, 'Why don't we start with what's closest, then move to what's further away?'

They decided in the end they'd begin with the neighbourhood of Mounira, in the Sayeda Zeinab district, and that the performance would be on Friday, right after the sunset prayer, so that the largest number of people could see it. The young people left, Ashraf checked the laptops, screens, and microphones, turned off the lights, locked the door, and went upstairs with Ikram to the flat.

Ikram had made no comment on the idea of the travelling show. She'd been waiting for the right moment. She had her own special way of dealing with Ashraf – a mix of her natural intelligence, her experience of men, the sensitivity of a mistress, and the tenderness of a mother. She could now see through Ashraf at a glance, knowing immediately when he was stoned, hungry, tired, or angry, or even when he was feeling aroused and wanted to make love to her, and for every state she was ready with the appropriate response. She never confronted him, but rather guided him adroitly to what she wanted. Sometimes she was prey to misgivings. What if he decided to return to his old wife and throw her out? What if he became embarrassed at her being a servant and decided to end the relationship? At such times, she'd seek refuge with him, so that he could set her mind at rest and assure her that he still loved her and would never abandon her. Sometimes she'd cry because she was so afraid for him and sometimes she'd cry because she loved him so much. Her love for him was so strong that it often confused her. Her love

379

for him was more than love. There was emotional love and there was physical passion, and she had never known such ever-renewed, burning, tyrannical love as she knew with him. There was also a deep feeling of gratitude. This man had taken her in from the streets and was spending thousands of pounds to rid her of the evil of her husband Mansour, the pill and Max addict. Also, he loved Shahd as though she were his own daughter or granddaughter. Ashraf had become the axis around which Ikram's life revolved from the moment she woke to the moment she went to sleep, and she cared for only two individuals in this life, Shahd and Ashraf. Whatever she did, she did with Ashraf in mind, starting with taking care of her heels, which he liked to be smooth, and ending with the blood pressure pills she gave him every morning, following his health crisis on the day of the Maspero events. She'd even succeeded in convincing him of the importance of the popular remedies that she'd learned from her late grandmother. What a scene it was, difficult even to imagine! Ashraf Bey, the aristocrat and scion of pashas, lying naked and submissive to the hands of Ikram, the maid, as she spread pages of newspapers over his chest and then covered them with a woollen vest to absorb the dampness, or when she gave him a drink that she'd made with leaves brought from the apothecary's, to lower his blood pressure. Ikram would corner Ashraf with the glass and whisper silkily, 'Come on now, there's a good boy. Drink up!'

Ashraf appeared to enjoy the situation and would say, grumbling like a child, 'This concoction tastes terrible. I want a reward.'

Ikram's face would then light up with a smile and every time he took a sip, she'd give him a kiss. Sometimes, desire would mount, Ikram would put the glass on the nearest table, and they'd start a bout of passion.

That night, when they returned to the flat, there was something hanging in the air between them, something Ashraf knew she was going to say. Despite which, or because of which, Ashraf talked about other topics, telling her he'd noticed that Shahd was drawing beautiful shapes and he'd therefore decided to buy her a big box of crayons, and if she turned out really to have talent, he'd sign her up for drawing classes.

'Shouldn't she learn to draw first?' said Ikram, jokingly.

He explained to her in detail why it was necessary to foster a child's talent early. Ashraf was convinced of what he was saying but was also trying to put the other subject off. Ikram took her evening bath and returned in a blue nightdress and wearing make-up. Ashraf had smoked a couple of joints, which had put him into a contemplative, almost joyful mood. She lay down next to him on the bed, he couldn't stop himself, and they fell into a passionate embrace. When they were spent, he lit a cigarette and kissed her on her cheek, and she said, 'Are you really going to go out with the young people on the campaign?'

He looked at her in amazement and said, 'Of course.'

'You know the government may send thugs to beat you up?'

'The youngsters have taken that into consideration and there will be security details.'

'Do you remember the doctor telling you to avoid excitement?'

He didn't reply, so she went on heatedly, 'The doctor told you that if you subjected yourself to major excitement, your blood pressure could go up suddenly and you'd get ill, God forbid.'

He looked away and said, 'If I don't go out on the campaign, I'll get even more worked up.' He was silent for a moment, then continued sadly, 'It's the least I can offer the young people whom I saw being run over by personnel carriers and shot before my very eyes.'

Something in Ashraf's tone made her feel that her attempts to dissuade him from going with them would never work. They slept in one another's arms. As the following day was a Friday, Ashraf spent the whole day with Shahd. He played with her and asked her to draw him simple shapes, rewarding her each time with a sweet, and then hugging and kissing her. Ikram was listening to Shahd and Ashraf talking while she was in the kitchen making food like any ordinary housewife. After lunch, Ashraf slept for an hour, waking to find Ikram and Shahd in outdoor clothes. He looked at them in astonishment and Ikram said, 'I'm going out but I'll be back soon.'

'Where are you going?'

'I'm going to leave Shahd with my neighbour in Hawamdiya, so I can go with you.'

Ashraf was on the point of objecting but a broad smile from Ikram silenced him. Then he kissed Shahd, took a shower, got dressed, and, by the time he was finished, Ikram had returned, and they went down to the street, where they found the young people waiting for them. There were three other cars in addition to Ashraf's, plus a small truck they'd hired to haul the chairs as well as the timbers and cloth that would be used to set up the marquee. The procession of vehicles proceeded along the Corniche, then crossed Garden City to Qasr El Eini Street. They'd chosen a dead-end street next to the French Centre. They unloaded the chairs and began erecting the marquee. After a few minutes, a number of people appeared, asking what it was for. One of the young men said, 'We're a group of young people and we're holding a cultural seminar.'

This was the response they'd agreed on to avoid getting into arguments with passers-by that might prevent them from putting up the marquee. After about half an hour, everything was ready. The marquee, the seats, the spotlights, and the two screens had been hooked up to the laptops. The seats were about half full, and many people, driven by curiosity, were standing around at the entrance to the marquee, as though they were watching a quarrel in the street. Ashraf had agreed with the young people that he'd begin the talking, and his voice now echoed from the microphone as he said, 'Good evening. My name is Ashraf Wissa. I'm an Egyptian Copt and I want to ask you a question. Isn't it the duty of anyone who sees a crime to report it? In Christianity, in Islam, and in the law, anyone who sees a crime and doesn't report it is considered a participant in it, exactly like the criminal. The aim of this seminar is for us to report to you. We have seen horrible crimes committed against innocent Egyptian citizens, and so as not to be participants in them, we've made a video for you, which we're going to show you now.'

60

'Providing security for the cement lorries we can do. Two security guards armed with automatic rifles can go with each lorry. I'm concerned about something more important.'

The man was in his fifties. His head was shaved, his expression piercing and probing, his body athletic, all of which gave him a military appearance, despite the fact that he was wearing civilian clothes. He was sitting in the large armchair in the living room of Mazen's small flat, which consisted of a bedroom at the back and the small living room containing a number of chairs and an arabesque table that Mazen used for eating and reading. The walls were painted white and hung with pictures by artists both international and Egyptian. Mazen looked at the man and asked, 'What do you mean?'

The man smiled and said, 'Can you tell me how the thugs know, every day, the route the lorries will take?'

Mazen didn't answer, and the man went on, 'The only explanation is that you have people inside the factory who inform the thugs of the route. It follows that it's not enough for you to provide security, because the attack could be switched to inside the factory, and your security guards aren't qualified to handle that.'

Mazen thought for a little, then said, 'Very well. So what is your suggestion?'

'My suggestion is that the factory should sign a comprehensive security contract with me. If you do that, you'll have a hundred security guards, armed and trained to the highest level. Security operations will cover the lorries, the furnaces, the mills, and every stage of the production process.'

'How much would it cost?'

'I'll do the sums and send them to you by email.'

'Can you do them now? To be honest, it's urgent.'

'Very well.'

The man opened his laptop and became engrossed in making the calculations. Suddenly, the doorbell rang. The man seemed nervous and asked, 'Are you expecting guests?'

Mazen shook his head, then rose and cast a quick look around the place. He didn't keep any information or papers at home, and even his mobile phone and laptop were stripped of anything that might give a clue to his activities. The doorbell rang again, and Mazen looked through the peephole, astonishment appearing on his face. He opened the door and Asmaa entered, saying, not yet having noticed the presence of a third person, 'Thank God I've found you! Why don't you answer your phone?'

'Please come in,' Mazen said, once he'd got over his surprise.

Appearing embarrassed, the man said, 'We can continue the meeting at some other time, if you like.'

'No, not at all,' Mazen replied. 'This is Asmaa, our colleague. The brigadier has a private security firm, and we're making an arrangement for protection of the factory.'

Asmaa nodded and threw herself into the chair that was furthest away. She seemed despondent and completely absorbed in her own thoughts. Mazen returned and sat down in front of the brigadier, who was busy writing on a piece of paper, which he soon gave to Mazen, saying amicably, 'I've included the security charges for the entire factory and given you a 10 per cent discount as my contribution.'

'I have no objection to the amount. Security will save us millions. But my colleagues on the four-man committee will have to agree, and we'll have to get the consent of Legal Affairs.'

'At your service.'

'I'll get back to you tomorrow at the end of the day. If we agree, when can you start providing guards?'

'If we sign the contract and you make the first payment, you'll have guards the same day.'

'Great.'

Mazen fell silent and looked at the brigadier with a smile, as if to indicate that the meeting was over. The brigadier excused himself, shook Mazen's hand warmly, and said goodbye to Asmaa, who responded in a low voice. No sooner had Mazen closed the door than he went quickly over to Asmaa and said, cheerfully, 'What's this lovely surprise?'

Asmaa looked at him for a moment, then said quietly, 'I've left home.'

61

Danya took no longer than the time needed to reach Maasara. She arrived at Uncle Madany's house accompanied by a professor of psychiatry she knew from the Gezira Club; she'd phoned him, and he had come immediately. They met at Roxy Square, where he left his car and got into hers. On the way, she told him everything. The moment they knocked on the door, Hind came out and whispered in panic, 'Dad just keeps talking on and on. He doesn't want to sit down or sleep or eat. I speak to him and he doesn't reply, as though he can't hear me. He's been saying the same things since the moment we were in court.'

The doctor calmed her down and they agreed that they'd introduce him as a professor at the Faculty of Medicine who'd been abroad and had heard of Khaled's death when he'd got back, so he'd come to offer his condolences. They entered and found Uncle Madany standing in the living room in the same clothes he'd worn in court. He appeared tense and stared at them straightaway. The moment he saw the doctor, he said, 'Sir, I have a question, if you don't mind. When my son is murdered in broad daylight, and all the witnesses say that the officer Heisam El Meligi killed him, I have the right to talk to the judge, don't I, and it's his duty to listen to me, isn't it? Right, sir?'

Hind cried out in a tearful voice, 'Dad, all the lawyers told you that the judge couldn't give his opinion on the case or he'd be disqualified.'

As though he hadn't heard her, Madany said, 'I said two words to the judge and he went and cut me off. He said the court was adjourned!'

The doctor signalled to Hind not to continue with the conversation and went up to Madany, shook his hand affectionately, introduced himself, and expressed his condolences. Uncle Madany looked at him and suddenly became excited.

'You taught the late Khaled, sir? Welcome, welcome!'

He invited him into the guest parlour and asked what he would drink, insisting until the man asked for coffee, which Hind went off to make. Madany sat down in front of him and greeted him again: 'Welcome, welcome, Doctor!'

They sat together for about an hour, during which the doctor was able skilfully to conceal his probing glances behind his smile and his talk, which appeared normal and appropriate to the situation. Then he excused himself, with Danya, and Uncle Madany bade them a warm farewell. Hind went out with them and stood outside the flat, where the doctor spoke to her in a whisper, a serious and entirely professional expression on his face.

'Uncle Madany has what's called post-traumatic stress disorder. When a person is subjected to a violent shock, he is likely to suffer certain disorders. He will have a tendency to withdraw, meaning he will speak little and show no interest in anything. Then, suddenly, he'll suffer a strong reaction, which will last for a long time. But Uncle Madany has retained his memory and his powers of concentration completely. Thank God – his condition could have been much worse. I'll write you a prescription for a tranquilliser that he's only to take if he has trouble sleeping. At this stage, we have to keep an eye on him without letting him feel that anything is wrong with him. The Lord be with him.'

62

The battle that now ensued between Nourhan and Basant was so packed with ferocity, hatred, and bile, that it took on a somewhat animalistic character, as though the women were two beasts fighting for survival, one of which had to die for the other to live. It took place under a concentrated mutual bombardment of phrases of extreme vulgarity. Nourhan initiated the attack, pulling Basant violently by her arm so that she tottered and almost fell, while with her other arm she was able to tear off her hairpiece. Basant shrieked and began insulting Nourhan's mother, only to quickly discover that Nourhan's Islamic dress provided her with protection from her blows, which led her to begin kicking her with all her might on her shins instead, using her pointed, metal-tipped shoes, time after time and in the same place, to make the wound deeper. Nourhan was able, however, despite the pain, to get her hands on Basant's face, digging her nails in and then dragging her powerfully towards her, after which she brought her mouth down onto her shoulder and bit it with all the strength her teeth possessed, causing Basant to emit successive, piercing screams.

At this point, the channel's staff arrived on the field of battle and were able to separate the opponents. Basant's wounds were severe: her face had been scratched in more than one place by Nourhan's long fingernails, while Nourhan's bite on her shoulder had torn the skin right open, and this was not to mention her many blue bruises. Nourhan's injuries, however, amounted to no more than a few bruises on her legs from Basant's shoes. The odd thing is that Hagg Shanawany, in front of whose office door the terrible battle took place, never emerged to see what was going on. Some attributed this to poor hearing as a result of his advanced age. The truth, though, is that he heard everything but had realised – in view of his long experience of life – that to interfere in a battle of this ferocity would be to take a risk, the outcome of which could not be guaranteed. He stayed in his office, following the situation via a phone call from a member of the channel's staff, until Nourhan pushed the door open and entered, yelling and crying.

'Save me, Hagg! I've been beaten and insulted, and I want my rights!'

At precisely the same time, Basant was making a phone call to her friend the general who advised her to proceed immediately to the October police station and there make an official complaint against Nourhan, as well as requesting a medical examination to document her injuries. On arriving at the police station, Basant found the station chief waiting for her so that he could take her statement personally. She was also able to obtain a medical report to the effect that her injuries required treatment for at least twenty-one days, a finding that required the prosecutor's office to refer Nourhan for trial. The two women disappeared from the channel, and the oldest of the male presenters took Nourhan's place, apologising to the viewers and telling them that she had had to take a week's holiday owing to work-related exhaustion. The channel's staff enjoyed themselves going over the incident numerous times, at different rhythms and with amusing additions and comments, and in the end found themselves faced with the question that mattered most: which of the two women would emerge from the war victorious? No one testified in support of Basant. Those who did appear before the prosecutor asserted that Madame Nourhan had been the victim of a mean and uncivilised assault by Basant. Most of the staff were certain that Nourhan would win, because her husband was the owner of the channel and his influence within the state was solid, not to mention that he was 'like a ring on her finger' that she could put on and take off as she pleased. This group rushed to announce its absolute support for Madame Nourhan, praising her morals and her devotion to her religion. They also hinted that Basant was known for bad conduct and surrounded by deep suspicions as to her morals, which their piety prevented them from mentioning, given that, in keeping with popular belief, they didn't like to talk about women's reputations in case someone someday should impugn those of their own daughters. They knew that every word that passed their lips would reach Madame Nourhan and attract to them her benevolent regard. Some staff members did believe that Basant might win because her friend was a general with State Security, but these took refuge in a prudent silence, not announcing their support for either side and remaining neutral, anxious to avoid the worst scenario, given that their sole concern was to put bread on the table and raise their children, no more, no less.

The women kept up their pressures on the general and the hagg and word went around that the general had activated contacts at the highest level to demand the restoration of Basant's violated, unavenged rights. Hagg Shanawany's response was slower, perhaps owing to the wisdom granted him by his advanced years or perhaps because he knew that his wife was the aggressor. Nourhan did not, however, give up, and after she had screamed and wept, and shown him her injuries (on her marvellous legs), she decided, for the first time since they had got married, to deny him his conjugal rights. Thus, after Shanawany had returned from Friday prayers and they'd had lunch and he'd preceded her to the bedroom, Nourhan donned a nightdress, put on her make-up as usual, but then lay down beside him in a strange state of despondency. When he extended his hand to fondle her breasts and inaugurate the encounter, as was his custom, she moved away and said, with the fury of one wronged, 'Sorry, Hagg. I can't. I know that the Messenger, God bless him and grant him peace, said that the woman who refuses her husband in bed will pass the night cursed by the angels, so please, forgive me. I don't want the angels to curse me.'

With the last words, her voice quavered and tears shone in her eyes, and the hagg was moved to tell her, with a tenderness mixed with arousal, 'Darling, calm yourself.'

At this, Nourhan could no longer contain herself and burst into tears, repeating, 'I have been insulted, Hagg, and dragged through the mud, and you haven't got me my rights.'

The message was clear. Nourhan would never give up her feud and would take it out on Shanawany at just that moment of pleasure he looked forward to the whole week. And, because the solution to any conflict reflects the relative strengths of the competing powers (to employ the language of political science), a compromise was reached whereby, in return for her giving up her case against Nourhan, Basant's services at the channel would be dispensed with but she would be compensated with a job at another channel with the same salary and privileges. Nourhan made a show of being displeased with this solution, but realised, given her intelligence, that it was the best that could be achieved: on the one hand, the general, with his influence, could have Basant appointed to any other channel anyway, while, on the other, Nourhan considered that she had won, as she had expelled Basant from their channel after first beating her and dragging her honour through the mud in front of everyone.

The incident would remain fixed in the minds of anyone who might have thought of being cheeky to Nourhan, who called a meeting of the staff on the first day of her return and spoke about work-related matters in an ordinary fashion without alluding in any way to what had happened. (She believed that this mysteriousness would enhance the awe with which she was regarded.) The period after the battle would also see intensified activity on the part of the Authentic Egypt channel, under the leadership of Nourhan, who was called into the office of the supervising officer, who said to her, 'Starting next week, I want you to do a segment called "The Blacklist".'

Cheerfully she asked, 'And who would you like to have on it, sir?'

The officer looked at her almost with reproach and said, 'This segment may be the most important you ever present. There is a group of public figures who took part in the 25 January conspiracy. Most of its members have international contacts and are known around the world, from which it follows that it would be difficult for us to arrest them at the present time. We want to inform public opinion that they are traitors and agents of foreign powers who have taken money to destroy the country. The rest is up to you, Madame Nourhan.'

Advertisements for 'With Nourhan' began to appear the next day, announcing the new segment: 'Watch out for "The Blacklist"!' Nourhan didn't have to expend any effort in putting the segment together: everything came to her prepared with precision by the supervising officer. Nourhan would read the written paragraph from the autocue, while pictures of the opposition figure in question, in the company of foreigners, appeared. Then she'd say, 'We shall now listen to proof of the treason.' A recording of a telephone call between the same figure and a foreign person would then be transmitted. This would then be cut off and she would read, 'We have now heard with our own ears the traitor speaking to an official of the CIA.'

Nourhan added her own touch at the end of the segment: she agreed with the director that the camera should zoom in on her face, which would show deep emotion, and that she would then smile and say, 'Dear viewers, I find it difficult to imagine that anyone could betray Egypt. For what are you betraying your country? For dollars? For a job? For international prizes? Is it nothing to you that Egypt gave you food and drink, raised you and educated you and made you a human being? Traitor! Despicable wretch! Dear viewers, I ask of you one thing: should you see any of these traitors, let them know that you reject their treachery! Tell them, "You are a traitor!" May God forgive us all!'

She went to the officer to ask for his opinion and he laughed out loud and said, 'Bravo, Madame Nourhan! If you keep this up, not one of them will be able to leave his house. People will beat them with their shoes in the street!'

63

My darling Mazen,

Whether I die today or live a hundred years, I shall never forget what happened yesterday and shall always hold it in my heart and head. I shall remember the low lighting in the entrance to the flat and the sound of the music (you told me it was a piece by Chopin, right?). I shall remember shaking your hand before I left. Everything appeared normal but suddenly I felt a strange and violent trembling. Then I saw your face coming close to mine and I became aware of the scent of your breath. Then I found myself embracing you and kissing you – it felt as though it was the kiss of a lifetime, as though it erased all that went before so that we could begin a new page in our love. What amazed me was that I felt no shyness at our kiss. On the contrary, I was proud of it. When I left your place, I wanted to stop people in the street and tell them, 'I kissed my darling Mazen.' I'm going to let you in on an amazing secret now: at the moment when you kissed me, I was totally prepared for you, like a rose that has opened and is ready to give away its nectar. If you had pulled me inside, I would have followed you in total obedience and given myself to you and been happy. I swear I wouldn't have felt an instant of regret because I actually consider myself your wife. I am yours and you are mine, even if we haven't registered our love at the Civil Registry. What is the value of official papers? They are proof of legal rights but they are not proof of love. You may have felt what I was feeling at that moment when I embraced you so hard, as though seeking refuge with you from everything in this aggressive, stupid world that pursues us. I am certain that you controlled yourself so as not to make my life even more complicated than it already is. It's what I expected of you – always noble and gentlemanly. I am still living that moment, Mazen. I shall remain in it forever because I shall love you forever.

You asked me yesterday about my father and mother. I told you that I love them, of course, but that I had had no choice but to leave the house. I couldn't abandon the revolution, or live under surveillance. And worse than all that was what my father said about God having used me to afflict him. I felt very sorry for myself. What had I done that my father should consider me the cause of his problems? Is it because I'm honest, with myself and with others? Is it because I rose up, like millions of Egyptians, for the sake of justice and freedom? What I didn't tell you yesterday is that my father and mother went that evening to a relative of my father's to offer condolences for a death. I had prepared everything, so I took my suitcase and left the house. I left a note for my father that I stuck on the refrigerator door in which I said, 'Dear Father, I cannot abandon my colleagues who are dying for the revolution, and since you say that I'm a disaster with which God has afflicted you, I have decided to relieve you and leave your life for ever. Goodbye.'

Can you believe I was crying as I left the house? I gave it one last look, as I don't know when I shall return. I don't regret my decision. I shall phone my mother to confirm to her that I'm well but I shall never go back to them, ever. I went to my girlfriend Asmahan's, on Murad Street – I don't know if you remember her. She's a teaching assistant at the Media Faculty, Cairo University, and a member of the National Association. I took my suitcase. We'd made arrangements over the phone and I found her waiting for me. I took out my clothes and put them in the wardrobes, then took a shower and had a coffee with Asmahan. Then I felt that I had to see you. I couldn't wait. I wanted to see you, no matter how, as though I needed to draw strength from you. You were the one who could reassure me

396

*that I was doing the right thing. I phoned you but you didn't answer,
so I had two options: go to the factory or to your house. Of course,
the house was closer, even though the likelihood of your being there
was slight. I had to put up, naturally, with the stare of the waiter in
the café downstairs when I asked him about your flat. He looked at
me as though I were a prostitute. I didn't get upset. It's part of the
stupidity that we rose up against.*

*Let me tell you about my new living quarters. The flat consists
of a living room, a small kitchen, a bathroom, and two bedrooms.
Asmahan sleeps in one and she's given me the other. My new room
is spacious and clean, and the window looks out over the zoo. The
building is old and luxurious, and Asmahan tells me that the small
flats like hers were what the rich in the past rented to hide their
mistresses in. I started imagining my room, and one of the feudal
landowners meeting a dancer there in the forties. You know me,
I have a fertile imagination (I still haven't shown you my short
stories). Asmahan comes from a rich family from Tanta, and her
father, a doctor, rented this flat for her. He must be an enlightened
person because he let his daughter study whatever she wanted and
live on her own, even though they're always visiting her. I woke up
early today and went to the sit-in that has moved from Muhammad
Mahmoud to in front of the cabinet building. The Military Council
insists on staying in power. Following the massacres it carried out,
it opened Mubarak's cupboard and brought out a mummy called
Ganzouri to be prime minister. We moved to the cabinet building
to prevent this prime minister from the old regime from entering his
office. One hour spent with my fellows who are conducting the sit-in
convinced me of the truth of what you said, Mazen. This revolution
will be victorious, God willing. Everyone you know sends greetings.
They know you're fighting a difficult battle at the cement factory.
This morning, I met Ahmad Harara. Can you believe he never stops
smiling? I took a good look at him. From where does he get that*

strength? *According to normal calculations, this young man has lost everything. He was a successful doctor from a comfortable family. He lost one eye on the Friday of Rage. Then he took to the streets again, on Muhammad Mahmoud Street, and lost his other eye. His professional future is over but he's still optimistic and he's still smiling. We cannot be defeated as long as we have people like Harara among us. He asked me to say hello to you, by the way, and to tell you, 'Stiff upper lip!' I left the sit-in and went to school with mixed feelings. After I left home yesterday and met you and joined my fellows at the sit-in, I felt stronger. I no longer care what the teachers say about the revolution. Let them say what they want. As I told you yesterday, 'We're on the way in and they're on the way out.' We're the ones who are going to change Egypt. I taught my classes as usual, and the strange thing is that none of the teachers made any problems for me, as they have been doing recently. I'd expected that they'd talk about the sit-in at the cabinet building and accuse me of treason, and this time I was completely ready to answer them and silence them with my arguments, but no one said a word. It seems they're scared of me. Can our psychological state be transmitted to those around us even if we say nothing? I'm now at my best, psychologically, and completely optimistic. I feel free because I'm not obliged to go home early and I'll never have to lie again. I feel happy because I love you and you love me. I'll spend the evening and part of the night with our colleagues at the cabinet building. We will never accept the appointment of a prime minister from the regime against which we rose up. It's unthinkable. We will bring this Ganzouri down and force the soldiery to go away and we will form a civilian presidential council to last till the presidential elections. I believe, like you, that our revolution will be victorious. Do you know what I wish for now? To kiss you the way I did yesterday.*

  Bye, darling.

  Asmaa

64

Despite a few cries of objection, the young people were able to show the video in full. The audience consisted of about fifty people. Some were seated and some were standing but all watched the film to the end. The lights were then turned on, and the young man standing next to Ashraf Wissa said into the microphone, 'I thank you for giving us the opportunity to present the truth. Once again, I stress that we are not against the army. All we are demanding of it is that it put all the individuals who committed these crimes on trial, whether they gave the orders or carried them out.'

'How do we know these pictures are real?' shouted out a stout man wearing a galabiya. 'They could be completely fake.'

The young man replied, in a calm, clear tone, 'We have the full names of the victims. They're on our website, with telephone numbers for anyone who wants to contact their families, whether to offer their condolences, or to help them, or to confirm the truth.'

Voices rose posing other questions, but the young man didn't respond. This was all the discussion that was allowed. The second part of the mission consisted of taking down the marquee as quickly as possible and loading it onto the lorry, while the young men outside ensured the security of the withdrawal to the cars. The planning had been precise and was well thought out. The scouts had spent a full day exploring good places for the show. These had to be well frequented but not extremely crowded, and without a lot of traffic, so that there wouldn't be any problems. It also had to lend itself to the provision of security for the withdrawal after the show. In the evening, the scouts would return and propose a number of places, one of which would be selected. On the chosen evening, young people would be awaiting the campaign in the chosen place so that they could warn off their colleagues if anything untoward occurred. The erection of the marquee took place with the utmost speed and care was taken to avoid getting into any discussion that might lead to a clash. While the marquee was being put up, curious citizens would always turn up and ask insistently, 'Who are you and what do you want?', to which the young people's response was always short and polite: 'We are volunteers who are setting up a cultural seminar.' If they were asked, 'What's the subject of the seminar?', the answer would be, 'Come, and you'll find out.'

There was no objection to exchanging light-hearted comments with these curious onlookers so long as no specific information was given to them.

As soon as the marquee was ready, Ashraf Wissa would introduce the show because his age, smart appearance, and refined manners made a good impression. During the showing of the film, the young people in charge of security would surround the marquee on all sides, to prevent any hooligans from entering. As soon as the show was over, the young man would make his closing statement and everyone would leave quickly. The element of surprise was the secret of their repeated success. Their calculations had been precise and correct. Informing the police and sending thugs would take two hours at least, during which time they would have shown the video and gone.

At the meeting held to launch the campaign, Ashraf said, 'Our task isn't to convince anyone. Our task is to present the truth and leave people to the dictates of their conscience.'

The campaign had a success even the most optimistic hadn't expected. They were able to do ten shows in two weeks. They limited themselves to one show per day, to avoid any follow-up from the security forces. In the end, thugs would arrive, usually while the marquee was being dismantled or loaded onto the lorry, but would find the young people's security waiting for them. Most of these were ultras and had considerable experience of street fighting, and others had been chosen because they practised martial arts. The clashes with the thugs would continue until everyone had managed to load up the equipment and get into their cars. Then, finally, the young people would withdraw. The only possible mistake made by the campaign was to return to the neighbourhood in which it had started – Sayeda Zeinab. This time, the scouts had specified a place on Reda Street, a small street leading to Port Said Street. The scouts went, as per the plan, and found nothing to worry about, so they gave the go-ahead for the campaign team, which arrived. However, as the young people began unloading the chairs and poles for the marquee from the lorry, they were surprised to see people emerging from the surrounding shops and approaching them. There were a number of car repair garages next to one another on the street as well as, on the other side, a place selling tyres and car batteries, and next to that an old-fashioned grocer's bearing an ancient, battered sign on which was handwritten 'Ali Salama and Sons, Groceries'. The people who emerged didn't look like thugs from the security force. They looked ordinary and they didn't ask the usual suspi-cious, inquisitive questions, but they surrounded the young people and their expressions were grim, their looks challenging and aggres-sive. The oldest of them, and the largest, was about fifty and wore blue workers' overalls, while his hands were completely covered with grease. He went up to the young people and asked in a loud voice, as though launching into a stage role, 'What do you want?'

The rest gathered around him as though waiting to see what the conversation would reveal. One of the young men said, 'We've come to hold a cultural seminar.'

'Who are you holding it for?'

'For the people in the street.'

'Thanks, but we don't want seminars.'

The answer was unexpected. The young man said nothing for a moment. Ashraf came forward, shook the man by the hand, gave him a friendly smile, and said, 'Hagg, these are a group of young people who have a video that they want to show. If anyone wants to watch, they're most welcome, and if not, that's their business.'

The man answered, 'We're from the area. We don't want seminars and we don't want videos. Be so kind as to buzz off.'

Ashraf said, 'May I know the reason?'

The man now shouted angrily, 'Because you've come to insult the army and we're for the army. Got it?'

The others standing around responded to the man's words, their voices rising and mingling. One of the young people said in response, 'We're for the army too but there are people in the army who have committed crimes and they have to be put on trial.'

'And who are you, sunshine, to put the army on trial?' asked a worker.

Ashraf intervened, saying, 'I'd like our discussion to be conducted respectably, if you please.'

'How come, when you aren't respectable people?' one of the workers shouted.

Shouts of objection rose among the young people and Ashraf gestured to them to calm down. He was saying something, but the workers' boss shouted again, 'Look, son, and all the rest of you, the army can do what it wants. I swear to God, if anyone says one word against the army, I'll cut his tongue out!'

Ashraf said, 'How come, Hagg? Aren't soldiers and officers humans who can make mistakes? So when they make mistakes, we have to hold them to account.'

The man took a step closer and shouted, 'Tell you what . . . why don't you buzz off? Pick up your things and say bye-bye. It'll be better for you if you leave quietly.'

An angry murmur ran through the young people, and one of them shouted, 'You don't have the right to stop us from showing the video. The street belongs to everyone, it's not your private property. We're going to put on the show and if you don't like it, don't watch.'

As though the workers had been waiting for him to say this, they pounced as one on the youths and a bruising battle began. Some of the workers hurried over to the workshops and brought back tools and iron bars and began hitting the young people very violently, and one rushed forward waving a metal shovel and fell with all his strength on Ashraf. Ikram stretched out her arms to protect his head and screamed in a voice that resounded down the street, 'Shame on you! He's an old man, and sick. What kind of person are you? An infidel?'

65

Beautiful Asmaa,

I apologise. I wasn't able to phone you because events have been moving so fast. The attacks on the lorries have increased an extraordinary amount. On Thursday, five lorries and their loads were stolen. The four-man committee took the decision to stop transporting the cement in lorries until we can provide security for them. Every lorry that is stolen along with its cargo costs the factory tens of thousands of pounds in losses. Expecting help from the police or army is pointless. They simply do not want to provide security for the factory. The strange thing is that the head of the security company (whom you met at my house) vanished completely after we'd agreed to his asking price. I phoned him a number of times but he didn't answer. I was surprised he'd disappear when he was in a hurry to complete the agreement. I sent him a message saying that convention required that he at least reply to me, even if he'd changed his mind. He responded with the following brief, weird message: 'I apologise, Mazen. I cannot provide security for the factory and I cannot give the reasons. You're into something very big. God be with you.'

I haven't tried to contact him since. I found his response strange. What did he mean, 'You're into something very big'? He knew the magnitude of the security required and he assured me he had the capacity to do it. I was very exhausted so I decided to go home for a little while. Being at the factory always makes me very tense, which affects my thinking and my behaviour. When I feel like that, I go home and spend a night, or even just a few hours, and go back to the factory in good spirits. I went home, took a hot shower, and went into the bedroom in the hope of sleeping a little. I did indeed go to sleep, but I awoke to the sound of the telephone ringing (I keep it turned on, as you know, in case of emergencies). It was five in the morning. The workers informed me that the army had closed the factory. At first, I couldn't believe it. Then I confirmed the news. Troops had closed the gates. The officers had kept a few engineers and work-ers to close down the furnaces and forbidden the rest of the workers to enter. They told the workers that the factory's management had decided to close it because of the losses and the breakdown in secur-ity. At this point, the picture became clear to me. All the events I'd lived through passed before my eyes like scenes from a film that I was seeing in its entirety and understanding for the first time. I finally understood the meaning of the message from the head of the security company, 'You're into something very big.' I got dressed and hurried to the factory. I decided I'd go to the head of the military police. I found the officer on duty, a major. It was past 6 a.m. and he looked tired from lack of sleep. As soon as I broached the subject of the fac-tory, he said, 'The area commander took the decision to close the factory at the request of the Italian company.'

I asked him the reason. He smiled politely and said, 'To tell you the truth, I didn't bother to find out. This particular file is in the hands of the colonel. I think there's a problem with providing secur-ity to the factory and it's causing losses.'

I told him about the attacks on the lorries and said I'd presented a memorandum to the military police and nothing had happened. He responded with polite generalities. I realised that talking to him would get me nowhere. I shook his hand and left. It's now almost seven. I'm sitting in a café here in Turah, behind the factory. Thank God I have the new laptop with me. I'm going to send the news about the closing of the factory to the movement's media person. It has to be published in the largest possible number of papers and web-sites. We have to put pressure on management and the army using all possible means. I'm going to wait until the change of shift at 8 a.m. I'll call on the workers to hold a sit-in in front of the closed factory. We will never surrender! When the morning shift workers come to start work, they'll be surprised to find the factory has been closed. That's when we have to start the sit-in. Can you believe that, despite the crisis I'm experiencing, I feel at ease, just because I've told you what happened? I feel that our love and the revolution mean the same thing: we share the same battle and the same trench. In a little while, I shall join the workers in our decisive battle, and we shall be victorious, God willing.

I love you.

Mazen

P.S. I've heard that the army is going to break up the sit-in at the cabinet building by force. Take care, and my greetings to all the colleagues.

66

Later, Ashraf and Ikram would often recall that moment. Divine providence saved them. The worker fell on Ashraf, who was able to leap out of the way, while Ikram raised her arm to protect him and received the blow – from the flat end of the shovel, fortunately, not the shaft. The two of them ran to the car, and Ashraf drove off at high speed, to escape. The worker didn't chase after them but turned to take part in the fierce battle that was ongoing between the young people and the locals. Ashraf asked Ikram about her hand, and she assured him that it was fine. They went first to fetch Shahd from Ikram's neighbours' house in Hawamdiya; as soon as she was put into the back seat she went to sleep. When they reached home, they were silent. Ikram put Shahd down to sleep in her bed and made a cup of coffee, which she took to Ashraf in his study. Then she excused herself to change her clothes and take a shower. Ashraf smoked a joint and made several telephone calls. After a little while, Ikram returned, having put her hair up and wearing a housedress. Ashraf looked at her and said sadly, 'They arrested three of the young people from April 6.'

'And the rest of them?'

'Three are injured and at Mounira Hospital and the rest went home.'

'What are we going to do?'

'Lawyers have been to see the ones who were arrested and there are others with the injured.'

'We should go and see them.'

'We must. I just need to think a little. What happened today was strange.'

'Not at all. They were government thugs, like all the other times.'

He lit another joint and said, 'The people who attacked us today weren't hired.'

Ikram thought and said, 'You mean the government wasn't behind them?'

He looked at her and said, 'Unfortunately, Ikram, they attacked us on their own initiative. These were ordinary people who hate the revolution.'

Ikram remained silent, and Ashraf said in a low voice, as though talking to himself, 'I understand why the rich hate the revolution: it threatens their interests. But the poor in defence of whose rights the revolution came about – how can they hate it?'

'Shall I make you another coffee?'

Ashraf nodded, but noticed for the first time that Ikram lifted the cup with her left hand. He asked her once again about her hand but she made light of the matter. All the same, he insisted on taking her to the Ramses Hospital, which was nearby. After taking X-rays, the doctor there told her, 'You're lucky the blow didn't break your wrist.'

The doctor put a pressure bandage on her hand, and when they got home and as soon as they'd passed through the door, Ashraf hugged her and they lost themselves in a long kiss that ended in bed, where he tried hard not to bear down on her injured hand. The next day, Ashraf forced Ikram to take a rest and did the housework himself. He woke early, made sandwiches for Shahd, did her hair, and helped her get into her school tunic, then he took her to the kindergarten. Before leaving the flat, though, holding Shahd's hand, he looked at Ikram, and said to her cheerfully, 'If they ask me at the kindergarten, I'll say I'm her grandfather, and if they insist on knowing my name, I'll tell them that in our family we have Copts and Muslims, all mixed together!' He gave a loud laugh and went off with the girl. When he got back, Ikram came close to him, looked at him, and said, clearly moved, 'Even if I were to serve you for the rest of my life, I wouldn't be able to repay your kindness.'

Ashraf kissed her head and whispered, 'I'm the one who should thank you, for so many things.'

During the days that followed, Ashraf kept up his non-stop activities. The committee continued its meetings and decided to postpone the video campaign for a few days so that what had occurred could be studied and avoided in the future. He went with the lawyers to visit the young people who'd been arrested and found that they were in good spirits. He visited the injured daily; two of the young people had left the hospital and one was still there, to be discharged the following week. He stopped taking Ikram around with him on his outings on the advice of the doctor, who asked her to reduce her activities until her hand was back to normal. One day, he came home close to 6 p.m. He let himself in with the key and found Ikram standing in the hall as though waiting for him. The moment she saw him, she said in a worried voice, 'Your children are here.'

While Ashraf looked at her in astonishment, she whispered, 'Butrus and Sarah are waiting for you in the reception room.'

67

Mazen left the café at seven thirty on his way to the factory, going over in his mind what he was going to say to the workers. He intended to say that the four-man committee that represented them had been the target of a plot by the Italian management, the army, and the police; he was no longer afraid of calling things by their proper names; the workers had to understand that the Military Council was heading a counter-revolution that sought to bring about the failure of the revolution in every sphere. What he said wouldn't be hearsay. He had decisive evidence that the attack on the cement lorries was organised and that the security services had been negligent in protecting the factory. He would tell them about the complaints that he'd signed at the police station and the memo that he'd presented to the military police. He'd tell them that no one from the army or the police had done anything to save the factory. He mustn't speak for more than ten minutes. After reviewing the plot in all its details, he'd call on the workers to hold a comprehensive sit-in in front of the locked factory. He'd call on them to bring their wives and children to the sit-in, as the workers of Kafr El Dawwar had done. The presence of the women and children would remind the regime that these would be the first victims of the closure of the factory and would make it difficult for the authorities to break up the sit-in by force: if they assaulted the women and children, their ugly face would be on display to the entire world.

Mazen had settled on what he wanted to do, but when he approached the factory, he saw a strange sight. Hundreds of workers were massed in front of a platform that had been set up in front of the main gate and some of the workers were standing on it. Uncle Fahmi was speaking into a microphone.

'We want to eat, and raise our children. They made problems and headaches for us and in the end the factory was closed. Who's going to provide for our families now? We took the wrong road. All the members of the four-man committee are from the revolution and they want to put the country to the torch. We had rights provided by management. We could have asked for our rights politely and we would have got them, one by one, without problems. What we don't get from management today, we'll get tomorrow. What did the four-man committee do for us? They staged a revolution inside the factory and some of us, unfortunately, went along with them. We got involved in demonstrations and strikes until the factory was closed down and we lost our livelihoods.'

An excited cry rose from the workers. From the middle of the crowd, some of the workers who supported the committee began shouting, 'Not true!' and 'The workers have to take over management to get their rights in full.'

It was clear that those who supported the four-man committee had become a minority. Uncle Fahmi had been able to have an impact on most of the workers, and Mazen's supporters stormed towards the platform, shouting, 'Let Mazen speak!' and 'We want to hear Mazen!'

Uncle Fahmi picked up the thread and said, his eyes roaming over the massed workers, 'Chief Engineer Mazen Saqqa would like to speak? By all means! And what is Mazen going to tell you? He's going to tell you we should have sit-ins and strikes. Again, Mazen? We've already seen where your advice gets us. The factory, as you can see, has been closed down and now we're on the streets. Are you happy our children are going hungry? Have mercy on us, Mazen! Mazen, leave us alone to earn our livings. I want to ask you something, Mazen: now that the factory is closed, who's going to cover your expenses? Who's going to spend money on you and the youth in Tahrir who turned the country upside down and left it in chaos? Even if Mubarak was corrupt, at least there was security. Now the thugs and criminals are everywhere and we're afraid for our children. Our livelihoods have been cut off, so what are you going to do for us, Mazen? If you're going to get money from abroad, bully for you, but we're simple workers and all we have is our work at the factory. Get out of our hair, and no more problems! We want to open the factory so we can have money to buy things for our children.'

Voices rose and mingled. A minority of the workers around Mazen were demanding that he be given the floor while the majority were against letting him get up onto the platform. Uncle Fahmi went on, 'You want common sense? I've written a petition to the owners' representative in which we undertake not to strike and not to hold sit-ins and we agree to let a new director for the factory be appointed, with his knowledge, in return for the reopening of the factory. Agreed?'

Cries of agreement rose and Uncle Fahmi said, 'Let's get down to it, then. The petition's down there. Please, each of you, sign it. The owners' representative has promised me that if you sign the petition the factory will reopen in two days maximum and he's promised me you'll receive full pay for the days when the factory was closed.'

It seemed to Mazen that everything had been prepared ahead of time. Below the platform there was a table where an employee sat to take the workers' signatures. With the exception of Mazen's small group, the workers were pushing one another aside to sign the petition, obliging some to intervene and organise them into a long queue, after which each one signed his name alongside his national ID number. Mazen approached the queue, and some of the people standing in it averted their faces to avoid looking at him, while others gestured at him angrily and muttered disapprovingly. Mazen stood there a while with his supporters, then suddenly turned to them and said, 'I'm going.'

He didn't wait for their reply and didn't shake their hands. He walked slowly till he had left the factory and crossed the road to the embankment, where he found a minibus taxi and got in, heading for the city centre.

68

Was Asmaa dreaming or living reality?

She felt she was halfway between sleeping and waking. Everything she saw around her was imprinted on her mind in the form of vague, tattered images. The only thing she was sure of was that she hurt – extreme, unbearable pain in every part of her body that would die down a little in one place to be renewed in another. She was sure that her right arm was enveloped in a thick covering of plaster of Paris. She recalled the face of the doctor as he wrapped her arm in the plaster but avoided looking at her. She was sure, too, about the metal shackle that connected her left wrist to the back of the bed. With her tired mind she followed the faces of the young nurses who went in and out, giving her pills and changing the compresses without talking to her. And finally she remembered the head nurse, the expression on whose face, brimming with hatred and contempt, she would never forget, as she would never forget how she came close to her and said, slowly, enunciating the letters as though jabbing her with a knife, 'Slut! Traitor! You and your like have taken money from America to destroy the country. I wish they'd killed you all and spared us the headache. Your kind ought to be killed so that the country can be clean again.'

Asmaa could say nothing in return. Speaking hurt. Every movement hurt. There was plaster on one hand and a handcuff on the other and together they made moving impossible. One kind-hearted nurse would come to her when she was alone in the room (as though she secretly sympathised with her), smile, bend over her, and whisper, 'Do you want to pass water?'

Asmaa would nod, and the nurse would bring her a metal chamber pot and put it beneath her. She avoided going to the bathroom as much as possible because it was a complicated process. There was a soldier, who undid the handcuffs and escorted her, a wheelchair to which she was transferred, causing her extreme pain, and a nurse, who would go in with her and sit her on the toilet. She was absolutely exhausted. She'd lose consciousness for a while, then open her eyes and find the same pale light, the same white-painted walls, and the same empty bed in front of her. She didn't know whether it was night or day. Sometimes, without warning, she'd remember what happened and pant and sweat and feel she wanted to scream. She'd see herself at that last moment: she was standing talking with Karim, Asmahan, and some of the others at the sit-in in front of the cabinet building, then heard the uproar and the screams and one of those standing there shouting as he ran, 'The army's attacking!'

Everyone fled. Karim and Asmahan ran in the direction of Tahrir. For some reason, she ran in the opposite direction. She'd thought that the army was attacking from Tahrir. After running a few metres in the direction of Qasr El Eini, she was detained. She'd never seen soldiers in such huge numbers before (it was a special army unit called, she found out later, 777). The soldier didn't speak to her and didn't ask her any questions. He grabbed her by her hair and dragged her over the ground, while his colleagues set about hitting her with batons they had in their hands, then took her into the Shura Council building. There they led her to 'the Ladies' Department', as the officers called it, where she saw more than twenty soldiers beating seven female demonstrators as hard as they could with their batons. A girl would try to fend off the blows with her hands, exposing her body, and a hail of blows would descend on the exposed part. Then she'd fend off the blows from her body and the soldiers would go back to hitting her on her head. Asmaa was subjected to the full reception party, and then the officer came. She

415

remembered his piercing eyes, his moustache, and his gruff voice. He pointed to her as she lay there on the ground and shouted to the soldiers, 'Bring me that one!'

They had dragged her, while continuing to beat her, to a side room where she was left on her own with just the officer and three soldiers. The officer laughed and said, 'What's your name, champ?'

She couldn't remember how she'd answered but he said, 'Listen, Asmaa. Today, you're our bride. We're going to party with you.'

The officer fell silent and looked at the soldiers. As though this was a signal, a hail of blows rained down upon her without stopping, blows that fell on every part of her body. She started screaming and continued until her voice gave out. It hurt so much she wished she could lose consciousness. The officer gestured to them and they stopped, and he came over to her and said, 'Would you like me to stop the beating? Say, "I'm Asmaa the Whore"!'

She didn't answer, so he gestured to the soldiers and they resumed the beating with all their might, and the officer's voice grew louder, saying, 'I swear to God, you little bitch, we'll beat you to death if you don't say "I'm Asmaa the Whore"!'

She couldn't take it anymore, so she cried out in a tearful voice, as though apologising, 'I'm Asmaa the Whore!'

The officer stopped the beating and said, 'I can't hear you. Speak louder!'

She cried out, 'I'm Asmaa the Whore!'

'Again.'

'I'm Asmaa the Whore!'

'Again.'

'I'm Asmaa the Whore!'

The beating ceased and the officer gave a quite normal laugh, lit a cigarette, and said, 'Okay, Asmaa, if you're a whore, why are you so upset?'

He looked at the soldiers and said, 'Strip the whore.'

Two of the soldiers came forward, the third at their side. Asmaa didn't resist any further. She didn't cry out. She surrendered. She let them do to her whatever they wanted. They took off the trousers and woollen blouse she was wearing, so that she was now lying in her underwear. The officer said, 'Take off her bra, private!'

The private took her bra off roughly, causing it to rip. Her breasts hung down. 'Give her tits a tickle!' the officer said.

She remained stretched out and completely silent. The private approached and started grabbing her breasts with his fingers. Then he pulled back and looked at the officer, who said, 'I want each of you to play with her tits. One by one.'

The second soldier now came and bent down and started grasping at her breasts with his fingers, then the third, who just touched her breasts quickly. The officer shouted, 'Tickle them properly!'

The third soldier now rubbed away at her breasts. She noticed for the first time that he was crying.

'Is that good enough for you, whore?' the officer said. 'No? Not enough?'

In a hoarse voice, as though issuing an order of execution, he shouted, 'Grab her cunt, private!'

She felt the first soldier's fingers playing around between her thighs, and then the second soldier came and put his fingers in. The third soldier didn't move; his weeping had turned into sobbing, and he started saying, 'Enough, Basha! That's not right, Basha!'

The officer's voice rose in anger and he cried, 'Carry out the order, faggot!'

The weeping soldier approached her and put in his hand, trying to touch her gently.

The officer went up to her as she lay there on the ground and said, in a calm voice, 'Do you see, Asmaa, how little you're worth? You're worth nothing. I've had the soldiers play around with your tits and your cunt and I could have them fuck you now in front of me and you wouldn't be able to say no. You're nothing, Asmaa. Nothing. Know your worth, then, and don't be impertinent to your masters. Got it?'

69

The judge refused to allow the journalists and the cameras of the satellite news channels to enter the courtroom, so they gathered in a mass outside. The only people allowed to enter were the lawyers and families of the accused and the witnesses. The accused officers entered the dock, making an attempt to appear natural – waving to their families in the courtroom, whispering to one another, and smoking – but none of this could conceal their nervousness. A single glance was enough to distinguish the poor families of the victims from the families of the officers, with their smart clothes and the costly sunglasses on the faces of the ladies. This time the session took only a few minutes. The usher cried, 'Court in session!' and the judge and assistant judges entered and took their seats, and the judge began to read the names of the accused, followed by the articles of the law on which the charges were based. Finally, he said in a loud voice, 'The court finds all of the accused innocent. Court dismissed!'

The judge hurried to his chambers, the assistant judges behind him, while screams and wails broke out among the families of the victims, and trills of joy among the families of the officers, who started hugging one another and crying 'God is great!' It took Uncle Madany a few moments to absorb what had happened. Then he began yelling, 'What do they mean "innocent"? The officer Heisam killed my son.'

Khaled's colleagues gathered around him to calm him down. Hind screamed 'Shame on you!' and burst into tears, and Danya embraced her. Everyone was then surprised to see Uncle Madany rush from the courtroom. He passed through the door of the court

and went out onto the street, the others running after him and calling out. They caught up with him as he was trying to flag down a
taxi.

'I've had it. I'm leaving this country. I'm going to the post office
to take out my money so I can go abroad.'

They tried to calm him down but the idea had taken such a firm
hold on him that he was no longer listening to anyone. He started
stopping passers-by. He grabbed a young man and said, 'My son
was your age. A student at the Faculty of Medicine, called Khaled.
The officer Heisam El Meligi killed him in front of his colleagues
and the judge found him innocent.'

Voices could be heard from the passers-by:

'That's the way it is in our country.'

'God alone can help us!'

'May God recompense you!'

'Even if they find him innocent, where can he go to escape God's
accounting?'

At the top of his voice Uncle Madany yelled, 'I don't want to stay
another day in this country! I have sixty thousand pounds in the
post office, my life's savings. I'm getting them out right now and I'm
leaving in the morning.'

Some of the passers-by, along with the lawyers and Khaled's colleagues, tried to calm him down, but he kept on shouting the same
words over and over again. He appeared to have lost all self-control.
Danya spoke to Hind, then went over to Madany and took him by
the hand, saying, 'Enough. Come along with us, please. We'll go to
the post office.'

70

My darling Asmaa,

 This is the first time I write you a letter on paper rather than an email since the Friday of Rage, when they cut the communications networks, and the first time I'm writing you a letter of any sort in two months. When the workers agreed to submit to the Italian management, I felt frustrated for the first time. I felt the same disappointment I felt as a child when we were building beautiful sandcastles on the shore at Alexandria and a wave would come and knock them over and they'd disappear in an instant as though they'd never been. I called you that day but found your phone was turned off. I wrote you an email telling you what had happened. Believe me, I'm not angry at the workers. Each of them has commitments to his family and they can't gamble with their children's daily bread. At the same time, the media, which deluges them with lies, has unfortunately made them hate the revolution. I believe they will soon discover the truth. My father taught me to put my trust at the end of the day in our people's own capacities. Even if they are misled for a while, they will quickly return to the truth. You can't fool people forever. Tomorrow, or in a week, or in a month, the Egyptians will understand what happened. They will, inevitably, turn again to revolution. I haven't the slightest doubt of that. Asmaa, when I rode the minibus to go home, I felt that they were going to arrest me. I thought that if I were in the authorities' place, I'd arrest us now. Once public opinion had been turned against us and our reputations had been blackened, once everyone had been persuaded that the revolution was a conspiracy and they'd been terrorised and made to feel that the alternative to the old regime was chaos, the time had come to arrest us. Perhaps you'll ask me, if I was convinced they were going to arrest me, why did I go back to the house? Why didn't I hide out somewhere far away, with one of my friends or relatives? I was still suffering from the shock of the workers' submission to management and I couldn't bear feeling that I was running away. If I hid, I might avoid detention but for sure I'd never be able to escape the feeling that I'd run away from the field of battle. You're free to reject that logic and say I should have saved myself. I wasn't capable psychologically of doing so. I went home and was so exhausted I fell asleep. I woke up in the late afternoon, took a shower, and drank a glass of tea. The strange thing is that, when I heard the knocking on the door, I knew for sure they'd come. I opened and found an officer accompanied by a number of police goons wearing civilian clothing. The officer said politely, 'Mr Mazen, we need to have a couple of words with you.'

I asked him to wait while I quickly got my suitcase ready and he agreed. I went downstairs with them and we got into a minibus. The moment the bus started moving, they beat me painfully. I don't want to remember the details of the torture to which I was subjected. For forty-two days I was cut off from the world. The officials at the Ministry of Interior and the military police denied to my lawyers that they had arrested me. I stayed at a Central Security camp whose location I don't know because I was blindfolded when they moved me. I was subjected to hideous torture, Asmaa. Their goal was to force me to confess that we got our funding from the CIA. The officer would present me with a list of the names of foreign officials so that I'd sign a confession that I'd received money from them. After each round of torture, they'd show it to me again and I'd refuse again, so the torture would begin once more. Once I yelled in his face, 'You're wearing yourself out for nothing. If you want to kill me, kill me. I shall never betray the revolution.'

Suddenly, after forty-two days, the torture stopped. Either because *they'd despaired of getting me to sign false confessions or because Essam Shaalan's interventions with high-up officials had been successful or because our colleagues had made such a row over my detention in the Western press or for all these reasons. A colonel whom I hadn't seen before summoned me and told me he was sorry about the mistreatment I'd received and asked me to please bear in mind the delicate circumstances through which the country was passing. He assured me that, in spite of everything, they didn't doubt my patriotism, even if our views differed. It's just a common practice executioners use to give you hope, after which they start torturing you again, so that you're destroyed utterly. I said something ordinary and meaningless to him and he told me that I'd see for myself how my treatment would change and that I'd be leaving tomorrow for Turah prison, where conditions were much better and I'd be getting my first visit within a few days. I didn't believe him. However, contrary to my expectations, I was indeed moved the next day to Turah and two days later received my first visit, which was from Essam Shaalan, as a mark of respect for whom the prison director left us alone in his office. I'll never forget the first moment when Essam saw me in my prison clothes and with the marks of torture on my face and body. Can you believe he embraced me and burst into tears like a child? It was only at that moment that I realised how much I love the man. The visit was supposed to be for a quarter or half an hour but the director left us for two whole hours. Essam still has strong relations with the security apparatuses, and he told me that he'd heard about my detention and had tried to see me, but they'd told him, 'Mazen Saqqa is a dangerous and influential element. Leave him to us for a few days.'*

At Turah, everything changed. The torture stopped, even though the deputy director would slap me from time to time just to assert his authority, as though telling me, 'Essam Shaalan may have intervened on your behalf but I can still hit you anytime.'

After Essam, I was visited by my mother and my sister Maryam.

423

I was impressed by my mother's toughness, Asmaa. Can you believe she didn't cry? Can you believe that she told me, 'Hang on, Mazen. You're in the right.'

Can you believe she told my sister off when she cried? She asked her in a loud voice, 'What are you crying about? Don't give these criminals a chance to insult us. Your brother's a hero.'

Of course, I'm sure she'll cry for a long time at home, but she was fantastic. She held up in front of me so as not to affect my morale. When I thought about it, I realised she must have learned this toughness from her life with my father, who spent years in detention. Two days after my mother's visit, Karim the lawyer came, and it was he who told me everything. He told me what happened to you at the cabinet building and the hospital. I felt great pain for you, Asmaa. I wish I could have been with you but I was detained a few hours before the sit-in was broken up. Essam Shaalan visits me every Friday, and he will send you this letter once I've got your address from Karim. Essam has assured me that I'll be referred to the public prosecutor and be released on bail. After a while, they'll arrest me in another, major case, and I'll get a heavy sentence. Essam says, 'Don't think that there's such a thing as a prosecutor's office or a judiciary. It's the security forces that rule Egypt. They want to get rid of you forever. We have to be cleverer than them. The moment you're released, you have to go abroad. I can get you a visa quickly and as soon as you get out, go to any country in Europe.'

I refused, of course. I told him I'd rather die than flee but he keeps going on at me. Once he even yelled in my face, 'Are you going to be your own worst enemy, boy? I tell you, I heard about this set-up from a general in National Security. They're putting together a case charging leadership elements like you with seeking to overthrow the state, and you'll get life sentences. Would you mind telling me what heroism there is in staying and waiting for them when you know they'll throw you in prison for twenty-five years? Be sensible this once, if only to show you can!'

Of course, I'm smiling as I write this because I know I can't flee. You know me. I don't know what the circumstances were that made you decide to go abroad, Asmaa, but I cannot leave Egypt, even if I have to spend all my life behind bars. I'm still optimistic, Asmaa. I'll tell you something that happened so that you can understand how the officers think. The prison director is a kind-hearted, traditional type, even though that doesn't stop him from torturing people if need be. I asked if I could meet him and I told him, 'I've noticed that some of the criminal prisoners are illiterate. With your kind permission, I'd like to hold literacy classes for them.'

The director looked at me in astonishment and said, 'I don't understand. You want to teach the prisoners to read and write?'

'Exactly.'

'And what do you get out of it?'

'Every educated person in Egypt owes a duty to the illiterate.'

'Forget the empty slogans. What exactly do you want to get from the prisoners?'

'I want to help them.'

'Go help yourself first, son,' he replied sarcastically.

All the officers make fun of me for the literacy project. I feel a kind of rage behind their mockery. They're angry because we haven't been broken. I'm optimistic. The revolution will be victorious in spite of everything we've been subjected to and in spite of all the murder, torture, violations, and defamation campaigns, because they'll never be able to break us. Even the Egyptians who were misled by the media will soon discover the truth. The revolution continues and will be victorious. Don't doubt our victory, Asmaa, for an instant. You'll find Essam's address inside the letter. Send your letters to him and he'll deliver them to me at our meetings.

I love you more than ever.

Mazen

71

The surprise left Ashraf confused for a few moments. He hadn't seen Butrus and Sarah for more than a year. He gave them a warm and emotional reception, hugging them and patting them and gazing at them at length. Sometimes, he felt that they were he. He saw himself in them. Sarah was a slim young woman, with smooth black hair that hung down over her shoulders, and had inherited her mother's beauty. Sometimes, though, when she turned, or looked hard at something, he would see in her something of himself. Butrus, on the other hand, was a copy of his father – 'with improvements', as Ashraf would say jokingly.

'Would you like something to drink?' Ashraf asked them, after the greetings.

Butrus muttered 'No thank you,' and Sarah shook her head in a tense way that brought Ashraf back to a thought he'd been trying to dismiss from his mind since the beginning. There was silence for a few moments and then Sarah said, 'We've come to make sure you're okay, sir, and Mummy too.'

'You're most welcome,' Ashraf said.

In English, Sarah went on, 'Can we speak English, so that the lady who opened the door to us can't understand?'

Ashraf nodded, the situation now perfectly clear to him.

With the fluency of one who has prepared her speech beforehand, Sarah said, 'You know how we love you, and Mummy. To be honest, we're worried. We were saddened when we heard of the differences between you. You were always such wonderful parents. What happened?'

Ashraf's voice, speaking in English, sounded strange to him. He said, 'I don't know why you're asking me that. Your mother's the one who left the house and I invited her to come back more than once but she refused.'

Butrus said nothing but Sarah, who seemed to be leading the opposition, replied, 'She says that the house isn't safe now.'

'If the house isn't safe, that's all the more reason for her to be with her husband, if she loves him.'

Sarah looked at Butrus as though urging him to speak, so he said, 'Mummy says that the youths you're hosting are wanted by the police . . .'

Ashraf interrupted him sharply by saying, 'Listen. I'm not going to let myself get dragged into any discussion of the revolution. I've explained my position to you both over the phone and I've explained it at your grandmother's house. How often do I have to repeat myself before you understand?'

Silence fell once more. Sarah cleared her throat, then passed her hand over her hair and said, 'To be honest, I think your problems with one another go beyond politics.'

'What do you mean?'

'I mean that there's another woman,' Sarah responded without hesitation.

Ashraf answered angrily, 'You have no right, Sarah, to hold me to account.'

'I have a right to know.'

'Your mother and I were never happy. I think you know that. If it weren't for the complications created by the church, we would have divorced long ago. That's the truth.'

Sarah looked at Butrus, who said nothing this time, so she went on, 'You have the right to manage your marital affairs as you please, and you have a right to love another woman and Mummy to love another man. The problem is that when I learned who the other woman was, I was shocked.'

Ashraf smiled bitterly and said, 'You're contradicting yourself. If you believe I have the right to love another woman, then the identity of that other woman shouldn't matter. Anyway, I have nothing to hide. I love Ikram and I'm living with her and her daughter.'

'Ikram the maid?' Butrus asked, sounding upset. 'Do you think that's normal?'

'You're still young,' Ashraf said. 'When you get older, you'll realise that a man can love a woman irrespective of her job.'

'She's a Muslim, right?' Butrus said.

Ashraf said firmly, 'Yes she is. She was born a Muslim just as we were born Christians. Neither she nor we chose our religion. But I chose her because I love her. She makes me happy and I shall stay with her because she's the only woman I have ever loved.'

'I can't believe it!' Sarah cried out. 'She's a maid and a Muslim and married!'

'It's clear your mother has given you all the facts.'

'Everyone knows.'

'I have no interest whatsoever in other people's opinion.'

'Such behaviour angers Christ.'

He laughed bitterly and said, 'You believe that Christ only gets angry when you do. Leave Christ and me to one another. I love him, and he loves me and understands me and blesses me.'

Trying to control herself, Sarah said, 'Naturally, we don't have the authority to separate you from that woman, but we do have the right to inform you of our feelings towards the situation. We feel shocked.'

Ashraf was silent for a moment. Then he lit a cigarette and said, 'If you're here to inform me of your feelings, then I shall inform you of mine. I disapprove extremely, in fact, of your position because you have adopted your mother's position against me, as you always do.'

Butrus muttered some objection, but Ashraf shouted, 'Don't interrupt me! I'd understand if you'd come all the way from Canada to make sure I was okay during the days of the revolution, when people were getting killed every day. You were aware that I was taking part in the demonstrations and might die at any moment. I'd understand if you'd intervened to persuade your mother to come home and not leave me alone in those difficult circumstances. But you come now, to rescue me from my madness? The truth is you have only come now, at your mother's request, to rescue my money, which you will inherit after I die. You dropped everything and came to get to me in time, because you're afraid for my money, afraid I'll play the role of the old man who squanders his money on his mistress and her daughter. The fact is you've come to defend your own interests.'

'That's not true,' Butrus said.

'Very unfortunately,' Ashraf responded, 'it is. You think like your mother: you're incapable of understanding life in any terms but numbers.'

Sarah, who was now furious and looked like a copy of her mother, said, 'We aren't obliged to prove to you that we love you.'

'You love me in your own fashion, which is Magda's fashion. There's another way to love. This woman whom you despise because she's a maid and a Muslim, this woman who opened the door to you – did you notice that her hand is wrapped in a pressure bandage? Do you know why? Because she defended me and took a blow for me from a metal shovel which would have killed me on the spot if it had landed on my head. That kind of love is different from your kind.'

Sarah stood and so did Butrus, and Ashraf rose, went closer to them, and said, 'Fine. You want to leave because your mission has failed. By all means, go. Despite everything, I'll go on loving you and I'll be happy to see you any time.'

72

My darling Mazen,

I can't describe how happy I was to read your letter. I'm sure the people sitting around me in the café must think I'm mad, because after I'd read the letter I took to sniffing it and kissing it, more than once. How I've missed you! I used to phone Karim every day to find out how you were. I'll be indebted to Karim for the rest of my life. Sometimes I ask myself how a young man of no more than twenty-five can behave with such wisdom and courage. I was in the hospital, utterly destroyed both physically and in spirit. They had chained me to the bed so that I couldn't escape, even though I was unable to move anyway. Then the attorney from the prosecutor's office came. I could tell at first glance that he was an arrogant young man and a client of the regime. I didn't ask him to make an official record of my injuries and he didn't ask to do so, of course. I answered all his questions with the single phrase 'It never happened.'

Provoked by my replies, he asked, 'Is that the only thing you know how to say?'

I was released on bail of three thousand pounds pending trial. Our colleagues collected the money and Karim paid it. Then I left the hospital, after signing a statement to the effect that further treatment would be my responsibility (as though they really cared that I get treatment). Karim was of the opinion that the public prosecutor was going to issue an order at any moment banning me from leaving the country and that I should, therefore, go abroad quickly, because there'd never be another opportunity. Fortunately, I had a five-year visa for Britain that I'd obtained two years before so that I could visit my uncle who lives in London. Asmahan paid for the ticket on British Airways and Karim and Asmahan went with me to the airport. Can you believe that I travelled with a face still swollen from the beating and my right arm in plaster, and that I could walk only with difficulty? Every part of my body hurt and I was exhausted and so completely unable to concentrate that, in retrospect, my time at Cairo airport feels like a dream. The pain attacked me when I was on the plane and I took painkillers that I had on me. Can you believe that the moment I reached London, the British air hostess informed the management at Heathrow and they brought me a wheelchair and a doctor to examine me, and a hostess went with me to help me complete the immigration procedures? I never asked them for anything. It was just that as soon as they noticed that I was injured and in pain, they offered me this service. Can you believe that the British doctor said, as he examined me, 'You're going to be fine, and it'll be the last accident you ever have'?

He said this jokingly, to make me feel better, but I burst into tears. Really, Mazen, I wept. I wanted to tell him that I hadn't had an accident and that the ones who'd done it to me were Egyptian soldiers. I wanted to tell him, 'This is what my country, which I loved more than anything else in this world, did to me – my country for which I'd faced death, never fearing and never hesitating for an instant.' Yes indeed, it was my country that had violated me and abused me and humiliated me. Believe me, Mazen, I didn't leave the country because I was afraid of the big legal case that they're faking up against us. I left because I knew the truth, because the officer who abused me with his soldiers had said to me at the end, 'Now do you understand, Asmaa, that you're nothing?'

It's the truth, Mazen. I really am 'nothing' and all the young people who took part in the revolution are 'nothing'. They did to us, and will go on doing to us, whatever they want. They will kill us and abuse us sexually and put out our eyes with shotgun pellets and no one will bring them to trial and no one will hold them to account.

431

Do you know why? Because we're 'nothing'. Because we mounted a revolution that nobody needed and nobody wanted. I know you still believe in the People. I, though, will never believe in them. This people, whose freedom and dignity the best among us gave their lives to defend, doesn't want freedom and dignity. You used to ask, 'Why the hatred that we see on the faces of the officers as they kill us?' Because they hate what we represent. Because we're demanding to be citizens, not slaves. The people for whose sake we rose up, Mazen, hate us and hate the revolution. I shall never forget the hate-filled look on the face of the chief nurse and how she accused me of treason. I shall never forget how she wanted to kill all the young people of the revolution so that the country could cleanse itself, because we're agents and traitors. I shall never forget the comments of the teachers and the accusations of Mrs Manal. I shall never forget the taxi driver's abuse of the revolution and the suspicions of my father, who believes that we held sit-ins in Tahrir so we could have sex. You will tell me, of course, that that's all the effect of the media, but I will tell you in turn, 'I will never let myself be fooled again.' The Egyptians were influenced by the media because they wanted to be influenced. The majority of Egyptians are happy to be oppressed. They consent to corruption and have become a part of it. They hated the revolution from the beginning because it embarrassed them in front of themselves. They hated the revolution first, then the media gave them reasons for their hatred. The Egyptians live in the Republic of False Truths. They live in a mass of lies that they treat as if they were true. They practise the rites of religion, so they look 'as if' they were religious, though in reality they're totally corrupt. Everything in Egypt appears as if it were true but it's all lies, starting with the president of the republic who holds power through elections that are fixed but which the people congratulate him for winning, all the way to my father, who pours out praise by the bucketful for the Saudi sponsor who humiliates him and abuses him and robs him of what he's owed, to the headmaster of my school who halts teaching for the noon prayer but is the most corrupt of people, and to the supposedly pious teachers with their beards and their headscarves and face veils who fleece poor girls for their private lessons. Everything in Egypt is a lie, except for the revolution. Only the revolution is true, which is why they hate it, because it shows up their corruption and their hypocrisy. Egypt is the Republic of False Truths, and we presented the Egyptians with the reality and they hated it from the depths of their hearts. I left the country because I will not agree to live in a country where I am treated as though I were 'nothing'. In London, I'm a human being with dignity and with rights. No one will ever abuse me, no one will accuse me of treason, and no one can force me to take off my clothes so that they can play about with my body. I've now discovered that, when I was in Egypt, I was never a human being, Mazen. I was a 'nothing'. The officer who abused me taught me the truth.

In London, I went to live for two weeks with my uncle, his Scottish wife, and their daughter. Then I found a cheap, clean room in a small hotel in Paddington. The owner of the hotel is an Egyptian called Medhat Hanna, an elderly and very kind-hearted man who reminds me of Mr Ashraf. I will never go back to Egypt, Mazen. I shall work and study here, because I prefer to be a human being in a country that is not her own to being a 'nothing' in my own country. I know, of course, that you'll never agree with what I'm about to ask you, but I still have to: please, do as Mr Essam says and leave the country the moment you're released. Doing so isn't running away from the battle at all. We've lost the battle, not because we weren't brave enough but because the Egyptians let us down and abandoned us – the Egyptians for whom we rose up and for whom thousands of us died or lost eyes while defending their rights. These same Egyptians watched us being detained and killed and abused, and they clapped with joy and enthusiastically encouraged the massacre. I will never again make a sacrifice for those people, for one simple reason: they don't deserve

433

sacrifice. They love the dictator's stick and don't understand any other kind of treatment. The mighty revolution was an impetuous outburst, a single, strange, beautiful flower appearing out of a swamp. Our revolution was a sudden unexpected divergence from the path determined by Egyptian genes, after which everything quickly went back to normal and we found ourselves out of context, disowned, wanted by no one, sympathised with by no one and regarded by everyone as the cause of all their problems. Congratulations to the Egyptians for aborting the revolution and congratulations to them for discovering that we are agents of foreign powers and traitors! They will never know that the revolution was their sole chance at justice and freedom, which they thwarted with their own hands when they let us down. They regard us as traitors just for demanding the trial of the soldiers who committed murder. They organise demonstrations in support of the Military Council that murdered us and abused us and ran us over with armoured personnel carriers. No matter how much we explain, they will never understand that we do not hate the army but we do hate injustice. They will never understand because none of them gives a damn if the army kills other people's children, so long as it doesn't kill his. They will never understand that we prefer dignity and freedom to life itself, while they are prepared to give them up for a crust of bread. They are perfectly willing to let any authority run over them so long as they survive to raise their children. The Egyptians will never understand us and we will never be like them. What is the meaning, or the benefit, of your sacrificing your liberty and your life to defend a people who hate you and consider you a traitor? Leave them to their own devices, Mazen, and come to a country that respects your humanity and where you can feel you have some value, that you are not a 'nothing'.

I love you and am waiting for you and know that you will come.
Your beloved forever,
Asmaa

73

From the time Captain Heisam El Meligi left the Central Security camp on the Alexandria highway till it brought him to his house in the Muqattam, he'd driven without concentrating because he knew the road by heart. When he'd married Hadya seven years before, his father, General Ezzat El Meligi, former Cairo Security chief, had made him a present of a duplex on Road 9, which Hadya had taken a fancy to because it was spacious and attractively laid out. The living room, reception room, and dining room were on the ground floor, while the three bedrooms were on the second. There were four bathrooms, two on each level, one of them en suite with the marital bedroom to allow greater privacy. The couple had had their son Islam first, followed by Nadine, and Hadya had put both of them into the American Kindergarten as she worked at the Arab-African Bank and didn't get back to the house before five in the evening, not to mention Captain Heisam's continually shifting work hours. Hadya would never forget how scared she'd been for her husband during the revolution, when he'd stayed on the streets for three whole days. He'd phoned her just once, to tell her that the country was fighting a conspiracy and he didn't know when he'd be back. Following the fall of Mubarak, Hadya had lived through all the saddening details of her husband's trial. True, he hadn't spent a single day in prison – he hadn't even stopped working, in fact – but the idea of his being put on trial for murder threw a gloomy shadow over the household. Hadya avoided talking about the matter as much as possible. Just once, she'd asked, 'Is it true you killed that young student?'

Heisam hadn't been expecting the question, so without thinking he turned his face away and said, angrily, 'A police officer defends the whole country. It's perfectly possible he should kill someone, if the need arises.'

Hadya hadn't opened the subject again, but she did, of course, take time off from her work at the bank to attend the hearings, and when Heisam was found innocent, cried out in joy, 'Thanks be to God! God is great!' and hugged the wives of the other accused officers in congratulation. The same week, she had a bullock slaughtered and its meat distributed to the poor of the El Zelzal neighbourhood of the Muqattam.

The day after he was found innocent, Heisam was summoned by his commanding officer at Central Security. He entered and saluted, and the general smiled and said, 'Congratulations on the verdict!'

'Thank you, sir,' Heisam said, smiling back.

A serious expression now appeared on the general's face, and he removed his spectacles and ran his finger over his nose, then said, 'The finding of innocence regarding you and your colleagues is a message to all of Egypt's officers. No officer whosoever will come to harm so long as he carries out orders. And by the way, I've awarded you an exceptional pay rise.'

'Thank you, sir. I'm very grateful.'

The general dismissed him and Captain Heisam's life returned to normal. Hadya would go to work at the bank and then pick up Islam and Nadine from the kindergarten, while Heisam's hours were, as usual, variable. Sometimes he'd stay on duty the entire night and sometimes he'd work during the day and return and have dinner with them. On this particular day, it was past four in the morning when he drove his car onto the Muqattam highway. The road was completely empty, and Captain Heisam was tired, so he drove fast. He wanted a hot shower and dinner with Hadya, who always woke up and greeted him, no matter what the hour. He drove until he reached Midway Hill, and it was there that the unexpected occurred. He found a large rock in the middle of the road. Luckily, he noticed in time and was able to stop the car. The rock seemed to have fallen from the mountain, blocking the road. No sooner had Captain Heisam stopped than he noticed figures moving towards him. There were three of them. They came at him fast and he could see rapid-fire rifles in their hands. One came up to the window of the car and shouted, 'Get out!'

Heisam thought quickly of the revolver hanging at his left hip but, as though reading his mind, the man, whose face was covered, released a hail of bullets from his rifle that passed clear over the car, and he shouted, 'Get out, if you want to live!'

Heisam opened the door and got out slowly, and two more masked men came up and pointed their rifles at him. One of them said, 'Put up your hands!'

Heisam raised his hands and the man approached, put out his hand, and took the revolver off him, saying, 'Where's the phone?'

'In the car,' replied Heisam, in a voice that sounded strange to him. The three men moved confidently, as though accustomed to what they were doing, or as if they had been trained in it. The man entered the car, took the phone and opened it. Then he took out the SIM and, advancing a few paces towards the mountain, flung the phone with the full force of his arm. It fell far away and the man returned to his companions. One of them took the driver's seat, and they placed Heisam in the back, with one of the men, whose rifle was trained on his head, next to him. The third man got in next to the driver, his body turned to face Heisam and his rifle at the ready. The car turned and went back the way it had come, as though it was going to leave the Muqattam area. Heisam spoke once, his voice shaking: 'If you want the car and my money, take whatever you like.'

The driver laughed and said in a heavy tone, 'Shame on you,

Basha! Are you going to cry like a child? Pull yourself together!'

Heisam knew from the man's voice that he was under the influence of drugs, so he took refuge in silence. The car went down a slope, then drove fast for about ten minutes and came to a stop in front of a half-finished building. Heisam had decided to obey the kidnappers, mindful that a single pull on a trigger by any one of them would release a round of bullets that would kill him instantly. They led him to an unfinished flat on the second floor.

The walls and the stairs were made of cement and the flat had neither door nor electricity, but they brought a large paraffin lamp that gave out a dim light, which cast their shadows in ghostly forms moving over the walls. Everything had been prepared. Two of the masked men took on the task of tying Heisam to a wooden chair with rope, while the third left. Heisam looked at them and said, 'I agree to anything you ask.'

One of them shouted 'Shut up!' in a drugged voice. 'Don't give me a headache! Open your mouth again and I'll kill you.'

The two men remained silent, their rifles pointed at his head, while Heisam held himself rigid, afraid the kidnappers might misinterpret any sudden movement and open fire. After a little while, he heard footsteps on the stairs and soon the third masked man appeared and with him a man carrying a medium-sized suitcase. Heisam hadn't been able to make out the face of the newcomer in the dim light, but when he approached and stood in front of him, Heisam recognised him. Uncle Madany seemed angry and his eyes were shining. 'Hello there, Heisam Basha!' he shouted.

As though suddenly grasping what was happening, Heisam said in a tone of supplication, 'Hagg! Please don't kill me!'

Madany let out a strange-sounding laugh and said, 'Who says I'm going to kill you? You're a basha. Who can kill a basha?'

Heisam stared at Madany, his face trembling. Madany's voice rose again.

'I must say, you've cost me a lot. These men who brought you here are from our neighbourhood, from Maasara. They're known as "the killers". They kill to order. It's their job. Did you know that, if they kill you now, they're the ones who will take care of your body? It's what they do. Tomorrow morning that car of yours will be broken up and sold as spare parts. No one will know what happened to you and not a trace of you will be left.'

Heisam began to cry, his pleas for mercy overcome by his tears. 'I beg you, Hagg, don't kill me! I have a boy and a girl who need me. I've got lots of money. I can pay anything you ask, but don't kill me!'

Madany stared at him and said, 'What are you talking about, kill you? I came here specifically to talk to you. I have things I want to show you. May I?'

Heisam was in no condition to reply. Madany bent down, opened the suitcase, and took items from it. He began talking, fast and with laboured breath:

'So have a look, Basha. These are the first trainers I got Khaled, when he was in primary school. He was delighted with them because they light up. See – as soon as you press on them, they light up. Look at this. This is Khaled's certificate that he got when he came out top of the whole district in the primary school leaving exam. We had his certificates hung up in the living room but I took them down and brought them to show you. And here, my dear sir, we have the notice from the university placement board saying that Khaled had been accepted by the Faculty of Medicine, and this is his first suit, which I bought him when he entered the faculty. You know, the first day, when I saw him wearing the suit and setting off for the faculty, I cried for joy. And his mother, God rest her soul, cried and kept praying for him. This, now, is a music recorder with headphones. To be honest, I don't know how to pronounce its English name. I got it for Khaled so he could listen to music while he was studying.'

Madany suddenly let the recorder fall to the ground, approached Heisam until he was face to face with him, and shouted, 'Why did you kill my son?'

Heisam began weeping and begging, saying, 'Forgive me, Hagg! I kiss your feet! Please don't kill me!'

As though he couldn't hear him, Madany shouted, 'You shot my son. The bullet that you fired with this hand of yours right here pierced his head. I picked up a bit of his brain in my hand as I was washing him. I picked up his brain with this hand of mine.'

Uncle Madany sighed and bent his head as though he'd suddenly thought of something. Then he averted his face, bent down, and began gathering the things up and putting them back in the suitcase. He started with the trainers, then the primary and secondary school certificates and the placement notice. Then he folded the suit and placed it carefully inside, followed by the recorder and the headphones. Finally, he closed the suitcase and, without speaking, picked it up and left. He began descending the cement steps with care. Before he had reached the doorway, the roar of a rapid salvo of bullets reached his ears. Then there was silence.

Glossary

Abd El Aziz Street	A well-known commercial street in the older part of central Cairo.
Abd El Men'em Reyad and *Abd El Men'em Reyad Square*	An area of streets and flyovers that extends east from the Nile south of Maspero.
Adly	Habib Adly, Egypt's minister of the interior from November 1997 to January 2011.
Al-Ahram	One of Egypt's oldest daily newspapers (established 1875) and its newspaper of record, government-owned since 1952.
the Alliance	The Alliance of Egyptian Centrist Parties, a grouping of seventeen political parties created in 2012 to back the presidential candidacy of Mahmoud Husam.
the American University	The American University in Cairo, an English-language private university founded in 1919 whose historic campus stands on Tahrir Square.
April 6 and *the April 6 Movement*	An activist organisation created in the spring of 2008 to support a workers' strike in Mahalla El Kubra in the Delta; banned in 2014.
Ataba Square	A large square in central Cairo, between the medieval city and its nineteenth century expansion westwards to the Nile.

the Barrages	Two low dams on the Nile just north of Cairo and a popular picnic spot.
Basha	(1) Formal title awarded, under the monarchy (1805–1954), to large landowners, high-ranking civil servants, and other prominent figures; (2) Courtesy title used today to ingratiate the speaker with police officers and other figures of authority.
the Battle of the Camel	An incident that occurred on 2 February 2011, when men mounted on horses and camels attacked demonstrators in Tahrir Square in coordination with other attackers using firebombs, reportedly resulting in the deaths of several demonstrators and the wounding of at least 600; the name evokes an important early Islamic battle (659).
Bey	A rank lower than *Basha*, in either usage.
Bukhari	Muhammad El Bukhari (810–70), a renowned compiler and evaluator of Traditions.
Central Security	The Central Security Forces, Egypt's riot police.
Copt	A member of Egypt's Coptic Christian minority, the majority of whom belong, like Ashraf Wissa, to the Coptic Orthodox church.
the Corniche	A large road running along the eastern bank of the Nile from Cairo's northern to its southern suburbs.
Dar El Salam	A poor district of southern Cairo.

444

Downtown	Roughly the districts of Cairo between the medieval city on the east and the Nile on the west, which grew up between the second half of the nineteenth century and the Second World War.
Ein El Sukhna	A tourist development on the Gulf of Suez, about 140 km south-east of Cairo, started in the 1960s and greatly expanded since the 1990s.
the Emergency Law	The law (dating to 1958) under which a state of emergency was declared in 1981 and subsequently renewed every three years, and which gave extended powers to the police while suspending numerous constitutional rights.
Enan	Sami Enan, Chief of the General Staff of the Armed Forces from 2005 until August 2012 and deputy head of *the Supreme Council of the Armed Forces*.
Enough!	Arabic Kefaya; informal name of the Egyptian Movement for Change, a broad-based political protest movement founded in 2004 that grew out of opposition to then president Hosni Mubarak's attempts to assume a fifth term in office and to promote his son Gamal Mubarak as his successor.
the Feast	The annual Lesser Feast, or Lesser Bayram, with which Muslims celebrate the end of the fasting month of Ramadan and for which they traditionally buy new clothes.
Feisal Street	A major commercial thoroughfare (and the crowded middle- and lower-middle-class residential streets around it) in *Giza*; the street runs parallel to Pyramids Road and the district grew up in the 1970s.

the Fifth Settlement	A major new residential development to the north-east of Cairo.
galabiya	A long closed gown.
Ganzouri	Kamal Ganzouri, an economist who held a number of ministerial posts under Hosni Mubarak, and served as prime minister from 1996 to 1999; he served again in that position from 7 December 2011 to 26 June 2012.
Garden City	An older, upscale residential area south-west of central Cairo, on the Nile.
the Gezira Club	A long-established and prestigious sporting and social club on the island of Gezira in the Nile opposite central Cairo.
Giza	Cairo's sister city on the west bank of the Nile.
Guidance Office	A body consisting of some fifteen of the highest-ranking members of the Muslim Brotherhood, which functions as a sort of cabinet for the organisation.
hagg (for a man), hagga (for a woman)	Title of a person who has made the pilgrimage to Mecca.
Hawamdiya	A town south-west of Cairo, on the west bank of the Nile.
Heliopolis	An upscale suburb to the north-east of central Cairo, established in the early years of the twentieth century.

Ismailiya	A city on the Suez Canal.
Kafr El Daw-war	An industrial city near Alexandria in the north-west Nile delta; the scene of labour unrest following the 1952 revolution that led to the execution of two activists.
Khaled Said	A young man from Alexandria who died after being beaten by members of the Egyptian police forces and whose killing led to a broad wave of popular anger.
Kosheh	A village in Upper Egypt where a massacre of Copts by Muslims took place on 21 December 1999.
Maadi	An affluent suburb south of central Cairo on the east bank of the Nile.
Maasara	An industrial suburb south of central Cairo and *Maadi* on the east bank of the Nile.
Mahmoud Said	Egyptian painter (1897–1964), known for his depictions of voluptuous women of the lower classes.
The Maid Is the Solution!	A play on the Muslim Brotherhood slogan 'Islam Is the Solution!'
Mansoura	A major city of the Nile Delta, on the eastern branch of the river.
Marinab	A village close to Edfu where a newly built church was burned down by a Muslim fundamentalist mob on 30 September 2011.
Masarra	A northern suburb of Cairo.

Maspero and *the Maspero Building*	The headquarters of Egypt's state television and radio broadcasting system, on the east bank of the Nile.
Max	Common name for 4-Methylaminorex (4-MAR, 4-MAX), a stimulant drug also known as 'Euphoria' and 'Ice'.
Medinet Nasr	A north-eastern suburb of Cairo, built in the late 1950s to absorb overflow population from older districts of the city.
the Mère de Dieu	The Collège de la Mère de Dieu, a historic French-language school for girls run by nuns, founded in 1880 and based in its current location in *Garden City* since 1921.
the Military Council	*The Supreme Council of the Armed Forces.*
Mounira	A middle- to lower-middle-class neighbourhood in south central Cairo.
the Museum	The Egyptian Museum, at the northern end of Tahrir Square.
the Muslim Brotherhood	An Islamist religious, political, and social movement founded in Egypt in 1928 and banned there in September 2013; its head is referred to as the Supreme Guide.
the National Association and *the National Association for Change*	A loose grouping of progressive Egyptian political forces and individuals headed by Mohamed El Baradei and active from 2010 to an undetermined date.

the National Party	The Democratic National Party, Egypt's ruling party from the party's foundation in 1978 until the overthrow of its then leader, Hosni Mubarak, on 11 February 2011; dissolved 16 April 2011.
new rent	A new-rent flat is one whose rent increases annually, as opposed to 'old' fixed-rent flats; new rents were introduced in the 1990s, and apply predominantly to newly built properties.
the North Coast	Egypt's Mediterranean coast between Alexandria and Marsa Matrouh, developed intensively for tourism beginning in the 1980s.
October and *October City*	6th of October City, a major upmarket residential development on the west bank of the Nile south-west of Cairo.
Omar Makram Mosque	A mosque named after a revolutionary figure of the early nineteenth century, that stands on the southern edge of *Tahrir Square*.
Palace of Culture	Any of the institutions run by the General Authority for Palaces of Culture, under the Ministry of Culture, with the aim of promoting culture among the masses.
Qasr El Eini	A neighbourhood in south-central Cairo, home to a large hospital complex and to Cairo University's Faculty of Medicine.
Qasr El Nil	One of central Cairo's main thoroughfares.
the Revolutionary Socialists	A Marxist–Trotskyite political organisation that played an active role in the organisation of sit-ins in Tahrir Square.

Saad Zagh-loul	Saad Zaghloul (1859–1927), nationalist politician and leader of the Wafd ('the Delegation'), a political party.
the Saints Church massacre	The massacre at the Church of the Two Saints, at Sidi Bishr in Alexandria, where bombs exploded on 1 January 2011 resulting in the death of twenty-one people and the injury of many more; following the 2011 uprising, documents surfaced that indicated the involvement of the minister of the interior in the attack.
Salah Salem Road	An arterial road skirting Cairo on the east.
Sayeda Zeinab	A traditional and lower-class neighbourhood on the south-western edge of Cairo's medieval district.
the Settlement	see *the Fifth Settlement*
Sheikh Zayed	Sheikh Zayed City, an upscale residential development west of Cairo established in 1995 and named after the late president of the United Arab Emirates.
the Supreme Council of the Armed Forces	A body created in 1954 and consisting of senior officers of the Egyptian armed forces, which convenes at times of national emergency; it took over power from deposed President Hosni Mubarak on 11 February 2011 and relinquished it on 30 June 2012 following elections.
Supreme Guide	see *the Muslim Brotherhood*

Tahrir Square	A large, irregularly shaped space on the southern edge of central Cairo that became the main focus of demonstrations during the uprising that began on 25 January 2011; the name means Liberation Square and was given following Nasser's 1952 revolution.
Talaat Harb Street	One of central Cairo's main thoroughfares.
Talkha	A town in the Nile Delta.
Tantawi	Field Marshal Mohamed Hussein Tantawi, commander in chief of the Egyptian Armed Forces and head of the Supreme Council of the Armed Forces, who served as de facto head of state from the resignation of President Hosni Mubarak on 11 February 2011 until the inauguration of Mohamed Morsi as president of Egypt on 30 June 2012.
Tradition	Arabic hadith; an authenticated saying of the Prophet Muhammad, taken by believers as a guide to their conduct.
Turah	An industrial area south of Cairo on the east bank of the Nile.
Uncle	An informal title of respect for social inferiors.
the Wafd	A political party (literally, 'the Delegation') founded to argue for the independence and unity of Egypt and Sudan at the Paris Peace Conference of 1919. Though its participation at the conference was denied, the Wafd went on to spearhead Egypt's nationalist movement until banned in 1952.

Wahhabi	Pertaining to the ultraconservative interpretation of Islam preached by Muhammad ibn Abd El Wahhab (1703–92) and followed by the Kingdom of Saudi Arabia.
Zahret El Bustan café	A café on Talaat Harb Street, close to *Tahrir Square*.
Zamalek	An upper-class residential district on the island of Gezira.